PRAISE FOR WIN BLEVINS'S RENDEZVOUS SERIES

"Blevins has done his research and knows the mountain men as well as anyone could—to read this tale is to get a true sense of what their ordeal and adventures must have been like."
—*Library Journal* on *Dancing with the Golden Bear*

"A rousing installment in a fine epic of the American frontier."
—*Publishers Weekly* on *Beauty for Ashes*

"His gritty fiction brings to mind the fur-trading novels of Frederick Manfred *(Lord Grizzly)* and Vardis Fisher *(Mountain Man)*. The glory years of frontier life, fresh and rich."
—*Kirkus Reviews* on *Beauty for Ashes*

"Win Blevins's novel about venturesome Sam Morgan and the fur trade and mountain men of the 1820s is both authentic and entertaining. It will be a welcome addition to any collection of Western fiction."
—*The Dallas Morning News* on *So Wild a Dream*

"Author Blevins, an expert on early American fur trade, introduces his Rendezvous series with this entertaining, vivid portrait of frontier America as seen through the eyes of an impressionable youth."
—*Booklist* on *So Wild a Dream*

CHAPTER

Heaven Is a Long Way Off

Also by Win Blevins

Stone Song
The Rock Child
ravenShadow
Give Your Heart to the Hawks

RENDEZVOUS SERIES
So Wild a Dream
Beauty for Ashes
Dancing with the Golden Bear
A Long and Winding Road

This is a work of fiction. All of the characters, organizations, and events portrayed in this novel are either products of the author's imagination or are used fictitiously.

HEAVEN IS A LONG WAY OFF: A NOVEL OF THE MOUNTAIN MEN

Copyright © 2006 by Win Blevins

A Forge Book
Published by Tom Doherty Associates, LLC
175 Fifth Avenue
New York, NY 10010

www.tor-forge.com

Forge® is a registered trademark of Tom Doherty Associates, LLC.

ISBN-13: 978-0-7653-4484-7
ISBN-10: 0-7653-4484-X

First Edition: October 2006
First Mass Market Edition: September 2007

Printed in the United States of America

0 9 8 7 6 5 4 3 2

Heaven Is a Long Way Off

A Novel of the Mountain Men

WIN BLEVINS

A Tom Doherty Associates Book
New York

To Meredith,
all my harem in one

Acknowledgments

Dennis Copeland, archivist of the Monterey Public Library, provided materials. New Mexico historian Stan Hordes saved me from errors. Three books about Nuevo Mexico were invaluable: Marc Simmons's *Coronado's Land,* L. R. Bailey's *Indian Slave Trade in the Southwest,* and Paul Horgan's *The Centuries of Santa Fe.*

I couldn't write without the help of friends and family. Heidi Schulman helped me along. Eric Stone guided me to an 1820s map of the Los Angeles area. Lana Latham was my point woman for interlibrary loan. Jan Blevins helped me with the French language. Dick James was my particular advisor about mountain men. As always, Dale Walker, Richard Wheeler, and Clyde Hall were my companions and consultants on the journey. My wife, Meredith, my agent, Nat Sobel, and Dale Walker read the manuscript and steered me toward the truth. I am grateful to all of them.

Rideo ergo sum.
(I laugh, therefore I am)

—*Hannibal McKye*

A Note About History

This book begins by following the second journey of the Rocky Mountain fur traders to California, a major event in their history, and then swings into the further adventures of Sam Morgan, which are imaginary.

The events involving Jedediah Smith, especially the massacre and escape at the Mojave villages, are dramatized on the basis of the documentation we have. The quotations from his journal are what he wrote. The captain's troubles in California are depicted accurately; his epistle in Chapter Ten, while invented, is based on a letter he did write.

The picture of Nuevo Mexico in 1828 is drawn from history, including the sketch of the Indian slave trade, which was horrific, and continued under American rule and even beyond the Civil War.

Likewise my depictions of the fur trade at this time, and of the rendezvous of 1828, are intended seriously.

The heart and soul of this novel, and of all in the series, is the heart and soul of Sam Morgan.

Introductory Note

Okay, you're in a spot. Here you hold the fourth novel in a series in your hands. (I hope they're eager hands.) You have no way to know what wild adventures you've missed in the first three volumes, what achievement and failures the Rocky Mountain fur trapper Sam Morgan has marched through. You don't know his friends or enemies, his loves or his dislikes, his heart, his soul.

Here are some notes to help you get started.

SYNOPSES OF THE FIRST THREE VOLUMES, 1822–1827

In *So Wild a Dream,* challenged by the half-breed Hannibal, Sam follows his heart west. After traveling to St. Louis with the con man Grumble and the madam Abby, he goes to the Rocky Mountains with a fur brigade and begins to learn the ways of the trappers and the Indians. At the end he is forced to walk seven hundred miles alone, lost and starving, to the nearest fort.

In *Beauty for Ashes,* Sam courts the Crow girl Meadowlark. Helping Sam in a daring feat to win her hand, one of her brothers is killed. Seeking peace, Sam goes through the rigors of a sun dance, and Meadowlark elopes with him. Her family takes her back by force and kicks Sam out of the village. But Meadowlark runs away to join Sam, and at the trapper rendezvous they are married.

Dancing with the Golden Bear launches Sam and Meadowlark to California with a fur brigade. After terrible hardships crossing the desert, they reach the Golden Clime and the ocean. But Meadowlark dies in childbirth. As he embarks on a harrowing journey across the Sierra Nevada and the deserts beyond, Sam passes through the dark night of the soul.

CAST OF CHARACTERS
of the
Three Preceding Books

SAM MORGAN, an eighteen-year-old Pennsylvanian who leaves home for the Rocky Mountains.

HANNIBAL MCKYE, a scholar and an Indian, born to a Dartmouth professor and a Delaware woman. He's also a former trainer of circus horses.

GRUMBLE, a con man of erudition and style.

ABBY, a beautiful and clever madam.

MEADOWLARK, a Crow girl who marries Sam.

BLUE MEDICINE HORSE and FLAT DOG, her brothers.

GRAY HAWK and NEEDLE, her parents.

RED ROAN, son of the Crow chief and rival for Meadowlark's hand.

GIDEON POORBOY, a bear of a French-Canadian, Sam's trapping partner.

SUMNER, a slave who claims his freedom and follows Grumble into the con life.

JULIA RUBIO, daughter of a California don, later Flat Dog's wife.

CESAR RUBIO, her father, owner of Rancho Malibu.

COY, Sam's pet coyote. In a huge prairie fire Coy led Sam to safety inside the carcass of a buffalo, and they've been inseparable since.

PALADIN, Sam's mare, trained in the skills of circus horses.

HISTORICAL CHARACTERS

JEDEDIAH SMITH, an educated and religious Yankee, one of the principal leaders of the mountain men, later co-owner of the main trapping firm.

WILLIAM ASHLEY, the entrepreneur who opens most of the West to beaver trapping.

JAMES CLYMAN, a trapper friend of Sam's who sometimes tells the stories of Shakespeare's plays.

JIM BECKWOURTH, a mulatto and a trapping companion of Sam's.

TOM FITZPATRICK, an Irishman who becomes a brigade leader.

JIM BRIDGER, trapper, brigade leader, and yarner extraordinaire.

BILL SUBLETTE, a trapper and partner of Jedediah Smith.

HARRISON ROGERS, ROBERT EVANS, SILAS GOBEL, and other trappers of the California brigades.

FATHER JOSÉ SANCHEZ, head of the mission at San Gabriel, California.

Heaven Is a Long Way Off

One

THEY WERE LATE arriving, and the last of the sunlight spread red-gold across the summits of the western mountains. A fresh, damp smell lifted up off the river, a promise of a blessing as evening came to the desert. A breeze stirred among the willow branches along the banks. The finger-shaped leaves caught the light of the sun and tossed it, red-gold-green, into the soft evening air.

Along the top ridges the cinnamon mountains turned the color of candied apples, and grew amethyst shadows on their lower slopes. The Colorado flexed and muttered on its journey from the mountains to the sea.

Sam Morgan looked around. Again he found the desert strange and alluring. He said to himself, *What the hell am I doing here?*

"On the adventure," said Hannibal. Sam's friend had an irritating habit of reading his thoughts.

Village leaders were riding out to meet them. It would be impolite to go closer to the village before courtesies were exchanged. Impolite even though these were the Mojave villages, where the fur brigade had spent a couple of weeks last autumn and knew the Indians were friendly. So Sam, Hannibal, and Captain Jedediah Smith sat their mounts in this place. Sam cursed. He squirmed in the saddle, itchy from his own sweat after the long ride. His pet coyote, Coy, sat in the shade of a creosote bush and panted.

"There's a sorry piece of the adventure."

Sam turned his head. A few paces into the brush three Mojave boys had built a small fire and were torturing horny toads.

The biggest boy reached into a hide bag, plucked out a toad, flat and ugly and the size of a palm. The creature had dagger-like spikes all around its head, and it was fighting its captor.

The boy laughed and threw the toad onto the fire.

Coy barked.

The toad skittered out of the fire like a stone hopping across water.

The smallest boy snatched the toad up and held it close to his nose. The toad sprouted blood from its eyes—Sam had seen this trick before. The boy jumped and threw the toad into the air.

Another boy snatched the creature on the fly and tossed it onto the fire.

The small boy wiped blood off his nose and grinned.

The toad came lickety-split out of the flames and slithered under another boy's knee. The boy grabbed the toad coming out the back side.

Coy squealed, like a plea for mercy.

A picture floated into Sam's mind—damnedest thing, he couldn't imagine why. He saw his infant daughter suckling at the breast of Sam's . . .

Meadowlark. Dead.

He shook his head to make the picture go away. But it stayed right where it was.

The biggest boy took the toad from the younger one and dropped it into the flames.

This time it first blew itself up big, and then, amazingly, never moved again.

Coy growled.

Sam started to rein his horse toward the boys. Hannibal put his hand out—no. Sam stopped. "What made them like that?" whispered Sam.

"A bad one leading good ones," said Hannibal.

Sam's eyes asked for help. Sometimes Hannibal knew things. Some of the men called him Mage, short for magician.

"Let's go," said Jedediah.

Sam handed Paladin's reins to the magician and fell in behind Captain Smith on foot. About fifty yards off several leaders of the tribe waited to meet the trappers, and beyond them on the willow flat Sam could see the brush huts and crop fields of the village.

Safety, he thought.

Sam took a last glance at the boys. They were still mesmerized by toads and fire. *Life goes topsy-turvy into death.*

He forced himself to turn and study the Mojave leaders. There was Red Shirt, front and foremost, smiling broadly, wearing the garment that gave him his name. As far as Sam knew, it was the only shirt among the Mojaves, and worn only on state occasions. The Mojave men wore only loincloths, and the women only short skirts of bark.

Sam was not glad to see Red Shirt, not after he stole Gideon's wife a year ago. But it was Sam's job as *segundo* to stay with Diah, see how he handled things, learn what to do. Diah wanted Sam to be a brigade leader soon. Also, Sam had a knack for communicating with Indians, in sign language or even gestures and grunts.

Alongside Red Shirt was Francisco, the Mojave who had been to the Spanish settlements near the ocean and knew some Spanish. Behind these two stood three other leaders.

"*Buenas tardes,*" said Francisco. "*Bienvenido, Capitán! Bienvenido, White Hair!*"

Sam's hair had been straw-colored, almost white for all of his twenty-two and a half years. He said, "*Gracias. ¿Como esta ustedes?*"

Francisco extended his hand to Sam and then to the captain, showing that he remembered this white-man nicety. When they shook, Red Shirt grinned broadly. His entire face was elaborately tattooed with dots in vertical lines. When he grinned, the lines queered their way into strange curves. Sam didn't know if the dots were supposed to make a picture or pattern, but he knew the effect when the mouth curled the lines—it gave Sam the willies.

Francisco had a simpler tattoo.

Neither Sam nor Francisco spoke fluent Spanish, so they now resorted to gestures and single words to settle the rest. Sam laboriously asked permission for the brigade to trade and to rest its horses. Francisco translated into Mojave. Red Shirt said the people of the village were glad to give their hospitality to its friends, the men who hunted the beaver.

Now Red Shirt spoke what was probably his only word of Spanish. *"Bienvenido,"* he said, grinning. The grin made his tattoos squirm like snakes.

Captain Smith waved to the rest of the brigade to come forward.

"¿Bienvenido? Welcome to what?" said Sam in English.

"Maior risus, acrior ensis," said Hannibal. The Mage liked to say things in Latin.

"What does that mean?" asked Sam.

"The bigger the smile, the sharper the knife."

THE TWENTY-ONE TRAPPERS and two Indian women set up camp hastily on an open spot by the river they used for a campground last year. Just upstream of them was the circle of brush huts, several hundred of them, that made up the village. All around them were the vegetable fields of the Mojaves. The Indians planted close to the river, and rises in the Colorado irrigated the crops.

Last autumn, when they arrived in much poorer condition, the brigade stayed two weeks with the Mojaves to rest their horses and put some meat back on their ribs. On the men's ribs too—they traded for corn, beans, melons, pumpkins, everything the Mojaves had to eat. Then the trappers had known them as the Amuchabas. Now they thought of them as the Mojaves, the name for them in the Spanish settlements, and the name of the desert that faced all who would travel on to California, as this brigade intended to do.

The captain walked off to trade for corn, beans, and some of the bread the Mojaves made from the honey locust bean.

The other trappers rigged the camp. They unpacked and unsaddled the horses, led them to the river for water, and then penned them in a rope corral. They set up, laid out bedrolls, and put their possibles in the tents.

"Want to put a guard on the horses?" Hannibal asked Sam.

"Only at night." These Indians could be trusted. Sam and Hannibal, however, kept their personal mounts, Paladin and Ellie, staked by their tent.

Exhausted, as he seemed to be the whole trip, Sam propped himself against a cottonwood and napped. Coy curled up against his thigh.

"Garden sass!" said Hannibal, shaking Sam awake.

Sam got up and stepped to the low fire. Everyone gathered around and boiled and roasted the vegetables.

"Never thought I'd get tired of meat," Silas Gobel said, chomping down on an ear of corn. Though the Indians ground their corn dry, the trappers liked to boil it and then grouse that it didn't taste as good as sweet corn.

"That dried meat is *dry*," said Polette Labross. Everyone called him Polly. They'd had nothing else to eat from the Salt Lake all the way down through the redrock country to the banks of the Colorado River, dried meat and not enough water.

"Even my pecker is dry," said Gobel. He gave a sly smile. "But not for long around here."

"Sailors on the loose in port!" said Bos'n Brown.

Last year the Mojave women were as eager as the vagabond trappers. Sam thought, *I won't be partaking.*

"Bitterness bites the man who puts it on his tongue," said Hannibal.

Sam shot him a glance. *Reading my thoughts again. Are they scrawled across my face like words?*

He looked around the fire. Friends all, and he was damned glad to have them. When you rode the mountains and plains and deserts, your friends saved your life, and you saved theirs.

Coy looked at the boiled corn, boiled beans, and bread. He whapped his tail on the ground. He whined.

"He wants a blood sacrifice," said Hannibal.

Sam had gotten an education from following Hannibal's sayings. Maybe some day he'd get Hannibal to teach him to read and write. He fished in his possible sack and tossed Coy a little dried meat.

These five men gathered to eat and sleep together every evening, for no particular reason other than they liked each other. Sam was a Pennsylvania backwoodsman; Gobel, a king-sized blacksmith; Bos'n, a man who'd spent his life at sea; Polly, a grizzled mulatto; Hannibal, a man of mixed blood, white and Delaware Indian.

Trappers were always a jumble of races. Sam liked that. Among the Frenchies and their Indian wives you might hear French, Iroquois, Cree, Shoshone, and English oddly mixed in one or two sentences.

Captain Smith was odd himself. On the one hand he was a book-learned Yankee who carried a Bible and nearly wore it out with reading. On the other hand, most of the trappers thought he was the smartest, toughest man in the West. No leader was more respected. He'd been Sam's first brigade captain, and their bond was strong.

Sam thought the most intriguing man of the lot was Hannibal McKye. Since his father was a classics professor at Dartmouth College and his mother a Delaware, Hannibal grew up speaking two languages. He learned to read not only animal tracks but Greek and Latin. He could discuss Greek philosophy, Caesar's wars, and Shoshone beadwork. To top it all off, he worked in the circus and learned their horse tricks. It was partly his wizardry with horses that made the men call him the Mage.

Sam and Hannibal had crossed trails from time to time on the plains and in the mountains, but they'd never traveled together until now. Hannibal wanted to see California. Sam had a reason to go back, a reason that was very good and very bad.

"I need sleep," said Sam. He walked to the river, filled his hat with water, and took it to Paladin. The mare looked strong for this stage in the trip. She was a fine-looking Indian pony, white with a black cap around the ears, a black blaze on the chest, and black mane and tail. The Crows called this kind of pony a medicine hat.

When she'd lapped the crown of the hat dry, he led her out of the rope corral and staked and hobbled her on some good grass near his bedroll. Since she was specially trained, he kept her close every night.

He lay down on his blankets, looked at the stars, and then let his eyes blur. His bones sagged into the ground. Coy lay beside Sam's head, as always.

Maybe it's just the trip, he thought. *Maybe a few days' rest . . .*

This journey had been so much easier than last year's. Both times they left rendezvous in mid July. Last year they got to the Mojave villages in early November, this year in mid August. The difference was knowing the route and where they could find water. When they got here last year, half the horses were dead and the men were gaunt. This year the horses were gaunt but alive and the men were fine.

Except Sam. He thought about tomorrow's task, which he didn't look forward to. Then he let himself picture the reason he was going back to California.

Esperanza, my daughter.

"SPARK!"

The woman looked up from weeding the pumpkins.

As Sam approached, a quirk twisted her face. No, she wasn't glad to see him.

"I'm glad to see you," he said, walking forward.

Francisco tagged along. It was like Sam had two pets, Coy and the Mojave interpreter.

"What you want, Sam?" she said with a gleam in her eyes.

So she was turning it into a flirtation. Spark was no one's idea of a romantic figure. She looked a bride's well-used older sister. Her face was a little mashed, her bare breasts were narrow and pointy, and she now sported the Mojave look—a tattooed chin. Five parallel lines curved from her mouth to under her jawbone, with some sideways squiggles. The Shoshone woman had declared herself Mojave.

"Just to say hello." He squatted. So did Francisco and Coy, and after a moment Spark. She had decent English from her three months with the brigade last summer and fall.

He broke a slab of dried meat into three pieces length-wise, gave one each to Spark and Francisco, and ate. Meat of any kind was a treat for the Mojaves.

"Thought you might want news of Gideon."

She gave a flirty wiggle of her eyebrows.

He was tickled, thinking, *It's not going to work, lady.*

They looked at each other, munching, waiting. He decided to change the subject to her new man.

"How is Red Shirt?"

"He is good man. Big man." Sam wondered how many wives he had. With the Mojaves' fields of crops, at least Spark wouldn't go hungry.

Sam nodded to himself. Out with it. "You broke Gideon's heart."

"I am woman. Put man's moccasins outside lodge when I want."

Sam stared at her, thinking, *You barely let his moccasins inside.*

She'd been a slave in the Ute camp at Utah Lake when they found her. Jedediah bought her, and as the brigade journeyed south, she and Gideon fell in love. Or so everyone thought, and Gideon thought. They'd shared a lodge for a couple of weeks—married, in the fashion of the country.

Then, when the brigade started west across the Mojave Desert, she slipped off and joined Red Shirt's family.

First Gideon had nearly lost his life. Did lose his leg. And then the one-legged man lost his new wife. He dived into despair.

"He's doing well now," Sam said.

She concentrated on the meat, which took a lot of chewing.

"He became an artist in California." He realized she wouldn't know what "artist" meant, and probably didn't care either. "He makes very beautiful earrings and necklaces from gold and silver and turquoise and shells." That should impress her.

She looked at him proudly. "I make baby."

She didn't have a child on a blanket or a cradle on her back. Then Sam realized. The stiff bark of Mojave women's skirts always stuck out behind, a little comically. Spark's also stuck out in front. Her belly was bulging.

The name came like a pang. *Esperanza* . . .

Sam tried to remember. Was Spark with Gideon's child, or Red Shirt's? Did it matter?

She looked at him with huge satisfaction.

"You broke his heart," he said.

She waited a moment and said, "Thank you for the meat. Now I weed the pumpkins." She got up and walked away.

Sam and Francisco ambled back toward the trapper campground.

Francisco said in Spanish, "See Captain Smith?"

SAM THOUGHT FRANCISCO just wanted to cadge a present of some kind, but he had something else in mind. He sipped his hot coffee, grimaced, and said, "*¿No dulce?*"

Sam answered that the party had no sugar.

Between small sips of hot coffee Francisco slowly informed them that this past winter a band of Mexicans (Spaniards, he called them) and Americans had come from Nuevo Mexico down the Gila River and up the Colorado to these very villages.

Sam and Jedediah looked at each other. They had been first into this country, but not by much. Trapping brigades were heading west out of Taos and Santa Fe, they knew that, but they didn't know any had come this far.

"Find out if they crossed to California," Diah told Sam.

After more sips of coffee, Sam told the captain no.

"That's a relief." Jedediah wanted the California beaver country for his own company, Smith, Jackson & Sublette.

"Francisco says the trapping outfit took beaver from the Colorado and didn't want to pay for it. They quarreled and split up here. Some of them went up the Colorado River. He doesn't know where the others went."

Now Diah indulged one of his real passions. He got out the notebook where he wrote his journal and his maps. In the sand he drew the Colorado as it came down from the north to these villages. He got Francisco to draw it farther south, to the mouth of the Gila. The Yuma Indians lived around the mouth of the Gila, Francisco said, and Jedediah made a note. Then the interpreter drew the Gila coming in from the east, and where the Salt River flowed into it. But he didn't know where either river headed up. He said the Colorado emptied into the ocean several sleeps below the mouth of the Gila.

Jedediah copied the information from the map in the sand into his notebook and closed it with a smile.

THAT NIGHT THE men were boiling for a dance.

On the long trip south from rendezvous Sam had found a new musical partner—Polly Labross was a peach of a fiddler. A black man from Montreal and once a *voyageur,* Polly knew French-Canadian songs. Sam had learned to pipe the melodies on his tin whistle, and had even learned some lyrics in French.

The trappers moved up to some flat ground near the huts. When Polly started tuning the fiddle, Mojave women gathered to watch. Polly scraped out a verse of "Ah, Si Mon Moine Voulait Danser," and a dozen women crept close.

Sam played a second verse and chorus while Polly double-stopped harmony. Polly looked like a sly old dog, his hair mottled gray and his beard black, with a shape that seemed almost Chinese. His soft eyes hinted at a wisdom that embraced thousands of secrets he wouldn't tell.

"Let's go," hollered Bos'n Brown. He grabbed Gobel's arm and set out jigging. Gobel was Goliath, Bos'n a small and lithe David. Bos'n was a sassy fellow, quick with a quip. Now he took the woman's role—he hopped, he bounced, he swung his bottom like a girl's, he even jumped into the air. Gobel swung him 'round. They had a big time.

The Mojave women, remembering last year's affair, started dancing in place. The dance style of the fur men was nothing like their own, but they liked it.

Sam sang in a light, clear voice over Polly:

If my old top were a dancing man
A cap to fit I would give him then

chorus:
Dance old top, dance in
Oh, you don't care for dancing
Oh, you don't care for my mill la, la
Oh, you won't hear how my mill runs on

As Polly explained it to Sam, it was a tease. The dancers were asking a monk to join them. In every verse they tempted him with something different, a cap, a gown . . .

If my old top were a dancing man
A gown of serge I would give him then

In the next verse they tempted him with a Psalter, then a rosary, and so on, but the monk never danced, and they hooted at him.

No one gave a damn about this story, but the tune was lively.

Now Bos'n spun away from Gobel and held out his hand to one of the women. She grabbed hold, and around the circle they went, the woman . . .

It was Spark! She followed clumsily but eagerly.

Well, Sam reminded himself, he'd told Bos'n that she danced with several men last year, and went to the bushes with at least one, Red Shirt.

Polly jumped faster into the tune, and Sam took a break.

Other Mojave women joined in, and several men. Among them—surprise! Last year two teenagers had tried to steal Paladin, Skinny and Stout, Sam called them in his mind. He had gotten her back only by chasing them halfway across the river, and one nearly drowned under a cottonwood log beached on a sand bar. But Skinny and Stout were dancing now, and apparently having a good time.

A pretty woman held out her hand to Sam, smiling. She was smiling, and she said something in her language, probably asking him to dance.

He couldn't help looking lingeringly at her breasts. "No," he said.

She said whatever it was again, and reached out and fingered his hair. Women always seemed to like Sam's white hair.

"No," said Sam again, and took her hand away. He wished he wanted to touch a woman, hold a woman, lie down with a woman.

She turned to the next man without a hint of regret. It was Robiseau, one of the French-Canadians, and he whirled away with her. Sam thought of Robiseau as Merry One Tooth, for the number of dentures he had in the upper front, which he showed off in a perpetual lunatic grin.

When Merry One Tooth danced off, his wife glared after him. Then Red Shirt came up and motioned to her, and she danced off with the chief. Robiseau winked at her.

At least half the trappers now were bouncing along, and both trapper wives were dancing with Mojave men.

Polly changed the tune to a sea shanty, a slow capstan song that would give all the men a chance to ease the women close:

> *When Ham and Shem and Japhet, they walked the capstan*
>   *'round,*
> *Upon the strangest vessel that was ever outward bound,*
> *The music of their voices from wave to welkin rang,*
> *As they sang the first sea shanty that sailors ever sang.*

"Don't you want to dance?" said Hannibal.

"Think I'll turn in," said Sam. *Away from temptation,* he thought, *and with my memories.*

"Sure."

As Hannibal disappeared into the darkness, Sam wondered if his friend wanted a woman. Probably so. Even magicians liked sex.

He stretched out on his blankets, reached to where he knew Coy would be, and scratched the coyote's head. In the dark, when he couldn't see, the smell and sound of the river were stronger. He remembered the brute force of its current—pound and splash, spin and suck. Its whirlpools pulled him to its bottom and to sleep.

SAM LOOKED AT his arms, which were all scratched up. Sweat was running into the scratches—the August sun felt like coals in a woodstove. He frowned across at Hannibal, who grinned. Hannibal's arms were probably worse than Sam's.

They were standing ankle deep in the river cutting more cane for the two rafts. It took a lot of float power to carry twenty-three people and their cargo across the swift, turbulent Colorado. This gear included barrels for water, blacksmith tools, tomahawks, traps, kegs of gunpowder, and much more. There were the trade goods for Indians. And the trappers bore their own gear. A typical man had a rifle, a butcher knife, two horns for powder, a blanket, an extra pair of moccasins, and a pouch containing a bar of lead, a tool for making the lead into balls, a patch knife, a fire-striker, char cloth, and so on, altogether another ten percent of his body weight.

Sam and Hannibal shouldered the last loads of cane on both shoulders and labored upstream along the bank. When they got to where the other men were binding the cane into the rafts, they dumped their loads and sagged onto the ground.

Coy mewled. He often seemed to pity men doing hard labor.

The Mojaves were gathered around to see the trappers off. Red Shirt was there, Francisco, Skinny and Stout, Spark, seemingly most of the village, hundreds of men, women, and children. Partly, Sam supposed, they wanted to see how the trappers built a cane raft. With trappers working and calling to each other and Mojaves talking, everything was hubbub.

"Captain," called Sam. Smith looked around. Whenever Sam addressed Diah in an official way, he called him by title. "Hannibal and me, we'll swim over with the horses."

"You?" Jedediah asked at large, "Who's a strong swimmer?"

"Me!" said Hannibal and Virgin at once.

Tom Virgin was old, Sam guessed probably in his forties, but he was tough and strong. Sam liked him.

"Hannibal, Virgin, ride the river with the horses."

"Captain, I'm sticking with Paladin."

Smith looked at Sam and knew his *segundo* wouldn't be denied. "All right, three of you. Sam, hang on to that horse."

"Let's go," said Hannibal. All thirty-some-odd mounts, including Paladin and Ellie, were rope-corralled a hundred paces downstream.

"Hold on," said Diah. He was looking across the river. "You feel sure of hitting that sand bar?"

"It'll work," said Sam.

The trappers would set out in the rafts and pole across. The current would bear them downstream. Remembering last year, Jedediah and Sam figured they would float about as much down the river to the bar as across it. They allowed a good margin for error.

Now the first raft was loaded—eight trappers plus the captain and half their gear.

Sam, Hannibal, and Virgin started downstream to run the horses into the river. Coy tagged along.

"Wait!" said Sam. He ran to the raft that was still on the bank and lashed the rifle his father had left him, The Celt, to the bundle of rifles there. Most of the men had wrapped their rifles in canvas and tied them to this second raft. This rifle was important to Sam. It was the only memento he had of his father, Lew Morgan.

"Me too," Hannibal and Virgin said together. A man swimming the Colorado didn't want something as heavy as a rifle in his hands. Hannibal roped both rifles in.

Off the three hurried down to the river.

"Push off!" cried Jedediah.

Coy barked once in the direction of the raft and scooted after Sam and Hannibal.

The trappers on the raft shoved hard against the bank with their long poles, and the raft surged into the river. The current grabbed them hard. The raft spun in a full circle, making some of the men fall down. Everyone laughed. A big wave lifted the raft, and it dropped down the back side with a belly-sucking lurch. Men made whoopsy noises.

At that moment all the Mojave men yelled fiercely and attacked the ten men left on the bank.

The first blows whisked through the air. Two men got pincushioned, others were wounded here and there.

Spears were hurled. Polly Labross went down with a shaft through his chest, blood gouting from his mouth onto his gray beard.

Warriors rushed in and struck with spears and knives.

Silas Gobel was slashed by at least two knives but roared, picked a man up, and threw him at the other treacherous warriors.

Mojaves ran into nearby brush and came out brandishing war clubs.

Several trappers got off shots with their pistols—the rifles were lashed to the beached raft—but the Mojaves swarmed on them.

Jedediah and eight other men watched in horror from the river. It was like seeing ants rush onto a dying mouse.

The current yanked them relentlessly downstream. "Pole, damn it!" yelled Jedediah. He set an example.

The trappers had been gaping at the attack. Now they stuck their poles deep into the water, found the bottom, and shoved.

Two men pushed upstream.

"We can't go against the current," shouted Jedediah. "Pole for the other side!"

They did, hard.

From a hundred paces downstream Sam, Hannibal, and Virgin, armed with only their pistols and butcher knives, sprinted back to their comrades. Coy ran ahead of them, growling and yowling. Sam saw Bos'n Brown fall, and two Mojaves pounced on him. Robiseau staggered out of the melee, his back sprouting arrows.

Before they were halfway back, a score of armed Mojaves ran toward Sam, Hannibal, and Virgin.

Coy turned and dashed the other way.

Sam fired, and a man dropped.

Hannibal fired.

Suddenly everything was chaos.

A capricious wind whipped up a dust devil. Sand and smoke swirled around the trappers.

Warriors ran into the dark pall, screaming and swinging war clubs.

Virgin went down, his skull bloodied.

"Run!" yelled Hannibal.

Sam and Hannibal sprinted toward the horses, a dozen Mojaves after them.

Sam thought, *I'm dead*.

He ran like hell and caught Hannibal and got half a step on him. Coy fell in with them.

Suddenly, out of the brush downstream, the horses stampeded. Three or four Mojaves ran behind, driving them.

Salvation! thought Sam.

He put his fingers to his mouth and gave a loud, piercing whistle, rising low to high.

Hannibal did the same, looping from high to low and back twice.

Paladin and Ellie cut out of the herd and ran toward Sam and Hannibal.

Thank God! Sam's mind screamed.

The herd followed Paladin and Ellie. "Hallelujah!" shouted Sam.

When Paladin got close, Sam grabbed her mane and swung up bareback. Hannibal did the same on Ellie.

Sam saw Virgin staggering toward the river alone, holding his bleeding head in both hands. Coy ran toward the old man, then pivoted and came fast after Sam.

An arrow caught Paladin. She fell, and Sam pitched over her head.

Hooves rat-a-tat-tatted all around him. Dust and horse manure flew everywhere. Coy poised himself and yipped furiously at the horses pounding by.

A sharp edge slashed Sam's hip.

He whirled and swung his fist.

The Mojave jumped back, cocking his spear. It was Stout, who had the face of a snake.

Sam grabbed his butcher knife and thrust forward.

Stout slammed his spear into Sam's wrist.

The butcher knife went flying.

Stout grinned in triumph.

Sam grabbed his empty pistol and threw it at Stout's head.

Stout ducked and the pistol sailed by. Stout laughed.

Yes, you bastard, I'm disarmed.

Sam fingered his trick belt buckle. Coy barked furiously at Stout.

Sam smiled. "Right. Hey," he told Stout out loud in English, "look what I'm doing." He jerked at the buckle, and his breechcloth dropped.

Stout's eyes darkened at the insult. He bounded forward. Coy launched himself at the warrior's groin. Somehow Stout thrust the spear.

Sam spun.

The point nipped his ribs.

When Sam came full circle, he crowded inside the spear point. His belt buckle had turned into a steel blade in his hand, and he drove it into Stout's belly.

He jerked it out, looked at the blood, picked up his breechcloth, and wiped the blade.

Stout sat down hard and loose.

Sam looked with satisfaction at his glassy eyes.

Coy gave a last bark and snipped at Stout's face.

"Thanks, Gideon," he said.

His friend had smithed him a dagger with a belt buckle as a handle. Sam slid the blade back into his belt, deep, fastened the buckle, and put his breechcloth back on.

He walked over and picked up his pistol. Since The Celt was lost, the pistol was essential. He looked around. The herd had run off toward the hills, and the Mojaves were chasing them. *Thirty horses,* he thought. A huge triumph for them.

Where was Hannibal? Sam didn't know. If he could, Hannibal would have led the herd into the river. Where was Paladin? With the herd. Injured.

All right, no Mojave was close. A grove of cottonwoods marked the bank. Sam loped toward the water, Coy bounding alongside. He hit the top of the bank in stride and made a long, flat dive.

The river was a turmoil. Waves slapped him in the face. They rolled him over. Suck holes grabbed at his legs.

He flailed at the water with his arms, he kicked at it with his feet. He fought the goddamn water. He battered it. He punished it. The river laughed and tossed him up and caught him. It jerked him under and let him up.

Sam whacked at the river with arms and legs.

Long minutes later, minutes he couldn't remember, a mewling woke him up. Coy, he realized. Consciousness picked at his brain.

A hand touched him. He opened his eyes. Hannibal. They were on the far bank.

"I'm checking your wounds."

He prodded at the gash in Sam's hip and the slice along his ribs.

"You'll be fine."

"Where's Paladin?"

"Don't know."

"Where's Ellie?"

"Dead. Let's get up to the others."

"Dead!"

Hannibal pulled Sam to his feet. "The ass cut Ellie's throat. I cut his."

They stumbled upstream, splashing in the shallows, feet sinking into the sand bars. Pictures invaded Sam's mind, images of the handsome stallion lying on the sand, neck pumping out blood. Then he thought of Paladin and wondered how her hindquarter was. His blood prickled.

Around a couple of bends stood Captain Smith and eight

other men. Diah was looking across the river with his field glass. The trappers looked at each other with the bright knowledge of mortality in their eyes.

Diah lowered his field glass. Sam could hardly hear his words. "They're all dead." Sam looked across the river. Hundreds of Mojaves milled around. From this distance he could make out no one in particular. He pictured Red Shirt's face, Francisco's face, Spark's. *What in hell . . .*

"Why?" said Diah.

No one answered. These Indians were friendly last autumn. Why?

They looked at each other, mute and afraid.

Now the captain's voice of command came back. "Let's get out of here."

Two

THOUGH THEY'D LOST half their equipment, without horses they couldn't carry even what was left. They stared bitterly at the gear. The captain put their food in his own possible sack, fifteen pounds of dried meat—that was all they had to eat. Then he filled his sack with trade goods for Indians, beads, ribbon, cloth, and tobacco. He grabbed several traps. His possible sack got heavy.

He told the other men that they had to walk a dozen sleeps in blazing heat. Considering that, they should take whatever they wanted. "This was company property. Now it's your property."

Sam looked at Diah's sack and considered. Eleven men, fifteen pounds of meat, twelve sleeps (if they were lucky), that didn't add up. And there was no game out there.

Five men still had their rifles. Sam grabbed the single tomahawk and held it high. He knew how to throw one. *My anger will make it a vicious weapon.*

He barely paid attention to what the others picked up. Knives seemed to go first, then traps, then bridles, in hopes of getting horseflesh. Last, they picked up more items for the Indians. These men had learned a hard practicality about that.

When each man had the load he wanted to carry across the Mojave Desert, Jedediah said, "Scatter the rest across the sand. Tempt them."

They did. The thought of savages boiling over this equipment fevered the brain of every man. There was no point in asking how soon they would be here.

"Drink your fill," said Jedediah. "We have only one kettle to carry water with."

The men flopped onto the sand and sucked up all the river they could. Coy did the same. Sam refused to think of what it meant, starting across the Mojave with no water casks and only one kettle.

They started walking west.

"They know where we're headed," said Jedediah. "We have to get to that first spring."

The men chewed on that. They looked around at the barren country. Desert scrub, desert scrub, desert scrub, and no place to hide.

Fragments of ugly reality spun through their heads. The screams of their dead friends. The flash of knife, the silhouette of arm-cocked spear. The mud made by blood in the dust. The thump of human bodies on the sand.

They tramped. They waded through grief. They looked slyly toward their own deaths, which lay ahead.

Only Coy kept his head perked up.

After a few minutes Hannibal said, "You know why older women are better in bed than young ones?"

Sam was stupefied.

Hannibal went on, "Ben Franklin wrote this. I'm going to quote it."

"Hannibal!" complained Sam.

"Go ahead, Mage," said two or three voices.

" 'In your amours you should prefer old women to young ones. This you call a paradox, and demand my reasons. They are these: One—because they have more knowledge of the world, and their minds are better stored with observations; their conversation is more improving, and more lastingly agreeable.' "

"Conversation," someone mimicked.

" 'Two—because when women cease to be handsome, they study to be good. To maintain their Influence over man, they supply the diminution of beauty by an augmentation of utility. They learn to do a thousand services, small and great, and are the most tender and useful of friends when you are sick. Thus they continue amiable. And hence there is hardly such a thing to be found as an old woman who is not a good woman.' "

"I've knowed some wasn't good," said Isaac Galbraith. He was a Herculean man with a strong Maine accent.

" 'Three,' " Hannibal barged forward. " 'Because there is no hazard of children, which irregularly produced may be attended with much inconvenience.' "

"Sacre bleu," said Toussaint Marechal, "can you no speak straight out?"

" 'Four,' " persisted Hannibal, " 'because through more experience they are more prudent and discreet in conducting an intrigue to prevent suspicion. The commerce with them is therefore safer with regard to your reputation, and regard to theirs; if the affair should happen to be known, considerate people might be inclined to excuse an old woman, who would kindly take care of a young man, form his manners by her good counsels, and prevent his ruining his health and fortune among mercenary prostitutes.' "

"Zis *hivernant* me," said Joseph LaPoint, "I take whatever come." *Hivernant* was Frenchy talk for an experienced wilderness hand. LaPoint was called Seph by everyone.

"Godawmighty, Hannibal!" said Sam.

"This is good," the captain said softly to Sam.

Sam shut up. He noticed, though, that Jedediah was keeping a very sharp eye out.

" 'Five,' " said Hannibal, " 'because in every animal that walks upright, the deficiency of the fluids that fill the muscles appears first in the highest part. The face first grows lank and wrinkled; then the neck; then the breast and arms; the lower parts continuing to the last as plump as ever . . . ' "

"We're turning around," interrupted Jedediah.

He wheeled and headed back to the river at a trot. Every man followed him close. "The Mojaves are coming," Diah said quietly to Sam.

They would have a better chance in the cover of trees along the river.

WHEN THEY GOT to the river alive, they eyed each other as though sharing a secret joke. In a grove of cottonwoods they felled small trees, grumbling that they had to use knives, since Sam wielded the only tomahawk. They made a flimsy breast-work from these poles. Then, waiting, men began to lash their butcher knives to the ends of light poles, making lances.

No need to speak about the situation. Only five of them had rifles. Sam and Hannibal had pistols, useful only at short range. Since they got their powder horns soaked swimming the river and there wasn't time to dry it, the other men gave them powder. Three men had no weapons but the lances. The river protected the trappers' backs, but the Indians could attack from three directions. They would probably outnumber the trappers fifty to one. More than one trapper pictured the Indians' hands still dripping red with the blood of their comrades.

Sam said to himself several times, "Make them pay." That's all the defenders could get for their lives.

As he worked, he thought of other reasons to make them pay. The bastards had The Celt. They had Paladin. Probably Skinny would try to keep Paladin, but Red Shirt would claim her for himself, because of the wonderful tricks she could do, the routines Sam and the Mage had taught her. Sam grimaced. The chief wouldn't know how to signal Paladin to perform, and wouldn't understand why she didn't.

On the other hand, Paladin wouldn't get the fun of doing the circus routines again.

"Let me see those wounds," Hannibal said.

Sam turned his hip to his friend (this was the convenience

of wearing just a breechcloth), then raised his shirt to show the ribs.

Hannibal fingered both of them. "Tonight I'll put poultices on them."

Sam grinned at him. *Tonight—that's optimistic.*

"What's that blood on your belly?"

"A Mojave's." Sam whipped out the belt-buckle knife and mock-pointed it at Hannibal. "Gideon made this for me, said it was thanks for amputating his leg." The two friends held each other's eyes a moment.

Sam snapped the knife back into its belt buckle guise, and flashed it out again. "Easy to get out."

Hannibal inspected it. The blade was the sheathed part, fashioned in the double-edged style of a dagger and very sharp.

"So you have two secret blades," said Hannibal, fingering it. They each had a knife concealed as a hair ornament. "You ought to wash the blood off."

Sam thought about the stabbing, about Stout, and about his dead friends on the far bank. "No, I'll keep it for a while."

Coy barked. Head to tail he pointed toward the river behind them.

Five rifles trained on the brush in that direction.

"Hey!"

The voice came from the riverbank. Every man looked down his sights or held his lance in that direction.

"Hey!"

"That's English!" said Hannibal.

Thomas Virgin's half-bald head peeped out of the bushes. It was still bleeding.

Sam ran forward and supported the old man. His shiny head sported a lump nearly the size of a fist. The wound was still trickling blood. Sam remembered he'd been clubbed. A stone war club could do a lot of damage, often fatal damage.

Virgin was soaked, and he'd lost everything. His britches were gone (he preferred those to a breechcloth), his shot pouch was gone, his belt, his knife, and his belt pouch were gone. He lost his knife and pistol. The old man was nothing but flesh, moccasins, and a torn cloth shirt.

"I dropped ever'thing in the river, one by one," he said.

"You wouldn't have made it otherwise," said Hannibal. He and Sam helped Virgin up to the breastwork.

How had the old man made it? Sam wondered. The sight of him lifted his spirits. But it wouldn't for long.

Coy sniffed Virgin like he was something alien.

"Everyone keep watch," said the captain.

"The next voice won't be English," someone muttered.

The men eyed each other surreptitiously.

Five minutes ticked by. Ten. The men spent it by cutting brush and stuffing it into the breastwork. It wouldn't do much, but . . .

LaPoint said in a quavery voice, "Can we do it, Captain?"

Marechal snickered.

"Captain?" echoed someone else.

Sam grimaced. The men wouldn't ask if their blood wasn't running chill.

"We'll drive them off," said Jedediah.

His voice was calm, firm. Sam was amazed. He and the captain looked at each other, and Sam saw that Diah knew better. Knew for sure.

He and Diah had nearly died on the Missouri when the Rees fired down on them on an unprotected beach. Most of the men stayed on that beach forever. Diah and Sam and a few others escaped.

They almost died together just three months ago, crossing the salt waste from the California mountains to the Salt Lake. Bashed by heat and weakened by thirst, they actually buried themselves in the sand. But they rose from those graves and walked.

Sam said to himself, *Every man's luck runs out.*

Jedediah glassed an area south in the brush, then let the glass hang from the lanyard around his neck. Sam looked carefully and saw them even with the naked eye. Yes, the Indians were coming.

"Rifles, spread out across the breastwork."

Galbraith, Marechal, Swift, and Turner placed themselves where they could shoot in three directions.

"I'll call the fire," said Smith. "We'll always keep two rifles in reserve. I'll name two men, and those only fire."

The riflemen nodded. "Under no circumstances empty all rifles at once."

Coy stood stiff, facing south. He heard or smelled the enemy.

Sam's hands felt ridiculous without The Celt. Hannibal looked as edgy as he felt. Sam wished he and Hannibal had Swift's and Turner's rifles. Ike Galbraith was a great shot—he could knock the heads off blackbirds at twenty paces. Marechal was a good hunter. But Sam wasn't sure of Swift and Turner. *Goddammit! I'm the one to defend my own life!*

Indians showed themselves now, defiantly standing in the open and then ducking back.

"Galbraith, Marechal, ready," said Jedediah.

The shooters trained their sights on whatever targets they could. It was a long shot, over a hundred paces, but there was no wind. Four Mojaves were visible.

"Fire!"

Two Mojaves dropped. A third grabbed himself, perhaps wounded, and started running away.

A dozen Mojaves ran away. A score. A hundred.

Several hundred Indians bolted from cover and streaked away from the trappers, scurrying around rocks, bounding up hillocks. Their hide loincloths flounced in the afternoon sun.

"Rabbits!" called Hannibal.

"Rabbits!" yelled the other men. "Rabbits!"

The trappers stood up and shook their fists in the air. They clapped each other on the back.

"Sum bitch!" yelled one.

"We done it!" yelled another.

"Victoire!"

"Zey are tinned cowards!" cried Marechal.

Diah and Hannibal looked at each other, and everyone at them. They shrugged and started laughing.

"Tinned?" said Hannibal, slapping his thighs.

"Tinned cowards!" hollered Sam, shaking his fist.

They all took up the cry. "Tinned cowards!" They stumbled around like they were drunk. They embraced each other.

Everyone celebrated but poor Tom Virgin, who was unconscious.

"All right!" said the captain loudly. "Get a drink from the river and get back here! This might not be over!"

But it was. The trappers waited, alert, until nearly dark.

Jedediah got Virgin awake and spoke soft words to him. Virgin struggled to his feet.

"Let's go," said the captain.

THEY MARCHED THROUGH the night hungry and thirsty.

"Better than during the day," said Sam.

"Better than being dead," said Hannibal.

Sam kept an eye on Virgin. The wounded man weaved as he walked, but he managed to go slowly, steadily forward.

The trail was an old one, worn by long years of trading with people of the seashore. The Mojaves wanted the shells of the sea, and the coastal peoples wanted Mojave melons, pumpkins, corn, squash, and beans. The captain and Sam had ridden the stretch three times last fall, the first being a false start. It wasn't a hard trek, even in the dark.

Sam knew, though, that the sands blew, and blew, and signs of the trail would be wiped away in some places, perhaps for miles. Parties steered by landmarks of hills and mountains, which were murky and deceptive at night.

His spirits were low. As he tramped, he talked to himself.

We've got no way to carry water, said the nervous part of himself, and added mockingly, *one kettle.*

Gonna be parched all day, every day, said some other part. This part was more relaxed.

What if we miss a spring? said Nervous.

What if? said Relaxed.

We've got about one day's supply of food.

Shining times, answered Relaxed.

Ten- or fifteen-day trip, said Nervous, starving.

That's how I remember it too.
We've lost all our horses and nearly every damn thing.
Hallelujah!
Tom Virgin's going to slow us down.
Or he may die.
Why are you so easy about it?
Just crazy, I guess.

The outfit came to the spring before the sun got hot the next morning. They drank. They ate a little meat, very little. Because the August sun would get blistering hot, they stayed by the spring all day. Mostly they slept in the shade of bushes or rocks. For an hour in midafternoon Jedediah worked on his journal.

When he finished, Sam moved next to him. "What did you write?" As a brigade leader in training, Sam wanted to know.

"First, what happened when we pushed off into the river, and the names of the men who died." Diah looked at his own page. " 'Silas Gobel.' " Sam and Diah looked at each other. Gobel was one of the companions buried in the blazing sands two months ago. He rose up from that death only to walk blind into another.

" 'Henry "Boatswain" Brown,' " Jedediah read on, " 'Polette Labross (a mulatto), William Campbell, David Cunningham, Francois Deromme, Gregory Ortago (a Spaniard), John Ratelle, John Relle (a Canadian), Robiseau (a Canadian half-breed).' "

A checklist of slaughter. Sam took a big breath in and out.

"Next, a list of the men still with me." Sam could see the ten men around him—aside from Sam and Hannibal, Galbraith, Marechal, Virgin, Turner, Swift, LaPoint, Daws, and Palmer.

"Then an account of how we drove them off at the riverbank."

"Read it to me."

"Here's part of it. 'We survivors with but five guns were awaiting behind a defense made of brush the charge of four or five hundred Indians . . . Some of the men asked me if we would be able to defend ourselves. I told them I thought we would. But that was not my opinion.' "

The captain and his *segundo* looked each other in the eye. Hannibal walked over and sat close. Coy lay down against Sam's thigh.

"A wise man learns his letters, my friend," the magician told Sam.

"Yeah."

"A brigade leader needs a record," Jedediah said.

"That's what a clerk is for," said Sam. He didn't add that he wasn't eager to be a brigade leader. Something about it bothered him.

The brigade's clerk, Harrison Rogers, was ahead in California. Meanwhile Jedediah kept the ledgers himself, company property sold or given away.

"Learn to read or not?" said Hannibal.

"Learn to read," said Sam, "some time." He turned to Diah. "So what are we going to do?"

"Go to the Californians."

"Damn." He looked at Hannibal. "Last year they practically jailed Jedediah because we didn't have passports. They told us we could go only if we hightailed it out the way we came and stayed gone."

Jedediah spoke up now. "We left coastal California by the same pass. Then we went to a desert the Spaniards haven't settled and north to some mountains they haven't approached. I don't think they have any honest claim to that country."

Hannibal nodded, understanding.

"We can't go straight to the brigade?" said Sam.

"We need horses, we need food, we need weapons, we need a lot of things. Father Joseph will help us."

"He's the head of San Gabriel Mission," Sam told Hannibal. He looked back at Diah. "And the governor may arrest your ass this time."

Jedediah gave a thin smile. "We'll be quick on our feet."

Sam frowned.

"Sam, I know you're anxious to get to Esperanza. We said we'd be there by September 20, and we will."

Sam walked off. He thought. He fretted. He looked down at

Coy. He looked at Tom Virgin, who tumbled to the ground like
a rag and slept every time they stopped.

Sam thought, *Life goes topsy-turvy into death.*

THAT NIGHT, WANDERING among the desert hills, Jedediah
stopped the line of men. For a moment he looked around.

"You know where we are?"

"No," said Sam. They'd traveled this route only once, with
guides, and in the daylight.

Everyone sat down. Some sprawled, and Virgin seemed to
pass out. They'd trudged all night, zigzagging through creosote
bushes, dipping down into dry washes and clambering up the
other side, mounting hillocks and descending again onto flats
that appeared infinite, but flexed irritatingly up and down. Now
the captain doled out the liquid from their one kettle, a swallow
at a time for each man except himself. "I'm used to going
without," he said. He made Virgin sit up and take an extra
swallow. That was the last drop.

"God, more water," said LaPoint.

"Balm of Gilead," said Hannibal.

"We're lost," said Jedediah.

That got their attention. The captain didn't know where the
next spring was. Every man wondered if he would taste water
again.

"Daybreak soon. Let's rest until then."

Coy whimpered. *He thinks this is ridiculous,* thought Sam.

They stretched out. Some slept. Most couldn't.

At first light Jedediah said, "I'm going up that hill to spot the
trail." There was the advantage of the field glass Diah carried.

A while after sunrise he was back. Sam could see the result
in his face.

"I don't know. The trail goes on one side of that hill or the
other, but I can't tell which."

The men were too tired to grouse.

"I want one man to go with me to look for water."

"I'll go," Sam and Hannibal said at the same time.

"No." He looked around. "Galbraith, come with me. That

hill"—Jedediah pointed toward a much higher one—"that's the direction we need to go." It was the opposite direction of the rising sun. He pursed his lips, thinking. "If Galbraith and I don't come back, head that way. Sam, you're in charge. You'll recognize where the next spring is."

Sam let all this flap through his brain. *If Diah doesn't come back . . .* All right, the party had missed one spring and was hoping to hit the next one. If Sam could spot it.

"Understood."

Diah and Ike Galbraith walked off.

"I don't know if I've got any *move* left in me," said Hannibal.

"I'll carry you if you'll carry me."

They watched their friends disappear around a hill.

Sam studied Virgin, asleep, his mouth hanging open. The bulge in his skull looked terrible.

"All of us could easy die," said the Mage.

IN AN HOUR Galbraith was back, looking amazingly hearty.

"We found water. The captain's there sleeping."

"Zis man, my Ike, he has ze hair of ze bear inside him." This was Marechal.

"The water did it for me. Let's go. It's only gonna get hotter."

Sam roused Virgin and they tramped off.

The little spring was marked by a few bushes where fluid seeped from rocks at the bottom of a hill. Jedediah sat up as the outfit approached.

They were too dry to talk. Each man scooped a little water into his hands and slurped it up. The trickle was tiny, and they took a lot of time, one after another, filling their bellies with liquid. Waiting made them wild-eyed. Finally, they were lazing by the spring. They watered their stomachs over and over, and rubbed water onto their faces and arms and legs, and wadded their clothes up in the spring.

"We'll stay here today," said Jedediah. "Right now I'm going to climb that hill"—it was the highest in sight—"and look for the trail and the next spring."

Off he went.

"Hellacious almighty," said Galbraith, looking after the captain.

"We walk all night, no water," said Marechal.

Hannibal said, "We can't even piss."

"Jedediah walks up a hill and back by himself while we rest," said Sam, "and then he hikes off and finds water."

"Now," said Galbraith, "with me panting and desperate, he marches off to climb a big hill in the heat of the day."

"And he'll come back ready to walk tonight." Sam rolled onto his side to nap. "That's why he's the captain," he said.

THE CAPTAIN DID spot the trail in the glass, about five miles to the south, and he saw where the next spring was. That night he led the party straight across open desert, not bothering with the trail until they rejoined it at the spring. They rested there all day and all the next night. Jedediah rationed out a little dried meat, about a third of what a man needed for sustenance, every other day.

Sam was wondering if they could afford to rest, with food running out.

Marechal said under his breath to Sam, "Hardly no water, hardly no meat, no whiskey any, you *Americains* . . ."

The next day they trekked across the desert during the day. The heat was awful, but the risk of getting lost seemed worse. Jedediah remembered a shortcut pointed out by last year's guides, who thought it too stony for horses. Now they took it.

The sun hit them like a club. Every step was a struggle. They trudged, they wandered, they stumbled. Sam and Hannibal took Virgin by the elbows to steady him. All were too parched and too exhausted to utter one word of complaint.

Occasionally men got a little satisfaction by cutting off slices of cabbage pears and chewing on them. The juice was a blessing on the tongue, and when you chewed the fiber, you could pretend you were eating.

The men were disgruntled, discouraged, failing. Jedediah boosted them continually with encouraging words. "It's not far now," he would say. Tramp, tramp, tramp on the sand.

"There'll be a spring against the hill." Tramp, tramp, tramp. They stopped, and the captain glassed. "See the dark spot at the bottom of the hill there? Those are bushes, and bushes mean water."

Some men lifted their eyes and gazed blearily in the direction of the hill. Maybe someone saw the dark spot. No one mentioned the thousands of footsteps between here and the hill.

Late in the afternoon Virgin collapsed. Seph LaPoint plopped down beside him.

Smith bent over Virgin. "I'm done," he said. No more words came out.

"Me too," said LaPoint.

The captain studied them. Sam thought, *They don't have strength even for words . . .*

"Tom," said the captain, "you've soldiered this far. We all admire you." He looked back and forth from Virgin to LaPoint. "You've got grit. You'll both make it.

"Normally, I'd cover you with sand, keep you cooler, but we don't have any shovels." He thought. "Scoot into the shade of the greasewood here. When you can, dig in the sand with your hands. Make a shallow hole, get in it, and cover up."

LaPoint snickered.

"Seph, it's your job to dig for Tom and cover him."

LaPoint shrugged.

"Do it. Sam saved his own life this way."

"I will," rasped LaPoint. His voice sounded like a scrape on a washboard.

"I'll bring water."

They walked on. Sam's heart twisted at leaving, but he resisted looking back. The first time this happened, two months ago, he and Diah and Robert Evans left Silas Gobel behind. Gobel, who was now nothing but bones. The second time, Diah and Gobel had to go off and leave Sam and Evans. Both times Diah had found a spring, both times someone carried a kettle back, and both times the men were saved.

Sam checked the sky for buzzards. *I wonder if I'll have to see them circling over Virgin and LaPoint.*

Or these eight figures trudging across the Mojave Desert.

Just after sunset Diah led them to a spring.

"I'll go back," said Sam.

"Me too," said Hannibal.

Two men to carry one kettle, but Sam was glad of the company.

What a world, he thought, *where nightmares get to be routine.*

THAT NIGHT EVERYONE talked about the Inconstant River. Drank and talked and drank some more and talked about the Inconstant. Their thirst felt so wide and dry they didn't even miss food.

LaPoint wanted to know why it was called Inconstant.

Sam smiled and answered dryly, "Because the water disappears into the sands and then comes back up and disappears again."

"In lots of places you can dig for it," said Jedediah.

Sam held up his bare hands and looked at them. He said good-naturedly, "My hands are begging to dig."

The men chuckled. Anything for a chuckle, as downhearted as they felt.

"It flows out of the mountains to the west," Jedediah said. "One way or another, there's water steady enough up the river."

Sam added, "Last year there were Indians at the foot of the mountain. We traded with them."

"We can cross the mountain in two days," the captain said, "and we'll see deer."

Men slunk off to separate boulders and bushes to sleep. They didn't feel much like talking, didn't feel like company. Some were slipping off into a private place in their minds where they could die peacefully. Sam wondered whether Virgin would wake up in the morning.

He knew the men were bothered by a lot of things. They were starving. They were half-thirsting. Their bodies were wasting. If they traveled like this for long, they'd die, no question.

"I can tell you this," said Hannibal. "Death hath dominion here."

Sam shook off that thought. Something else was bothering him.

MOUNTAIN LUCK, THEY called it. Desert luck too, Sam supposed. Like mountain luck, it could be very good and very bad.

The river was drier than the year before. At first Sam was worried about water. But in the middle of that first day walking up the Inconstant, Hannibal spotted two horses.

The captain stopped the outfit and circled the mounts, looking for their owners. He found two lodges and eased up to them gently enough that the Indians didn't have a chance to run away. Paiutes, they said they were. He made them presents of some beads.

Then he brought the men up. The Paiutes trembled visibly, men, women, and children. Sam could see that every impulse was to run like hell, but they stayed. Slowly, Jedediah began to trade with them. He offered more beads, which pleased the women. He put out cloth, which thrilled them. He laid down a double handful of knives. In an hour or two he'd traded for both horses, some water pots, and big loaves of candy made from cane grass.

The brigade had this candy last fall. It was funny stuff, a loaf of sugar hard as a rock. You knocked off pieces with a tomahawk or your knife. Strange food, but the sweet tasted great and any nourishment helped.

The Paiutes told the trappers that the lodges of the Serranos were still at the foot of the mountain, where the river came out. All the beaver men were sitting in front of the Paiute lodges, sucking on chunks of candy.

"We'll be able to trade for food and horses there," Jedediah said with satisfaction. "The closer to the Spanish settlements, the easier to get horses."

Last year, Sam remembered, the Serranos made a rabbit drive through the desert, many hunters marching, and put on a feast for the trappers.

They loaded the horses, took their leave of the Paiutes, and resumed their march. The Serrano lodges were about three days ahead, and the horses, not the men, were the beasts of burden.

Sam looked carefully at the captain. Jedediah would never say it, but he was proud. His brigade had blundered into a disaster at the Mojave villages. Without water, without food, and without horses, he had brought them across the worst desert anyone had seen.

That night when they bedded down, they knew they were going to live.

First day up the Inconstant—the river was almost completely dry—but they had water in the pots. They found a standing pool to camp by. The men stripped and dunked their entire bodies in the liquid.

Second day, there was water enough in occasional places in the riverbed—they would have been fine even without the pots.

On the third day they walked into the cluster of lodges that made up the Serrano village. Their guides from last autumn weren't here, but the chiefs remembered the fur men well. Jedediah gave them presents, they gave the trappers dried rabbit meat.

The men fell on the meat like vultures. While the captain traded for two more horses, they gorged themselves. Then they napped and gorged themselves again. They lay down, slept, woke in the middle of the night, and filled their bellies once more. They acted ravenous and uproarious.

Sam ate as big as any man, and spent the night churning his mind about what he had to do. Every day this journey, going to California, bothered him. The only home he had, it wasn't here. And now things were about to get worse.

In the morning, while the captain was making sure of the hitches that held the gear and newfound food on the horses, Sam touched Jedediah on the shoulder. Smith turned to him.

"Diah, I have to go back."

"YOU WHAT?" THE captain's voice crackled.

Men were craning their necks to hear this conversation.

Jedediah took Sam's elbow and moved off. Hannibal followed.
Jedediah looked at him, hesitated, and then nodded.

"What are you talking about?"

"Paladin is back there. My father's rifle is back there. I can't
walk away."

"You are second in command here. You have a responsibility."

Sam poked the dirt with a moccasin. "One to myself too."

"Sam, you can't do this."

"If I have to, I'll quit." He paused and added, "Sir," the first
time he'd spoken that word to Jedediah in several years.

"It's too dangerous."

"It's risky."

"Water, food, you can't do it."

Sam just looked at him. They both knew the outfit had just
done it.

"You giving up on Esperanza, Flat Dog, and Julia?"

Sam's daughter, Meadowlark's brother, and his wife. "Not a
bit. I'll be along."

"Late."

"Yes."

Jedediah looked toward the horizon to the east, where they'd
just walked, and said, "Let's sit."

They did. Sam barged ahead. "I'm going to trade my pistol."
Sam pulled it out of his belt and put it in his lap. "The Serranos
will give me what I need for it. I'll have more than we did coming across."

Jedediah huffed out a big breath. "You mean it."

"Yes."

So they worked it out. The captain and Sam would make the
trade together, so the Serranos wouldn't know Sam was going
off alone. Even friendly Indians could be tempted by the vul-
nerability of a lone man.

They got their choice of the herd for the pistol, several of
Sam's .50-caliber balls, and a little powder. Hannibal picked
out a brown gelding for Sam. "This is a hell of an animal," he
said, "an athlete."

The men grinned at each other. The Serranos had owned

horses, but probably not firearms. Not that one pistol would do much good. With these balls a man might learn to shoot, but he'd play the devil getting more ammunition.

Jedediah provided a couple of knives and some beads to get Sam a stack of dried meat. He gave Sam a pot to carry water.

"I mean to steal some vegetables from the Mojaves too," said Sam.

All three of them chuckled.

"You'll be two weeks behind," said Jedediah. They'd spent seven days crossing from the Mojave villages to here.

"Or less," said Sam.

"I'll have to go in to see the governor at Monterey," said Diah.

"If they don't arrest your ass at San Gabriel."

The Mexicans thought Americans were their enemies. Sam chuckled. What a laugh. Twenty fur men against the entire Mexican army.

"While I'm gone, I'll leave the brigade on the Appelaminy, right where they are."

"I'll catch up."

Jedediah twisted his straight, thin mouth and thought. Finally he said, "I'm going to lend you something." He slipped the lanyard over his head and handed Sam the field glass. "You'll need it more than me."

Sam's heart pinged a little. The glass was a big item to Jedediah, not only useful but a symbol of command. He thought of handing it back, but then thought of scouting the Mojaves. It would come in handy.

He said, "Thank you, Diah."

By midmorning the brigade was ready to go west, Sam itching to get started east. They parted ways well outside the village, so the Serranos wouldn't know.

There Hannibal sprang his surprise. "I'm going with you."

"No. No way. This is my job."

"Two are safer than one," said Hannibal.

"A lot safer," said Jedediah, who was known for his lone journeys in the wilderness.

"I want to go," said Hannibal.

"Nothing in it for you."

"You're my friend."

Sam slid up onto the unfamiliar brown gelding. "He was *my* father."

Off he rode, alone.

Three

AT FIRST LIGHT Sam lay in the shallows and dunked his face in the water. The Colorado. Hallelujah, praise be, the river. He drank when he felt like it. He craned his face back out of the water. He rolled over and wet his back side. He lolled and soaked himself.

Coy lapped at the edge and stayed back. Standing between man and coyote, the brown gelding slurped and slobbered and stamped and splashed all three of them. Sam had named the pony Brownie.

Sam had managed the return trip in five days, two less than coming over. Knowing the route and the springs, and having a waxing moon, he'd traveled long and hard every night. Resting during the day, neither he nor the horse sweated away so much water. Half the time he rode, and half he walked. Sometimes he felt like loping alongside the horse, but he resisted. He needed all his strength, and the mount's. He thought he was a good plainsman, a good man in the mountains, and he was getting to be a good man in the desert.

He had about ten pounds of dried meat, and he ate a pound or so every day. Coy hunted mice and pack rats and devoured them. The grass near the springs was plenty for a single horse. The trip seemed easy, actually. Sam told himself it was easy because it was the right thing.

Now he had to get the job done.

For watering man and beasts, he'd carefully picked a spot blocked from the village by a river bend. Now he tied Brownie to a tree, crept through the willows, and glassed the collection of huts downstream. He sat and watched until the sun cleared the eastern horizon. He didn't want the sun to reflect off the lens and give him away. Keeping low, he walked back to his horse, scrunching up his mouth. He hadn't learned anything new.

Sam knew he could find the horses, which would be kept herded somewhere beside the river. He didn't know where The Celt was. That would take some scouting.

He pulled the horse's stake and walked upstream. Somewhere above and on this side he would sleep all morning. Later he would swim the river, drifting down with the current, and take a look around. He'd find the horses and scout the village. He'd look for Red Shirt too. Ten of Sam's friends had been murdered here, and Red Shirt was the chief.

SAM HAD TO laugh.

He lay on a ridge watching the horse herd. He was so close he didn't even need the glass. Today the horses were south of the village, between two hills that sloped to the river, where the critters could get to water. They were loose-herded now and would be close-herded at night. Every week or so they'd be moved because the desert grass was so scanty.

The Mojaves kept the horses well guarded because they were enemies of the Yuma tribe, which lived downstream at the mouth of the Gila River.

Right now, Sam thought, *you boys got your eyes on the wrong enemy.*

He hadn't been worried about finding the horses, just his rifle. There were four or five hundred Mojave warriors. They'd stolen a baker's dozen rifles, but just one Celt. How would Sam ever find it?

Now he was grinning because the problem had just solved itself.

The Mojaves must be big on show.

Two guards were keeping an eye on the horses today, one tall and skinny like a reed, the other stocky, with a limp. And for no earthly reason those guards were carrying rifles. It made no sense. They wore no shot pouches, no powder horns. Which meant they couldn't actually fire the rifles. Probably they hadn't even figured out how yet. Still, they carried the weapons, probably proud of their symbols of thunder-striking.

Sam didn't recognize one rifle, might be anyone's. The other one was The Celt, and it was in the hands of the reedy fellow. That gave Sam a tingle.

He watched Paladin. Her white coat and black markings gleamed in the strong sunlight, black cap around the ears, black shield on the chest, and black mane and tail. "Hello, gorgeous," Sam whispered.

He watched her move around, grazing. She looked fit, her hip healed.

Suddenly he thought, *I hope she's carrying Ellie's foal.*

Sam and Hannibal had put Paladin together with the stallion, and had seen Ellie cover her.

Damn. If she wasn't in foal, she would be after a couple of weeks in this herd.

He decided he better check that The Celt hadn't been damaged. A man who didn't know how to fire a rifle wouldn't know how to take care of one.

He made sure the sun was behind him and trained the field glass on The Celt. The rifle looked fine. Hammer intact and not cocked, triggers still there, stock all right, butt looking normal. This glass was something. He felt like he could almost make out the name on the engraved butt plate, THE CELT. Celt was one of the few written words he knew. He inspected the rifle one more time. He'd have to make sure that Reed hadn't stood it on its muzzle instead of its butt and clogged the barrel with dirt. He'd also have to check that the ball, patch, and powder he kept in The Celt were still seated in the barrel. He wouldn't want to have a need, lift his rifle, and find out he was just pointing a stick at someone.

He smiled to himself. As things were, he could walk right up to Reed in broad daylight. Reed would aim The Celt at the intruder, intending to unleash lightning. The flint would go *click!* against the pan, and nothing would happen. While Reed was puzzling things out, Sam would drive a blade into his innards.

Sam considered that thought. Yes, he wanted to kill someone. These Mojaves murdered ten of his friends. And not in an honest fight—through treachery. No, he didn't mind his heat for revenge. But when it came to the actual killing, his stomach would churn.

It was midday. Probably the guards would be changed at dusk. Reed and Limp would go back to the village, and The Celt would go with them.

He could make his move now. Sam's way was to be daring, to act without planning everything out, to strike whenever opportunity seemed to open and ride out the storm. The edge always went to the bold.

Yes. He could take the guards out quietly one by one. He could grab The Celt and Paladin, swim the river, and ride hellaciously for California. He might also run the horse herd off. If he did that, the Mojaves would either have to take time to gather the horses or chase a well-mounted man on foot.

He'd be giving up the chance to get more rifles back, and to get even with Red Shirt, but . . .

He got to his hands and knees. He felt it rise in him. *I need to act.* He saw what to do. Guards had to drink, especially on a sun-blasted day like this one. He would wait by the river and take the first man in silence.

The second . . . ?

It took time to slip back into the ravine, circle the herd on the upstream side, and get into the cover of the brush alongside the Colorado. He dropped to his knees and drank deep.

Coy lapped gingerly. He never seemed to need much water.

Sam surveyed the ground, which would become a killing field. The other advantage here, he noted, was that the rush-rush of the current would cover the sounds of his movements.

He slipped back through the willows, searched for the guards, and got a nasty surprise.

Four guards stood together talking.

Sam waited and watched. They chatted. Reed and Limp waved, walked away toward the river.

Damn, they were changing the guards. In the middle of the day.

This thought gave Sam a chill. As he'd slipped down from the ridge to the river, he'd crossed paths with the arriving guards.

Reed and Limp strolled casually through the brush, worrying about nothing.

Sam put a hand on Coy and kept low in a clump of willows. Reed was carrying The Celt. Sam ached to jump out and grab his rifle. But it didn't feel right.

Reed and Limp drank from the river, looked around, laughed about something, and headed along the bank toward the village.

Sam followed on the sly.

HOURS LATER, BACK at his bivouac, Coy resting and Brownie grazing nearby, Sam added up his information. He knew the spread of the brush huts on the sand flat thoroughly. Now he'd seen that Reed's hut was on the northern end, and he had a pretty wife with a child on the way. The wife had a mole next to her left nipple, what among white women might be thought of as a beauty mark.

The Celt was tucked into the hut—not lying directly on the sand, Sam hoped. Reed sat on a cottonwood log with other men, all of them straightening arrow shafts. Beauty Mark puttered around the hut. Then she went to work the fields by the river with other women. Sam followed them, bush to bush. For a moment the hut was unattended. But Sam's white skin and white hair would be spotted.

He slipped back here to rest and wait for the cover of darkness. Surely The Celt would be in the hut tonight. He pictured the dome of brush. It was outlying; it faced east. A fire pit blackened the sand in front of the door, evidently where Beauty Mark did the cooking. A shovel leaned next to the entrance. That shovel irked Sam—Jedediah had traded shovels to the Mojaves just a couple of weeks ago.

It would be dicey to slip into the hut with the couple sleeping there, dark or not. And if he woke them, he'd have a hell of a long run to reach the herd and get Paladin.

Would the Mojaves guess the horses were a target? He thought so. Then they would boil around him like hornets. He couldn't take the chance.

On the other hand, he did have a trick that might let him get Paladin out of the herd . . .

He shook his head to clear it of doubt. Hell, maybe the Indians would have a get-together tonight, some sort of ceremony, and his rifle would be unwatched.

One comfort—the camp dogs wouldn't get excited about Sam or Coy. After the days spent around each other, the dogs were used to them.

Oh, didn't he miss his pistol now? He was thinking of how the Mojaves panicked at the firing of two rifles on the day of the slaughter. But he traded his pistol for Brownie, who was essential.

Well, he thought, *maybe I'll just have to do what I like to do, start the trouble and then improvise like crazy.*

On that note he took a cat nap.

THE NIGHT WAS chill. Lying on a boulder, Sam hugged himself. Coy was all eyes on the village, and Sam was riveted on a single hut, Reed and Beauty Mark's.

Curiously, the horse herd was more closely watched than the village. Looked like enemies in this country were more likely to steal horseflesh than to attack such a big camp.

Everyone was asleep, had been asleep for hours. Sam didn't see a good opportunity yet. *Damn, If I don't get a chance by first light, I guess I'll just go like a berserker.* That was a word he'd learned from Hannibal the magician.

Oh, cuss and to hell with it.

Sam stood up on the boulder. *Now.*

He looked at the moon, sagging down the western sky, full-bellied. Now was the time. Maybe the moonlight would be enough to find The Celt.

He slid off the rock, and Coy leapt down. Sam padded slowly, carefully toward the hut. He kept balanced. He avoided touching the limbs of bushes. He made sure of every foot placement. After every step he waited and listened.

He circled the hut and approached the back side. The moon shone bright here. The willow leaves, dry on the branches, let speckles of moonlight into the hut.

A dozen feet behind the hut Sam squatted. He could make out nothing in the interior but shadows. He couldn't even be sure where the sleeping figures were. If they were like Crows, Reed and Beauty Mark slept at the rear of the lodge.

He studied the area above where the couple's bed probably was. Crows, Sioux, most Indians of the plains and mountains hung their rifles from leather thongs at the rear, well off the ground. Maybe . . .

He thought about it.

He covered his face with his hands so his eyes would let in more of the faint light. He popped his hands away. Yes, he was pretty sure. Parallel to the earth, three or four feet off the ground, at the very back of the lodge he could see a long, rod-like shape.

The Celt.

He hardly dared think. Could he do it? Slip both hands silently through the branches? Yes. The branches bent to shape the lodge stood well apart. Hold The Celt with one hand and cut the thongs with the other? He probably could. Slip The Celt back out of the branches? That would be tricky. *But what a hoot, if I can get away with it.*

He cautioned himself. *When I get it, I can't fire it.* There was no telling whether the muzzle might be blocked with something.

He stood up again. Step by step he eased forward. Coy stood

to one side, sniffed, and watched curiously. Every step closer, every step closer.

Now he could almost smell the sleeping couple, almost hear the deep, rhythmic breaths. He could hardly believe that The Celt was within reach.

He snaked his right hand through the lodge branches. Silence. Had he done it?

He grasped the rifle.

Except it wasn't The Celt. He had his hand on . . . a flint spearhead.

Sam smothered a laugh and almost peed on himself.

He was holding Reed's spear!

"Mmmm!"

Every hair on his body squiggled.

He jerked his hand out and leapt back.

Someone spoke.

Sam jumped. He breathed and calmed himself. A female voice. Sounded like "ark-fart," but he knew only about twenty words of Mojave.

He padded slowly backward, watching the hut.

Now the man's voice sounded.

The woman's.

He lost his poise—he turned and sprinted back behind the boulder. Coy trotted at his heels.

He crouched and listened.

Nothing. He seemed to have disturbed no one. No movement came from Reed and Beauty Mark's lodge, and no sounds loud enough to hear. He tried to melt into the rock.

Silence. Waiting. Breathing again.

Soon a surprise. Across the village he saw tinder flame up. An infant fire lit the face of a woman bending over it.

He watched and waited, every sense super-alert.

Beauty Mark came out of her hut, got down on her knees, and started making a fire. The way she was going about it, it looked like she would singe her bare nipples.

Around the village other fires spurted up, a dot of orange here, a flicker there.

Beauty Mark hung a metal pot over the flames on a tripod, a pot the fur men had traded to the tribe. She poured water from a clay jug into the pot. She dumped something else in.

Sam understood. He'd seen the women picking beans yesterday afternoon. Now they were boiling them. They probably did the cooking early so they wouldn't have to lean over fires during the heat of the day.

Sam noticed that night was lifting, the sky easing from black to gray. First light.

He made a very simple choice. Go berserk!

He gripped his tomahawk in one hand and his butcher knife in the other. He sprinted toward the hut pell-mell, bellowing as loud as he could.

Beauty Mark jumped back in alarm.

Sam ignored her and went for the lodge. He leapt with both feet onto where he thought Reed would be stretched out. His knee hit what felt like a raised head.

He jumped into the air and came down ass first on the center of the lodge. Branches splintered. Sam and the lodge dome banged to earth.

From inside Reed roared. Beauty Mark was shrieking.

The broken lodge branches rippled. Sam could see Reed crawling toward the entrance. He kicked and hit a butt. He looked sharp, kicked again, and seemed to catch a neck.

Beauty Mark jumped onto his back.

Sam roared and threw himself over backward onto the branches. He came down square on Beauty Mark's chest, and heard the breath *whumpf!* out of her.

Reed was crawling out of the smashed entrance.

Sam clubbed him with the flat side of the tomahawk.

Reed got to his feet but staggered sideways. Sam slammed the tomahawk blade at his shoulder.

Beauty Mark came at Sam clawing.

He put his hands on both of her breasts and shoved fiercely. She went flying backward.

The whole camp was aroused. People howled. Men ran toward him with weapons in hand.

Sam spotted The Celt's butt plate sticking out of a hide

wrap on the dirt floor of the hut. He heaved the rifle out and ran like hell.

Two arrows whistled by his pumping arms. Coy dashed at the attackers, barking ferociously.

Sam whirled. The Mojaves slowed down or stopped. He raised and pointed The Celt. The warriors hurled themselves to the ground, behind bushes, or behind lodges.

Fooled you! The rifle wasn't even cocked.

Sam whooped and ran. In an instant Coy was alongside him. They dodged around bushes. For now the brush would save him. No one could get a clear shot.

Fifty yards into the brush Sam turned hard to the right to head for the herd. Paladin . . . He ran like a madman. *Paladin will save us.*

He jumped into a dry wash, bounded across, and scrambled up the other side. There he faced a grove of cottonwoods—and forty or fifty armed and angry Indians.

He stopped. *Oh, hell, I can't berserk my way out of this one.* He jumped back into the wash and fled upstream.

A dozen, two dozen, three dozen Mojaves jumped in and called out their war cries. Others ran along the banks. They came at him like baying hounds.

Come on, feet, do it.

Sam sprinted for everything he was worth. *I can't slip out of this one . . .*

When he put one foot on a fist-sized rock, it turned and he went down hard. His shoulder plowed a groove in the gravel.

Rising to a knee, Sam saw a huge Mojave bearing down on him. The man cocked his spear.

Sam lifted The Celt.

A gun roared.

Blood squirted from the Mojave's chest, and he crashed to the ground like a felled tree.

What the devil? A gun? He almost checked The Celt's muzzle for smoke.

From the left bank, the direction Sam came from, a cloud of white mist floated over the wash.

All the Mojaves ran back toward the village.

A head rose over the bank.

Hannibal?

Another head appeared.

Hannibal on Brownie!

The Delaware jumped Brownie into the wash, galloped to Sam, and skidded to a stop in the gravel. Sam hopped up behind Hannibal.

The horse labored out of the wash and ran toward the herd. As they went, Hannibal reloaded his pistol.

"We've got them buffaloed," he yelled, grinning hugely. "You all right?"

"The horse sentries heard that shot."

"We'll take them."

Brownie and Coy topped the next to last ridge and plunged into the ravine.

A sentry loosed a flock of arrows at them.

Sam and Hannibal dived off the horse in opposite directions and scrambled behind bushes. They were too close, maybe twenty-five paces, and too exposed.

Pain lightninged up Sam's arm.

His left hand sprouted a shaft and feathers. He yelled, and his knife clattered to the ground.

A second sentry rose on the ridge, pointing a rifle at Sam and Hannibal.

Sam cackled loudly. "What do you mean to do," he hollered, "scare us to death?"

Hannibal stood up, leveled his pistol, and shot the arrow warrior square in the chest. His body lifted and dropped backward.

Instantly Sam and Hannibal charged the rifleman.

The fellow threw the rifle down and ran.

From the top of the ridge Sam threw his tomahawk at the man. It hit him handle-first on top of the head and bounced forward. The Indian hightailed it for the hills.

Hannibal grabbed the abandoned rifle.

Sam whistled piercingly, low-high.

Paladin tossed her head and cantered toward them.

Hannibal smiled. "Magic."

Sam touched her muzzle, jumped joyously onto her back, grabbed her mane, and rubbed her ears.

Brownie trotted up to join Paladin. Hannibal grabbed the rope bridle and vaulted on.

"Let's go!" Sam yelled, and kicked Paladin toward the river.

Hannibal said, "I'm going to get something for our trouble."

Quickly, they separated a group of seven horses from the main herd. Hannibal drove them toward the water. Sam dashed Paladin at the rest of the herd, shouting and waving his hat. They broke like a flock of sparrows and ran in all directions.

Sam put Paladin to a gallop after Hannibal and the seven stolen horses. From the bank he saw their heads bobbing up and down in the river. Without missing a step, Paladin leapt into the shallows and soaked Sam. In a few steps she was swimming. The cool of the river was a blessing.

Four

"WHAT THE HELL did you do?"

"Saved your ass. Let me see that hand."

Sam showed him the puncture wound. Back by the Colorado, Hannibal had pulled the arrow through. Coy tried to lick the hand, and Hannibal shoved his muzzle away.

"I'm going to poultice and bandage it now."

"You followed me?"

"No need. I knew where you were going. I came along far behind."

Hannibal made a paste with ground herbs from his belt pouch. He wrapped them in cloth, dunked them in a water jug, and applied them to the wound.

"This is damn likely to fester, but we'll do our best."

"Why did you follow me?" Sam would worry about his hand later.

"It's my fault you're in this country at all."

This was a kind of joke between them. On Christmas Day nearly five years ago Hannibal found Sam moping over a girl and dared him to do what he really wanted to do, go to the West.

"That's it for now."

They were stretched out in some rocks a hundred paces above the first spring. The nine horses were rope-corralled a quarter mile away, on poor grass.

Sam and Hannibal scooted onto their bellies and rested their barrels on rocks. They made sure priming was in the pans and that the rifles were on half cock. They made sure their cover was good and their sight lines were good.

The Mojaves, if they followed, had to use this spring. Then two good riflemen would have some fine targets. Hannibal didn't know the rifle he'd snatched from the sentry, but that made an extra firearm.

"I've still got those words written down."

"Too bad you can't read."

They both chuckled.

"They're getting hard to make out."

Sam opened his shot pouch, spread out a patch of rabbit fur, unrolled a piece of oiled cloth, and unfolded the piece of paper within. The hand was stiff and achy and the bandage felt cumbersome. He handed the paper to Hannibal.

"Illegible," said the Delaware. "Too many times wet, too dry, too much folding and unfolding."

" 'Everything worthwhile is crazy,' " quoted Sam, " 'and everyone on the planet who's not following his wild-hair, middle-of-the-night notions should lay down his burden, right now, in the middle of the row he's hoeing, and follow the direction his wild hair points.' "

"What bit me in the tail that night?"

"Maybe you'll write it down for me again."

"Sure. When we don't have enemies hot behind us."

Sam looked to the east and pointed with his bandaged hand. From these rocks they had a fine panoramic view back toward the Colorado River.

"I see them too," said Hannibal. "We don't get to slip out of anything."

"I wouldn't have it any other way."

Waiting was the worst part. Watching your enemy. Mulling on his intent. Picturing blood and torn flesh. Hurting in your middle, because you know that the blood might be yours.

Sam flexed his hand. He hoped the damn thing didn't make it hard to shoot. But he had confidence—The Celt shot dead center.

They watched the Mojaves ride up to the spring at a lope. A half dozen of them carried useless rifles. Sam and Hannibal grinned at each other.

The Indians held their horses back from the water while two scouts inspected the tracks around the spring. Francisco was one of the scouts, and Red Shirt seemed to be the war leader. Handsome, friendly, slick Francisco. Treacherous Francisco. Quickly the interpreter found the tracks of the mounts moving along the foot of this rocky spur toward where they were corralled.

The Indians let the horses drink first. When the men dismounted and stepped toward the water, Hannibal fired.

Red Shirt thudded to the ground.

Sam saw no need to hold his fire. The Indians couldn't scramble up these rocks before he and Hannibal reloaded. He pulled the trigger and Francisco went down.

Sam thought grimly how easy this was, with the barrel resting on a big rock.

A few Mojaves jumped onto their horses. One man yelled at the enemy and waved a rifle.

Hannibal fired, and the yelling man got knocked under a horse and trampled.

The rest of the Mojaves jumped on their horses, and all skedaddled, taking three riderless mounts with them.

"What do you think?" said Hannibal, reloading fast.

"We'll be able to watch them halfway back to the river," said Sam.

While Hannibal made sure the Indians were riding away, Sam walked to the horses and brought them back to the water.

Hannibal dragged the three bodies in a pile away from the spring.

The two took turns all afternoon, sleeping and watching. The Mojaves stayed gone.

Being near the three dead men gave Sam the willies. He didn't want to get an angle where he could see Francisco's and Red Shirt's bodies. He imagined they stank already. He was mad at the buzzards circling overhead, eyeing the dead.

"What are you thinking about?" asked Hannibal.

"Esperanza," lied Sam.

Then, however, he did think about his daughter. Over and over he imagined holding her. And embracing Flat Dog, her uncle. And Julia, her aunt.

When dark fell, Sam and Hannibal rode toward the next spring.

"SISTER SUSIE PICKED a peck of peppers," said Hannibal to the plop of the horses' hoofs.

"A peck of peppers Sister Susie picked," answered Sam.

"Plenty of peckers," put in Hannibal, "Sister Susie plundered."

Jedediah grinned at him. "McKye," he said lightly, "you put a cloud into a fine day."

"Sister Susie deemed them dapper Daves."

The eighteenth day of September was in fact fine. Sunny and warm, views of what the Mexicans called the Sierra Nevada stretching for miles to the east, the river hard by, and miles of wheat-colored grasses in every direction.

Sam felt heady. In a few hours he would see Esperanza, and Flat Dog, and Julia. Jedediah, Sam knew, was happy. He'd told Rogers, the brigade's clerk, to hold the brigade in that camp on the Appelaminy until September 20. If the captain didn't appear by then with supplies and more men, Rogers was to consider him dead, take the remaining men in to the Russian fort at Bodega Bay for supplies, and make his way home however he could.

They would arrive this afternoon, two days before the deadline.

And Hannibal? He seemed to like the world every day, however it came. Sam looked at his friend's face. Sometimes it made him twist with envy, the way his friend seemed to enjoy everything. He had a saying for it. "Life is a whirling devil of trouble, thanks be to God."

Only a little while more.

ROGERS, ART BLACK, and Joe Laplant stood up, waved, and came running. "Good to see you, you old coons!"

Then they looked behind the captain at the other riders, and their faces changed.

Jedediah saw it. "We have nothing," he said. He'd promised to come with a pack train of supplies of every kind. Instead he brought ten riders, half of them without rifles, not a single pack animal, and no equipment.

"Hellfire," said Rogers.

The captain and his clerk looked at each other, speaking without words.

Art Black, though, was looking sheepishly at Sam.

Jedediah reached down to shake Black's hand, and Art didn't even notice.

"They're gone," he said.

Sam opened his mouth and nothing came out.

"Disappeared," Black said.

Rogers kept his eyes down and kicked at the dirt.

"Esperanza?" Sam squeaked.

Black nodded. His eyes ached the truth up to Sam.

"F-F-Flat Dog and Julia?"

"Gone. Probably kidnapped. No idea where they are."

"When?"

"About two months ago."

Gone. Sam almost fell off Paladin.

Rogers changed the subject. "The rest of the men are out hunting." He looked at the ten gaunt riders and their mounts. "We have plenty of meat but we're out of everything else. They'll be back before dark."

"I'm sorry," Black said to Sam.

Art Black was a decent man. Sam had never liked Rogers.

The two outfits greeted each other, one by one. They hadn't seen each other in over a year. The men from Salt Lake, intended to be rescuers, were the ones who needed rescuing.

Whatever they were saying, Sam could see their mouths move, but he couldn't hear the words. He got off Paladin and led her down to the Appelaminy.

The mare drank. Sam had the illusion, repeatedly, that he was tumbling head over heels into the river.

His infant daughter, gone.

One of his best friends, gone.

His best friend's wife, disappeared.

He sat down by the river for a long time. He rubbed Coy's head. He listened to the water and watched it turn and swirl. Paladin splashed in the shallows. When he was ready, Sam staked the mare on some grass and walked back to the fire. The hunters were back, and everyone was gathered around and feeding on elk.

"Give me the story," Sam told Rogers.

Head down, the clerk began. "The child was colicky all the time," he said in a tone that suggested it wasn't his concern. "Señora Julia wanted a *médico* or a *curandera*. She had a notion about some herbs or something." Sam didn't know whether the tone was contempt for Mexicans or the irritability one married woman can cause in a camp of rough men.

Rogers looked up from his food at Sam and smiled eerily. "Some Indians led them toward San Jose. They thought they'd come on a rancho, either mission or private, and get some help. Didn't figure they'd have to go all the way to San Jose.

"Indians come back, said the party stopped at a farmhouse a day's ride that direction." He indicated west with a vague wave. "Men took 'em at gunpoint. I rode over there with some of the boys. Farmer said, 'People in Monterey wanted them,' wouldn't say nothing else."

Sam glared at Rogers, thinking the clerk would have done

more if it wasn't an Indian, a Mexican, and a half-breed child. He clenched and unclenched his fists.

Coy tensed, glaring at the clerk. Rogers gave the coyote a nasty look.

"Give me that liver," Hannibal said to Rogers.

Sam snapped his head toward his friend.

Rogers picked up the liver with the tip of his butcher knife and extended it to Hannibal.

"Hannibal, I . . ."

Hannibal interrupted. "Eat. Eat good. You're going to need it."

Sam got up and walked down to the river, Coy trotting along.

After he stared at the dark water for a while, Hannibal sat down next to him and tossed a hunk of meat to Coy. "Color prejudice shows in all sorts of ways," he said right off. "Even in people who say they don't have any."

Sam didn't answer.

"We'll find them."

"Yes." He turned a grim face to Hannibal. "That bastard at Monterey got them."

"I know the story. Let's get back."

The celebration that night was pathetic. The men left waiting here were down in the mouth about what the captain hadn't brought—everything a trapper needed, from goods to trade to the Indians to critical items like powder, lead, traps, knives, and coffee.

The men who came from the Salt Lake were miserable about their friends killed by the Mojaves, and having to tell the story.

Everyone grumbled in their food. They traded piece after piece of news, sometimes personal information, sometimes an item that bore on their mission to trap beaver, sometimes a story that was funny or nutty or unbelievable.

Jedediah caught up on the business news from Rogers. The men left behind had had an easy time, fine weather, lots of good hunting, Indians that were both peaceable and honest. Good beaver trapping, except in the summer.

The captain didn't say it, but he knew that Smith, Jackson &

Sublette had paid wages both summers and the men hadn't had a chance to earn the firm a dime.

Sam sat in a deep pool of unbelief.

"The Spaniards," said Rogers, meaning the Mexicans, "sent some riders up here from San Jose. They wanted to know what we were doing in the territory. I told them hunting beaver."

"Did that satisfy them?"

"Seemed so." Rogers's eyes said, *But they're Spaniards, and you never know.*

Hannibal said quietly to Sam, "Let's get some rest. We leave in the morning."

SAM LOOKED OVER his breakfast coffee cup at the captain. "We're going to Monterey."

"Why don't we ride together?"

Sam mulled. He knew the captain had to go. He needed to ask for passports and for permission to trade for the equipment the outfit needed.

The governor would tell the captain he had no right to be in the country, and he was probably a spy. "Why," the governor would press, "did you come back after you promised to leave the country and never return?"

At least something was worth a smile this morning. Sam said, "You may end up in the *calabozo.*"

"With you. Listen—wait. I'll leave in two or three days. We'll stop in Saint Joseph, maybe you'll get news there, and I'm sure they'll make me go on to Monterey to see the governor."

Sam shook his head no. "I'm too worried."

Jedediah raised his eyes to Sam's. "I give you a lot of rope, you know."

This brought Sam up short.

"Sometimes you act like you don't work for Smith, Jackson & Sublette. As if you just hang around with us when it's handy."

Sam dropped his head. "I guess so."

"A brigade leader can't do that. The company comes ahead of the personal."

Sam nodded. He looked the captain straight in the eye. "Not with me."

Coy whimpered.

"Go on then," said Jedediah, his tone edgy.

Sam and Hannibal were gone within the hour.

Five

AS THEY RODE to Monterey, Sam thought, *I need to get my daughter to her country, Crow country.*

To the music of Paladin's hoofs he walked through the dark door of memory and looked at the unbearable past. Meadowlark died of childbed fever. Sam had a daughter and no wife. He buried her at the mission in Monterey. After the friars had said their words, he spaded the dirt back onto her coffin, thunk after thunk after thunk.

Then the handsome son of Don Joaquin Montalban arrived, asking for Señorita Julia Rubio. With a cunning smile, he extended his false invitation. Would she care to visit an old family friend at their rancho?

Julia understood what was going on. These old family friends were in league with her father, who had spread word that his runaway daughter was to be found and returned. So she answered firmly: "My husband and I will gladly receive the don this evening at the mission."

The young don looked contemptuously at the Indian who presumed to be the husband of the beautiful youngest daughter of the great Rubio family of Rancho Malibu. He looked at their rough fur trapper companion, Sam Morgan. "Not possible," he said. Then he gave his bodyguards orders to seize the señorita.

In the fight the young don died, two of his three bodyguards died, and his carriage driver fled.

Now Sam looked at Coy, trotting beside Paladin. He was envious. "You don't remember," he said to the coyote. *At least not in the haunting way that I do.*

Sam ran the pictures through his mind over and over—the surprise of the bodyguard when Sam's belt buckle turned into a knife. The slash of glinting blade, the kick of foot, the spout of blood, the fall and roll, the lifetime of events that spun themselves out across a minute or two.

The deaths.

His indifference, his utter indifference to everything.

And now Don Joaquin or other agents of Julia's father had kidnapped Julia. And her husband, Flat Dog. And Esperanza.

All Sam wanted to know was whether they were dead or alive.

He had advanced beyond indifference. Revenge bubbled in his throat like lava.

FROM THE SUMMIT of the Santa Lucia Mountains the Pacific stretched before them to a horizon where sea misted into sky. Sam's dad's voice sounded in his mind—*Forever.*

Monterey Bay itself was a small dollop of ocean cupped by pincers of land on the north and south. Near the southern pincer lay the presidio, the arm of the Mexican government, and farther south the mission, the arm of the church. The presidio was a stockade a couple of hundred yards long. Originally, all secular intruders into this Indian land had lived within the fort. Now buildings leaned against the outside of the stockade, and a town was springing up nearby, a few adobe homes forming a plaza, and other adobes and thatched huts on the hills above. Compared to the mission, all of it was rough and tumble, dirty, and crowded.

The mission where Meadowlark died, far from her home . . . Where my daughter was born, far from home.

Sam jerked himself back to the present. He looked at Coy and touched his spurs to Paladin.

He had ridden for three and a half days chewing on one question: *Are they alive? Has Montalban killed them?* He didn't speak of it to Hannibal. They rode in silence. But he obsessed about it. Sometimes he told himself he knew: Flat Dog had been murdered, mother and baby spared.

Two brothers. Blue Medicine Horse went with me to the Sioux villages and got killed. Flat Dog went with me to California and got killed.

He did not let himself think consciously of Meadowlark. *The family will despise me.*

Walking Paladin down this slope, he felt a chill.

"No way to know what we're coming into," said Hannibal.

"Let's be careful," said Sam, "and head for the mission."

As they approached Mission San Carlos Borromeo de Carmelo, Sam felt its enchantment. The buildings were elegant adobe structures in a Moorish style, with arched walkways, red-tiled roofs, and a handsome central quadrangle with a fountain. These sun-struck adobes were an ideal of beauty to Sam. The church was even more impressive, built of dressed stones and adorned with bell towers.

They passed the barracks and Sam kicked Paladin to a trot. Soldiers made him edgy.

Sam's eyes roved the mission. He loved it and hated it.

"How many soldiers?" asked Hannibal.

"Not enough to control the Indians."

"So priests enslave their souls."

Sam and Hannibal put their horses in the corral.

Then, by unspoken consent, they walked to the small cemetery. Sam stood by the small, grassy mound, hat in hand, Hannibal behind him. Coy curled up in the grass at Meadowlark's feet.

Her grave was marked with a simple oblong of wood. MEAD-OWLARK MORGAN, it read, 1808–1827, REQUIESCAT IN PACE.

Sam hadn't seen the marker before. He and Flat Dog had been obliged to leave in a hurry, after the Montalban trouble.

He took thought now. "The Indian converts are buried here."

Hannibal looked at him questioningly. "This is consecrated ground. But she was not a Christian."

Sam just looked at the grave. He hadn't understood at the time. There was a lot he hadn't understood.

"This must be the kindness of the priest. Those Latin words, they mean, 'Rest in peace.' "

Then the feelings swelled in Sam like music, a sorrow inex-pressible in words. He swam into the sounds, a depth and breadth of loss beyond comprehension. Tumbling feelings, pictures of Meadowlark, brushes of her flesh, hints of the smell of her skin. In exquisite pain he held her. She felt warm. He loved her. Then she felt cold, as on that day. He loved her. He hated living without her.

He forced himself to the surface of consciousness. He told himself once more, as he had many times—so commonplace, a fever after childbirth. So commonplace. Dead.

Coy yipped.

"I am sorry to interrupt," came a voice behind them. Sam turned and saw Padre Enrique, the brown-robed head of the Franciscan mission. In decent English he said, "Sorry, Sam. You have no idea what danger you are in. Come with me."

SAM FELT SURE he would never forget the picture before him. In the mission library at a table sat Flat Dog, reading a book.

Flat Dog jumped up and braced Sam by both shoulders and shook Hannibal's hand.

"Reading?"

"Father Enrique is teaching me." He gestured at the book-lined walls. "There are two thousand volumes here."

The priest set down a flagon of wine and four glasses. "I re-gret to interrupt, but we must make plans. Trouble will come." He sat at the big table and motioned for his guests to sit.

The padre poured. Sam didn't particularly favor wine, but out of politeness he drank.

Padre Enrique was a tall, thin priest with a huge, hooked nose and enormous brown eyes filled with intelligence and kindness. He moved jerkily, like a marionette. Sam had not been surprised, four months ago, to discover that the priest could lead a large enterprise successfully, hold hundreds of Indians in sway, run huge herds of cattle and sheep, and manage vineyards, orchards, and fields of beans and corn. He had been surprised by the kindness.

"I'm sure you have . . . apprehended what happened. Don Joaquin gave out word that anyone who found the so-called murderers of his son would be rewarded handsomely. The manager of the farmhouse where Flat Dog, Julia, and Esperanza went for help, he betrayed them for the gold."

Flat Dog put in, "Julia is with her father at Rancho Malibu." The deadness in his voice chilled Sam. "Esperanza too." Then his face changed somehow, streaks of hope and bitterness. "She's carrying our child."

"Child!" said Sam.

Flat Dog managed a sort of smile. "Yes, child."

"Let's go get her."

The priest said, "Flat Dog is here under arrest."

"Arrest!" said Sam.

"They let me out of jail during the day to study Christianity."

"Flat Dog is an excellent student," said the Franciscan.

"My marriage vows were to become a Christian."

Sam looked to see if Flat Dog's eyes were merry, but his friend kept his face blank.

"We are making the progress daily," said Father Enrique. "Literary and spiritual."

Sam couldn't believe it. *Flat Dog is learning to read before me. Is he really becoming a Christian?* Then Sam remembered that he himself had become a Crow for Meadowlark's sake.

"Why in jail?" said Hannibal.

"He is charged with the murder of Agustin Montalban y Romero, son of Don Joaquin Montalban y Alvarado."

"And two ruffians," said Sam.

"Yes."

"Why haven't they hanged him already?" asked Hannibal.

"Because I intervened. I told the governor that I saw the fight, and Flat Dog acted in self-defense. Also Montalban is not pushing for a quick trial."

"Why not?" asked Sam.

"Because he is using Flat Dog as . . . a bait to lure you here."

"You, amigo," mocked Flat Dog, "are the real killer. You snatched out your belt buckle and cut a man's throat. You sliced his faithful servant from his collarbone to his balls."

"So we have stepped in the dung," said Hannibal, "and good."

"Yes." The priest's eyes grew intense. "Sam, your white hair is a flag. The stable hands saw you, others saw you. Soon the whole mission will know, and soon, possibly this evening, certainly tomorrow, Montalban will know." It was already late afternoon.

"Then?"

The priest shrugged. "Perhaps I can protect you for now. I can arrest you and jail you. If that works, in eventuality, Montalban, he forces a trial."

The priest sipped his wine and considered. "Already I have spoken a falsehood. I said I saw what happened and that both of you acted in self-defense. In fact, I didn't see it, and cannot give that testimony officially. Therefore conviction and execution."

"You have kept Flat Dog alive . . . why?"

"Justice," said Father Enrique. "I believe in justice." The Franciscan smiled a little to himself. "And I want to save his soul."

Sam's spirit spun like a dervish.

"So Sam and Flat Dog will hang," Hannibal said.

"I doubt it. Why would Montalban wait for a trial?"

Sam and Hannibal studied each other.

"Do you . . . ?"

Father Enrique said, "Yes, I have suggestions. For the sake of justice I will help you."

*   *   *

HE OFFERED THESE suggestions over dinner. Huge, steaming platters of food were served, enough to fatten up men starved by the desert—three kinds of meat, beans, corn, squash, and huge loaves of bread, pudding, plenty of wine and water. Other brown-robed priests set to with a will. Sam couldn't imagine how Father Enrique stayed so skinny.

The father had permitted Coy into the dining room, and everyone tossed him scraps. Sam wondered how the padres treated the slaves who served the food. Indians, he noticed, and curiously one black. They padded about invisibly. *Slaves,* Sam thought to himself, a skeptical eye on Father Enrique.

"Why do you imagine Montalban will exempt you from his wrath, Señor Hannibal?" asked the padre.

"Haud facile me interficere."

"What?"

"You know Latin." He translated for Sam and Flat Dog. "I'm hard to kill."

"You look like an Indian," said the Franciscan.

"I am Indian. One who intends to stay in possession of his soul."

Avid curiosity flushed the padre's face, and Hannibal had to explain to him that his father was a professor of classics at Dartmouth College and his mother a Delaware, a student at the college. "I grew up speaking English and Delaware, and reading Greek and Latin."

"Amazing!"

Sam pitched in. "Don't get ideas about sailing him to Europe with a sign that says, 'WHAT CIVILIZATION CAN DO FOR THE RED MAN.'"

"Of course not," said the priest.

That's exactly what you were thinking. Sam covered the thought by turning away and feeding Coy.

"Padre, guide us," said Hannibal.

"I want to put you on El Camino Real at first light," said the priest.

"El Camino Real?"

"The trail that runs from mission to mission, called the

King's Highway. You will go south, toward Rancho Malibu. Is that not what you wish?"

"Damn right," said Flat Dog.

"A long journey, more than a hundred leagues."

"More than three hundred miles," translated Hannibal.

"There are nine missions, counting the one nearest Malibu. I will give you a letter of safe passage for the heads of the missions. I am the ecclesiastical head of all the California missions—they will give you whatever you need."

"Sounds sweet and easy," said Sam. That wasn't what he was thinking. His mind was thrumming, *Another long journey in the wrong direction.* But he couldn't go home to Crow country until he had Esperanza.

The black slave slid a pudding in front of Sam with what seemed to be a flourish. He wore a pancho with a hood.

"It is not easy. It is a very long ride. You have enemies. And that hair of yours." The priest touched it. Coy mewled. Sam tossed his head, flicking the hand away.

"And your outfits. You would be easily identified as foreigners, even at a distance."

"What will we do?"

The priest leaned forward with a conspiratorial smile. "We'll dress you in disguise," he said. "And we'll take care of that hair."

"How?" said Sam.

An oratorical voice came from behind them. "With the help of a master of disguise and deceit."

Sam started. *Who the devil . . . ?*

A round priest approached the table and bent over Sam. Then he threw his cowl back.

"Grumble!" yelled Sam, and jumped up and hugged him.

An elegantly dressed woman stepped from the shadows next to them.

"Abby!" said Sam. He hugged her too.

Everyone else exchanged greetings. Coy wagged his tail and accepted head-patting.

"I agreed to your friend's little charade," said the priest.

Grumble swept on, "Our party would not be complete without . . ."

The black slave came around Abby, flipped his hood back, and stuck his head theatrically into Sam's face. "A black man, you white folk don't hardly notice him."

"Sumner!" Sam shouted.

THE WHITE-HAIRED TRAPPER and the eggplant-colored youth traded *abrazos*.

"We have business," said Grumble.

"Yeah, we got to save they white asses," said Sumner.

"My red ass begs your pardon," said Hannibal in a silly tone, pointing at his bottom. They introduced themselves.

"Don't call mine white neither," said Flat Dog. They clapped shoulders.

"Business!" said Grumble firmly.

An Indian slave dragged a trunk forward. Sam knew it well. He traveled with it on two steamboats from Pittsburgh to St. Louis. He was sure it was still full of costumes, decks of marked cards, jewelry both real and fake, and other accoutrements of a con man.

"How did you three get here?" said Sam. He could barely stand still. Grumble and Abby were the two oldest friends of his five years in the West. Sumner had come to California with the brigade last fall, as a slave.

"All that will wait," said Abby. She was a vision—hennaed hair, pale lime gown, and a sky-blue scarf.

"We're going to get you disguised," said Grumble. He studied Hannibal and Flat Dog. "In fact, Mr. McKye first. Padre, can you get the clothes of a mission Indian of his size? Those shirts of rough cloth you give them, hideous stuff, and loincloths. He's dark and black-haired, so . . ."

Abby said, "He's already wearing loincloth and moccasins."

Grumble regarded Hannibal. The breechcloth seemed to make him shudder. "Just a different shirt, much shabbier. I have something else for Flat Dog later. Meanwhile, will you show Sam, Abby, and me to a room where he can be dressed and made up in private? Sam is the trickiest."

FLAT DOG READ aloud in Spanish. He went slowly, sometimes correcting himself, but he was having fun—showing off. Father Enrique translated the words into English for Hannibal and Sumner:

"I believe in one God, the Father, the Almighty, maker of heaven and earth, of all that is seen and unseen. I believe in one Lord, Jesus Christ, the only Son of God, eternally begotten of the Father, God from God, Light from Light, true God from true God, begotten, not made, one in Being with the Father . . ."

Hannibal chuckled. "The Nicene Creed. Let me get this straight. His native language is Crow, and he speaks good English, but he's learning to read in Spanish."

"It seems best to teach the Indians in a language that itself represents the height of civilization," said Father Enrique.

"You can always tell a height civilization," said Sumner. "They got slaves."

Hannibal and Flat Dog suppressed smiles. "It has been so many years . . ." Now Hannibal grinned and began as hesitantly as Flat Dog, *"Credo in unum Deum, Patrem omnipotentem, factorem caeli et terrae, visibilium omnium et invisibilium."*

"Too many Christians around here," said Sumner.

"Not including yourself?" the priest asked.

"Got better sense. But I can read and write English."

Father Enrique nodded. "You are three exceptional . . . men," he said. They all wondered if he'd been thinking of saying "savages." "Nonetheless," he said to Flat Dog, "your soul is not yet made safe in the hands of God."

He looked at the ormolu hands of the ornate clock on the wall. The pendulum ticked like a nun correcting their ways. "It's getting late. I wanted to wait for our friends, but . . .

"Flat Dog, I will give you your freedom on one condition."

All three "exceptional men" tensed.

"Before you leave, you must be baptized, make your first confession, and take Holy Communion."

"Why?"

"I will save your body. God will save your soul. Are you willing?"

Flat Dog hesitated.

Sumner was grinning broadly.

"Remember your marriage vows. Father Sanchez consecrated your union with Julia on the condition that you become a Christian."

"I'll do it," said Flat Dog.

"Now," said the priest.

GRUMBLE AND ABBY sat Sam in a chair. They brought out a corked bottle of a brown liquid. One portly figure and one slender figure bent to the task. "Walnut juice," Grumble said.

Coy gave them a peculiar look.

They rubbed it firmly into the skin of Sam's face, even the corners of the nostrils, the lips, and the edges of the eyes. "The craft is demanding," Grumble said.

Abby smiled. "This is what women do every day."

It was what she did, Sam knew. As a provider of liquors, games of chance, and seductive women, she had to look splendid, and she always took pains.

Sam forbade himself to wonder exactly what was going on. Walnut juice?

"What are you two doing here?" He'd last seen them at the Los Angeles pueblo. They headed north on an American sailing ship, looking for a home for their chosen enterprise. Abby managed the booze and ladies, Grumble the gambling.

Grumble began painting the grottos of Sam's ears with a fine brush. "We disembarked here, looked around, and discovered the town was in its infancy, though the setting is very beautiful. We sailed on to San Francisco Bay and found even less of a town."

"I'm building a home here, an adobe, and then I'll open my

usual sort of business." Abby gave an impish smile. "The mission is all holy men, but the presidio is all soldiers."

"I'll join her eventually, but the building period is boring. I want to go back to Los Angeles pueblo for a while. It's vulgar, but alive."

Abby said, "I like to sin in a beautiful place." She checked Sam's face. "Those white eyebrows will never do." With a tiny brush she dabbed something greasy and black onto them.

Grumble went back to the corked bottle. "Now your hands."

Sam stuck them out, and Grumble colored them. "Walnut juice?" whined Sam.

"Beautiful, isn't it? It's a little dark for most Californios. So handy. Too dark nips suspicion in the bud. The missions grow orchards and orchards of it." He smeared the juice up over the wrists. "You must not show your arms," he said.

Carefully, Abby covered Sam's neck with the brown liquid. "Why were you ready with my disguise?"

"Didn't your captain say he'd return by September 20? Flat Dog said you'd show up here. You're a few days early."

Sam smiled to himself. *Flat Dog knew I would come.*

Abby said, "Now use this mirror." She handed an ornate one to Sam. "Look for white spots. The costume will be the coup de grace, but we mustn't have any of those nasty little white spots."

Costume?

Coy tapped his tail on the floor. Sam understood the wagging was anxiety, not delight.

Sam studied himself in the mirror. *I'm a darkie.*

Abby piled his white hair on top of his head. With Sam's wooden hair ornament and long pins such as she used in her own coiffure, she fastened it up, stood back, and surveyed her work.

"No white spots except the hair," said Sam.

"Excellent," said Grumble. "Now . . ."

He draped a black wig on Sam's head. The hair was shoulder length and gleaming. Grumble made careful adjustments.

"You're not making me into a woman!"

"Scarcely."

Abby circled to Sam's front and let the bundle in her arms

drop full length. It was a brown Franciscan robe. "The cowl," said Grumble, "will even hide your face from prying eyes. Put it on over your clothes while I change." The con man disappeared behind a folding screen. "Be sure to replace the moccasins with sandals," he called.

Sam donned the robe. He tied it with the tasseled belt. Abby slipped the pectoral cross over his head and dropped it onto his chest. He fingered the rosary. He started laughing. They both laughed and laughed and couldn't stop.

Grumble popped out from behind the screen, arms wide in the declarative gesture of an actor. He wore an English gentleman's riding outfit, knee-high boots, leggings close-fitting on the calves and blousy around the thighs, a beaver hat in a serious business color. "Every inch a blue blood," he intoned in a plummy voice.

They hooted and clapped each other on the back.

Then Sam said, "You in costume? You're going with us?"

"Sumner and I," answered Grumble, "are your escort. You require our protection."

FLAT DOG STUDIED the water in the font.

"Holy water," said Hannibal.

"Wu-wu juice," said Sumner.

Flat Dog held these two odd thoughts, as though rubbing a stone between his fingers. "It's a relief to be in here," he said.

"Far away from the altar," said Hannibal.

"That thing done give me the willies," said Sumner.

None of them looked through the entryway down the length of the church at the huge, painted statue of the Christ, nailed to the cross and dying.

Now Father Enrique approached in white and gold robes. He looked into Flat Dog's eyes and spoke with gravity. "Do you understand that with these words you are embraced by the arms of the holy catholic and apostolic church of our Lord Jesus Christ?"

Flat Dog pictured Julia's beautiful face, her golden skin, her tawny hair. "Yes."

The padre put his hand into the shadowed water.

"Ego te baptismo in nomine Patris et Filii et Spiritus Sancti." As the priest spoke, he sprinkled holy water on Flat Dog's head three times—Father, Son, and Holy Spirit.

Flat Dog thought, *Now I am a Christian.* It gave him a chill. *I promised Julia.*

"Come to the confessional."

Flat Dog knelt in the small box and spoke of his many sins. He had killed people. He had fornicated. He had lied. He had taken the name of the Lord in vain. Since he was well prepared, he enumerated these sins quickly. The priest gave him a psalm to say as penance and absolved him.

Flat Dog shivered.

Father Enrique disappeared.

Flat Dog, Hannibal, and Sumner went into the nave and sat, as instructed, on the front pew, in front of the altar. Now the new Christian looked up at the God with the bleeding hands and feet. To him it was not credible or right that a father should sacrifice his son for the sake of strangers.

At the far end of the nave Grumble and Abby entered.

Father Enrique appeared in front of the altar with a flagon of wine and a gold plate that bore the bread.

"Christians are invited to the sacrament of the Eucharist," said Father Enrique.

Grumble and Abby genuflected before the altar and knelt at the table bearing the host.

The priest at the rear, oddly, slipped into a back pew.

Flat Dog came to his knees beside his roguish friends, who were apparently Catholics.

Father Enrique spoke words. Later Flat Dog remembered only "body and blood of Christ."

As the party treaded to the rear of the church, a brown robe came in and tossed back his cowl. It was Sam.

Flat Dog laughed and clapped him on the shoulder.

"You're a Christian now?" said Sam.

"Yes," said Flat Dog.

"Dumb slave religion," said Sumner.

"Christian and Crow," whispered Flat Dog. "Both."

Six

IN THE HALF-LIGHT before dawn they met by the corral. Shadows flitted across the dust and the rails. Horses stirred, restless.

Sam was bleary-eyed. Grumble, Flat Dog, and Sumner looked worse. Flat Dog dressed as an Indian slave.

"Black man don't need no outfit to make him look like a slave," said Sumner. But then he got an idea. Suddenly he spoke in an upper-class British voice. "I want to be a proper British servant," he said. "Once I am properly dressed, no one can deny me."

Grumble's chest provided the broadcloth of an English manservant, breeches buckled below the knee, stockings, and a dark coat. The wide-brimmed hat was a logical addition for a sun such as never shone in England.

Sumner looked down at himself, pirouetted proudly, and made a low bow to Grumble.

Coy barked vigorously at Sumner. Sam laughed out loud.

"You don't understand art," Sumner told the coyote.

"We clever gents," said Grumble, "now present the world with a British aristocrat and his attendants—a servant, a priest, and two mission Indians."

"The fair-skinned people of this continent are overfond of class distinctions," said Sumner.

"The don will be looking for three American fur trappers," said Padre Enrique. He sounded dubious.

Grumble surveyed them all. "All the actors are dressed for their roles," he said happily.

Coy barked at Flat Dog again. Then he dashed at the wagon wheels—it was more wagon than carriage—and pranced back, barking, eager to go.

Sam and Flat Dog got into their saddles. The rising sun was still behind the Santa Lucia Mountains. "Time to move," said Hannibal.

Abby gave Sam a good-bye peck on the cheek. When Sumner presented his face, she pinched his bottom.

The Delaware dressed as a mission Indian drove the wagon, Sumner beside him, Grumble seated behind and above the two of them, the gear in the box behind. The Franciscan priest had outfitted them generously—wagon, two draft horses, casks for water, dried meat, fruit, even a cask of wine. At Hannibal's request they also had a small keg of gunpowder, because their powder horns were half empty.

On the plank seat between Hannibal and Sumner perched the most visible weapon, a scattergun. Grumble had a pistol in his belt, which he might brandish foolishly at anyone who confronted them. The mountain-style rifles belonging to Sam, Hannibal, and Flat Dog were behind the passengers, laid loose under canvas, in case of emergency. No one knew what weapon Sumner might be carrying, or dared ask.

"Everyone clear on our story?" repeated Grumble. It was that the British blue blood, Grumble, was seeking contracts with the various missions for cow hides and tallow. The missions away from the coast were not yet involved in this commerce, very profitable for both sides.

"Go," he told Hannibal. The wagon lurched forward. "This cursed conveyance may bump us to death," Grumble said to no one in particular. In his pouch, to show anyone who asked, he carried the letter of safe passage from Padre Enrique to the heads of the nine missions where they would stop. Sam and Flat Dog had protested that the niceties of reception and hospitality at each mission would slow them down. Grumble insisted they'd need all the niceties they could get. Hannibal added that the party needed the safety missions offered.

As they rolled, Hannibal said, "You're a mystery."

Sumner smiled. "I done worked at it."

Hannibal laughed at the lapse back into slave English.

"And I assure you I can perform like a trouper." This was fancy talk again.

So they traded stories. Sumner said, "I was born near Santo Domingo, on a cane plantation. Since my mother worked in the big house, I grew up there, and played with the white kids. Our master was the second son of a viscount, or some such foolery. I grew up speaking the king's English. By serving meals, I even learned elegant table manners. I could pass myself off as, perhaps, the third son of a viscount."

Hannibal laughed.

Sumner shifted back to slave speech. "At night, though, down at our hut, we was with the other Niggers, including my father and his brothers and their wives, and they all spoke Spanish, nothing but Spanish. So I grew up talking both tongues."

"Two roles," said Hannibal.

"When I was sold to New Orleans, I done caught on to bow-and-shuffle English."

After Hannibal told about being born to a professor of classics and a Delaware student, raised speaking two languages and reading three, they agreed that they didn't know who had the stranger life.

SAM WAS NERVOUS about Grumble's little game. He didn't like not having The Celt in his hands. It made him feel naked.

He'd concealed his other weapons. A butcher knife and his belt-buckle blade were covered by his robe. The hair ornament blade was hidden in one sleeve. He wished he still had the pistol he traded to the Serranos.

He fussed with the robe between his legs and Paladin's saddle. He hated the damn thing—it made riding embarrassing. He glanced sideways at Sumner, and saw that the black was tickled at the modest white boy. Inside Sam's robe was folded Father Enrique's map of El Camino Real, its towns, and its missions. Grumble carried another copy in his coat.

Now Sam spotted the first place marked on the map, Montalban's rancho. "Be watchful," Father Enrique had warned him. "Don Joaquin is vengeful."

Actually, the rancho looked like nothing much.

The grounds were handsome, a fine lay of land on the far side of the Salinas River. The don had planted fields, orchards, and a vineyard visible from the road. Probably herds of horses, cattle, and sheep grazed the hills beyond. These hills were brocaded with grasses that looked too rich and tall to be real. They were bright as brass, thick as hair, and stood as high as a horse's withers. Sam had never seen such grass. But he was no herdsman.

The house, on the other hand, was unimpressive, an ordinary-looking adobe of modest size, without a courtyard or other beautification.

Coy drank out of the creek that ran through the property as though nothing was amiss.

"Father Enrique told me," said Grumble, "that the don complained greatly about having to build his house of mud. But there's not enough timber around here."

"He's rich," said Sam irritably.

"But he doesn't enjoy it," said the cherub. "The old man was a great landowner in Mexico. Montalban was one of the younger sons. When his wife died and his daughters were married off, he accepted exile to this miserable province to make his son what he could never be, the master of a grand estate." Grumble gave Sam and Flat Dog a look.

"The son of a bitch was trying to steal my wife," said Flat Dog.

"The pistol was his, and it went off accidentally," said Sam.

"What a comfort that must be to Don Joaquin," said Grumble.

Sam couldn't see any sign of life around the place. There must be Indians working the fields, but he saw no one.

"WHO ARE YOU and where are you going?"

From Paladin's saddle alongside the wagon, Sam had watched the four riders coming from the south, growing in his field of vision and on his nerves.

Immediately Sumner picked up the scattergun from the wagon seat. No one of either party misunderstood the threat. At that range it would be a devastating weapon.

Coy walked in front of Sam, growling, his spine hair sticking up.

Rising next to Hannibal, Sumner said in his fanciest English, "My master wishes to know who dares to ask such questions." When they just stared at him, he repeated it in good Spanish.

From behind, Grumble spoke in plummy tones, and Sumner translated. "Good sir, I present this letter of safe passage from Father Enrique Hidalgo, head of all the Franciscan missions of California."

He gave it to Sumner, who held it out. The lead rider had to dismount and look at it. Sumner kept the paper in his grip.

Sam knew damn well who this was, one of the ruffians from the time the young don tried to abduct Julia, the man Sam had slit from collarbone to balls. Too bad he'd lived. Sam kept his head down, his features hidden by his cowl.

Flat Dog recognized the fellow too. Sam could feel the anger radiating from Flat Dog's body. The two mounts minced nervously.

"I represent Don Joaquin Montalban y Alvarado. On the authority of the commandante of the Presidio of Monterey we are searching for two criminals who have escaped from Mission San Carlos Borromeo de Carmelo."

Sam got enough of the Spanish to be offended at this arrogant ass.

"We have every desire," Grumble said, Sumner still translating, "to cooperate with the authorities. I am Edward Muddleforth, second son of the Viscount of Piddleston."

Sam was surprised Sumner could translate this foolishness without a grin.

"These men comprise my retinue."

"Where are you going?" repeated Collarbone to Balls.

"We travel to Mission Nuestra Señora de la Soledad and other missions on business."

"I see." His disbelief curled his lips. But the sneer was probably a pose, Sam thought. Beneath it Collarbone to Balls seemed to be accepting the story.

"Have you seen other travelers on this road today?"

Coy barked once.

"None," Grumble answered truthfully.

"Three Americans dressed as hunters? Carrying long rifles?"

"No travelers."

Collarbone nodded slowly, thinking. "We ask you to be on watch. We will probably see you again as you travel south."

"Glad to be of service," said Grumble.

Collarbone pulled his reins to the side to ride around the wagon.

Sam breathed again.

Flat Dog reached to his hat. Sam saw his friend's face do funny things. Casually, he took the hat off, rubbed his hair back, and looked full face at the Mexicans.

Collarbone's face changed to a truly memorable look of recognition.

Then he looked at Sumner, who was holding the scattergun. The black man gazed at Collarbone without expression.

The sides of Collarbone's grin turned down. His mount edged backward. He squeezed words out. "We'll be on our way then."

As he rode around the wagon, Sumner turned to watch him, the gun following his body. The other three riders trailed after Collarbone with mystified faces.

When they were out of sight, Sam growled at Flat Dog, "What the hell did you do that for?"

"That son of a bitch stole Julia. He stole Esperanza. He put me in jail. I want to kill him."

"That's good," said Hannibal, "because now he intends to kill you."

Grumble added softly, "And the rest of us."

Hannibal said, "What he intends will be different from what he gets."

SAM AND HANNIBAL chose the battleground that suited them, a grove of trees along the river. It looked like a normal campsite, had a place where they could rope-corral the horses on grass, and offered a jumble of boulders for cover.

Coy trotted around the campground sniffing, like an inspector.

Sam, Hannibal, and Sumner made what appeared to be a normal camp, put up tents, gathered wood for a fire.

Flat Dog walked down to the river and sat alone. No one criticized him, but there was a lot of edgy body language as they prepared.

Grumble laid out a tarpaulin and had a picnic, pretending nothing was happening. It made Sam's nerves worse. The cherub should know a shooting war wasn't amusing.

Coy cadged scraps of dried meat from Grumble. Grumble kept looking up into the cottonwood branches and smiling.

"How many men do you think Montalban will bring?" asked Sam.

"All he can get," said Hannibal. "But not many of his Indians ride or shoot."

Sumner squatted and talked to Grumble. They both looked up into the trees, pointed, and whispered.

Sam got the scattergun and handed it to his black friend. "You any good with this?"

"I'm a con artist, not a gunman."

Sam was sure he was a good con man too, since he'd accepted Grumble's tutelage.

"Look, it fires a lot of pellets, and they spread out as they go." Sam held his hands a foot or two apart. "You don't aim it, you point it." He showed Sumner how the trigger, flint, and pan worked.

"That's all good," said Sumner, "but Grumble and me, we got an idea. A little surprise for the bad boys."

Grumble and Sumner sketched out their plan for Sam and Hannibal. Heads nodded, and smiles flashed. Sam and Sumner climbed the trees and began the rigging. Sumner moved through the trees like an athlete. Sam, bulkier and more muscled, was sure a branch was going to break under him. But they got it done.

Sam took off his robe—he wanted to fight in a man's clothes. Then he walked down to the river to join Flat Dog. The Crow had his sacred pipe out of its hide bag and was lighting it. Sam took thought. He started to get his own pipe out, but then he sat and shared Flat Dog's. They offered the pipe to the four directions, they smoked, and rubbed the smoke on themselves. Sam contemplated his Crow name, Joins with Buffalo. He thought of how buffalo never run away, but stay and fight to the last of their strength—that's what it meant to be a buffalo bull. This was what the medicine man in Meadowlark's village, Bell Rock, told Sam. He asked the powers for the strength to live up to his name, and he prayed that no one in his party would be hurt tonight.

When they were finished and the pipe bowl and stem were separated, so that the pipe was no longer a living being, Sam said, "Do you miss it? Crow country?"

Flat Dog gave a dry laugh. "We've been in a lot of places where a Crow's dog wouldn't even drink the water."

Sam's mind roamed back there—the land of the Wind River, the Big Horn Mountains, the Yellowstone River, the hot springs, the forests. "I miss it too," he said. "It's home."

Flat Dog gave him a look. "It will be Esperanza's home."

"It's where we belong."

"We're going," said Flat Dog.

"Very roundabout," said Sam.

He walked back into camp and surveyed the rigging. He thought the trick would work.

How will the don come? he asked himself.

Sam himself would scout and move stealthily.

But he was no fiery don.

THEY WERE SET. The campfire was down to coals. Around the fire lay five blanketed figures. If a curious person had taken time to look at the hats, he would have seen those of the Englishman and his manservant beside two blankets together and three Californio hats and saddles beside other blankets. Had this observer been curious enough to touch the blankets, he would have felt the stones underneath.

Don Joaquin Montalban y Alvarado, however, was not a man to come creeping up on his enemy. Riders, horses, and men of foot stormed the campground as a fire rages before the wind.

They came so suddenly, so swiftly that Grumble was nearly late with his knife. The don's horses roared into the campground, the men yelling out war cries and firing at the sleeping figures.

Coy barked furiously, but Sam held him back.

Grumble sliced hard at the rope.

The keg of gunpowder dropped straight down from where it hung below a limb and directly onto the fire.

The explosion hit like lightning. Tree limbs sailed through the air like torches. Sparks flew into the sky like fiery birds.

Eight enemies on foot brandishing axes and knives crashed at random into trees, boulders, and the earth.

The five mounted enemies were mostly beyond the campground when the keg blew, turning their horses to charge back among their blanketed foes.

The horses were blown backward, sometimes landing on the riders. As the attackers scrambled to their feet, Sam, Flat Dog, and Hannibal fired from behind boulders.

Well instructed, Sumner held the scattergun at the ready. Grumble held fire with his palm-sized gambler's pistol.

The firelight made sighting difficult, and only two out of three shots struck. Then the three mountain men charged the enemies still standing, or staggering, or trying to get to their feet. Two fired their pistols, and Sam swung his butcher knife.

Enemies died.

Coy hurled himself at enemies, snarling and biting.

Sam, Hannibal, and Flat Dog hacked wildly at the remnants of the enemy force with tomahawks and knives. They didn't know whom they cut, but they struck hard.

Eventually, the tornado blew itself out. All stood still, their eyes mad. Embers around the campground smoldered. Small clumps of grass smoked, crisped, and went out. Sam could smell the river air again.

Sam counted. Hannibal and Flat Dog stood near him. Coy rubbed against his leg. Grumble and Sumner came out from behind boulders. Grumble was holding his face. "He couldn't resist looking," Sumner said, "and he's a little burned."

Flat Dog knelt over a prostrate figure. Coy approached the figure's head, sniffing.

"Check to make sure they're dead," said Hannibal.

Sam had to swallow hard. *They came here to kill us.*

They were dead. Some of them were mangled, some dismembered.

Sam wanted to vomit.

Flat Dog walked to him holding a bloody scalp.

Sam raised an eyebrow at him.

"Montalban's," said Flat Dog.

Coy whined.

Montalban's. Sam didn't want to touch the thing. He hoped he could get rid of the memories.

DAYLIGHT CONFIRMED ELEVEN bodies. Grumble and Hannibal thought they'd seen thirteen attackers, which meant two escaped.

"I doubt that they'll be back," said Grumble, smiling. "Ouch!" His face shone from the grease he'd rubbed on his facial burns.

Five riders, two dead horses, two horses they were able to round up.

Four saddles. One was a gorgeous work of tooled leather and silver studs, probably Montalban's. On or near the bodies of the four riders they found four rifles and three pistols. From the riders and men on foot they took an assortment of knives and daggers. Each mountain man claimed a pistol. The rest of the booty they carried off in the wagon.

They got going as soon as they could. Even before the bodies ripened, death stood rank in their eyes and nostrils.

Hannibal said.

Seven

"I DON'T LIKE it," said Hannibal.

"I hate it," said Flat Dog, but he didn't mean the situation. He meant his fury about his wife.

Rancho Malibu stretched before them, wide plains on the inland side of ragged coastal mountains. Now, in October, golden grasses colored the flats along the creek and the steep slopes. Scrubby trees spotted the hills. The ranch house and buildings stretched along the creek. Planted fields, an orchard, a vineyard, and grazing lands spread away from the steep slopes of mountains.

Sam couldn't help thinking of what lay behind him, the vast Pacific Ocean. There he and Meadowlark camped on Topanga Beach, and their new friend Robber showed them the wonders of the tide pools. Meadowlark had been thrilled by the anemones and the sea horses.

A few days later Flat Dog and Julia eloped to that beach, borrowed the tipi, and spent several days exploring each other. Until Julia's father barged in and snatched away his daughter. He also gave Flat Dog a thrashing with a knout, a Russian lash with bits of metal embedded in the rawhide. Flat Dog's back would be bumpy as a plowed field for the rest of his life.

"Watching isn't getting us anywhere," said Sam. He could feel the rage coming from his brother-in-law.

"Let's do something," said Flat Dog.

Sam tried not to think what it must be like for Flat Dog to know his wife was in one of those two houses, full of their child, but he couldn't see her, talk to her, touch her.

The three of them had watched the rancho from this ridge for two full days. Having found out how practical a field glass was, Sam traded a captured pistol for one in Santa Barbara. Passing through eight missions on the way south, they'd been welcomed everywhere and protected along El Camino Real by Padre Enrique's letter. Funny world, to Sam, where influence counted for more than skill or good sense.

Two days of watching told them that Mexican hands worked around the rancho's outbuildings and in the vineyards and orchard. Occasionally, herders could be seen in the distance. Don Cesar, the *patròn,* rode the property each afternoon with his son-in-law Alfredo, and they were out on horseback now. They stopped at the vineyard to talk with an old man, then dismounted to inspect something. Then they rode on.

"Sumner would love this," said Sam.

"A life where you do nothing but watch your 'inferiors' labor for you," said Hannibal.

Now father and son rode to the corral, dismounted, and let a stable hand take the horses. Each man then strode to his own house. The don's adobe, by the Pittsburgh and St. Louis standards Sam knew, was not particularly grand. He remembered its comfort, and its one strange room, which housed Don Cesar's collection of weapons, and the don's pride in his instruments of torture and destruction.

Two days and no sign at all of Julia.

Reina, her sister, took her two children outside every day for a couple of hours. She and Alfredo shared the modest adobe next to Don Cesar's.

"Do they ever go anywhere?" asked Sam.

"Julia won't be traveling now," said Flat Dog. "She's almost eight months."

"Californio women, meaning rich Californio women," said Hannibal, "aren't like Crow women. Toward the end they don't travel. They lie in."

"I just want to go kill the son of a bitch," said Flat Dog.

Sam saw that in his friend's face.

"Not a good idea to kill your wife's father," said Hannibal, "no matter how much she hates him."

Flat Dog made a rude sound.

"We don't want to hurt him," said Sam. "Just to get her. And Esperanza."

Flat Dog was silent.

"Let's go talk to Grumble," said Sam.

They'd let Grumble and Sumner ride into Mission San Fernando alone. The mission was only ten miles north of the rancho. No point in adding Grumble to the watch party. "Just one more face someone from the rancho might recognize," Sam had said.

"Going in, that's risky," said Hannibal.

"I've got an idea," said Sam.

"You? That's plain dangerous," said Hannibal.

THE THREE BUMPED along in the open carriage.

"My dear," said Grumble, "you've never looked lovelier."

"Nuns don't have to be pretty," said Sumner. He adjusted the wimple around his head. "I hate this brown. It's the color of shit. And they's nuns 'cause they ain't pretty."

"Some men might want to try a nun," said Hannibal.

"Pervert," said Sumner.

Grumble had told him to steal a monk's robe from the laundry. In the dark Sumner had filched a nun's outfit. Which Grumble suddenly decided was even better.

"Let's get our minds on business," Grumble said. He was brown-robed as a priest, and all smiles at the disguise.

Hannibal drove the carriage. He'd never been to the rancho, so couldn't be recognized. He looked over one shoulder. Rubio and his son were in the vineyard and riding away from the house. He'd timed it right.

They'd gotten good information at the mission. Grumble and Sumner discovered that once a week a priest traveled to Rancho Malibu to accept confessions and administer the Eucharist, and a nun from the convent went along to tutor the boys in reading. Thus the plan.

Sam and Flat Dog were hiding along the road north to the mission, probably half mad with fear and doubt.

Hannibal reined in the carriage directly in front of Don Cesar's adobe. *Right in the lion's den,* he thought. His chest tightened. A stable hand appeared to help with the horses. A cigarillo jutted up into the air from his lips, unlit.

As Cigarillo carried the harness, Hannibal led the animals. He was outfitted as a poor Indian, so that no one would expect him to speak good Spanish and he would have no business near the main house. He looked back at his friends, making their way to the front door. Under his loose shirt Hannibal was armed with knife and pistol. *But I'll be at the corral, and damned little help from there.*

"I don't like this," said Sumner in a falsetto voice.

"You'll be amazed at how easily people accept a costume," Grumble said. "You can be a policeman, a sailor, anything you like. That's the charm of it."

Grumble rapped on the door and they were admitted. The maid seemed to accept the friar and nun as a matter of course. Since he and Sumner had met the don last winter, Grumble's face and hands were walnut-stained a deep brown, and from his trunk of tricks he'd put on a silver beard.

"I don't like this," Sumner repeated.

"Your falsetto is really very good."

To Grumble's relief it was Doña Reina who came to greet them. Two boys ran down the corridor behind her, playing at war. *As I am playing at war,* thought the cherub.

"Permit me to introduce myself," he said in his uncertain Spanish. "I am Father Lorenzo come to pay my respects to the family. This is Sister Annunzio."

"Come in," said Reina. Her face showed signs of wear and worry, and no interest in her visitors.

As they followed Reina down the corridor and into a parlor, Grumble felt a familiar rise in his energy. *I like a frisson of danger.*

Sumner lifted his wimpled head to him, as though to say, *This is more than any damned frisson.*

When they sat, Reina said, "My father and husband are out in the fields, but I'll let my sister know you're here." Her voice was lifeless.

When they were alone, Grumble said softly, "I relish deceiving people."

Sumner said, "I can tell you're nervous. You babble."

Grumble chuckled. "And you?"

"The life of a thief is more honest."

Julia walked in, one child in her arms and another big in her belly. *My God,* thought Grumble, *she really is near her term.*

Julia was a beautiful woman, with comely features, tawny hair, and golden skin, and she was quick-minded. Her eyes were bright and alert and—and perhaps suspicious.

"My child," Grumble began immediately, "I am Father Lorenzo. I am new to the mission, and come to pay my respects to the family."

At the sound of Grumble's voice her face grew wild. *She knows,* Grumble thought. He pursed his lips. *She spent plenty of time with us.* Julia's eyes flashed from one face to other, and her face mottled with color. He rushed forward with words. "This is Sister Annunzio."

"Buenas tardes, Señora," said Sumner.

Julia opened her mouth but nothing came out. Disbelief? Joy? Alarm? Grumble wished he knew.

Reina came in bearing two glasses. "You'll want some wine," she said.

Grumble and Sumner accepted the wine and sipped. Reina disappeared.

"Are you well, my child?" said Grumble. "Physically?"

Julia clearly couldn't speak.

"I'd be glad to accept your confession, if you like."

She nodded.

Reina came in and handed Julia a glass. Julia downed the wine in a single gulp. She looked around wildly and handed the baby to Reina.

The four sat and stared at each other nervously.

"I'm pleased to meet the two of you," said Grumble, "and look forward to meeting Don Cesar and Don Alfredo."

"Why have you come?" asked Julia. Tension thrummed in her voice. After a moment she added, "Father."

Grumble pretended. "I was born in Padua. I've been serving at Mission San Carlos Borromeo de Carmelo, near Monterey, and am newly assigned to Mission San Fernando Rey de España."

Reina looked oddly at her sister, turned back to her guests, and said, "Is Sister Annunzio also a newcomer?"

"I have seen the boys when they've been at the mission," said Sumner, "but this is my first time at the rancho. It's beautiful."

Julia's hand was about to shatter the wineglass.

"My child, perhaps it's time for you to make your confession now."

"Of course, Father."

IN THE SMALL room Julia sat on the narrow bed, not pretending. Grumble drew a chair close. "Flat Dog is waiting for you," he said softly. "Sam is with him."

Julia gasped. She clutched her hands around her belly as though to hold the child in.

"We are going to take you out of here right now. If you want to go."

Julia looked like she was going to burst with emotions. She managed to nod yes.

Grumble put his arms around her and held her. Her head thrashed wildly. Quietly, he told her what she was to do. From time to time she whispered, "Yes." She seemed tongue-tied, but at the end she got out one thought. "Trust Reina. She's on our side." She leaned into him and wept, great, heaving sobs.

Eventually, after Julia had cried long enough to recite the sins of a highwayman, Grumble softly told her the rest of the plan. She nodded yes several times. He said with a sincerity that surprised even him, "God bless you, my child." He wished he could give her absolution.

When Julia left the room to get her sister, her face was marbled red, white, and gold. *Good,* he thought, *she will be convincing.*

Reina came in and knelt. She looked up at Grumble, looked down, and began the ritual words, "Forgive me, Father, for I have sinned."

Grumble interrupted. "Doña Reina," he said, "I am not a priest and Sister Annunzio is not a nun."

Horror floated through Reina's eyes.

Grumble couldn't help smiling as he said, "I am Grumble, she is Sumner."

Reina jumped. Grumble put a hand on her shoulder to keep her from running off.

Julia glided into the room. "Let us explain . . ."

HANNIBAL CURSED. DON Cesar and his son were walking their horses back. *Just when I thought we might get off clean.*

He jumped down from the corral fence, trotted into the barn, and got the harness. Cigarillo gave him a peculiar look—like *Who told you to get the carriage ready?*—but the Mexican brought the two draft animals out of the corral. Together they started the harnessing.

Don Cesar threw Cigarillo an imperious look. The stable hand walked toward the dons, his shoulders swaying sassily, took the reins of both horses, and led them away for water and oats.

The front door of Don Cesar's adobe scraped open. Out came a horrendous moan, a ululating cry of pain.

Don't overdo it, Hannibal thought.

Two women came out, one of them Sumner in his nun's

getup. The other must be Doña Reina. They held the ends of a heavy blanket, which emerged in bright colors from the shadowed corridor.

The moan soared upward again. It came from the shape half wrapped in the blanket, apparently Julia.

Grumble staggered out, struggling to support his end of the blanket.

"The baby!" exclaimed Doña Reina.

The don's face rearranged itself from arrogance to childlike horror.

Hannibal ran to help. He grabbed Julia and lifted her out of the blanket. Reina took Esperanza from Julia. Hannibal hurried toward the carriage, bearing the stricken woman.

"What the devil is going on?" demanded Don Cesar.

"Papa, it's a month early! The baby is coming a month early!"

"Then why are you moving Julia?"

Sumner minced forward in quick tiny steps and put his hand on the don's forearm. "She needs help. It's very dangerous. We must get her to the midwife."

"Who in hell are you?"

"Sister Annunzio," said Reina, sounding out of breath. "Papa, we've got to get her help."

Hannibal deposited Julia in the carriage.

Again she issued a horrifying moan.

Good woman, thought Hannibal. He climbed up and took the reins.

"I'll ride to the pueblo for the doctor."

"Not enough time," said Grumble. "Quicker to the mission and the midwife, far quicker."

"Who in the hell are you?" snapped Don Cesar.

"Father Lorenzo, who is trying to save your grandchild's life. And your daughter's."

Grumble hopped into the carriage behind Sumner, and Hannibal lashed the horses into motion.

Don Cesar's policy was, When uncertain, shout. "Alfredo, get the doctor! Bring him to the mission! Now!"

The don himself snapped at Cigarillo to bring his horse.

Mounted, he trotted to the carriage and fell in behind. "What in hell . . . ?" he muttered. "What the devil . . . ?"

ABOUT A MILE along the dirt road the Indian driving the carriage stopped.

"What are you doing, you idiot? My daughter's life is at stake!"

"No," said the Indian, "yours is." He cocked the pistol and held it straight at the don's chest. "Dismount!"

The don did.

Two American beaver hunters ran out of the cluster of scrubby trees.

"Grumble, get the reins."

The priest did.

Grumble! The don recognized that name. He was beginning to understand . . .

Reina got down from the carriage with Esperanza in her arms. Julia stepped out next to her sister.

Don Cesar stared at Julia, uncomprehending.

Now the beaver hunters trained their rifles on the don's chest.

Don Cesar recognized them. Sam Morgan, the American clown with the Indian wife. Flat Dog, the Indian who usurped his daughter. And Sam's scraggly dog.

"Julia!" the don snapped.

The beaver hunters seized his arms.

She walked directly in front of him, glaring. She was perfectly well. His lips slipped into a snarl.

"Father," she said, "I disinherit you."

She cocked her open hand well back and slapped him.

The hands let him go, and he nearly fell.

Julia glared, challenging him.

Coy jumped forward and nipped at the don's leg. Rubio kicked at the animal. He looked rage at his daughters.

"Oh, Papa," said Reina, "you deserve it."

Flat Dog stepped up to Julia, embraced her, and kissed her, a huge kiss. Julia kissed him back with passion.

The don looked away.

Hannibal looked at Grumble, holding the reins, and nodded. Then he put his pistol in his belt, turned, plucked his rifle off the seat, and looked down its barrel at the don.

"Our friends will go on to . . . wherever they choose to go," said Flat Dog. "I, Julia's husband, the father of your grandchild, I will escort you home."

"And me," said Hannibal, prodding the don with his cocked rifle.

Flat Dog gave Julia one more kiss. He said softly, "I have to do this."

"I understand."

"Soon."

"Yes."

SAM MORGAN LOOKED into the carriage at Julia, Sumner, and Reina, who was holding his daughter. He reached for her and held her for the first time in half a year, almost her entire life. She yawned and closed her eyes. His mind went moony.

"She is a gentle baby," said Reina, "always peaceful."

Sam gawked at Esperanza.

DON CESAR CURSED Flat Dog and Hannibal all the way back to the rancho. He walked, led his horse, and cursed them.

Hannibal interrupted him. "You're impressive. Only a man of education has such magnificent imprecations."

The huge rowels on the don's spurs made his steps crooked and awkward. In a quarter mile his ankles were torturing him, and his creative energy waned.

However, his tongue was relentless. He denounced his captors. He denounced Julia and his grandchild. And he cursed the priest and nun who helped to perpetrate this atrocity. "I will make them pay," he said. "I am a loyal friend and supporter of that mission, and Father Antonio will stand by me. That priest and nun will pay."

Flat Dog and Hannibal smiled at each other and kept their guns on their prisoner.

Soon Don Cesar and the two riders came on an elderly Mexican in a big sombrero who was pruning a grapevine. The mountain men put their rifles across their laps, looking idle. Sombrero looked questioningly at the don. "It is all right, Miguel," the don said. "It is all right."

When they neared the house, Cigarillo came out of the barn, his unlit cigarillo an inch shorter but still jutting up to the sky. "It's all right," said the don. "I'm fine."

At the door of the adobe Flat Dog said, "Who is inside?"

"Two women, a maid and a cook," said the don.

"If there are only two," said Flat Dog, "fine. If there is a third or a fourth, you die." He glared at the don.

Don Cesar Rubio shrugged.

Flat Dog kicked the door open.

From the corral Cigarillo saw the American hunters pushing Don Cesar inside with their rifles. He decided that now would be a good time to relax somewhere else with a bottle of mescal.

The captors and the don stepped into the entry hall. "Call them," ordered Flat Dog.

"Lupe. Juanita."

Two women crept from separate rooms into the corridor.

"Is anyone else in the house?" said Hannibal.

The women shook their heads no. They looked terrified. "Lead me to the parlor. We will sit like guests. Have you ever been privileged to sit in that room?"

The women minced into the parlor, and Hannibal followed them.

"Down the hall," said Flat Dog, his rifle in the don's back.

He marched Don Cesar down the long corridor and into a special room at the end, where he kept his prized collection of weapons. The walls here were adorned with instruments of destruction—a conquistador's sword and breastplate; a matchlock rifle; two fine dueling pistols; a cutlass from a pirate vessel; a jeweled dirk belonging to a Spanish grandee; several styles of whips and lashes, including a cat-o'-nine-tails.

The don had displayed these marvels proudly to Flat Dog

and Sam last winter. "The cat," he said, "is preferred by the British. And this is the choice of the Russians. The knout."

He took it down to show them its nastiness. "Wire is interwoven with the rawhide, you see." Then he tapped the handle into his hand with an air of satisfaction.

Now Flat Dog took down the knout. Its memories crawled up and down the flesh of his back.

The don's eyes bugged and swelled. He remembered perfectly. He saw the eruptions of Flat Dog's skin, the spewing blood. He heard once more the Indian's screams, and remembered how he relished them.

"Down on the floor," said Flat Dog.

Don Cesar went.

"All the way. Flat on your belly."

Don Cesar obeyed.

Flat Dog leaned his rifle in a corner. Then he tapped the handle of the knout in his hand.

Eight

THE RAINS CAME.

That first night Sam, Grumble, Sumner, Julia, Reina, and the infant Esperanza drove to the pueblo of Los Angeles. They considered finding a place to stay there, but it would have been a hovel. As soon as they started on toward Mission San Gabriel Arcangel, rain started sluicing down. The road along Arroyo Seco turned to mud, and the dry creek bed trickled. Before Sam got the carriage to the mission, the horses were sliding around in the muck. Sam and Coy, in the open, were soaked and chattering.

Father Sanchez got out of bed to make them welcome. He even brewed hot coffee and poured them brandy to go with it. Sam silently wished blessings on the good Father Jose.

They all got into their beds quickly.

Sam insisted on keeping Esperanza with him. The child had been cheerful as long as the light lasted, and after dark slept.

Men went to one room, women another. Sam slept slouched in a chair, his arms around his daughter.

The next morning rain still sluiced down.

At midmorning Hannibal and Flat Dog came in. They'd slept a few hours and then ridden through the rain. They accepted bread, butter, and coffee. Hannibal took his food to bed. Flat Dog put an arm around Julia, and they headed for another bedroom.

"He's awful tired," said Sam.

"She's eight months along," said Grumble.

"I wager they'll have some fun," said Sumner.

Rain and gray, rain and gray. They napped and rested all day.

At dinner Sam looked at the friars and asked his friends in English, "What are we going to do? Rubio will come for us."

"Not for a few days he won't," said Flat Dog. He told the story of the knout-lashing. It came out flat and hard. He showed them all the knout, and the dried blood still on the rawhide and the metal studs.

"Father José is a good man," said Grumble.

"He married me and Julia."

"He knows what we've done, all of it," said Hannibal.

"But he can't protect us long," said the cherub.

"My father will pursue us wherever we go," said Julia. Reina nodded.

"Gentlemen," said Sumner, "the harbor. A ship."

They looked at each other. They nodded. "A ship," two or three of them said.

Not even a California don could attack an American or British sailing vessel on the high seas.

THE NEXT MORNING Sam and Hannibal had lunch in town. They'd left the mission while Flat Dog and Julia were still in bed, and before Grumble and Sumner got up.

A friend walked into the cantina.

"Ike Galbraith!"

Sam and Hannibal stood up at their table and shook hands with Galbraith.

"Sit and eat!" said Hannibal.

The big Mainer sat. Even seated, he was half a head taller than either of the two tall men. "Damn rain," he said. On this second morning it was still pouring.

"This un heard white men was at the mission." He did a second take on Hannibal. "Sorry, you know what I mean."

Under the table Coy whined.

"It's all right, Ike."

They poured Galbraith coffee and handed him tortillas.

"I hope everybody hasn't heard we're at the mission," said Sam.

"Damn silly hope," said Galbraith.

They told him how Flat Dog had gotten Julia back, and made Rubio pay.

"That shines," said Galbraith.

"He'll be coming after us," said Sam.

"After a few days," said Hannibal.

"Slow going in this rain anyway," said Galbraith.

"Hard even to ford the Los Angeles River," said Sam.

The road crossed the river just above the pueblo without benefit of bridge.

"That dinky thing, she's a-roaring," said the Mainer, chuckling. "What you beavers doing in town?"

"We sold some things," said Hannibal.

"One of the dons up near Monterey wanted to get me and Flat Dog hanged, or better yet bushwhacked," said Sam. "We sold most of his men's saddles, rifles, pistols, and knives."

Galbraith's eyes flashed his understanding. "Sounds more profitable than plews."

Sam and Hannibal smiled and nodded. Good to have something to smile about. Sam thought happily of the coins in his shooting pouch, a lot of them.

"We're alchemists," said Hannibal. "We turned our lead balls into gold."

"Think I'll come back to the mission with you," said Galbraith.

"We could use another hand," said Sam.

*   *   *

ON THE MORNING of the third day the rain fell in sheets.

They were putting their heads together, everyone at one big table. Father José had given them good news. "My American friends," he said in Spanish. "Good tidings. An American ship leaves San Pedro for San Diego on the tide tomorrow evening."

Sam fed Coy under the table. He'd discovered that the coyote would snap up a crust of bread if it was smeared thickly with butter.

"Right about now a ship would be a fine way to travel," said Grumble. He and Sumner had decided that Los Angeles wasn't safe for them either, not for a while.

"Safe to get there?" asked Sam. The harbor at San Pedro was a long, hard day's drive south.

"Two and a half days since Flat Dog whipped Rubio," said Hannibal.

"He's damn well not doing any riding yet," said Flat Dog.

Sumner said, "I want to take no chances."

"Let's do it," said Grumble.

Sam and Hannibal, Flat Dog and Julia—everyone looked at each other. They were agreed.

Julia squeezed Reina's hand.

"I'll be all right," she said. "Father rages, but he will never hurt me, and Alfredo would not let him."

A voice came from the outside. "Where are the Americans?"

Sam jumped up. He thought maybe he recognized that voice.

The heavy wooden door opened and Robert Dingley limped in.

Sam and Flat Dog said at once, "Robber!"

He looked like hell, face scratched and bruised, silver beard and hair matted and dirty, and one leg gimpy somehow.

Coy squealed.

"What happened to you?" said Sam.

"What's gonna happen to you, only worse. Rubio's men beat me up."

Introductions and explanations were urgently made. Robber

was an American seaman who had abandoned ship to live the carefree life in California.

"What are you doing here?" said Sam.

"Looking for you. Getting away from Rubio's men. Either or both."

The story was that he had been enjoying life in his shack up Topanga Creek in his usual way yesterday morning. Rubio's men showed up suddenly, demanding to know where Sam and Flat Dog went. "I couldn't tell them nothing. Been nearly a year since I saw you."

Robber's eyes asked where Meadowlark was. Sam wasn't ready to talk about that.

"So they beat me up."

"Don't you love them Rubios?" said Flat Dog.

"I'm through with this place," Robber said. "It was only a matter of time before Rubio run me off anyway."

"Come with us," said Sam. "We'll go to San Pedro, get a ship, get the hell out of here."

"Sure," said Robber, "and you better get going. Those men were heading back to the ranch to pick Rubio up and charge straight here."

"Rubio can't ride," said Flat Dog.

"They thought he could. And maybe they'll come without him. Either way, they're coming."

"Anyone in the pueblo will tell them where we are," said Galbraith.

The table broke into babble about how to slip down to San Pedro without getting caught. Everybody had an different idea—they agreed only that it would be dangerous.

"Listen," said Robber, but no one heard him in the talk.

"Listen," he said loudly.

They fell silent.

"I know where Rubio will never look for us."

They waited.

"In a boat. On the Los Angeles River. Which ain't never a river except now."

"Yes!" said some.

"But if he sees us," others said, "we'll be sitting ducks."

"It's a good idea," said Grumble. "Devious."

In a whirlwind of talk they came up with a plan.

They would borrow a rowboat from the mission. Robber would row Sumner, Julia, Esperanza, and Grumble down Arroyo Seco to where it flowed into the Los Angeles River just above the pueblo, and on downriver to the sea. Sam, Hannibal, and Flat Dog would ride along the bank above the river, on the lookout for Rubio and his men.

"I'll come along too," said Galbraith.

Sam liked that. Galbraith was the best shot he knew.

"When do we leave?" said Flat Dog.

"Now," said Sam.

Everyone stood up to get ready.

"Sister," said Julia in Spanish, "will you come as far as the sailing ship with me?"

"Are you all right?" said Reina. Julia's face was drawn, strained.

"Flat Dog?"

Her husband went to her, took her hand.

"I think the baby, it begins now to come."

RIDERS IN THE rain. Sam's eyes searched for dark figures in a gray world. Rain drummed on his hat and dripped off like a curtain. Rain slashed across the hills, the gullies, the landscape. He had trouble seeing, and that was dangerous.

He looked southwest along the dirt track, where the riders would probably come from. He looked west toward the hills, where they might show up. He looked every direction but down toward the water. He, Flat Dog, Hannibal, and Galbraith had agreed to keep their eyes off the stream, for that would give away the secret. There the frail boat tossed on the swollen creek called Arroyo Seco, a boat bearing friends, bearing women, bearing his daughter, bearing a baby striving to enter the world.

When he and Paladin forded the creek above, the surge felt rough. It looked rough and sounded rough. What a joke—Sam hadn't even seen water in that gully before.

Coy skittered along in front of him. Fortunately, the coyote paid no attention to the boat.

Sam hoped Robber was good with those oars.

He checked to make sure his powder was dry. He chuckled cynically to himself. *If Rubio's men show up, with or without the don, there'll be no talking things over.*

He looked at Flat Dog. His friend's horse slipped around on the wet track, just like Sam's, Hannibal's, and Galbraith's, and the packhorse that bore their gear. Flat Dog's eyes probed at the rain, and shadows in the rain. But Sam suspected the landscape he surveyed was inside. His wife was in labor down below, in the boat. His child was being born, maybe, in the rocking, plunging craft. Being born into a world of gray rain and black murderers.

That was enough to turn any man's insides into a desert.

JULIA CURSED. SHE cursed in Spanish, for her pains seemed to have squeezed away her English. The pains came every several minutes. When they did, she blanched, her body went rigid, and her curses outroared the flooding waters.

Mainly, and most eloquently, she cursed Flat Dog, the cause of these terrible pains, the one true culprit. She cursed the current, normally a trickle, now trundling along like a horse with a rough gait. She cursed the bumps and lurches. She cursed the rain, which soaked her. She cursed her need to squat. With the boat bouncing, she felt like she would bounce off to the left, or bounce to the right, and plunk into the river. But when she lay down, or took a seat on one of the hard benches, the pains were worse.

Every few minutes the boat bottomed out on a place too shallow to float. Everyone but Julia got out into ankle-deep water, dragged the boat through, and jumped back in before the jumpy thing got away. She damned them all, the grinding stop, the rough passage, and the jouncing as her fellow passengers jumped back in. She damned the lot of them, loudly and creatively.

Grumble, who had spent his life in low dives among vile-tongued men, was impressed at her eloquence. Sumner was much amused.

Except for Julia's magnificent performance, Grumble would have been grumbling. He had chosen a life of art, the art of the con. He was not a fellow for physical heroics, nor flight in wretched weather from enemies bearing the lust to kill.

Manning the oars, Robber hollered at Grumble, Sumner, and Reina from time to time to bail water out of the bottom of the boat. He had given them each buckets for the purpose. Julia cursed the water, which sloshed around and soaked her back and her bottom and the place where the baby was worming its way into the world. She cursed the baby, she cursed the bailing, she cursed the splashes, and she cursed the stupid rain.

Reina and Sumner took turns holding Julia in her squatting position and holding Esperanza. This child was showing her usual good spirit, looking around at everything with an expression of wonder. She never uttered a complaint.

Julia made up for Esperanza's reticence. She amplified her cursing now. She damned all male animals—they had those stupid appendages they just had to, had to, had to indulge—*Those damn things are the authors of pain in the world.*

"This creek is feisty," said Robber. "When we flow into the Los Angeles River, it might turn into a monster."

"I've never seen the Los Angeles River aroused," said Grumble.

"You ain't seen it after this much rain."

Julia denounced the curse God put on women in the Garden of Eden, the pain of bearing children, never to end, never to end. She cursed God himself, who was just another male. And she cursed His Holy Mother—*I don't give a damn why, I'm just cursing her.* At the start of every labor pain, or when she couldn't think of anyone else to curse, she returned to execrating Flat Dog.

Grumble heard oaths that were new on the horizon of his personal experience.

"Here comes the river," said Robber, gesturing to the right. He rowed the boat toward that bank. Where the new current plunged in, the water roiled, the waves tossing into the air. It reminded Grumble of a horse herd stampeding, their manes flying—it was as loud and scary as a stampede.

Robber heaved the boat through the roiling where the two currents met. The new, big current seized the small craft and turned it backward.

Robber yelled at the river, pulled fiercely on the oars, pivoted, and got himself faced downstream again. The boat rocked and bounced on the bucking river.

Everyone got splashed head to toe, as though they weren't already wet enough.

Then the water eased off to mere jostling, and full speed ahead, lickety-split.

Reina and Sumner patted Julia, held her, arranged the wool blankets tight around her. "They can't keep you dry," said Sumner, "but they'll keep you warm."

Julia swore bitterly.

Soon Robber warned his passengers, "The Zanja Madre dam is coming up."

"Dam?" said Grumble, Sumner, and Reina in one voice.

Robber looked at them. "How do you think the fields get irrigated? This dam makes the ditch."

"What are we going to do?" cried Grumble.

"Pull the boat out and portage it around."

Julia spewed out imprecations.

Grumble said, "Just tell me what to do."

Robber nodded, as though to say, *Good man.*

He stood up at the oars and peered downstream. "I can't see it."

They all looked downstream. The rain thinned, and the sound of the river blocked out . . .

"Oh, shit," said Robber.

He dropped to his seat and rowed like hell for the left bank.

"We're not gonna make it!"

Julia shrieked.

Now they all saw the dam of mud and brush. In a sheen of light the river thrummed straight over it.

Robber stood up and stared frantically at the dam. Frantically, he maneuvered, remaneuvered, got them a stroke this way and a stroke that way. "I don't see the best spot to go over," he hollered. "We may flip!"

The bow jutted into space. The bottom scraped.

"Oh, God," yelled Robber.

"Madre de Dios!" bellowed Julia.

Sitting in the stern, Grumble felt the waters swamp that end of the boat. "We're sinking!" he shouted.

Robber heaved on the oars, and the bow tilted downward.

They teetered over the dam.

Julia screamed.

The bow dived into the river several feet below. The undertow grabbed it.

The stern swung around the bow.

Robber rowed furiously, trying to jerk the stern downstream. Current boiled over the dam and into the boat.

Robber roared as he made a mighty heave.

With a sucking sound the bow popped out of the undertow.

All of a sudden their craft was small, flooded, and low and wobbly in the water.

"Bail!" shouted Robber.

The passengers bucketed water from the boat to the river. Bucket by bucket the boat floated higher. Soon it was on the water and not in it.

Finally, Robber could row to shore. He jumped out and held the boat with the painter.

Julia cursed Robber.

After Grumble, Sumner, and Reina clambered out, Reina holding Esperanza, Robber lifted Julia from the boat and set her on the ground.

She didn't protest. She was silent for the moment, her face grim and fixed, her mind riding toward the agony to come, plunging on the wild and stampeding stallion of pain.

Robber turned the boat upside down, then righted it, and pushed it back into the river. They got in, helped Julia get balanced in her squat, and headed downstream.

Grumble muttered to himself, "Heaven is a very, very long way off, and hell is hounding our heels."

*   *   *

THE WIND PICKED up and the rain fell harder.

"Look sharp," said Sam.

In Indian country you knew where enemies might be. In the underbrush along the creek. In the timber. Behind the ridge. Here they could come from any direction.

They turned the horses away from the river, along the irrigation ditch, to avoid giving the boat away.

Here on the eastern edge of the pueblo he could see too many hiding places. Crooked tracks led away from the bank, and hovels dotted the byways. A few structures were adobes. Any wall, any pen, any bush could hide an enemy.

No call for an honest fight here. Ideal spot for an ambush.

He didn't know whether he was chill from the rain or from fear.

An old woman came out of a hovel hunched over, a multicolored blanket draped over her head. She looked at the four riders passing along the river. Her mouth dropped into a U and she hurried back inside.

Sam strained his eyes down every track, around the edges of every building and fence, behind every tree, and saw nothing or everything. In the rain—streaming down, whipped by the wind—in the rain everything moved. Or nothing.

Long after the pueblo was behind them, his skin prickled. Turning in his saddle, he could see only hints of the village, dark shadows in the rain.

THE RAIN WAS the backdrop, unnoticed. Grumble paid it no mind, and the other boaters stopped grousing about it.

Though Julia's protests were unrelenting, Grumble accepted them as he accepted the rain and cold. Reina said, "The pains are coming closer together."

Grumble was tired. He couldn't remember, ever, being so tired. "How far?" he asked.

Robber didn't answer.

"How long to the harbor?"

"I don't know. By road from the pueblo, twenty-five miles. By river, I don't know. Longer." He looked at the current. "The river's going godawmighty fast, but it's a long way."

For an hour or so, the ride had been fast and uneventful. Grumble thought wearily, *Just the way I want it*. He grimaced.

"Will we make it tonight?"

"If we do, it will be way, way after dark."

"Julia's not gonna wait that long," said Sumner.

The men looked at each other. In the rain and the mud it would be one miserable night.

And the baby? Grumble wondered. *Can the baby survive?*

"The other river's coming up," said Robber.

"Other river?"

Robber smiled slightly. "The Rio Hondo."

Robber was a man of the waters, Grumble knew. He understood swells and tides, storms and following seas. It was no surprise that hills and the rivulets they formed, rains and the currents they created, these would be within his ken. People who didn't understand such things, well, Robber probably thought them a little silly.

Grumble didn't mind.

Robber pointed out the Rio Hondo coming in from the left, another lift to a current that was already bounding. "I'm going to hug the left bank," said Robber. "We want to feather into this new force as silky as possible."

Grumble was collecting Robber's jargon of the waters.

"It won't feel like a feather, though," said Robber.

It felt like they hit a rock. The bow bumped up and sideways. Julia yelled, and followed that with a spew of Spanish babble.

The river jabbered louder, and nattered and gabbled, and gurgled. It whacked the gunwales and slashed its waves over and into the boat, drenching the occupants. It slapped and jiggled the boat, squirreled it sideways, and teeter-tottered it. Robber was furious with trying to keep it straight. After a jigger-jerky ride, they slid into water that wasn't quite as rough.

Robber spun the boat sideways, so he could see upstream and down. His eyes rounded, his lower lip trembled, and he said, "Oh, shit!"

Grumble looked up the little *rio*. Toward them roared a wall about two feet high, a wall of churning water.

"Flash flood!" cried Robber.

Every eye was fixed on the roaring wall. They gasped for the last breath they might take on this earth.

The waters fell like an avalanche on the stern of their boat. The bow tilted toward the sky. The undertow grabbed the back end and ripped it sideways. The boat corkscrewed, the bow shot upward, and everything and everyone in the boat pitched into the tumult.

Grumble thought of nothing but grabbing Julia. He seized her under the arms and kicked like hell. Water ripped them, it rocked them, it buried them, it threw them high—it pummeled them and somersaulted them—it flung them like dirt from an explosion.

Yet being flung aside and whirled around meant . . . Grumble lay on his back and kicked like hell. "Kick!" he hollered at Julia, and felt her motions down below. "Kick!" He thrashed on his back, sometimes with his head underwater, Julia on top of him, faceup.

The eddy grabbed his shoulders and jerked them upstream. He made his last cry sound epic: "Ki-i-ck!"

Waves tumbled and flummoxed him. He kicked. Then suddenly he was sure they were going upstream instead of down. He fought for his breath, for his sanity. They bobbed along like corks. By God, they *were* going upstream. The current blasted downstream like a train of runaway wagons, and this eddy mildly eased its way the other direction.

He turned them toward the bank. In a few minutes he could actually stand up. It seemed like a miracle.

He took inventory.

Ten paces above them was Sumner, on his hands and knees in the shallows.

Another twenty paces above Sumner stood Robber, hip deep in water, his arms wrapped around Reina, her arms wrapped around Esperanza. They all had expressions of absolute stupefaction on their faces.

Reina fussed furiously with the blankets around Esperanza's face. The child sneezed, and everyone laughed.

Only the boat was missing.

THE ROAR OF wild waters, then the shouts—the four riders looked at each other, then whipped their horses down the grassy slope toward the river.

"Help!" Grumble yelled.

Flat Dog jumped off his horse on the fly, sprinted to the bank, and plowed through the water to Grumble and Julia. In a jiffy he had his wife on grass above the bank, resting.

"Blankets!"

"They're soaked," called Robber, who was holding Reina's hand and pulling her out of the river.

"Blankets anyway!"

Sumner staggered toward the bank.

Sam saw one dark shadow in the water. He jumped in and found the water was only waist deep. An arm's length beyond him it was raging. The shadow turned out to be a blanket, and he ran to Julia with it.

Ignored, Grumble crawled out of the water, crawled to Julia, and sagged to the ground.

Everyone hovered over Julia.

She said in Spanish, "The baby's coming now, the baby's going to come now, the baby's coming now."

THEY MADE CAMP right there. In a few minutes wet canvas was tented to make a sort of shelter, and Flat Dog had a small fire going.

Robber found the boat a quarter mile downstream, caught on some brush, and brought it back.

Sam and Hannibal staked the horses and went on foot to scout. Rubio or not, the party had to stay right here. Though the air felt swollen with moisture, the rain had eased off. They topped the rise behind the camp and looked up their back trail.

Mists hung low. Sam's eyes swept the grasses, bushes, and trees with his naked eyes. Then he lifted the field glass and swept them again. Coy cocked his head, as though listening.

Reina and Sumner made Julia comfortable near the fire. Grumble mumbled the prayers left from a Catholic boyhood in Baltimore.

In twenty minutes Flat Dog had coffee bubbling. Julia rejected it angrily, and glared and cursed her husband. The others were grateful for the tin cups of hot, steaming brew.

Grumble was warming his hands on the cup when Sam and Hannibal came treading softly into camp. Sam said, "They're here."

Nine

"WE CAN DEFEND this spot," said Hannibal.

It was a low rise between the river and the creek, which here ran almost parallel. A hundred paces below, the creek crooked hard left into the river, just below the camp. *Just below our people.*

The banks of the river and of the creek had plenty of cover, trees and bushes. This rise had almost none.

Sam and Hannibal crowded behind the one low tree on the rise. Flat Dog squatted behind a boulder that barely hid him. Galbraith lay in some high grass, the best he could do.

Coy kept prancing out from behind the trees and sniffing the breeze.

"How many?" asked Flat Dog.

"At least a dozen," said Sam. He was holding the field glass on them. They were strung out, dipping up and down on the hillocks, and he couldn't see them all at once.

Galbraith kept silent.

"Rubio there?"

"Out in front."

"He is some sumbitch," Flat Dog said from his boulder.

"They're on our tracks," said Sam.

"Leading them right to this spot," said Hannibal.

"And if they get by us," said Flat Dog, "leading them straight to the boat."

Sam's fantasy called up a crying newborn, and the child's cry floated like a croon to the murderers.

Sam surveyed the area. "I hate to give up the high ground," he said, "but . . ."

"No choice," said Hannibal.

"A cross fire," said Sam. "Right here, a cross fire."

Galbraith nodded once. Quick to act and slow to speak, he crawled off the rise, bent low, and took cover on the slope. The other three looked at each other. Flat Dog started after Galbraith, probably to be closer to Julia.

"Flat Dog," called Sam. "Leave Rubio to us."

His friend looked back and nodded.

Sam and Hannibal ducked down toward the creek. The cover was poor all the way to the willows along the bank. "In those cottonwoods," said Hannibal, indicating the far bank.

The men were sloshing through the water when Coy stopped at its edge. His spine hair rose, his tail pointed, and he growled.

Sam saw it. "Cub!"

Hannibal looked sharp, but could see only wiggling leaves of bushes. "Black bear or griz?"

"Couldn't tell."

They both watched the shrubbery where the cub disappeared. "Berry patch," said Sam.

Where there was one cub, there were probably two. Where there were any cubs, there was a sow. It was the sow who would be dangerous, very dangerous if you got between her and one of the cubs.

"Griz," said Sam. "Just saw her hump." A grizzly had a shoulder that, compared to a black bear's, tented up.

Coy snarled and gave a short, sharp bark.

The silvertip rose on her hind legs. The cub rumpety-rumped past her. Mama pivoted and padded along behind the cub.

"Hightailing it," said Hannibal.

Sam watched the spot. "I hope so. Sure gives me the willies," he said.

They picked shooting stations behind cottonwoods. Their barrels rested on limbs. The shots were a reasonable distance, wide open, and there was no wind. But the mist, which thickened and cleared from moment to moment, could ruin visibility.

"I don't like these odds," Sam said. The fur men had four rifles, which would take a minute or so to reload after the first volley. Rubio's men had a dozen or more rifles. Both sides had pistols.

Sam watched the rise. Turning his back to the berry patch made his skin tingle. Coy kept looking that way.

"Any strategy?" said Sam.

"Yeah. Blow hell out of them."

No need for the field glass now. Tense, Sam and Hannibal chewed their lips, rubbed their fingers, and stamped their feet. They watched for death to approach above. They listened nervously for the first sound of life arriving below. *And the damn griz is behind me,* thought Sam.

The lead rider came into view. From glassing him earlier, Sam knew it was Rubio. He looked along his sights.

"Take Rubio down with the first shot," said Hannibal, "so Flat Dog won't have to."

"Right."

"I'll hold fire."

TWO WORLDS FOR Julia, one black and one gray. In the black world she was a mote of dust spinning in a whirlwind of agony. She saw the whirlwind in ultra-clarity, the riffles of wind wild and glittering. Compared to any in real life, it was monumental, gargantuan, as big as the reach of the Milky Way across the night sky. Within this cyclone of energy the dust mote known as Julia Rubio Flat Dog gyrated around and around in unbelievable fury. And on this terrible power she rose up and up and up and up . . .

Then, abruptly, it set her down into the gray world, here on the ground, in this day of mist, on this soggy ground, in these wet blankets, with these two good, pitying people, Reina and Sumner, holding her hands on each side.

Julia knew she would die. The next time the whirlwind snatched her up she would break open, she would fly apart, and the life would spray out of her in bloody droplets into the savage air.

The baby will live, she thought. She didn't understand that, but the baby would live. She was glad.

And she was glad to die. Eager to die. Anything except . . .

The black world took her again. In an instant she was screaming upward into the whirlwind.

SAM KEPT HIS eyes on the riders. Coy pointed like a bird dog toward the berry patch where the griz disappeared. *Damn, I hate this.* Rubio was enough to worry about.

The foremost horse and rider loped into range. Rubio was reading the sloppy tracks himself. His mount cantered forward steadily. The shot was still long.

Rubio slowed his mount to a walk. *Dammit.* If the don was good at reading sign, he'd see the tale soon enough—horses cutting suddenly downhill toward the river, without any sense—moccasin prints among the horse prints.

It was time. Sam told himself, *Mexicans can't outshoot mountain men, no way.*

He squeezed the trigger, thinking clearly, *Surprise better be the trump card.*

JULIA FLAT DOG, born Julia Rubio y Obregon, made the supreme effort of her eighteen years. She gathered all her thoughts, all her juices, all her muscles, all her force, everything she was and a lot more, and—Madre de Dios—pushed!

Once! Twice! Reina and Sumner were exclaiming, cheering her on, but her fierce concentration made her deaf. Only the urge and the effort existed.

A third time! She teetered on the edge of success and fell back. Immediately, with a force she never dreamed she had, Julia made a huge fourth push and—*blessed virgin!*—she expelled the cursed, awful, alien thing from her body. It felt like excreting a melon.

"You did it!" cried Sumner.

Grumble, sitting at her head, applauded.

"*Es en muchacho!*" exclaimed Reina. It's a boy.

Robber joined in Grumble's applause.

Beaming, Sumner wiped and dried the baby.

Reina held Esperanza close to the new child. "This is your cousin," she said.

The new fellow roared out a protest at this strange world. He roared another one at the cold and the damp. Everyone chuckled.

Grumble cut the cord, and Reina put the baby to his mother's breast.

Julia was swimming back toward the surface of the ocean of awareness. She noticed a weight on her chest. She felt it with her fingers, and her mind rose toward the light. She held the weight where she could see it.

A baby. Her baby. A child, a human being. A living union of her and Flat Dog. A boy. He glowed with an angelic light. He was the most beautiful creature she'd ever seen.

Emotion lifted her on a huge wave, a swell of ecstasy. She clutched their creation to her bosom.

After a long while, she managed to say, "He is Azul Flat Dog. After Flat Dog's brother, Blue Medicine Horse, who died."

Happily, she unsnapped her blouse and put Azul's mouth on her nipple. As she felt the first suck at her milk, a rifle boomed.

CESAR RUBIO STOOD up in his stirrups to see the tracks. Then three waves crashed on him almost simultaneously—he felt an agony in his hip, he heard an explosion, and he crashed off his mount to the ground.

"Hell," said Sam, "he moved and it hit him low."

Two shots boomed from the direction of the river.

Rubio's men wheeled, looked, milled, raised their rifles, and saw nothing to shoot at.

One man was on the ground, another sagging and bleeding in his saddle.

A rider decided the creek was better than the river and charged down the short slope into bushes and trees.

All followed him.

Hannibal shot one man out of his saddle.

Hearing the blast and seeing the smoke, the line of riders angled upstream.

Rubio's mount came last in a jerky gait. The don's boot was caught in the stirrup, and his body dangled like an effigy, bouncing across grass, rocks, and mud.

Just as the riders disappeared into the cover, Sam shot again. The last rider flinched and grabbed but kept his seat.

"They're into the berry patch," he said, looking wild-eyed at Hannibal.

They both reloaded fast, fingers flying.

For long moments they heard nothing and saw nothing.

From the corner of his eye Sam saw Flat Dog and Galbraith crawl across the top of the rise, half-hidden in the grass, rifles ready.

The griz roared.

"If hell has church bells," said Hannibal, "they sound like that."

Eight or ten riders burst out of the thicket like a flock of ducks shotgunned by hunters.

Flat Dog and Galbraith fired from the high ground.

Sam heard an answering shot and saw the smoke, but the barrel seemed to be pointed straight up in the air.

More riders burst out of the berry patch. They wavered, gathered, and flew back north, the way they came, toward the pueblo, toward home. Anywhere gunfire and grizzlies might not tear hell out of them.

Rubio's horse came last, awkwardly, with Rubio's weight flopping along on one side. The don thrashed desperately to get his boot free. Suddenly, in a paroxysm of effort, he wrenched the foot loose and collapsed onto the muddy earth. His horse abandoned him at a gallop.

Sam looked at his enemy, now brought low.

Flat Dog started down the hill toward Rubio.

"Let him be," called Hannibal.

All four trappers waited. They watched. Coy grew rigid, pointed, and growled.

The sow griz approached the injured don with mincing steps. She was curious but wary. She stopped and looked. She sniffed the air, and the trappers felt glad to be downwind of her. She took several minutes getting to the crumpled figure.

She swatted it a couple of times, in a testing way.

Rubio flung an arm up in a half circle and back to the ground.

The griz roared and tore his shoulder with her teeth.

The two cubs crept close.

The griz roared louder. She whacked the body with her snout. She snuffled. She growled, bit, and waggled her head.

An arm came away in her mouth, hand up, accepting the rain.

Sam and Hannibal walked up the rise to join their friends. They looked at the bleeding bodies of the fallen. They looked at each other. They wanted to share their amazement, but there were no words.

They trotted away from the griz, toward camp. Not a man of them wanted to see more of what was happening with the griz and . . .

"Just before the first shot," said Galbraith, "I thought I heard a baby bawl."

Flat Dog ran toward Julia.

Ten

THERE ON THE bank of the river Hannibal took charge of telling the sisters. "Your father is dead."

"How?" said Julia, her voice shaking.

"It's strange," he said. "It's beyond strange. We fired at your father's party. They fled into a berry patch along the creek." He hesitated. "A grizzly bear attacked him and . . . It was almost beyond belief."

All of them looked at each other, wide-eyed.

"The others rode back where they came from. Fast."

Reina and Julia looked at each other. "Do you want me to go look?" said Reina.

Julia kissed Azul's head and then looked up at her sister. "No."

*   *   *

THE CAPTAIN OF the *Madison,* glad to have the gold coins for the passages, welcomed Sam's party to the harbor in San Pedro and his ship. "I was seeking you," he said, but did not yet explain.

The partings at San Pedro were brief and bittersweet. Reina wanted to return to her home, to rejoin her husband and children and see to the burial of her father.

All but Reina—Sam, Hannibal, Grumble, Flat Dog, Sumner, Galbraith, Robber, Julia, and the two infants—set forth on the evening tide on the *Madison* to San Diego.

Sam and Hannibal stood near the penned horses. The night was windy and the seas high. Coy watched the poor animals, who could do nothing but try to maintain balance as the boat switched from tack to tack and rocked from wave to wave. Sam was worried about Paladin, and the captain required that some one of the party watch the horses continually.

Sam looked westward upon the dark waters. China, he supposed, was out there somewhere. "I set out to find a home," he said to Hannibal. "I found it—Crow country. And now I'm as far from it as I can get. Hell, I'm even off the continent."

"Think about it. These waters began in Crow country. They came down the mountains and across the desert and joined this ocean. On the water you're always home."

Now Captain Bledsoe emerged out of the darkness. "I bring you a letter from Captain Jedediah Smith." He handed it to Sam, who passed it to Hannibal.

"Will you read it to me?"

Hannibal did.

To Samuel Morgan—
Dear Sir, and your companions Mr. McKye and Flat Dog,

I write in strong hopes that your fortunes have been better than mine. Leaving two days after you, I rode to Saint Joseph Mission, where I found in charge one Father Duran, a melancholy and thoroughly disagreeable man. He would not hear my request to pass through to the governor's residence in Monterey, and thus I could not join you there. Instead he put me in the guardhouse and told me that an officer would come from San Francisco to try my case. During the intervening days he made no provision for feeding myself or my men, and we were obliged to throw ourselves on the kindness of the elderly overseer.

It proved that an Indian had accused me of claiming the country on the Peticutry River. When the commander arrived, however, one Lieut. Martinos, instead of punishing me in accordance with the wishes of Father Duran, he sentenced the Indian to an undeserved flogging.

After two weeks the governor finally wrote from Monterey, bidding me to come there under guard.

In Monterey Governor Echeandia proved as difficult as ever. He gave me the liberty of the town, but no satisfaction with my problem. The town I found quaint, but the inhabitants too free and careless in their ways. There I received word of your difficulties at the mission and your journey southward to rejoin Flat Dog's wife and your daughter. I hope that effort has proved successful.

Through many discussions here the governor maintained his position that I am an intruder in the country, and my status can only be resolved by a journey to Mexico City. After some inquiries I determined that he meant for me to pay for my own passage to Mexico, and expressed my outrage that a man should be expected to take himself to prison at his own expense.

The governor further insisted that my men come in. I suggested that they were closer to San Francisco and wrote Mr. Rogers to proceed there.

The captains of four ships in port then kindly vouched for me and promised to be responsible for my conduct. Upon that event Echeandia gave me three choices, to go to Mexico, wait for instructions to come from Mexico, or leave the country by the route by which I entered.

More than eager to rid myself of California, I chose the latter. The governor signed a passport which enables me to purchase provisions. I am soon, therefore, to travel to San

Francisco on the *Franklin*, equip myself, and leave the country.

In these circumstances there appears to be no opportunity for you, Mr. McKye, and Flat Dog to take your places as employees of Smith, Jackson & Sublette. I have therefore discharged you as of the date you left our camp on the Appelaminy. I hope that we shall all greet each other gladly at the rendezvous next summer.

> Believe me
> your sincere friend,
> Jedediah S. Smith

Sam gazed out at the dark sea, stretching all the way to China. He turned and studied the wavy black line made by the coastal hills of California. He walked to the lee rail and looked at the country. Hannibal followed and stood beside him. Coy rubbed against the other leg. The men propped their hands on the rail and leaned out. Here you could hear the prow cutting through the water.

"A country of troubles," said Sam. "For me."

The memories were too fresh to be spoken. Meadowlark had died there. Sam had killed men there. "The authorities are probably looking for me too."

"Hell, the Mexican constabulary probably wants you, me, Flat Dog, Grumble, Sumner, Jedediah Smith, every American who's set foot in the province."

Sam felt the wind at his back, its scent strong with something . . .

Flat Dog walked up. "Time for my watch."

"I can stay longer," Sam said.

The Crow shook his head. "Look in on Julia, will you?"

Flat Dog's wife was facedown on the bunk in the small cabin, sobbing. Her sobs racked her whole body, and her cries drowned out the wind, the seas, and the noises of the rigging and sails.

Suddenly Julia twisted violently onto her back. She convulsed with sobs, over and over and over.

Hannibal gave Sam a look of warning.

She shouted, "I hated the *diablo!*" She slammed her fists against the bedclothes at her side. "I hated him!" She glared at Sam and Hannibal.

Coy yipped.

Esperanza woke up bawling.

Immediately Julia sat up. "Hand her to me."

Sam did.

Julia raised her blouse without hesitation, put Esperanza on one breast, and lay back down. "Stay with me," she said, "please stay."

Her chest began to heave again.

Sam and Hannibal sat down on the end of the bunk and looked at each other uncomfortably.

Sam glanced at Julia and for the first time admitted this thought clearly to his mind: *When I lost Meadowlark, I lost Esperanza.*

"It's true," said Hannibal.

Sam shot him a look. *Damn, get out of my head.*

"Sad but true."

Azul whimpered

Julia held her arms out. Sam put her son in them. In a moment she had a child on each breast.

I lost her.

Soon the children were asleep. "Take them, please."

When Sam did, Julia began to bawl again, and then to wail.

Sam curled up on the floor and tried to sleep.

Hannibal sat in a corner, leaned back, and closed his eyes.

TWO HOURS LATER they were back on watch with the horses, peering into the darkness.

Coy growled.

"A change in the weather, gentlemen."

Captain Bledsoe, evidently wandering his ship at night. The odor of his pipe was as strong as the smell of the sea. "It's time. They don't have four seasons on this coast, just dry season and rainy season. The storms can blow hard. This sea is not pacific." With a quick smile at his pun the captain continued on his rounds.

Sam smiled to himself. Odd how many people in his life gave importance to words. Pacific not pacific. Grumble treasured words, so did Hannibal. Sam's father, Lewis Morgan, had had a tongue voluble and creative. A Welsh tradition, said his father. *I should learn to read.*

"We already had our California storms," said Hannibal.

"I want to go home," said Sam.

"California is beautiful and languid," said Hannibal.

Coy whined and thumped his tail.

"One day it will be American."

Sam looked at Hannibal in surprise, and then back at the dark continent off the port bow. His single thought was, *What on earth do I do now?*

Hannibal said, "Let's drive horses to the mountains and sell them."

IT TOOK THEM a week to arrange things in San Diego.

First they brain-stormed their plans. The men had gold in their pockets, from selling the saddles, firearms, and other weapons. Since they'd all played the roles of fighters and rescuers, they would divide the booty equally.

Robber and Galbraith weren't interested in taking horses anywhere. They liked the little town and the easy life in California. They would stay.

"Who else wants what?" asked Sam.

"I think it might be well to take leave of California for a time," said Grumble.

"I goes where my massa goes," said Sumner, the apprentice con man.

They laughed at the darkie accent. Coy gave one sharp yip at all of them.

"Where are we going to go exactly?" said Flat Dog. "Winter's coming on."

"Winter's the time to cross the desert," said Sam. He would never forget that terrible June crossing with Jedediah, Gobel, and Robert Evans.

"Let's go to Taos or Santa Fe," said Hannibal. "Spend the cold months there before we head for rendezvous."

They considered and one by one the men nodded. Julia just listened. Since her one night of wild grief, she had seemed even-keeled. Flat Dog remarked to Sam that with two children to take care of, she showed less interest in men's doings.

"All right, we can probably buy horses from the mission," said Sam. Jedediah Smith had seen the huge herds when he was force-marched to San Diego last winter. The Californios had far, far more horses than they had any use for.

"What do you think we'll have to pay for them?" asked Sumner.

Grumble said, "At Mission San Carlos Borromeo de Carmelo we paid six dollars for a pair."

"And they were broke to harness," said Sam. "These will be unbroke."

Flat Dog said, "And at rendezvous we can sell them for . . . ?"

"Fifty to a hundred each," said Sam.

"That appeals to my larcenous heart," said Sumner.

"Can we get fifty animals?" said Flat Dog.

Hannibal shook his head. "We have to buy supplies."

"Say thirty," said Sam.

Grumble put in, "How many can we drive?"

Sam and Hannibal took thought. "Five men," said Flat Dog.

"Don't count me," said Grumble. The cherub hated riding, and hadn't forked a horse once on their entire journey. "I may walk the whole way."

"We could drive a hundred easily," said Hannibal.

"All right, here's a proposition," said Grumble. "I'll put my hand in my trunk and bring out enough coins to bring our horse count to a hundred."

"Grumble, you have that much gold?" said Sam.

The con man gave a dry smile. "For me money is a tool." He looked merrily at them. "This way we all get a handsome profit. Divided by five, up toward a thousand dollars each. But I get something in the bargain."

"Oh, no," said Sam.

"We'll winter in Santa Fe, yes?"

"Probably," said Hannibal. "Or Taos."

"Santa Fe is bigger, so let's head there. The deal is, one day or night a week each of you plays a little game with me."

"Chicanery," said Hannibal.

"Con games," said Sam.

"Exactly," said Grumble.

"Nothing that will get us arrested," said Sam.

"I am revolted by jails," said Grumble.

"It's a deal," said Hannibal.

One by one, they all agreed—Sam, Hannibal, Flat Dog, and Sumner. Coy gave another yip.

"Let's get mares," said Sam. "There'll be foals in the spring before we go to rendezvous."

"Good thought."

And on into the night they planned.

San Diego was a cinch. Aside from the mission and presidio, the town was only four adobes and about three dozen dark huts overlooking a fine bay. The letter of safe passage assured their hospitality at the mission. They avoided the presidio, where some officer might demand passports.

In a week they bought their hundred horses, got supplies, hired an Indian guide, and got started east across the Mojave Desert.

"Let's not go anywhere near the Mojave villages," Sam told the guide in Spanish. He was an older man, with a look of having seen everything.

"No," the man answered, "we go to the Yuma villages."

So they did.

For the first time since leaving rendezvous Sam thought, *I am headed home.* Roundabout, but home.

The desert was easy enough. Julia traveled almost as comfortably as a Crow woman, even with the two children. Sam felt like an old hand there now, and the guide knew where to find water. The crossing of the Colorado River wasn't bad—in November the river was low. Coy not only kept up with the herd but led the way—the little coyote didn't like swimming, so he did it fast.

At the Yuma villages they were welcomed as enemies of the Mojaves. They gave the Indians some presents, hired a new guide, and passed on rapidly. The route of the Gila River, said the Indians, had been used by other trappers, those from Taos.

Now they got the story of that trapping party and the Mojaves. The trappers worked their way up the Colorado, the Yumas said, to the Mojave villages. Red Shirt demanded payment for the beaver they'd taken out of the river. Incensed, for the Mojaves had no interest in the beaver, the trappers refused. In the ensuing fight several Mojaves were killed.

"And took it out on us," Sam said to Hannibal.

Up the valley of the Gila they went, clear to where the Salt River joined it, and above. Though the river was full of beaver, they didn't pause to trap. Their minds were on getting the live-stock safe to Santa Fe. Coy stayed near Paladin's hoofs and helped control the herd.

The Apaches watched them closely all the way, but didn't seem to want to make trouble.

Flat Dog, Julia, and the small children spent every night in a tipi. She fed both of them at her breasts, and tended to all their needs.

Spending his days alongside the herd, watching for trouble, Sam realized that he felt more like Esperanza's uncle than her father. He reflected that Julia and Flat Dog were the real family, and would be the parents in the eyes of the Crow people.

I have no family, he thought often.

That night, as all of them sat around a warm, crackling fire, he felt like playing his tin whistle. He hadn't touched it in California. He played an old tune in a minor key. Coy joined in with a mournful howl. Sam spoke sharply to him, and he fell into a resentful silence.

After one time through the tune, Hannibal raised his husky bass voice with the words, and Julia hummed a high, floating harmony over it all:

I am a poor wayfarin' stranger
A-wanderin' through this world of woe
But there's no trouble, no toil or danger
In that bright land to which I go.

I'm going home to see my father
I'm going there no more to roam
I'm just a-goin' over Jordan
I'm just a-goin' over home.

Sam thought, *It's how much I miss my dad, that's why I played this song.*

After singing the second verse, Hannibal put in the other chorus—

I'm going there to meet my mother
She said she'd meet me when I come . . .

Sam wondered if his mother, that good, weak woman, was still alive. If so, she was under the thumb of brother Owen.

When Sam put away the tin whistle, he realized how much he'd missed playing it. He reached down and scratched Coy's head. The coyote felt like an old, old buddy.

The next night Sam played again for a few minutes. Then he did something totally spontaneous. He said to Grumble, "Teach me to read."

Grumble and Hannibal competed for the privilege of teaching Sam. Grumble wrote out a list of the twenty-six letters of the alphabet. Hannibal taught Sam how to recite them to "Baa, Baa, Black Sheep."

"Now you can sing the alphabet while you ride alongside the herd by yourself all day."

Near the headwaters of the Gila they saw the rough road that led up to the copper mines, and wagons coming down. They crossed the divide above, coasted down the mountains into the huge valley, and turned north along the Rio Grande.

As they drove their herd up the river toward the capital city, Sam picked out his first words from a copy of the King James Bible, one of several books that Hannibal carried. He found reading frustrating, maddening, and worse. The way English is spelled made no sense to him.

By the time they passed the hamlet of Albuquerque, he was understanding his first English sentences. Soon he learned to pick out sayings he'd heard all his life—"Eye for eye, tooth for tooth, hand for hand, foot for foot."

"Not enough for me," said Sumner. "You take my eye, I take both yours."

Coy squealed.

"I abhor violence," said Grumble.

Sam sounded out the next one Hannibal had marked for him slowly. "Thou shalt love thy neighbor as thyself."

"The world chooses not to live by that admonition," said Grumble. No one disputed with him.

"Why can't they use plain talk?" said Sumner. " 'Thou,' 'thy'—it's dumb."

"He that is without sin among you, let him first cast a stone at her."

"I'd recommend that one," Grumble said.

"You're just afraid of getting stoned," said Sam.

"You white folks," said Sumner. Everyone looked at him. "Bible words," said Sumner, "made me dump that whole religion down the outhouse."

They all looked at each other around the fire.

Finally Hannibal shrugged. "Sam, if you want to know some gods, read up on the Greeks. Sex, murder, revenge, incest, the whole kit and caboodle."

Sam looked at Flat Dog. "What do you say about this? Give us a story about Crow gods."

"They're not really gods," said Flat Dog, "more like heroes."

Julia cleared her throat. Flat Dog looked at his wife. Her face gave warning. He smiled at Sam and shrugged.

"All right," said Sam. He turned to Julia. "What about you?"

"I am a Catholic. Religion is something I do, not something I analyze."

Coy whined and looked at Sam for attention. He cocked his ears forward and then backward. Sam scratched his head.

"So what do you want to *do*?" asked Hannibal.

"Go to mass on Christmas Day. Get me to Santa Fe in time to go to mass."

They rode into the city on Christmas Eve and close-herded their horses on good grass on the Santa Fe River above town. Flat Dog went with Julia to the Church of Our Lady of Guadalupe the next morning to celebrate the anniversary of the birth of Christ.

And Julia had more to do. The next day the priest baptized their son Azul into the Christian faith. At her request, which felt like a command, Sam Morgan stood as the infant's godfather.

Father and godfather, he thought. He didn't know what it all meant.

Eleven

THE PRIEST, FATHER Herrera, took them visiting. "This is the casa of the Otero family." Sam, Coy, Hannibal, and Flat Dog trundled along beside the priest. "Señora Luna, the sister of Señora Otero, is likely to help you, I think. Since it is the day of the birth of our Lord, she is in town."

Sam liked Santa Fe. It was perched on a high plateau below snowy mountains. The low buildings were all adobe, and columns of smoke rose straight up into a golden light that shimmered. The town was built along the river, and the streets wound out from the plaza unpredictably, twisting like roots of a tree. He had no idea where this winding lane would lead them, but the town was striking, even beautiful.

He hadn't seen so many people in several years, several thousand of them. The men of means wore huge-brimmed hats, the rowels of their spurs were enormous, almost comical, and they threw a blanket over one shoulder in a dashing style. Their horses were the same wiry Spanish ponies he'd seen in California.

"Señora Luna owns Rancho de las Palomas," the priest had said. "It is a splendid ranch of great size. The wagon trains, on El Camino Real from Santa Fe on the way to Chihuahua, they stop and trade there. The señora does an exemplary job running the enterprise." Sam's Spanish really wasn't up to words like "exemplary," but he got the point.

Hannibal raised an eyebrow at the priest.

"A widow," the padre said, "and an accomplished woman."

"Paloma?" said Sam as the three of them ambled lazily along. "That's a new one on me."

"It means 'dove,' " said the padre. "There is a fine Spanish novel called *Linda Paloma*. Beautiful dove."

"Here we are," said the priest, opening a gate into a courtyard.

The casa was handsome in the Santa Fe way, *vigas* jutting out above walls of plastered adobe. But they weren't going inside. Father Herrera led them into a courtyard and introduced them to two sisters, Señora Paloma Luna y Salazar and Señora Rosa Otero y Salazar.

"Excuse me a moment," said Señora Luna, finishing some sort of work with her hands. Sam was stunned. He'd expected a woman well along in years. The señora was in her early thirties, he guessed, and possessed of a grave beauty.

Señora Otero acknowledged the introductions, excused herself, and stepped into the house. The priest went with her.

Señora Luna came forward, holding a long string of red chiles. She hung it from a *viga*, retreated, and looked at it and the entire row of them along the house. *"Ristras,"* she said. "I find beautiful things irresistible."

Sam thought, *She is beauty.*

She made sure of each of their names, gave Coy a pat on the head, and invited them to sit. The winter afternoon was mild and the sun strong. "It's pleasant out here," she said. "Very well. Padre says you have a business proposition for me."

They explained. If Señora Luna would permit them to turn

their horse herd out on her grass, Sam and Flat Dog would train her horses as saddle mounts. "One horse each," Flat Dog offered. Sam couldn't have squeezed a word out.

He and Señora Luna gazed at each other.

"Also," said Hannibal, "you will get new blood for your mares."

Coy made a squealing yawn, perhaps in approval.

The señora snapped back into the conversation.

"Do you train with the *jaquima*?" she said.

"Sure," said Flat Dog. Since Indians didn't use bits at all, he and Sam were used to training riding horses with the piece of equipment called in English the hackamore.

"Sam is something special," said Hannibal.

Sam flushed red, which he always hated because his white hair made him look redder. The señora couldn't resist a smile of amusement.

"May we show you tomorrow?" said Hannibal.

"Yes, of course," she said. "I'm sure we can work something out." She gave them instructions on how to get to her rancho, which was down the Santa Fe River.

"I remember the place," said Sam. He was half proud that he'd found words and gotten them out.

Señora Luna rose. "Tomorrow, then, with your herd."

"Yes," said Hannibal.

"When will you take the horses to head for your fur hunters' summer rendezvous?"

"Early May," Hannibal said.

She thought. "Four and a half months." She turned to Sam. "I think we can form a profitable relationship."

Sam nodded.

"I'll expect you in the afternoon."

She stood. So did they, Sam tardily.

"You must call me Doña Paloma," she said. "We'll all be friends." But she was looking at Sam.

Walking back through the narrow streets, they talked about Doña Paloma. Sam had nothing to say. Flat Dog and Hannibal were full of admiration for her beauty, her low, husky voice, her intelligence, her business sense.

"Sounds like the girl for you," Sam said to Hannibal, and heard the foolishness in his own voice.

"Me?" the Delaware said, chuckling.

Flat Dog pointed to his eyes. "Sam, he has a pair of these, but he doesn't see."

"It's you she's interested in," Hannibal said to Sam.

Sam shivered, but could think of nothing to say to that.

SAM'S NERVES WERE tingling like a teenager's, and that was making Paladin skittish. She pricked up her ears and turned them constantly, as though she might be able to hear what was wrong with her rider. Her hoofs slipped in the soft surface of the river road—this afternoon was warm and a winter thaw was on. She swished her tail edgily. Once she even stopped and turned her head, maybe wanting to go back. But she had horses to lead, and she knew the job. Sam rode in front of the herd, Coy beside him. Flat Dog and Sumner rode flank and Hannibal came along behind. They were accustomed to this work—they'd trekked a thousand miles with the loss of only one animal.

Now Sam shook the memories of that long trail out of his head and came back to his job. He turned Paladin sideways in the road and waved at the horses, turning them into the road onto the north side of the señora's property. Hannibal pushed them from the far side, and Flat Dog herded them from behind.

Paloma Luna came out on a good-looking sorrel mare and helped herd the new horses back toward her band. She wore a skirt that was split for riding and big spurs. Across her shoulders, with artless grace, were tossed two colorful blankets.

Sam's first thought was, *She's much too old.*

And then he felt a flush of shame for what he'd been thinking.

Coy started a howl that came up short in a groan.

"Now. Would you like to take a tour of the rancho?"

They would.

It sat in a pleasant valley along the Santa Fe River. On broken land along the north side she grazed sheep, cattle, and goats and bred horses—"Trying to improve the line," she said, "my personal effort." On the south side of the stream she raised pigs, and chickens, grew fruit, and planted crops; she irrigated these fields out of the river via a *madre acequia,* mother ditch.

"We put this vineyard in," she said. "In two more years we will have some grapes, and soon enough to produce wine, which we will make ourselves."

A middle-aged man walked up, probably to see the strangers. "This is Antonio, my foreman." She introduced everyone, which surprised Sam. "Antonio will produce the wine. He is proud of the vineyard, his project."

Sam felt dazed—maybe it was the beautiful woman and her fine seat on her mare, or maybe the dazzling sun. Though he liked her elegant Spanish (she offered no English), he didn't seem to understand half of what she said. He gathered that this ranch had come down through her family, and now that her husband was dead, she ran it, with the help of half a dozen Mexican-Indian families who lived in the *casitas primitivas,* rough houses, on the property.

"I will establish a blacksmith here," she said, "and a wheelwright there. Along the creek we will build a mill. While my husband lived, the rancho did not progress. He was not interested in it. I love this land," she said, "and I am a serious woman of business."

As they rode back toward the main casa, the señora said, "What is this special thing that you want to show me?"

Hannibal grinned. "Watch. It takes a few minutes to set up."

Quickly they cut willow branches along the river and improvised a ring. Then Sam took the saddle and bridle off Paladin. He stood in the center of the ring. "Señora," Hannibal said, "if you will join Sam." She did.

Sam whistled. Paladin came to him immediately. With hand signals he set her to cantering around the ring clockwise. At another signal she reversed direction. He called to her and she stopped and faced him. At another call she pranced sideways, and then back to where she started. When he motioned down with both hands and stepped behind the señora, Paladin walked to the lady and bowed.

The señora laughed and applauded, delighted as a girl.

Then Sam whistled, Coy jumped onto Paladin's back, and around the ring the mare loped, the coyote standing up on her back.

"You are a magician!" said the señora. "Is Señor Flat Dog equally talented?"

"You bet," said Sam.

"Then please train any of my horses, train all of them. They will bring fine prices, so I will pay you well. Handsomely." She thought, hand in her chin. "Here is a proposal. Señor Flat Dog, you have a wife, two children."

"One child his, one mine," said Sam.

"Then you may live in one of my casitas. It is not occupied in the winter. You will be comfortable and close to your work."

Sam and Flat agreed with their eyes. "Sounds fine," said Flat Dog.

"The horses of mine you train, we will sell them just before you leave. Untrained, they are worth about two hundred fifty pesos. I will give you half of every peso above that amount."

Sam shot a look of gratitude at his teacher. Hannibal winked at him.

They went into the courtyard, which enclosed a well and an *horno,* an outdoor oven. They sat, and a servant girl brought them hot chocolate and *pan dulces,* sugared breads.

Sam felt like an idiot. As they chatted, the widow looked at him constantly. "Your white hair," she said, "on so young a man, it's charming." For a moment he thought she was going to reach out and touch it. Instead she turned away to the wall, looked over and said, "This is my flower garden and herb garden. It looks so sad in the middle of winter. But perhaps you will see it in the spring. I have transplanted the wildflowers of the region. They make rainbows of color."

She hesitated. "Señor Morgan, Señor Flat Dog, may I show you your new home?"

It was thirty paces away and indistinguishable from the other casitas. "Perfectly fine," Flat Dog said. "I will bring my family tomorrow."

Sam looked at Flat Dog edgily. He often spoke as though Esperanza were his own daughter.

"Señor Morgan, Señor Hannibal said you are learning to read. My father owned some English books. He spoke the language, and he loved literature. Perhaps you would like to see them."

Coy let out a squeal.

Sam nodded that he would like to see the books.

"You will find them in the *cuarto de recibo*. You may use them this afternoon," she said, "and stay to supper with us if you like."

Her gaze made it clear that Sam alone was the focus of the invitation.

"Thank you," Sam mumbled.

A stable hand took Paladin.

"Good day, gentlemen."

Paloma Luna turned toward the house, and Sam and Coy walked beside her.

Hannibal said to Flat Dog and Sumner said in English, "See what learning to read will get you?"

Sam thought he saw the señora suppress a smile—maybe she did speak English. Coy followed the two of them into the courtyard and the casa.

AT SUPPER PALOMA Luna smiled seldom. Sam wondered if she felt the sadness he felt, an undercurrent of melancholy that sounded in the heart of everyone who lost a spouse, and would never go away. He felt sure she did.

A gray-haired Mexican woman dished up the food and an attractive young woman served them. The señora introduced Sam to her servants—the cook was Juanita, the young woman Rosalita. Remembering his manners, Sam rose and said he was pleased to meet them. He caught a hint of a smile from the señora. "I don't like it when people treat their helpers like they're not people," said Sam.

"Then you'll be interested in Rosalita's story," said the señora. "You Americans are informal. May I call you Sam?"

He nodded yes.

"Will you call me Paloma?"

He nodded again.

Dinner was shredded pork in a green chile sauce on corn tortillas, with beans on the side, and boiled carrots diced with onions, and goat cheese. "I'm sorry we don't have fresh greens," said the señora. "This country is so high and cold. But I love it. I love the starkness of the earth here, the way the rock sticks out like bones. I love the red earth. Especially I love the quality of the sunlight—this light, it's like a diamond. When I was a child, my father took me to Chihuahua so that I could experience a real city. I saw light like this nowhere else, absolutely nowhere."

Sam looked at her in silence. He wanted to feed Coy pork by hand but didn't dare.

"My grandfather founded this rancho and named it after my grandmother, Paloma. In each generation the first daughter is named Paloma."

Except that you are childless, Sam thought. The melancholy throbbed within him. He thought of Esperanza, who would spend the winter here with himself, Flat Dog, Julia, and her cousin Azul. He tried to take comfort in that.

"I said you would be interested in Rosalita's story," said Paloma. She glanced toward the kitchen. Rosalita and Juanita ate the same food at a small table, just through a wide entrance from the dining room.

"Do you know about the big trade caravans?"

"No."

"We are a very remote province. The word 'provincial' barely begins to describe how far away we are and how little the government in Mexico cares about us. Everything we buy comes in big caravans all the way from Chihuahua, six hundred miles to the south, and is very expensive. My father and I traveled with one of the caravans. The road, El Camino Real, is the one that passes before my front gate.

"Chihuahua itself gets traders who come up from Ciudad Mexico through the mountains of central Mexico, where the mines are. The mines get vegetables, cattle, sheep, jerked meat—everything to eat, plus manufactured goods. Mining towns," she said with a grimace. "The men think of nothing but digging fortunes out of the ground. They don't even produce enough for themselves to eat.

"The traders do much business in Chihuahua, and a few come on to this small and insignificant place. They bring all the fine things we do not make for ourselves, delicate fabrics, shoes and boots, iron tools, copperware, pottery—all items manufactured, and some nice things, chocolate, sugar, tobacco, liquor, ink and paper.

"They take back what we have to offer—sheep, wool, salt, jerked meat, piñon nuts, Indian blankets, and the skins of beaver, buffalo, bear, and deer."

"Piñon nuts?" said Sam, grinning.

"Yes, any kind of food. It is a poor arrangement for us. Our traders are always in debt because of it." She sighed and looked toward the kitchen. The two women were cleaning pots and pans noisily and jabbering. "There is another, bigger item of trade. Slaves."

"Slaves?" Sam thought of Sumner.

"Yes. The traders bring to us Mexican women and children taken by Indians from their villages in Sonora and Chihuahua. Our wealthy families buy them."

Sam knew nothing of this.

"In return," Paloma said bitterly, "we steal Indian women and children from the villages and *rancherias* of our Indios and send them to Mexico. Families are destroyed both here and there. It is the most profitable part of the trade on the Chihuahua Trail—by far the most. Raid a village, kill some of the men, take all the women and children you can get." She breathed in and out. "Send Chihuahuans to this remote province, send Indians to Chihuahua."

Sam felt slapped in the face. His father, Lew Morgan, had always said slavery was a curse.

"In former times the big caravans came only once every two years. Now, because the traffic is so rewarding, the slave traders come several times each year."

"My friend Sumner was a slave," said Sam.

She nodded.

"I hate that. I helped him get free."

"It is barbaric," Paloma agreed. "The blankets you see all over my house—beautiful, aren't they? We call them slave blankets. Our wealthy families keep some of the Navajo women as slaves here, and they weave these blankets. I love them, but it makes me feel odd to buy them. I don't know whether my purchase encourages slavery or whether it makes the lives of the woman here better."

"I wouldn't know what to do either."

"Rosalita is a slave."

Sam just stared at Paloma.

"I set her free. I bought her two years ago and told her she was welcome to stay here on the rancho and work for a wage, or to go anywhere she wanted."

Suddenly Rosalita appeared at the table and put a small bowl in front of each of them. Sam looked carefully at her face, and she threw him a good smile. She didn't look oppressed.

"This is flan," Paloma said, "an egg custard with a sweet topping, sugar and butter melted together and burned a little. I am very fond of it."

Sam tasted it and said, "Terrific."

"With Rosalita this is not a fair arrangement. But it is the best I can do. As I have money to set more slaves free, I will."

Feeling like the words soiled his tongue, Sam said, "How much does a slave cost?"

"For Rosalita I paid one thousand pesos in trade goods—blankets, corn, and wool. She is attractive, so she cost a little more than a usual twelve-year-old." It was three or four months' wages for an ordinary working St. Louis man. "Her cousin, a girl cousin, was sold for two horses and six bushels of corn. I will buy her when I can afford her, so they can be together."

Sam tried to equate horses and corn to a human being. "Why doesn't Rosalita leave?"

"She would want to go back to her village, her family. But how can she get there? With one of the caravans that brought

her here? They would sell her as a slave. Walk alone for six
hundred miles? A girl?"

"I don't understand slavery at all."

Paloma looked at him for a long time before speaking. "You
have a certain innocence. It is one of your charms. May I show
you the rest of the house?"

The kitchen had what she called a shepherd's bed fireplace,
something new to Sam. He'd sat in the *cuarto de recibo,* which
seemed to mean the room where you receive guests, but hadn't
noticed the pen and ink sketch of the casa made by her grandmother. He also hadn't noticed the multitude of blankets, large
ones on the floor, smaller ones on the sofas and chairs.

"Yes, slave blankets," said Paloma.

"Thank you for letting me look at the books," he said. She
nodded. He'd looked at some verses in a collection of English
poetry. Though they'd been too difficult for him, he liked to
parse them out. He liked the sounds.

"Notice the stencils of birds on the walls," Paloma said. The
walls were plastered, white-washed adobe. "Palomas," murmured the señora. "The technique is called *tierra amarilla.* I
love it."

He was enchanted. Her spirit was so intense, but she was ut-
terly without guile, always direct.

"Now something special," she said, *"mi alcoba de dormir."*
They went down a short hall and into a bedroom. A fire was
burning in the small fireplace—Rosalita must have laid it. The
room held a bureau, a vanity, a full-length mirror, and her high
four-poster bed. She lit wall-mounted candles on each side of
the bed, and two more candles on the vanity. The room took on
a beautiful glow.

"Look at yourself in the mirror," she said, smiling. It was a
full-length mirror with an ornately carved frame. He picked
Coy up, but the coyote showed no interest in his reflection.
Paloma stood close to them, and they all smiled. Paloma
stroked Coy's head, and he nuzzled it into her hand. "You are
handsome," Paloma said.

Sam was lost for words.

The señora took Coy out of Sam's arms and set him down.

Then she turned back to Sam and kissed him fully on the mouth.

She took a step back, holding his gaze and her eyes holding the warm candlelight, and began to take off her dress.

THE NEXT DAY about noon, when they finally got out of bed, Coy whined desperately to be let out. They sat in the kitchen and drank coffee and ate sweet breads. Juanita worked at grinding corn, which Sam imagined was a never-ending job, and Rosalita cleaned the dining room. Sam felt a little uneasy, but the two servants acted like nothing was unusual.

Paloma saw the question in his face and said, "You are the first man to touch me since my husband died. I have been . . . in reserve for five years."

They went outside and to the casita to check on Flat Dog and Julia. "You are settling in well?"

"Fine," said Julia. It was one big room. Sam's guess was that she was relieved to be in a house instead of a tipi.

Paloma looked around the part of the room used for cooking. "Let me know if there's anything you need."

Sam picked up Esperanza and Azul and twirled around with them in his arms. The infants cackled.

Paloma came and looked closely at Esperanza's face. "She will be handsome, like her father. It would be perhaps better if she were beautiful." They all smiled broadly, and Sam and Paloma walked back to the kitchen of the main casa.

"Juanita, I will cook supper. Take the afternoon with your family. Rosalita, go do whatever you like."

Both women murmured *"Gracias"* and left immediately.

When they were alone, Paloma said, "Rosalita is being courted by one of the young men who works for me." She stood, came to Sam, and cupped his face with one hand and kissed him lightly. "You are a beautiful man. The crook where your nose must have been broken, it only makes your face interesting." She kissed him again. "Now I will start supper."

Sam sat in the kitchen with her and watched. First she cut the kernels off an ear of dried Indian corn. *"Chicos,"* we call these." She covered them with water, and set them on the cooking stove to simmer. The fire in the stove was strong, and the *cocina* felt good, a warm radiance in a cold house in January.

Now she took meat from a box cooled by ice in the bottom and began to dice it. "Mutton," she said. "This is a dish of the conquistadores."

She worked in firm strokes. Now she paused and looked directly at him. "I have a passion for you," she said. "For the time you are in Santa Fe, will you live at Rancho de las Palomas and be my lover?"

She waited.

She poured a little oil in a heavy skillet, put it on the stove, and began browning the meat. "I do not care about appearances," she said. "I care nothing for what the families on the rancho think, nothing about what my neighbors may think. I do not even care what the priest thinks." She looked up at him. "As for the sin, I will confess it." She shrugged.

Now she took three red chiles out of a canister, washed and cleaned them, and put them on the counter. She chopped the red pods and began to mash them in a heavy bowl with water. She looked at him. "This passion," she said, "I want to dive into it, to lose myself in it. Is your wish the same?"

"Yes."

She lowered her eyes to the chiles and ground hard. He noticed how strong her hands were.

"You may tell your friends who stay in town whatever you like about us, without flaunting it. They will understand."

"Sure."

She put the mashed chiles and water into a sauce pan, and put the pot on the rear of the cookstove. "It will make a sauce," she said.

She wiped her hands on a cloth, sat on a chair next to him, and took both his hands in hers.

"We both must understand, then, that it will end. Spring will come, the grass will turn green, you will go to your rendezvous of beaver hunters, and I will set this passion aside. We two are"—she hesitated—"not suitable. You are beautiful. Perhaps we even make an attractive couple. But we are not in the long term appropriate." She used the Spanish word *apropriado*.

Sam's mind tilted a little. What they'd just done in bed felt very damned appropriate to him.

She rose and poured water into the pot with mutton. "It is best when it simmers all afternoon," she said.

Sam shook his head. After five years in the mountains, taking care over cooking seemed foreign to him.

She dipped her finger in the red chile sauce and put it to his mouth. "Taste it."

He sucked the good taste off her finger. He'd liked chiles from the first taste, green more than red, not the heat but the flavor. He cleaned the finger well, smiling at her mischievously.

"I'll pour us some wine. You want to go to bed?"

He did.

THE NEXT DAY they rode the ranch, and she began to tell him about her life. Specifically, her husband. Coy trotted along with his ears perked, like he was listening.

"I was a silly young girl, seventeen years old. Miguel came for me like a whirlwind. He was a handsome man with a flair for the romantic gesture. Gestures, I later found out, he had practiced widely throughout Nuevo Mexico. We married when I was eighteen and he was thirty. My father warned me about him." Sam knew her mother had died giving birth to her sister.

"For a year, perhaps, I kept my illusions.

"He was good to me in front of others. He made love to me eagerly. In front of our ranch families he treated me like a queen, and to our friends in Santa Fe he showed me off as a great catch. I began to get impatient when he was gone on what he called the business of his family, which was actually to pursue other women and play at horsemanship games with his rich young comrades. His family, it turned out, had scarcely any enterprises left to run.

"It was not until we stood beside my father's grave that I realized, from Miguel's new imperial manner, that he had married me only to get Rancho de las Palomas."

They turned the horses along the *madre acequia*.

"The next years were very difficult. I hate to talk about them. The worst was that I miscarried twice. Now I am unable to bear children."

She grew thoughtful, and her voice changed. "Then, one morning, they brought the news. As he and his friends did their daredevil riding, his horse suddenly shied. Miguel landed headfirst against a boulder and was quickly dead."

She stopped, and Sam reined Paladin up beside her. Coy raised his head to Paloma. Her gaze roamed the grapes she had planted, but Sam knew they were not what she was seeing.

"You cannot imagine. In my anger I had thought I wanted to deliver a fatal blow myself. But when it happened, I was desolate. I stayed in bed, without even a candle, for days. I drank wine, all my stomach could keep down. I crawled deep into the cave of loneliness and self-pity.

"And I didn't come back to the world for months. Months."

She touched her heels to her mount, and they glided on.

"Finally, our foreman pointed out to me that the rancho was deteriorating. My people were willing to work hard, he said, but only if they knew I cared. Since I didn't seem to care, inevitably, the rancho would die. 'Dust, weeds, and wind, nothing else,' he said."

Coy made a sympathetic noise.

"So Rancho de las Palomas saved me. It saved my grandmother, the first Paloma. She dug the gardens with her own hands, she planted the cottonwoods by the house, she helped lay the stones of the walk from the well to the *cocina*. She nursed the land as she nursed her son and daughter. It gave to her as she gave to it.

"Women are not made to be alone, Sam. We can be in connection to a man, to children, to our whole family, we can even be mother and child to the earth herself. But we are not meant to be alone. My gardens, my orchards, my vineyard, my livestock, my workers—they saved me. Saved me for this moment, this passion that makes me alive." She looked at him for a long moment and finally tried to shrug lightly.

He wondered exactly what she was thinking at that moment. He would have bet it was, *For a short time I have this young man, this naïve foreigner. What comes afterward, what else my life may be, I will seize this.*

"Let's ride." She kicked her sorrel mare to a lope down the dirt track, across the road, and onto the north side of her land. They galloped across tablelands, through broken gullies, up steep hills. Coy scampered alongside them eagerly—he liked to run. Finally, when they came up into the timber, she eased her mount to a walk and came gently to the ridge. In front of them, far down the mountain, lay a lovely lake among pine trees, like a drop of dew on a green leaf. They sat for long moments and gazed. It was like drinking the cold lake with their eyes.

The winter day was mild, and they sat on the rocks of the ridge and looked at the water and talked, or for long periods didn't talk. Sam knew he was enraptured.

Finally, Paloma said, "Tell me about Meadowlark."

Sam did. He spoke slowly and considered his words, but the words came and came. How he met her in the Crow village, left on a trapping expedition saying he'd come back, and failed to keep his promise—"I got separated from the outfit, got my horse stolen, had hardly any lead for bullets. Ended up walking seven hundred miles to the nearest fort."

"Seven hundred? Alone?"

"Yes."

He thought for a moment. The story about the prairie fire would hold for later, and how he crawled into the buffalo carcass and got his Crow name, Joins with Buffalo.

"I went back to the village, and her parents said to bring eight horses for her. Getting the horses . . ." Here he paused, because this part of the story was still hard. "Getting the horses I got her brother killed, Blue Medicine Horse. Then her parents kept her away from me. But we ran off together."

He took big breaths in and out. "After a few days they came and took her back. I thought I'd lost her for good. I left, went to rendezvous." He waited for a beat. "She showed up there with her brother, ready to get married."

They let that sit for a minute.

"She wanted to see the Pacific Ocean, so we joined up with a brigade going to California. First that ever did that crossing." He stopped for a moment, and memories moved through him like hymns.

He shrugged. "She gave birth and it killed her."

Paloma considered that. Sam looked at her and thought of her childlessness.

Suddenly she said, "Let's go!" and jumped onto her horse. She loped back the way they came, and then it turned into a race. They shouted at the horses in glee and spurred them—down grassy hillsides, across rivulets, through arroyos. Coy sprinted alongside and sometimes barked vigorously. Paloma laughed at him.

At first Paladin fell behind Paloma and her mare, but Sam could feel that she was just biding her time. Few horses ran as often or as long as Paladin, and few had as much bottom. Still, the sorrel mare had sprinting speed, and Sam wasn't sure. His thought was, *Paloma wants me to beat her, but will do her damnedest to beat me.*

They roared onto the grasslands where the horses were grazing, the trappers' hundred with Paloma's, and the whole herd kicked up its heels and followed them. What a noise—Sam loved it, and it made him homesick for the buffalo plains, and the thunder of a buffalo stampede.

Suddenly Paloma turned her mare up a short, steep hill and through the underbrush into another small canyon. The herd didn't follow. *Too much work!* Sam thought happily. They crashed down a little creek, splashing themselves and whooping and hollering.

When El Camino Real came into sight, and the house beyond it, Sam slapped Paladin with his hat, and she charged. They passed Paloma the way a plummeting apple passes a drifting leaf. Sam wheeled Paladin to a skidding stop in front of the casa. When Paloma jumped from the saddle, she landed in Sam's arms. A stable hand took the reins, and Sam carried Paloma pell-mell to bed.

"WHAT IS GOING on inside my lover?" said Paloma softly. They were lying twisted in her sheets, naked, worn out by love. "I don't want your mind wandering. For this time we are together let it be with me."

He looked at the coals in the fireplace and answered truthfully, "Guilt."

Coy seconded the motion with a whimper.

She smiled warmly at him. "It didn't arrive until the fourth day. Not bad."

"Don't you feel guilty?"

"I feel triumphant. And so should you."

They looked at each other. Neither knew what to say.

"But your wife has been gone only . . ."

"Nine months. April to January."

Her eyes smiled at him. "Then it's time for you to be reborn, Sam Morgan. Time to emerge back into this world of the living, the world of things that still stand in the sunlight and grow." She gave him mocking eyes. "Things that rise from the dead, things that rise in the sheets."

"I miss her."

"I missed my husband for perhaps two years. He was a *pendejo,* but I missed him. Sometimes I woke up in the morning and reached for him. After a while I made myself sleep on his side of the bed, facing the edge. That stopped the reaching. Though I despised him, I expected him to be around every corner, and was always disappointed when he was missing. Always missing."

"I loved Meadowlark."

"You still do, the memory of her. But she's dead, Sam."

"Are you jealous of her?"

"As well be jealous of a mote of dust floating in the air."

She rolled over, tangled her hands in his white hair, and kissed him teasingly. "Let a woman who has walked this earth for a decade longer than you tell you this much. Life is for the living." She kissed him again. "The living. That's us. Can you let go of death for a while?"

She rolled him over on top of her.

"Yes."

Twelve

THE WINTER WAS a time of rest for the ranch, and the work was much less for everyone except Sam and Flat Dog. Every day they trained horses, and Paloma watched what was different about their technique, wanting to learn. They stood with the horse belly deep in the cold Santa Fe River until they got it to accept a saddle blanket, then a saddle, then a sitting horseman. "It is faster," she said immediately.

She sweetened the deal. "Please train as many of my horses as possible. Good saddle horses will bring me two hundred pesos more than wild ones. So I will pay you a hundred fifty pesos each."

They worked with a will.

Sam and Paloma, though, took some afternoons to ride her land. They camped one night by the northern lake. They rode downstream and explored the valley of the Rio Grande. They visited a pueblo of Indians down that river, and Paloma traded for some beautiful pots. "Do they steal slaves from this village?" asked Sam.

"No, these pueblo peoples, they accept the Holy Church. We Nuevos Mexicanos take slaves from the Navajos, who hold to their old religion, and the pueblo peoples help in the stealing."

They camped along the river on the way back, and since the next day was sunny, they lounged and stayed there all day.

They also established a life beyond the ranch and beyond their absorption in each other. Every Saturday morning they rode to Santa Fe. Paloma went to confession, spent the rest of Saturday with her sister and nieces, and on Sunday morning attended mass.

Sam spent Saturday afternoon at the lodgings of Hannibal, Grumble, and Sumner, working on his reading. He would recite the words out loud, and one of his mentors would offer corrections. Sam began to go from fumbling, word-by-word reading to making words into sentences that added up to something.

At first Sumner just listened with a half smile. Then he began to help Sam as well. Unlike Sam, the ex-slave had learned to read and write, and could do it very well.

Grumble always started with Sam on the Bible. Sam would sound out the sentences and Grumble would repeat them sonorously, in an actor's voice. Sam liked the big, rolling language. He also liked some of the stories of the Old Testament, but others seemed strange to him. "I don't know why I should like a story about Abraham putting his son on an altar and getting ready to drive a knife into his heart."

"A story about obedience," said Grumble.

"I don't think much of that either," said Sam.

"No mountain man would," said Grumble. "Nor any con man."

On another Saturday Sam read about how the pharaoh's daughter found Moses in a basket in the bulrushes and saved the child. "Some stories are more like children's fantasies," said Sam.

"You're becoming a wise man," said Grumble.

"And I hate this thing about Samson. He's strong—he can pull a whole building down. So how can a woman make him weak by cutting his hair?"

"Maybe it's not the hair, it's the larger situation, involvement with a woman. Submission to a woman."

Sam shrugged. "Meadowlark didn't do that to me." Neither of them said anything about Paloma.

When Grumble read the Psalms to him, Sam just floated along on the language. He liked the way words turned into a sort of music.

Another Saturday Sam told Grumble, "I don't get it about Jesus of Nazareth."

Grumble arched an eyebrow at him. "No?"

"He strikes me as a sort of pale, holy kind of guy who doesn't know how to enjoy life."

"I'm glad to see you enjoying life again."

"Sometimes Jesus reminds me of one part of Jedediah, all serious and no fun." Sam threw Grumble a grin. "Without the part of Jedediah who can go longer and harder than the toughest, who can lead men anywhere."

"Your Captain Smith is a remarkable man." Sam had the impression that "remarkable" carried two or three meanings. Maybe one of them was that Jedediah, yes, was tough, and maybe a little crazy.

The cherub smiled now and said, "Think about it, though. What could require more toughness than the Cross? And it's a great idea, that a God would suffer what mortals do, death, in order to give us what is immortal."

Sam held the thought for a moment and shrugged.

With Hannibal Sam read aloud verses of Lord Byron's that Hannibal had marked:

Maid of Athens, ere we part,
Give, oh give me back my heart!

"You could smoke the pipe and ask Meadowlark for your heart back."

Sam chuckled.

"Or does Paloma have it now?"
Sam gave his friend the evil eye.
Hannibal took the volume and read,

I live not in myself, but I become
Portion of that around me: and to me
High mountains are a feeling, but the hum
Of human cities torture.

" 'Become portion of that around me,' " Sam said. "I felt something like that once."
Hannibal nodded.
"When Coy and I hid inside the buffalo cow and she saved us from the fire. Felt it strong."
"You are Joins with Buffalo," Hannibal said. He handed the book back to Sam.

I stood
Among them, but not of them; in a shroud
Of thoughts which were not their thoughts.

"You feel like that?" said Sam.
"All the time," said Hannibal.
"Me too."

There is a pleasure in the pathless woods,
There is a rapture on the lonely shore,
There is society, where none intrudes,
By the deep sea, and music in its roar:
I love not man the less, but Nature more.

Sam took a breath and let it out. Coy squealed at him. "I felt that from the start. That's what I felt every time Dad and I went into Eden."
Hannibal made a sympathetic noise.
"The ocean, though, to me that means Meadowlark dying. She wanted to see it, she loved it, and it killed her. That's how it feels to me."

"Life is lived holding hands with death," said Hannibal.

"Is that a quotation of somebody famous?"

"Probably," said Hannibal.

Sam thought awhile, or sat in a place beyond thought, and went back to reading:

What men call gallantry, and gods adultery,
Is much more common where the climate's sultry.

"We need some sultriness," said Hannibal, "here in the Santa Fe winter."

"I got some." Sam grinned.

Let us have wine and women, mirth and laughter,
Sermons and soda water the day after.

Sam laughed. "My mom used to give my dad soda water when he got into the whiskey."

Man, being reasonable, must get drunk;
The best of life is but intoxication.

"Now that," Sam said, "is a verse the fellows would like."

"We don't need whiskey to be intoxicated," said Hannibal.

Hannibal also promised to get Sam some more books, so he could read on his own. That thought made Sam sad, because it reminded him that he and Hannibal wouldn't always be partners. Hannibal liked too well to go his own way.

ON HIS SATURDAY nights in town Sam kept his promise to Grumble and earned his share of the horses Grumble paid for—he helped with the cherub's deceptions. Here in Santa Fe, where Grumble wanted to stay for a while, that meant nothing more elaborate than card games. Certainly, though, no one could call what Grumble did either playing or gambling.

Every day Sumner worked on his card skills under Grum-

ble's tutelage, practicing dealing off the bottom of the deck
for hour upon hour. "Look here," he said, when Sam walked
into their lodgings one Saturday afternoon. He put the two
black aces on top of the deck and the two red aces on the bottom. Then he dealt Sam a four-card hand—all aces. Sumner
did it several times. Sam and Hannibal watched intently, but
neither of them could ever see that Sumner was dealing from
the bottom.

Coy barked sharply, whether in applause or protest none of
them knew. Sumner chuckled. "He wants to play. That coyote
be a gamblin' man."

"Next step," said Grumble. He told Sam to put the four aces
together, split the deck, and tuck them directly into the middle.
Sam did. Grumble dealt a three-card hand to each man, three
cards being the right number for the most popular card game in
Santa Fe, called brag.

Each man got an ace.

"You gotta be a witch to deal out of the middle," said Sumner.

None of them had imagined such a thing could be done.
They watched as Grumble did it again, and again. None could
spot it.

"All right, teach me," said Sumner.

Sam could hear lust in his voice.

"When these greenhorns aren't here," said Grumble. "We
con men want to keep some secrets within the fraternity."

"I'll never play cards for money again," said Hannibal.

"Best not," said Grumble with a sly smile.

Grumble said nothing about his biggest card secret. Abby
had a Baltimore manufacturer make her decks of cards from
her own design. Though the swirls and whorls on the back of
each card looked the same, they were not. When Abby saw the
backs, she knew what every card was.

Grumble possessed one of the decks, an advantage in card
games that could not be beaten.

"Now, this last is what you might call an honest trick. In
some games it's a big advantage to know which cards have been
dealt and which are still in the deck, especially the face cards."

He handed the deck to Sam. "Sam, pick any thirteen cards, any thirteen, and lay them face up."

Sam did.

Grumble studied them for a few seconds. "Now pick them up. Hold them so Hannibal and Sumner can see them and I can't."

Sam and Sumner split the cards and fanned them.

"King, two queens, ten, three eights, seven, six, a pair of fours, trey, deuce," recited Grumble.

He was exactly right.

"Now I can memorize the face value of thirteen quickly. One day I'll be able to memorize the value and the suit."

No one had a word to say.

"Of course, as Sam knows, winning at gambling is child's play. What's fun is what you might call the more elaborate cons. Deceptions that become works of art."

"And we won't do those here, not while we plan to stay here," Sam said.

"As you wish." Grumble smiled. "Merely winning is a little dull, but we've managed to attract some monied gentlemen who see losing as a challenge to rise to. I look forward to tonight. Along about seven, as we say in Nuevo Mexico."

"DON GILBERTO, WELCOME!" Grumble called. A Mexican gentleman bounced up to their table, fat and dressed like a fop. This man's style was to think everything in the world was funny, including losing a hand. Which was a good thing, because he lost lots of them.

"Don't you ever take the game seriously?" said the American who sat across from the Mexican. This man, whose name was Charles, or Don Carlos to the other dons, played with a fierce American competitiveness and lost almost as often as Don Gilberto, and with a good spirit. Sam thought his gravy-dripping accent was comical. The man hailed from New Orleans.

Sam had discovered he didn't much like cards or smoky cantinas. But he got a kick out of seeing Grumble play the pigeons for all they were worth.

The pigeons tonight were Don Carlos and Don Gilberto. Grumble said the men of the upper class were all disenfranchised *hidalgos,* sent to this most remote of Spanish outposts as punishment, and so treated life as a bitter joke.

Sam couldn't remember Charles's last name. A Creole and a Catholic, he had come from St. Louis with a trading outfit on the Santa Fe Trail, taken Mexican citizenship, and set up a trading company. According to Paloma, all the traders dealt in slaves.

Two pigeons tonight, then, plus Grumble and cappers, "what we in the con game call our helpers." Grumble liked to put on the air of an elegant, wealthy alcoholic, always sloshed, and win only an occasional hand himself.

On one night Flat Dog and Hannibal would leave with full pockets, another night Sam and Sumner. And most nights one Santa Fe local would break even or win a little, and two would lose big. Which just made them more avid to come back another night and get even.

Brag was a simple game. Grumble predicted that within a decade a more complicated version called poker would dominate. Every player put a coin in the pot for ante and got three cards. Then, clockwise, the players bet—you got no more cards, and you either had to bet or fold. Sam didn't make his own decisions—he waited for a signal from Grumble. Around and around went the bets, and when only two were left, they showed their hands. The best possible hand was a pair royal, or "prial," three of a kind.

By Grumble's minute signals—he was reading the backs of the cards—he told his cappers when to fold, when to match the bet, and when to raise.

Though Sam was bored by the cards, he was intrigued by the men.

Now Grumble dealt, and on his left Gilberto made no one wait. "I play blind," he said. This meant he would bet without looking at his cards. "*Dos* pesos." The fat man liked to take big chances and laugh a lot. He'd probably lost fifty pesos so far tonight, a modest amount by his standards.

Don Carlos played cards the way he carried himself, tightly

and stiffly. At the table or on the street, he always seemed to have a suspicious set of mouth and an eye eager for an edge. He caught up with the bet and added five pesos.

Sam and Flat Dog watched Grumble's small signals and built up the pot. When Sumner's turn came, he made a show of it. "Ah likes this," he said in his slave English, "Ah likes it fine, just fine. I see . . . how many to me, Mr. Grumble?"

"Thirteen," mouthed the cherub. His lips pursed. He thought these displays of Sumner's too ostentatious, but half of him enjoyed them.

"Thirteen to me. Thirteen pesos, that is, oh, don't I wish it was thirteen dollars. I don't hold with these no-account pesos."

"Suh," said Don Carlos. He disliked Sumner, and these antics only made it worse. "In front of that man," Sumner had confessed to Sam privately, "Ah loves to play the Nigger."

Now Sumner stood up, beaming, taking his moment in the sun. "Do NOT interrupt me. Do NOT get in my way. I am a man came to play and I will PL-A-A-A-Y." He made the word into a whinny.

Coy gave a short bark at him.

Slurring his speech, Grumble said, "Place your bet, sir." Sam never knew what Grumble did with the brandy—winners bought rounds constantly—but he knew very well that Grumble was sober and sharp.

"Thirteen, I say," and Sumner put those down, "I say thirteen"—he picked up his pile of coins—"and I raise, I raise . . . *ten*."

Ten was the agreed limit.

Grumble pushed out his coins crookedly, as though even his hand couldn't help weaving. He gave the table a cupid smile.

Around and around the table the bet went. After another round, Gilberto folded, still not having looked at his cards. "I must see what's going on in the kitchen," he said. "It smells delicious."

At his turn Sumner stood up again. He preened. He took a breath and held it. His eyes grew huge. It appeared that he would explode if he held his words inside any longer.

Carlos looked so irritated that Sam thought he needed watching.

"I FO-O-O-LD," said Sumner grandly, and sat down.

Coy whined.

Grumble, whose head now seemed to sag toward his belly, said, "You can't beat this company for bonhomie." He winked at Sam, because it was a word he'd taught Sam just today. The cherub pushed his coins out, and the betting went on.

When only Flat Dog and Don Carlos were left, they raised each other over and over. Finally the Louisianan lost his nerve and called.

Flat Dog smiled and slowly plunked his cards down on the table, one by one—three jacks. It was a hand to bet big on, for sure, but now the Crow waited. Not only could a prial of queens, kings, or aces beat him—by rule the best possible hand was three treys.

Carlos spilled his hand onto the table faceup. Three nines.

Everyone laughed and congratulated Flat Dog loudly. The pot he collected was two months' wages, and he was the big winner for the night.

Sumner got up and clapped both his shoulders from behind. "What a man! What a man!"

Don Carlos gave the black a sour look.

Sam was tickled. If Grumble enjoyed gulling anyone the most, it was Carlos. Aside from being arrogant, Grumble said, "The man is infected with racial hatred."

Whenever Sumner won, which was seldom, he scooted all the coins into his hat, stood up, did a dance, held the hat over his head, jingle-jangled the coins, and sang, "This child done won! This child done won!"

Sam said to him outside the cantina one night, as they walked home, "Don't you worry about going too far?"

"Black man can't go too far playing the fool. White folks nod their heads and say, 'Look at that Nigger. What a fool he be.' Believe anything, them white folks."

Grumble nodded in agreement.

Now it was late and Sam was weary of cards, weary of the brandy, weary of the smoky room. "Just one more hand," he said.

"Give this child of God that deck," said Sumner. It was his turn to deal. Though he was under strict instruction from Grumble not to try dealing seconds or bottoms yet, Sumner always grabbed the deck with great enthusiasm, as though he could make something special happen. "I have a very good card here for my friend Don Gilberto." He snapped a card facedown in front of the don, who was almost too drunk to keep his eyes open.

"And equally good cards for"—he clicked them down in front of each man—"my friends Sam, Carlos, Flat Dog, the stodgy old Grumble, and my humble self." He stroked his own card as though it were a pet, and made a cooing sound.

"Now!" he said, pausing dramatically. "That first card is a beauty. Any one could be a winner. The question is the second. Here's for you, Don Carlos. What do you say, is it good?"

Carlos didn't touch his facedown cards.

"Our Louisiana friend has nothing to say."

Sumner dealt the other cards and paraded out questions for every man. Gilberto was loud in his confidence. Sam said, honestly, that he was too tired to care. When he peeked at his cards and saw two queens, he still didn't care.

Grumble said, "The dealer should not be a performer."

Sumner laughed and dealt himself the last card. "A card of genius, I assure you all. Without looking, I can tell you I have a pair."

Grumble's face didn't change, but Sam saw a glint in his eyes.

Sam slid his third card off the table, saw the third queen, and put it back down. He looked words at Sumner. *You're dealing off the bottom, you devil.*

Coy gave a short, muffled bark.

Sumner grinned at Sam. Was he proud of the three queens? Or did he know Sam's thought? *This is dangerous.*

Carlos went for a raise of five pesos whenever it was his turn to bet. Sam raised quietly, one or two pesos, without emphasis. Grumble had taught him to keep the suckers in the pot.

Sam was getting uneasy. Sumner wasn't just pretending to have fun. There was something here he really liked.

Coy shifted from lying at Sam's feet to sitting up. He also smelled trouble coming.

Round and round the bets went. Finally, three players were left, Sam, Don Carlos, and Sumner. The pot was huge, probably eight hundred pesos.

Suddenly Don Carlos dropped words into the air like individual stones plopped into a pond. His voice curdled with something that gave Sam a chill.

"I think the Nigger is cheating."

Quick as a snake, Sumner's hand dived inside his coat.

Just as fast, Grumble locked his forearm in a fierce grip. "Let us all remember our manners," the cherub said casually.

Everyone at the table tensed, ready to dive for cover or grab a weapon. Coy growled, and Sam thought that if he snapped out a bark, everyone at the table would attack everyone else.

"My dear sir," said Grumble to Don Carlos, "I think you know better. This child of nature has neither the guile nor the intellect to commit such chicanery."

Carlos's face was boiling red. Everyone waited, poised.

"I will prove it," said Grumble. "Sam, show us your cards." His voice was as smooth as a hand stroking a cat.

Sam turned over three queens.

It seemed like the whole table gasped. A prial, and a high one.

"Don Carlos, my esteemed friend, now your cards."

Carlos hesitated. Then, one by one, a sneer on his face, he turned them over.

King of diamonds.

King of hearts.

King of spades.

Now the gasp was louder. A higher prial.

"And last let us see what the good Sumner's cards are." Grumble reached out and turned them over himself.

Ace of spades.

Ace of hearts.

Ten of clubs.

Everyone laughed uproariously. No one had seen anything so funny in his life. Don Gilberto, not Don Carlos, seemed to enjoy it the most. He guffawed, tried to drink his brandy at the same time, and spilled the brandy all down his front.

Everyone hee-hawed louder. Two of them were laughing out of relief—Sam and Flat Dog knew damned well that Grumble had palmed that third ace and dropped the ten in its place.

"Take your pot, sir," said Grumble to Don Carlos.

Carlos raked the coins toward himself.

"The finest pot of the night, it appears," said the cherub. "And I believe this will make an evening for me. Good night, gentlemen."

Carlos scooped the whole pot into his hat, stood up, held the hat over his head, jingle-jangled the gold and silver loudly, and did a mocking dance. All the while he fixed his eyes fiercely on Sumner.

Sam wanted desperately to go, but Grumble's rule was that they leave one by one, to put off suspicion of collaboration. Still, after two more hands Sam was on the street in the cold night air, breathing freely.

As they all crawled into their blankets later, Grumble said nothing to Sumner about the event except, "It would be well if you don't attend the games for a week or so."

So WENT THE winter for Sam. He spent five days a week with Paloma at the rancho, training her horses, teaching her his training methods, getting to know her in every way. Every weekday he had lunch with Flat Dog and Julia so he could be around Esperanza. One day while he was dandling her on his knee, Julia said, "Do you realize you are never quite comfortable with Esperanza?"

"I'm fine with her," said Sam.

Julia shrugged. "It doesn't seem so. Do you resent her for causing Meadowlark's death?"

"Sure not," Sam said quickly.

Julia cocked an eyebrow at him.

Sam picked up the child and turned away from Julia.

He spent weekends with his other amigos reading and gambling. At Rancho de las Palomas he earned some money, and at the gambling table he got hold of more. Though he spent some on cute baby clothes, his hunting pouch held a lot of coins, and he kept more in a pouch hung around his neck.

The best of the winter, though, was that he healed. Sam's body got its first rest, really, in a year and a half. He gained weight and fleshed out some hard edges on his body. Though Meadowlark's death still felt like a spike driven into his chest, he found a way to live with the pain. He knew that what healed him, mostly, was Paloma's love. Love in the physical sense and love, even if she never said so, in another and better sense. In her eyes he was a good man.

He improved his reading more and more, because he liked it and he worked at it. He even started picking out written Spanish words. When he and Paloma rode or walked the streets of Santa Fe, she would tell him the meanings of the signs in front of the shops. To help with pronunciation, she explained what sounds each of the letters made and had him speak the words after her.

One afternoon Sam and Paloma sat in the courtyard in the sun. Sam read one of her father's books in English. "English," she said, "what an ugly language, all full of sounds that grate on the tongue. And when you look at the words, you have no idea how to say them." Though Paloma's father did teach her some English, and she understood it, she disliked the language and declined to speak it.

"The only advantage of Spanish," he half mumbled, "is that the rules make it easy to figure out how to say the words."

"Spanish," she said, "is a lovely language of classic beauty. It flows as water runs smoothly over rocks. The Spanish language *is* beauty."

"I like English," he mumbled.

"Ha! I will show you."

She went into the house and brought back a book of Spanish proverbs. "I will read to you of love," she said, "and we will make beauty into beast by translating it into English."

She read, " '*El hombre es fuego, la mujer estopa; llega el diablo y sopla.*' "

They wrangled out the English together: "Man is fire, woman dry grass. The devil dances by and blows."

"Do you hear?" said Paloma. "The Spanish is liquid—*'diablo y sopla.'* The English, it is bumpy."

"It has a nice punch, though." Sam couldn't help wanting to defend his native tongue.

"Another," she said. " *'Juramentos de amor y humo de chimenea, el viento se los lleva.'* Listen to that, how beautiful it is—*'el viento se los lleva.'* "

Again they wrestled it into English. "Promises of love, smoke from a chimney—the wind whisks both away."

"You are right a little bit," she said, "the English has nice muscles."

Sam kissed her lingeringly.

"Now I tell you one of my favorites," she said. "The way the sounds roll, it is beyond compare. *'Amor es en fuego escondido, una agradable llaga, un sabroso veneno, una dulce amargura, una delectable dolencia, un alegre tormento, una dulce y fiera herida, una blanda muerte.'* "

Sam replied by kissing her again, sensuously, and fondling her breasts. Her chest heaved deep and strong, and then suddenly the breaths came short and fast. She took Sam's hand, and led him fast into the casa, into the bedroom, and into love.

Afterward, they sorted out an English version of her proverb. "Love is a concealed fire," she said, her eyes aflame.

He bent and licked her nipple, murmuring, "And a lovely sore."

"A tasty poison," she whispered. She raised his lips to hers and teased his tongue with hers. "A sweet rue."

Sam put her hand where he wanted it. She smiled wickedly and squeezed. "A delectable suffering," she said. She squeezed harder and harder. "A happy torment, a delicious wound."

Sam rolled on top of her again. "And a soft death."

Much, much later she said, "English lacks music, but our bodies sing together beautifully."

They napped.

When they woke blearily, Sam gave her sweet kisses.

"Let me tell you one more proverb," she said.

"What?"

" *'Más fuerte era Sansón y le venció el amor.'* "

"Which means?"

She enunciated clearly in English, "Samson had even more muscles than you, and love whipped his ass."

Thirteen

DURING HOLY WEEK, which was in the second half of April, Sam didn't see Paloma for four days. They rode up the river road to town on Wednesday instead of Saturday. "Holy Thursday," she said. "We have the Eucharist in honor of the day Christ held the first one. Then Holy Friday, mass on the day he gave his life for all us mortal sinners. On Saturday the vigil, at dawn on Sunday the Resurrection and the mass to celebrate this great event."

"Vigil?"

Paloma laughed. "You are such a barbarian. The vigil is the blessing of the new fire, the lighting of the paschal candle, a service of lessons that we call the prophecies, the blessing of the font, and then the long sitting in the church, each person holding a candle, waiting for the great moment of the Resurrection. There, you see? I always go."

Not only went, it turned out, but spent the entire time with her sister and her family, and didn't see Sam at all.

The result for Sam was a lot of reading with Hannibal and Grumble, some wandering around Santa Fe with all his friends, and five nights of playing brag. The whole trip felt like a thorn whose tip had broken off in his hind end. The one good part was that he ended up with a lot more gold coins in his hunting pouch.

On Monday morning, as Sam and Paloma rode back down the river road together in the fine spring weather, he felt extra aware of the way she sat in her saddle, the way she turned to watch the river roaring downhill, leaping over rocks and making suck holes on the back side. She stopped and led her mare to the river. While both horses drank, Paloma watched the current surge. "I am enthralled by its power." Riding on, from time to time she pointed out the wildflowers in bloom on the side of the road, the orange cups of globe mallow, purple rags of locoweed, and the red bristles of Indian paintbrush. "They are getting ready to open, see?"

Coy pranced about wildly, as though the greening grass, the leafing trees had brought up the sap in him, and he couldn't just walk.

Farther along a sound came to Sam's ears that he could hardly believe. "Oh, Sam, this is . . . I can't describe it. Let's ride and find a good place to watch." She whipped her horse up onto a knoll, and he was right behind her. In a few minutes the caravan came. The racket was an assault. "That noise is the big wheels turning against the axles," said Paloma, almost shouting. "As you can tell, it is heard even a mile away. If they greased the axles, it would be diminished. But the muleteers say the sound is like music to them. They call them the singing carts."

In the forefront came horses and mules, hundreds of them. Behind this livestock trudged human beings, Indians, Mexicans, or mestizos, Sam couldn't tell which. Their hands and feet were shackled. "Slaves," said Paloma.

Paladin pulled on the reins, impatient. But Sam couldn't take his eyes off these people. There were three women, one perhaps in her thirties, one in her twenties, one a teenager but physically mature, and seven children who were probably between the ages of eight and twelve. All the women and children walked with the look of those who have been not only defeated and humiliated but beaten beyond despair into utter hopelessness, a state where life offers nothing but dreariness, darkness, and pain.

Sam felt a sharp burning in his heart.

The slaves trudged on and on. Nothing would ever change, and they knew it. They probably resented the bodies that enabled them to walk to their own debasement.

"It is hard to bear," said Paloma.

"Who will buy them?"

"Landowners like me. The only wealth in this province is land, which comes in grants from the government. Slaves work the land, or clean the houses, or do the labor of making crops ready for the table. Slaves do everything, if you are willing to have them, which I am not. From the look of these, most of them will also bear children who will also become slaves."

"Why don't they run screaming at their captors?" said Sam. "Why don't they break away? If you die, so what?"

"I asked Rosalita that. She said it is not possible at the time, not quite possible, to believe that death is better than where you are. But death would be better—that's what she said."

Now the slaves were out of sight, blocked by the carts and the mules and oxen that pulled them—hundreds of carts, it seemed to Sam. The screech was now almost unbearable. The wheels were huge rounds of cottonwood in one big piece.

"What do they have to trade?"

"Whatever we cannot produce, household utensils, candles, tallow, nice textiles, coffee, sugar, liquor—oh, it's such pleasure to see all the fine things and buy them."

They watched the carts wobble and creak on their way, and the dirty, dusty drovers pushing them along.

"How long have they been on the road?"

"It's about six weeks from Chihuahua. These traders are daring—they must have started as soon as the weather warmed up a little. This is the first caravan of the year."

She looked at him with girlish glee in her eyes. "Sam, let's ride back to town tonight. First the afternoon in bed and then back to town. It will be so much fun, you cannot imagine. The whole town will come to the *baile*."

"Sure." He was thinking that the bed sounded better than the *baile*, but . . .

"We will even stay in town. We will be wicked and take a room for the night. We'll have such fun."

Sam looked far up along the train of carts, but he couldn't see the slaves.

"Tomorrow we will go to one of the great ranchos and see something you'll never forget. You'll hate it, but you'll never forget it."

LOLLING TOO LONG in bed, they got to town long after the grand entry. "It is a wonderful sight," Paloma said. "The cara-van men drive the carts along the river straight to the plaza. When they get there, they circle the plaza as fast as they can go, cracking their whips. From the uproar you would think it is a war. The children get very excited.

"As the caravan hurtles through the streets, the people hear the carts squealing and pour out. They run after the caravan on the way to the plaza, singing and shouting. From all directions everyone rushes to the plaza. We are all excited to see the fine things, to be able to trade for a pot of copper for the kitchen, to get new shoes for the family, to get a beautiful piece of silk that will make a skirt that may catch the eye of a certain man . . . And the merchants, after the first burst of trading, they stock their stores with the rest."

Now the *baile* was in full swing. The high-born, the mer-chants and tradesmen, the peasants—everyone thronged all over the plaza. Cantinas poured El Paso brandy and Taos whiskey liberally. Two groups of musicians competed to see who could play the loudest, with the most style, and attract the most listeners. Actually, the most dancers.

Hannibal waved at Sam and Paloma, and they crowded into

the table with him, Grumble, and Sumner. Grumble ordered more brandy, and they all drank fast. Sam was feeling wild.

"Get ready," said Hannibal. *"Nemo enim fere saltat sobrius, nisi forte insanit."*

"What does that mean?"

"Only crazy people dance sober."

"Have you had enough to drink? Do you know the fandango?" said Paloma, a dark, sexy look in her eyes.

"I'm woozy," Sam said, "but for you I'll pretend."

"You will do much better than that. You will *dance.*" She took one of his hands and led him out among the couples in the plaza. "These are *fandanguillos,* more festive versions of the fandango. They are dances of . . . courtship would be the polite word. You direct Americans would say seduction. They are exuberant, unrefined, born of the desire of all creatures for fertility. It is not for talking but for doing."

Without warning she began and Sam followed, feeling like he was in a whirlwind. She tapped out a rhythm with her feet and snapped her fingers. He couldn't copy her steps, but he matched her attitude. She rose and, stepping high, they pranced past each other, shoulders almost touching, and faced each other once more. She teased and challenged. He pursued, she slipped away. He held her eyes piercingly. With her hands, shoulders thrown back, she shook her skirt in a taunt.

The music accelerated, its rhythm accented by castanets. Paloma clapped her hands and stomped her feet. Sam followed as though in a trance. The music itself seemed to tell him what to do. Now the music swirled faster and faster, like a waltz in three beats, but free of all drawing rooms, free of civility, as primal as a roll of thunder.

Stop. A total halt to the music. Paloma and Sam and all the other dancers froze. Tension throbbed.

Music again! Animated by the notes, the dancers grew wild. Passion surged through their poses. Arms and faces teased. Eyes, torsos, and hips challenged. Back and forth they soared, faster and faster, ever more passionate, ever more daring, and yet again faster.

When the orchestra stopped, silence clapped the ears. The dancers froze—sexual electricity charged the air.

Again the music charged forward, and Sam charged with it. He whirled, he grabbed Paloma, he slung her to the length of both their arms, he brought her back, she clung to him. Gently, gradually, she arched backward in his arms. The music came to a climax and was over.

Sam was dazzled with what he had done, and limp.

Paloma embraced him and whispered, "I want you to be like that inside me tonight."

His groin throbbed.

They went back to the table, drank more brandy, ate tortillas with pork and green chile sauce, and drank more brandy. Grumble paid for everything, and everyone had a great celebration.

Sam noticed that, as at the Los Angeles pueblo, dancers often went slinking down side streets, wrapped in a single serape. Paloma whispered in his ear, "How many children do you think will be conceived tonight?"

A gentleman in the garb of the Mexican elite, and with the arrogance, came toward them.

"*Buenas noches, señora.*"

"*Buenas noches, Gobernador.* Won't you join us?" Paloma made the introductions. "Gobernador Armijo is our former governor."

"Oh, señora," said Armijo, "must you call me a ruler in front of these democratic Americans?"

"My American friends are traders," said Paloma. "They have brought a herd of horses from California. Governor or not," Paloma told her friends, "Don Miguel is a great man in Nuevo Mexico. We have five preeminent families, and he is the head of one of them."

"The head of a donkey still brays like a jackass," said Armijo. Everyone laughed at this self-mockery, Armijo the loudest. He had two more bottles of brandy brought to the table, and proposed several rousing toasts. He sported a conspiratorial smile hinting that they were all devils together.

He made the company laugh several times more before saying, "Señora, shall we dance?"

Paloma gave Sam a smile, slightly nervous, he thought, and walked into the plaza on Armijo's arm.

Sam watched Armijo do the fandango with fascination.

"He barely moves," said Hannibal, "but his whole body bristles lust."

Sam watched his thick, high-arched eyebrows and drooping eyelids. He and Paloma, facing each other, moved sensuously, suggestively. Sam felt a stab of jealousy.

"That's a man who would come to power by any means necessary," said Sumner.

"And assume that anyone else would do the same, if they have ambition and daring," added Hannibal.

"He's like a child, swept up in his own desires." said Grumble.

The fandango ended, and Armijo led Paloma back to the table. "I must be off," he said to the group.

"I wish you well in your conquests," said Paloma, with a smile, "of every kind."

The ex-governor beamed and strode away, leering.

"It is Armijo's rancho we will go to tomorrow," said Paloma. "You are all invited."

"To what, señora," asked Grumble.

"A slave auction," said Paloma.

Sumner's eyes flashed, and his nostrils flared.

"Do you care to come?" she asked in a light tone.

Hannibal and Grumble hesitated and murmured, "Yes."

Sumner said, "Damn right."

Fourteen

SAM AND PALOMA dismounted in front of Armijo's casa. "Last year, when he was governor," she said, "Armijo would not have dared to host an auction on his own property. The government supports slavery, very much so, but the policy is not discussed." Sam tied Paladin and Paloma's sorrel to the hitch rail.

Now Grumble, Hannibal, and Sumner got down from their carriage. The cherub and the black man had ridden inside in style while Hannibal drove—that tickled them. Grumble liked to travel in the style of a gentleman. Actually, he enjoyed mocking and employing pretensions of gentility at the same time.

Paloma led them through a gate into a large courtyard. It was not a place of utility, like Paloma's, but scene of beauty, with a central fountain and beds of wildflowers. About a dozen men were gathered there. One or two gave Paloma odd looks. They walked over and greeted Don Carlos and Don Gilberto, the American trader and the pumpkin-shaped Mexican, their gambling friends. A couple of the other Mexican men stared at Sumner. He affected not to notice.

Coy wanted to sniff out the people he didn't know, but Sam told him to sit.

Don Carlos introduced his American friends to the other dons. Most of them seemed indifferent to making new acquaintances. One gave Sam a truly sour look and whispered something to his companion about *"cabello blanco,"* white hair.

"Yes, Don Emilio," said Paloma, "isn't it beautiful?" She touched Sam's hair and flashed Emilio a smile that left no doubt that she was in possession of this splendid young man.

Don Emilio, a cadaverous-looking man with a sallow complexion, scowled at her.

Paloma and the Americans took themselves a few steps off.

"Like my outfit?" asked Sumner.

He was dressed the fanciest Sam had ever seen him, in a fine coat of dove-gray broadcloth and a cravat of gold silk with an edge of lace.

"Why, suh," Sam faked a genteel Louisiana accent, "you must be . . . Perhaps you are a planter from Santo Domingo."

They laughed together. In Santo Domingo Sumner had been a slave, not the planter.

"You and Grumble have been rummaging in Grumble's trunk of costumes, I can tell."

"I am a self-made man," said Sumner. "Whatever I want to be."

Sam thought, *I envy him just for saying that.*

They stood around and drank Armijo's brandy and chatted for a few minutes. Nothing seemed to be happening. Sam was so nervous his breathing was shallow. Then a man he recognized as a lead rider in the caravan came in through the back gate. A Spaniard, not an Indio, the way the Mexicans figured things. He was light-skinned, and his jaw outlined by a red-brown beard.

"Evil men should not be handsome," said Paloma.

Sam didn't think the fellow was a bit handsome, not with that harsh flash in his eyes.

An assistant oiled his way through the gate. By one hand he

led a teenage girl by a chain between the shackles on her wrists. In the other he carried a whip. He looked at the girl and ran his tongue across his lower lip.

Something in Sam's stomach lurched upward.

Armijo walked to the center of the courtyard and addressed everyone. "Gentlemen and Señora Luna, this is the trader José Cerritos, of Chihuahua."

Coy growled

"Buenas dias," said the red-bearded man. "We have business to conduct." His words were lightly ironic, and his manner said, *We are men together. Let us revel in the pleasures of men.*

He gestured toward the girl with one hand, an invitation to the eye. "This lovely creature is one part of our business. Maria comes all the way from the province of Chihuahua for your . . . consideration."

Paloma spoke softly. "Apaches probably stole her from her village and sold her in El Paso. It would have been months ago."

"She is healthy," continued Cerritos, "and she has learned to be submissive. With discipline you can teach her willingness to work." He seemed to put thoughts of pleasure into the word "discipline." "But she is not good enough for any of you, not yet." He looked at his audience with a bizarre mixture of contempt and something Sam couldn't decipher. "Maria is a virgin."

"Madre de Dios," said Paloma. "I have heard of this, but . . . Madre de Dios."

Cerritos turned and pulled her toward him by the chain. With a large key he undid her shackles, feet and hands.

The assistant fiddled with his whip, lust in his eyes. *Lust for sex or for blood?* Sam couldn't tell. Maria fixed her eyes, huge and black, straight ahead. Sam was sure her mind was on nothing but the whip.

"Not a chance of virginity, not after these two or three months," said Paloma. "In front of me. I can't believe this."

Cerritos untied at the collarbone the shirt of rough cloth the girl wore. With an absurdly delicate gesture, as though handling silk, he slipped it over her head.

Sam looked at Maria's fine, small breasts. *Stop it,* he told himself.

Cerritos pulled apart the strings of the bow tie at her waist, and with a gesture like a bullfighter handling a cape, he snapped her full skirt away. The girl stood naked. She stared at nothing. Though she struggled to keep her face still, tics rampaged across it.

Sam burned with shame.

Cerritos took her elbows and lowered her to the ground. Maria collapsed like sticks and lay flat, knees up, without protest.

Coy barked.

Sam looked at her closed eyes, her pursed lips, and her fingers clawing silently at the ground.

She hates it. Her rage boomed through him.

Cerritos knelt between her legs and dropped his trousers. He fondled her breasts and pinched her nipples hard. When she grimaced, he leered sideways at his audience. Then he leaned forward onto his elbows and stuck his stiff cock at her.

At the last instant her hips jerked sideways, as though to avoid him.

Cerritos laughed, reared his hips back, and thrust hard into her.

For a minute, two minutes, three, Cerritos rammed himself into Maria over and over. Sam could not look away, but he was glad that the rapist's arms blocked his view of her face. Mostly he saw Cerritos's body thrashing and the girl's knees rocking, like a boat being rowed.

"No," Paloma told him quietly, and held him back with a hand on his arm.

Cerritos finished, lingered an instant, and sat back on his heels.

Maria lay perfectly still, a corn-shuck doll.

Cerritos stood up, raised and belted his trousers, faced his audience with a hard face, and suddenly, strangely threw them a grin. "There," he said. "Now she's good enough for you."

Suddenly the tableau of watchers was released—an odd energy animated them. They moved about, touched each other on the arm, leaned over and whispered to each other.

Coy howled, drawing looks of displeasure from some of the Mexican men.

Armijo walked forward and stood next to Cerritos, staring at Maria. She knelt in the dust, put her clothes back on, and rose to face her audience. She put on a face that was blank as dried mud. It hurt Sam's heart.

He could not look at Paloma. Or Grumble, Sumner, or Hannibal. He felt deeply ashamed.

Why are some of us like this?

"The worst is past," Paloma said.

Armijo looked at the men, and one woman, he had invited to this event. His face sparkled with power. His thick lips gleamed with desire. His body said, *I am a man with the audacity to seize the good things in life. Are you?*

"He is voracious as a baby," said Paloma, "but not a bit innocent."

"Is he getting a share of the money?" Sam whispered.

"Of course."

An impulse ran through Sam. *Armijo needs killing.*

"I would suggest a starting bid of a thousand pesos for this fine specimen," said Armijo.

"Seven hundred," said Don Emilio.

Sam give the cadaverous don the evil eye. "Buy her," he told Paloma.

She shook her head. "I have pledged what money I have to buy Rosalita's sister."

Sam's mind roiled in anger. Armijo bid, Don Gilberto bid. The American trader abstained. Sam could not, did not, follow the bidding for Maria.

Suddenly Paloma left his side. She exchanged whispers with Don Emilio, several exchanges. It nettled Sam to see their faces so close together. But when she returned, Paloma wore a smile on her face.

"If he wins the bid," she said, "I will pay him a thousand pesos, and he will give me Rosalita's sister Lupe."

"He's probably tired of her in his bed," said Sam.

Paloma gave him a sympathetic look but said nothing.

Now Sam kept a keen ear on the bidding. The final price was *mil*-something pesos, over a thousand, but the numbers flipped by too fast for Sam's Spanish. The voice was Don Emilio's. He stepped forward, grasped the chain between Maria's wrists, and led her out of the courtyard. She hung her head and followed docilely.

Coy squealed.

"We will pick up Lupe on the way home today," said Paloma.

Sam's breaths came freer. He turned and told his friends what was happening. Hannibal and Grumble murmured their approval, but Sumner said nothing. His eyes were on fire. Sam couldn't look him in the face.

Next came a group of slaves, the oldest woman and her three children, girls who appeared to be about eight and ten and a boy who looked about eleven. "They would bring a higher price if the oldest was a girl," said Paloma.

More alkali in Sam's mouth.

The bidding barely passed a thousand pesos and stopped. Gobernador Armijo waddled forward to take possession of the four people.

Sam didn't think he could stay in this place. "Why are we still here?"

"Because leaving would offend Don Miguel," said Paloma.

Next came the woman in her twenties and two children. Sam couldn't bear to listen to the bidding, or watch the faces of any of the bidders, or of Armijo or Cerritos, or the so-called slaves. He didn't hear the price these people sold for.

"Last we have two boys, unfortunately without mothers," said Cerritos.

"If their mothers were captured, they probably died on the way," said Paloma. "Lots of them die. And when the women and children are stolen, the fathers are killed."

The boys were about ten and twelve, and they didn't look like brothers. Ragged, dirty, miserably dressed, one looking listless, the other rebellious. Looking at this boy's body, his rigidity, Sam realized he was all rage.

"What is offered for these fine young men?" said Cerritos. "They will grow into excellent workers in the fields. Also, they can be trained for any skill, blacksmith, wheelwright, whatever is needed. Very valuable. I ask five hundred for the pair."

"Two hundred," said Sumner.

Sam looked aghast at his friend. Was an ex-slave now going to own slaves?

Armijo glared at Sumner.

Cerritos said smoothly, "Two hundred, the man says. That is . . . silly." He gestured with his hands, a motion that said, *Come to me with other bids.*

"Two fifty," called Don Gilberto.

"Two seventy-five," said Sumner.

"What are you doing?" Sam stage-whispered.

"Spending my money the way I want to."

"Three hundred," someone rasped.

"Are you going to free them?" asked Sam.

Sumner said, "Three and a quarter." He threw an irate glance at Sam. "I want to cut the head off slavery. I'm sure not going to support it."

Don Gilberto bid again.

Sam could hardly believe what came out of his mouth. "I'll split it with you," he said.

Sumner gave the biggest grin Sam had ever seen for him. He called out some bid—Sam didn't register what it was.

Someone topped Sumner's bid.

Sam stood shakily, dizzy with his own behavior.

"Let me take over," said Grumble, and he called out a number.

Sam weaved on his feet, stupefied, as voices called back and forth, spending his money—exchanging human beings for bits of stamped metal.

In the end Grumble won the bidding and walked forward to take charge of the boys. Fat Don Gilberto didn't look angry. There was courtesy between people who bought and sold human beings.

Now they all walked to the carriage, and Grumble brought the boys behind. Sam took the key from him, knelt down, and unlocked their hands and feet. Then he looked into their faces. "You'll be all right," he said gently. He tousled their hair with one hand. "You won't be slaves. We'll set you free. You'll be all right." He stood up.

Don Emilio walked by, saw Sam on his knees with the boys, and arranged his face into disapproval.

Grumble told the boys, "Get in the carriage."

Meekly, they did. The older one moved like a marionette.

Grumble said to Sam, "We'll settle up later. Your half is twenty-five dollars."

Sam could hardly believe it. For twenty-five dollars he had bought a human being, with bones, blood, mind, heart, and spirit.

Fifteen

THEY RODE BY Don Emilio's rancho to pick up Rosalita's sister Lupe. When they unloaded and dismounted in front of Paloma's casa, Sam thought, *We're overrun with people.*

Inside the scene ran to chaos. Everyone crowded around Paloma's dining table, and Juanita the cook set big pots to steaming—a big supper for all, maybe followed by full beds and bedrolls all over the casa.

Sam realized he felt invaded, and smiled wryly at himself for thinking of himself as the papa of Paloma's house. Coy trotted to the kitchen and begged, accustomed to getting treats from Juanita's pots.

Rosalita and Lupe ran to each other, embraced, swung each other at arm's length, and launched into a jabber of ultra-fast Spanish. "The kitchen," suggested Paloma. The two of them sat at the small table there, arms stretched across, hands clasped, words leapfrogging over one another.

"They have not seen each other in more than a year," said Paloma.

Flat Dog and Julia came in from their casita, with the children. Sam reached to pick Esperanza up, but she toddled away. She had been walking for about a month and had a mind of her own.

Paloma turned to Grumble. "Excuse us." He made room for her and Sam to sit next to the boys who were recently slaves.

She looked at them very directly. "I am Paloma Luna. You may call me Doña Paloma. This is my ranch, and you may stay here for a while until we decide what you will do."

One looked at her with a baby face and puppy eyes. The other, older, taller, and more muscular, was all eyes that blazed with anger. They both had dark skin and blue-black hair. *Indios,* thought Sam, *not Spanish, in the dumb way Spaniards arrange reality.*

"You are not slaves, do you understand that? Some bad men captured you, but we have freed you. Isn't that right?"

Sam, Sumner, Hannibal, and Grumble all said it was. Flat Dog and Julia watched curiously from the far end of the table. Julia was breast-feeding Azul.

"Juanita, please, bring *atole*. These boys look hungry."

Rosalita set big bowls of the gruel in the middle of the table for all. Lupe poured everyone drinks from two pitchers of aromatic hot chocolate.

"What are your names?"

"Pedro," said the one who looked perpetually frightened. He sipped gingerly at the chocolate.

"Tomás," said the bigger one. He drank directly out of his bowl, looking around like a wolf, half ready to fight for its food, half ready to run off.

"Pedro, Tomás, you are only boys, not ready to be on your own. We won't turn you out into the world by yourselves, do you understand?"

Pedro nodded that he did. Words seemed hard for him.

"We don't give a damn about that," said Tomás.

Sam bit his tongue. Who did this kid think he was?

Paloma ignored the rudeness. "For now this is your home,

Rancho de las Palomas. If you are ever away from here and someone asks you, you live at Rancho de las Palomas." She looked at them hard. "You understand? Say it, Rancho de las Palomas."

Pedro mumbled the words. Tomás pronounced them loudly and sarcastically.

Both boys began to eat eagerly. Sam noticed that they didn't look at each other. Whatever else had happened on the Chihuahua Trail, these two didn't seem to have formed a bond.

"*Bueno.* Now you must meet your new friends. This is Sam Morgan, who paid a lot of money, enough to free one of you. This is Sumner, who also paid a lot of money for you. Say thank you."

"*Gracias,*" each boy said. Tomás seemed to think it was nastily funny.

"Tomás, where do you come from?"

He named a village no one had ever heard of.

"Pedro, do you come from the same village?"

The boy shook his head no.

"Where is your village, Tomás?"

"In the Sierra Madre."

"Like saying in the Rocky Mountains," she told Sam. "The province of Chihuahua then?"

"Yes."

"Pedro, is your village also in the Sierra Mountains?"

"No, near the Rio Grande."

So they hadn't been around each other long.

Paloma went on. "I must tell you. The one thing I cannot offer is to send you home. If I gave you to a caravan going south, they would sell you to the first buyer who wanted you, just as happened here. You would be slaves again. So that cannot be. Do you understand?"

Both of them nodded yes.

"But hear me. You are free to go wherever you like. You are free, free as a bird to fly from tree to mountain, be sure of that."

She waited for them to mumble yes.

"If you choose to stay at my rancho, and that seems to be a

good idea, I will make sure you have plenty to eat, clothes to wear, and a warm place to sleep. You understand?"

Mouths full, they nodded again.

"If you stay here, you must also know that there will be certain rules to follow, and chores to do. Just like for Rosalita, Lupe, me, everyone. And just like at home, no?"

Sam saw no particular reaction to the word "home." He guessed they'd given up on home. Maybe they'd seen their parents killed, their family houses burned to the ground, the entire village destroyed.

Juanita spoke to Rosalita and Lupe, and the two teenage girls began to bring platters of food to the dining table.

"*Bueno*," said Paloma. "Now we eat, then we sleep, and tomorrow maybe we have some fun. How does that sound?"

"*Bueno*," said both boys, their eyes on the food. It was the most positive sound Sam had heard from them.

The boys stayed up until everyone went to bed, Grumble and Sumner in the guest bedroom, the boys on pallets in the warm kitchen.

"Stay with us tonight," Flat Dog said to Hannibal.

"Sure."

Sam and Paloma walked to the casita with Flat Dog, Julia, and Hannibal. Sam offered to hold Esperanza's hand for the steps through the darkness, but she said "Papá!" and ran to give her finger to Flat Dog. Her other word, Sam had noticed, was "mamá."

She spoke no Crow or English at all. *Not yet*, Sam told himself.

At the door of the casita Sam picked Esperanza up and kissed her on the cheek. "I love you," he said, and handed her to Julia.

As Sam and Paloma strolled back toward the main house, she said, "That's the first time I've heard you say those words to her."

Sam looked up at the millions of stars—so many were visible at this altitude—and thought how far apart they were, how much empty space stretched between them. "It's been coming to me more and more," he said, "that she's the one way Meadowlark is alive."

"Good thinking," Paloma said.

"Now there's more to think on," Sam said. He walked a few steps. Even in April the night air was cold. "I've taken on responsibility for the lives of the two boys. What the hell am I going to do now?"

He smiled ruefully. She chuckled.

Though Paloma mostly preferred not to be touched while she slept, that night they spooned close to each other. Sam slept fitfully, and was grateful for her warmth.

His last thought was the memory of the Mojave boys who tortured the toads. *Why?*

THE NEXT MORNING Tomás was gone.

"Señora," said Juanita, "only one boy was here when I came in."

Sam knew that Juanita got to the kitchen well before dawn to start the day's tortillas.

"This other one, he was rolled right up against the legs of the stove, sucking his thumb. I couldn't work until I made him move."

Pedro was still rolled up in his blankets, against an interior wall now, looking at them all with wide, dark eyes, too frightened to be reached by Juanita's disapproval.

Paloma went to hunt for Tomás all over the house, though she had no hope that the boy was here. She asked all her guests if they'd heard anything. Sam went outside to search for the boy, or sign of him.

They met in the kitchen again with the same word, "Nothing."

"Rosalita," said Paloma, "go to the casita. Tell Don Flat Dog what has happened, and that I ask him to help Don Sam with the search."

Now Juanita was feeding Pedro hot chocolate and *atole*. Rosalita and Lupe were serving everyone else at the dining table. Grumble and Sumner were glum. Hannibal was rushing through his breakfast so they could get going. When Flat Dog came in, he and Sam ate on their feet.

"Unfortunately," Paloma told everyone, "I have no idea about this."

"Maybe one of the slave owners stole him," said Sumner.

"Impossible. It is a club, and I am a member. If they catch him, they will return him."

"Worse for the wear," said Sumner.

"Beaten," said Paloma.

"If he has headed down the Chihuahua Trail," said Hannibal, "someone will put shackles back on him."

"Absolutely. And if he goes to a pueblo, the same." Paloma added, "Though it is a soft kind of slavery there."

"If he's hiding somewhere?" asked Sam.

"In this rough country," said Hannibal, "he can't hold out long."

"He'll come back hungry. That's probably our best hope," said Paloma. She shooed the three of them out through the kitchen. "Go. Find Tomás. Tell him I will help him."

Sumner looked at Pedro, who was now squatting against a wall near the kitchen stove. The boy's hands were shaking.

Grumble handed Sumner a deck of playing cards.

Sumner grinned. "Hey, Pedro," he said. "Come here. I got something to show you. It's fun."

The boy edged as near as the archway.

Sumner waterfalled the cards. "Look here, see these pictures." He held them up to Pedro. The boy came close enough to see.

"See this card in my hand? It's called the king. Whoops! It isn't there. Look, both my hands are empty." Sumner showed the boy his hands, palms up. Then he reached up to Pedro's ear. "Look, here it is."

Pedro gaped his mouth open.

"Now it's gone. Where did it go?"

"*¿Donde?*" said Pedro, the first word they'd heard him say this morning.

Sumner reached into the waistband of the boy's pants and drew out the king.

Pedro giggled.

Paloma nodded at Sumner and Grumble in gratitude.

"Pedro is ruined for life," said Grumble.

NO ONE HAD seen Tomás. No horse gear was missing from the stable. Flat Dog, the best tracker, could find no signs along the riverbank. "There's no sense in looking for sign on that road," said Hannibal.

"Not with the traffic on it," Sam agreed. Coy mewled.

With Paloma they inventoried the house. The blankets the boy slept in were missing. Juanita said a bowl of *atole* was eaten and the bowl left on the counter, some leftover tortillas taken. That was all. She opened a couple of drawers, looked, and closed them. "Looks like he took my cleaver too."

"He's on foot," said Hannibal, "he has something to keep him warm at night. He took a little food, not much. Maybe he wanted the cleaver for self-defense."

"But why?" said Sam. "Why would he leave, with nowhere to go?"

They interrupted Sumner's card tricks to quiz Pedro. "Did he say anything about going anywhere?"

The boy shrugged, eyes on the floor. "No, señor."

Sam, Hannibal, Flat Dog, and Paloma looked at each other in frustration.

"So up the road or down the road?" said Sam.

"Up," said Hannibal. "He's damn well not planning to walk all the way to Chihuahua."

The miles upriver to Santa Fe revealed nothing. The town itself revealed nothing. They asked a dozen people along the main road—hell, they asked a score of people—but who would remember one Indian-looking boy out of so many? And it was impossible to ask everyone in a town of six thousand people.

Sam, Hannibal, and Flat Dog wandered around Santa Fe. They checked with the priest at each of the churches. They had lunch outdoors on the plaza where they could see. They rode up and down streets at random. They looped back on themselves, and circled back where they came from. When Coy looked at them quizzically, they ignored him.

Just before dark they trundled into Rancho de las Palomas discouraged.

Paloma stood in the doorway, blocking it. "Suppose you'd been captured and your parents killed and been hauled six hundred miles to be sold as a slave. Suppose you could get away for a day or two. What would be on your mind?"

"Kill Cerritos," said Sam.

"Then he's gone to Armijo's place," said Paloma.

She handed Sam a bundle of warm tortillas wrapped in cloth.

They ran for their horses.

Sixteen

TOMÁS GUERRERO, A boy from an insignificant village on an unimportant stream flowing east from the Sierre Madre Occidental, had one strength. He knew absolutely what he had to do.

His father had taught him the meaning of the name Guerrero, warrior. Now the men of this family grew corn, beans, and chiles in their fine irrigated fields, and the children looked after their few goats. It was a good place, and the men of this village had for generations defended their families and their village against many enemies. With bow and arrow, with spear, with club they had acted when necessary as men, as *guerreros*, warriors. That was the blood that coursed through the body of Tomás, and through his mind and will. At this moment he bore a warrior's courage, a warrior's determination, and a warrior's fierceness.

He was waiting only for complete darkness. He had walked most of the day. He followed El Camino Real for a mile or two so that his tracks would be indistinguishable from others, and then walked through the sagebrush, through the trees, across rock, wherever he would be hard to track. He didn't know who was more likely to come after him, the men who would make him a slave again, or the foolish woman who would make him into a household servant or a farmboy. He was determined to elude everyone until he fulfilled his purpose. He kept the cleaver stuck down the back of his pants, covered by his loose shirt. He didn't want anyone to know he was bringing trouble.

At midmorning he made a wide circle around the city of Santa Fe. No city was important. What mattered was carrying himself as a man.

Once this afternoon he stopped to ask directions. He found himself uncertain which road led along the plateau to the rancho of the don, the man who arrogated to himself the power to own other human beings, to subordinate their desires to his own, to use them as his playthings.

A simple man who was cleaning an irrigation ditch told Tomás, "The road is there, beyond those fields and across the creek." The way to the rancho of the powerful man Tomás despised.

Later, when he got to the top of the rise and looked down at the rancho, he saw that it would be hard. First Tomás observed, noting everything and memorizing the arrangement of buildings, tracks, and gates. Then he crawled to the creek, concealed himself in the willows, and waited. When he saw a clear chance, he sprinted to the back side of a building. Then he crept behind a wagon. He slipped into a corral with some horses. At last he got into the barn and up into the loft, where he could see into the casa. These movements took him all afternoon, but he was very, very patient. His father had taught him that the first strength of a warrior, as for a hunter, is patience.

He was frustrated. From the loft he could see into the courtyard and through windows into the kitchen, the dining room, and even the room where rich people sat prettily and received their guests. He had seen two such houses in his lifetime, yesterday and today, but he was smart and able to put the layout firmly in his mind. He would be able to find his way around this one in the dark. His stomach was sour with contempt for the rich who lived in high style while others plowed their fields, planted, and did all the other labor that supported the *ricos*.

He was burning with two questions: Where was this particular *rico* now? And where was the human being he intended to make his slave?

In the rooms Tomás could see from this perch, he got no hint of an answer to either question. And now that the sun was down, the sky fully dark, and the house lit only by candles, he could see less.

On the other hand, the darkness would make it possible for a warrior to approach undetected, and to enter in stealth.

He climbed down the ladder and padded softly between the stalls. He inhaled the musty smells of straw, dung, and hay, and looked at the dark shadows of the necks and heads of the horses sticking over the stall doors, peering at the intruder.

The night was brighter than the barn, even though the moon was dipping toward the western hills. He moved quietly and told himself he had the confidence of a warrior. No one would be stirring now, unless the cook came outside. The don was probably at his meal in the dining room—with *her*, Tomás supposed. Even wicked men liked the company of a pretty woman.

Otherwise, probably, the don was alone. The children must be grown and gone. All afternoon he'd seen no family members at all, only the cook and a serving woman near the house, and elsewhere just field hands. He wondered if they were slaves. He hadn't seen the don, or her. It drove him mad to picture how they were probably spending the hours.

Already he had decided how to make his approach. The house was two long wings that made an L, and the two walls of the courtyard completed the square. He ignored the front door, far to the front left. He tiptoed past the gate into the courtyard, which gave access to the door that led to the kitchen. He treaded quietly along the wall outside the courtyard, where he had seen ovens, a well, and at the far end a fountain and ornamental plantings of cholla and chamisa. Facing the courtyard where the two wings met were several windows. He wondered what that room was—where the master slept, with a view of his garden? He circled around the back of the house to the far corner and tiptoed all the way to the back corner, where the two wings joined. He was only guessing, but . . .

Yes, there was a small door here.

He slipped the cleaver out of his waistband and held it high. From now on he must be totally alert and completely ready. If he came on an enemy unexpectedly, he knew what to do. His father told him over and over.

"When I was a boy, or barely a man, fourteen," his father said, "we fought the Apaches. They came to steal our families, many of them. They rode into the village in the middle of the day, when the men were working in the fields. They rushed into our houses and seized our women and children. If the men ran in from the fields in time, they killed them. Even the boys my age, if we tried to fight, they killed us.

"My older brother, not yet married, he had walked into the village to get food for the men. When the Apaches came, he was stepping out of the door of our house. He threw down the food and fought with his knife. I grabbed a cleaver from the kitchen and rushed to fight beside him. He screamed like a madman and swung his blade in every direction. I did the same, I became a *loco*. By that fighting, I learned a great lesson. The Apaches shot their arrows at us and threw their spears, but we stood untouched, warriors. As a result they did not go into our house. We were too much trouble. They stole children from the neighbors instead. So if ever you must fight, Tomás, do it like a *loco*. In his madness, a *loco*, he is protected by the saints."

Tomás took off his sandals and set them down. Barefooted would be quieter. He squeezed the handle of the cleaver and gently opened the rear door. He stood outside a moment, listening. Nothing.

He eased his head in the opening and peered down the corridor straight ahead. Nothing that he could detect, but the corridor was dark. He slipped through the doorway and stood very still, looking down the other corridor. There warm candlelight flowed through two open doors, making the hall a checkerboard of darkness and light.

Good, thought Tomás, *probably I will find them in the dining room.* He breathed deep. *Like thunder and lightning I will fall upon him, and I will bless her like a warm rain.*

He glided along the inside wall, his back to it. When he came to the first door, he stopped, waited, and quieted his heart. Slowly, he craned his neck into the entryway. To the left his vision was blocked by the door, which stood half open. In the middle of the room there was a long table, apparently for dining. Against the wall at the far end stood a high cabinet with glass doors and full of plates, bowls, cups, and glassware. Tomás felt a spurt of disgust for people who owned many sets of dishes, while a family like his had to eat from cheap bowls of clay.

Suddenly, the kitchen door swung open and a serving girl walked briskly through, carrying a covered dish. Tomás jerked his head back. He didn't know whether she'd spotted him, and his heart pounded.

By her footsteps he could tell she walked to the left end of the table, the one hidden from view. Words were spoken— "Here you are, sir" in a female voice, and in a man's, *"Gracias."* He let out a huge sigh. Evidently, the girl hadn't seen him. The footsteps tick-ticked again, her figure appeared with her back to him, and she disappeared into the kitchen. From there an older woman's voice said something sharply, and the younger woman's gave a clipped answer.

I am within a few steps of her now. He pictured her sitting meekly next to the old man, answering meekly when spoken to, obeying when instructed. She had been obeying since they were stolen from their home, which drove him mad.

Yet at the same time he loved her.

Can I do it?

He crossed to the outer wall. Then, facing the dining room, he crabbed sideways across, visible to anyone who might raise their eyes in his direction.

No one was there to look. He couldn't even see the don and his sister at their places at the table.

He slid swiftly to the far door to the dining room. This door also stood ajar. And he found a blessing—he could peer through the crack between the door and the facing.

At the head of the table sat the don, alone. *Where is she?*

He slumped in his chair, picking at his food without interest, staring at the dark windows that bordered the courtyard garden. His sallow complexion looked even more yellow in the candlelight.

Diablo, where is she?

He scoured his memory of the other long hall, the one on the left.

He half ran back down the hall—foolish speed, he knew. He sped by the other dining door without hesitation. Not before the corner at the end of the hall did he slow down.

He glanced down the hall and jerked his head back. Nothing but gloom. The first door stood partly open, and moonlight pooled on the floor. The far end of the corridor was inky.

He walked silently to the open door and peered in. The window facing the courtyard let in enough light to see. A small, plain bed, a table, a wardrobe, nothing more. Pole rafters held a flat ceiling. Candles stood in their wall holders, but he had nothing to light them with.

He slipped on to the next door, closed. Slowly, quietly, he pushed down on the flat handle. When it stopped at the bottom of its turn, he waited. The mechanism had been silent.

He eased the door open, waited. No one shouted, no one rushed at him.

He poked his head in. The room was identical to the other. Neither appeared to be in use. He closed the door and went on. Maybe the don lived alone in this big house.

He stepped quietly to the last door on this hall. He'd guessed that this was the large bedroom, for the master and his . . . woman. He reminded himself that he didn't know.

He palmed the handle, turned it, and held it down. After a deep breath in and out he opened the door and stepped in.

And glimpsed a figure. In front of the big window on the opposite side, aglow in the moonlight, hung the nude body of a woman.

Tomás weaved the few steps forward. He looked up at the head, and the cord that suspended her from the rafter. He reached out and touched the hand. Cold.

That cold coursed through him, pumped by his own heart.

"¿Maria?"

A voice in the corridor!

"My dear?"

The horror.

Tomás jerked his head around and saw the glow of candlelight. He froze.

Two candles came into view, each held by one hand. Behind them in the soft aura of light was the face of Don Emilio.

Aghast, Tomás turned back to his nude sister. Her head was crooked forward and her small feet dangling above the floor. The breeze from the window made her black hair stir against her limp forearm.

"Maria!" screamed Tomás.

As he screamed, he whirled to Don Emilio. Two faces, stunned, glared at each other.

"Murderer!" bellowed Tomás.

All of his rage at life raised the cleaver straight over his head and with both hands Tomás swung savagely down onto the don's skull.

Seventeen

HE SIMPLY MATERIALIZED in the doorway. One moment Sam saw an empty rectangle, the next a space filled with the dirty, skinny, bloody form of Tomás.

Paloma rushed to him and embraced him. Then she threw a look at the dining table that quelled everyone there: Do not ask this child any questions, not yet. Quickly she pushed Tomás through the dining room into the kitchen. "Scrub this boy in hot, soapy water," she told Juanita the cook, "and bring him right back to the table. He's probably starved."

Tomás gave Rosalita and Lupe, the serving girls, a funny look. They giggled, probably at the idea of him being stripped down and washed vigorously. Juanita, with her grandmotherly age and sergeant style, would be perfect for that.

In a few minutes Paloma got things arranged. She dispatched Flat Dog, Julia, and the infants to their casita. Pedro tagged after them. She reheated the stew of pork and green chiles herself and popped the tortillas into the warming oven.

Tomás sat, clean and in a robe of Paloma's. Juanita took his clothes, dirty and speckled with blood. His eyes darted from Paloma to Sam to Hannibal. Sam was sure the boy felt outnumbered. Which was good.

"All right, Tomás," said Paloma, "what has happened?"

Sam watched Tomás decide how to play it. He decided on defiance. "I killed the *diablo*." His lips curled as he said the words.

Rosalita put food in front of Tomás, and he pitched in.

"Killed who?" said Hannibal. They had ridden to Armijo's rancho, had talked to Cerritos, and knew the slave trader was in disgustingly good health.

"The one you call Don Emilio."

The adults flashed their eyes at each other. Why Emilio?

Tomás ate enthusiastically and gave them a weird, quivery grin.

Sam looked at Tomás and thought, *This attitude isn't going to last long.*

"I killed him with the cleaver." Tomás picked up the big knife and threw it flat onto the dining table, where it clattered, quivered, and grew still. The blade was caked with dried blood.

The boy looked at them with what he intended as pride.

Sam put a hand on his arm. "Why?" he asked.

"Why?" Tomás looked down at his plate. He dropped his spoon into his bowl of stew. He stared at it. Then he dumped the whole bowl in his lap. He stood up, food dribbling down the robe. Maybe he tried to scream the next words, but they came out as a series of hiccups. "Because the *hijo de puta* killed Ma-ma-ria."

Then the tears burst forth. Tomás wept, he sobbed, he shook convulsively.

Paloma put her arms around him. Sam patted his shoulder. Hannibal watched Tomás's face closely, tenderly. Then, slowly and patiently, the three adults drew the story out of the child and put it together:

The girl that Cerritos raped in front of everyone, the one

"not good enough for you yet," she was Maria Guerrero, the older sister of Tomás. And all the other men had raped her, as often as they wanted, at least one every night, since . . .

"Maria, she . . ."

The first time they raped her, Tomás threw himself on her attacker. They laughed, beat him, and then did everything they wanted to do with her loudly, mocking him and laughing. When he threw himself on the rapist again the next night, they held him fast, brought him close, made him watch, and then beat him senseless. After that they separated the two completely. They were not permitted to walk together, to talk, even to sleep near each other.

Tomás did not know what would happen when they finally got to Santa Fe. He was hoping they would be sold to the same family and could escape together.

"But Cerritos, he made a point of it. When he sold her, he did not want anyone to know I am her brother, know she had any family nearby. Cerritos, he said these words, 'A tasty morsel, unprotected . . .'"

Hannibal and Sam looked at each other and reached an understanding. To help this boy they needed to know . . .

"You walked to Don Emilio's rancho?"

"Yes." They realized he'd seen it when they went to get Lupe.

"Then what did you do?"

Tomás had honest pride in the next part of the tale. He told how he watched, figured things out, approached, sneaked through the casa until he found the don at his table, explored the rest of the house in the dark, and discovered . . .

"She was in his bedroom. Naked. He came down the hall calling her '*Querida*.'"

A term of endearment—Sam felt it like a sting.

"I knew he soiled her all day long."

Sam sensed something wrong. "She was still in his bed?"

"No, she . . . No, she . . ." And he wailed and sobbed again. Some minutes and much soothing were needed to get the next part of the story.

"She was hanging in the moonlight, naked, by a cord from one of the rafters. *Muerto*."

For long moments no one could speak. Tomás looked from face to face. There were no words.

"You said he came down the hall?" This was Hannibal.

"Yes, just after I found her. Perhaps he heard me and thought it was her. He came carrying a candle in each hand. They showed me my target, they framed his head for me. I took that cleaver and . . ." He pointed to the big knife, raised his hands over his head in a double fist, and swung them viciously down. The blow rattled the dining table, and the equilibrium of his listeners.

"Are you sure she is dead?"

"I touched her."

"Sure he is dead?"

"I split his brain in two." The words danced to dark music in Tomás's eyes.

Sam, Paloma, and Hannibal looked at each other, understanding.

"My child," said Paloma, "you must rest." She put an arm around his shoulders and guided him toward the doorway. "We will talk about everything tomorrow."

SAM AND HANNIBAL spent the next day in Santa Fe and came back with a different story. "We didn't have to ask anyone," said Sam. "It's the talk of the town."

Paloma brought cups of coffee. As she started to sit, she said, "Wait, I'll get Tomás. He's done nothing but sleep all day."

"Maybe that's not such a good idea," said Sam.

"It is," said Paloma. "If he's old enough to kill a man, he's old enough to hear what comes of it."

When Tomás was across the table from them and fully alert, Sam started to give him the news.

Tomás held up a flat hand. "I don't care about the *cabrón*. Tell me about my sister."

Sam said gently, "We brought her body in the wagon. We stopped at the Church of the Virgin of Guadalupe, and the priest said the proper words over her."

To Sam the words felt like thrown stones.

Tomás's face was naked.

Paloma said, "Tomorrow, if you want, we will bury her outside the chapel here."

"Good." Tomás looked lost for a moment. Then he said with a twisted smile, "Now tell me about the *viejo hediondo*."

"Don Emilio is barely alive," said Sam. "No one knows whether he will live or die. He mumbles but says nothing that makes any sense. The doctor says maybe he has a fractured skull, or maybe he's only missing a big piece of scalp on the left side of his head. Either way, he's weak from loss of blood, and he has a high fever. No one will know anything for several days."

"Unless I get at him," said Tomás.

"Stop that," Sam said. He gave the boy a hard look.

"I will kill him," said Tomás bitterly.

"You won't," said Sam.

Tomás lashed out. "He might get well. He might remember me."

"You don't know what it is to kill a human being." Sam wished he didn't.

"He might send the *policia*."

"We'll plan for that."

Paloma held Tomás's hands and looked deep into his eyes. "We will protect you."

Sam added, "No more killing."

He watched Tomás's face carefully, and later he thought the boy's expression was relief.

Eighteen

DON EMILIO DID not cooperate. He neither lived nor died—
he lingered. Though his servants listened carefully and the police asked often, nothing came from his delirium but
babblings. Sam knew, because Grumble had a friend in the
comisaria de policia and kept close touch. The police, naturally, were properly concerned about an outrageous attack on a
prominent citizen. Such behavior could not go unpunished.
But they had no suspects, not even a hint of who the culprit
was. Nothing had been stolen, though the house was full of
valuables, especially the chapel. Don Emilio was a widower,
he lived alone with his herds and crops—why would anyone
want to kill such a man?

After a week, Sam decided he had to speak up to Paloma.
"We need to get started."

They were getting undressed for bed.

She looked at him, and he couldn't name all he saw in her eyes. Recognition, sadness, a sense of rightness.

She slipped into bed in her nightgown and patted the pillow next to her. "I know today is the first of May," she said. "Leave the candles on."

Sam slid in next to her naked. He didn't own enough clothes to have nightwear.

"How soon?" she said.

"A week maybe."

"All right. Today is Thursday. We have our horse sale next Monday. I will send a man to let everyone know. It's going to be quite a show, and you, sir, will make some money. Then you will be able to buy supplies to take to your important rendezvous and make a good profit."

That much was true, but it wasn't what Sam wanted to talk about. "It's going to be hard to say good-bye."

He saw warmth in her eyes as well. Maybe she felt comfortable with good-bye—he didn't. "What do you want me to say, Sam? That you must sell your horses to the other beaver men and make your bonanza? That you need to get back to the business of hunting beaver? That you must take your daughter to her grandparents, to the Crow village where she belongs?" She waited. They both knew all that.

Finally, Sam said, "I want you to tell me why we're inappropriate."

She just looked at him. "I've thought and thought about that. When I said it, my big thought was, I'm ten years older. Or it's because I'm Mexican and you're American. Or because we are from different class backgrounds, different education. I was raised to love things cultivated for beauty, you to love nature in the raw. And all of that is true."

She hesitated.

"But . . ."

"You tell me why we should be appropriate."

He tapped his chest with his fist. "I have a fire in here for you."

She just looked at him.

"When I look into your eyes, I see that you have fire for me."

She smiled. "That's just candlelight, sir."

"Talk true," he said.

After a long moment she said, "I think you've touched directly on it. Each of us has a fire in the heart. Mine is the fire of the hearth. I love my home, I love making a nest, I love creating a beautiful place to live.

"You, though, your fire is for adventure. It takes you hither and yon. You've been from the Atlantic to the Pacific. One day, when I see you again, I'll bet you've looked upon the Arctic Ocean."

Actually, Sam knew there was fur-trapping even up there— by the Russians.

She kissed him lightly on the lips. "You, *mi amante,* are a true adventurer, an explorer. You may dally with a nurturer like me. You even find peace and love at my hearth. But one day before long, your nature will require you to go wandering."

He was stuck for words.

"Husband? Not yet. Father? Maybe not yet either."

Now he was truly stuck.

She put both arms around him, buried her head in his chest, and said, "Don't go into that head of yours. Make love to me."

Nineteen

GETTING READY FOR the sale was a furious time. Over the three days Sam, Flat Dog, and Hannibal put Paloma's horses through their paces again, getting them all sharp. Sam found only one he wouldn't want himself, a gelding that was a knot-head. "One in every crowd," he told Flat Dog.

They also checked out the mounts of their own they'd trained for sale. Hannibal had made a list of Santa Fe prices of the most important supplies—powder, lead, coffee, blankets, traps, knives, foofaraw, brandy—and figured out they could turn a nice dollar on trade goods. If they could sell some of their horses at a good price here, they'd use others to pack goods to rendezvous and earn more money.

"I'm for it," said Sam.

"You're becoming a trader," Hannibal told him.

"Indians can't run off supplies like they can horses," said

Flat Dog. Both Sam and Hannibal looked at him funny for saying "Indians."

Flat Dog chuckled. "Indians," he said, "means every tribe but Crows."

The good news about getting ready was that Tomás worked hard at helping. While Pedro went to town and stayed with Sumner and Grumble—"No doubt learning card tricks," said Sam—Tomás worked with the horses. He'd ridden his father's mule a lot, always bareback, because the family didn't own a saddle. As a result he had good balance on a horse. Sam told Flat Dog, "I think he's a natural rider."

"Natural athlete," said Hannibal.

Tomás would be able to demonstrate, during the sale, how well trained the mounts were, so gentle that even a boy could handle them. He also showed a willingness to work at learning English. When Sam and Hannibal spoke English among themselves, he asked what certain words meant, and they explained.

The fun was getting ready for the showy part. Sam, Hannibal, and Flat Dog knew that if they could get the buyers and watchers excited and inspired, the bidding would spiral higher and higher. So they rehearsed all their routines—Paladin and Brownie showed off their liberty training. Coy did his stuff. Sam and Hannibal did all their tricks on both of them. Flat Dog demonstrated a stunt he'd developed on his own. The riders could tell what an impression their show would make—Tomás and Paloma gasped and applauded.

At the end of the first day, over supper, Tomás said, "I don't want to stay here with Paloma. I want to go with you."

Everyone noticed that he said it to Sam, not to the three men, Julia, and the children. Sam thought, *Well, I paid for him.*

"You're in trouble. You may not have much choice about where you go," said Hannibal.

"But I want you to know you're welcome here," said Paloma.

"If the police aren't chasing your tail," said Flat Dog.

Everyone grinned, but no one thought it was funny.

"I want to go with you," Tomás repeated. "I want to be a mountain man."

Sam wondered what Tomás thought that meant—trick riding?—but he didn't answer.

All day Saturday and Sunday they worked on combining their various stunts with music. Antonio, one of the ranch's field hands, accompanied them on guitar, and Sam sang while he rode. In the evenings Sam and Hannibal taught Antonio the songs the horses knew. While Paloma went to Santa Fe on Sunday, to go to mass and remind everyone about the sale, they fine-tuned everything.

Tomás brought it up again that night—"I want to go with you."

"You're still a kid."

Tomás made a face.

From the size of the crowd that showed up Monday at noon, they knew that the word had spread far and wide: Something special was about to happen at Rancho de las Palomas. Gobernador Armijo came and announced that he was looking for fine stallions. Don Gilberto and Don Carlos presented themselves with eager faces. The other great families of the region—Chavez, Otero, Perea, and Yrizar—sent representatives to buy good breeding stock. Merchants of Santa Fe appeared, perhaps to buy well-trained saddle mounts, perhaps just to watch the show. It seemed that every Santa Fean who loved horses came out for the event. Paloma sent Rosalita and Lupe through the crowd to pour brandy liberally.

At last Grumble called for silence. He was splendidly American in a plum morning coat and fawn beaver hat, which Paloma had ornamented with a wide, sky-blue ribbon to mark him as master of ceremonies. "Antonio," he declared, "give us a fanfare."

To Antonio's music Sam and Hannibal dashed into the improvised forty-two-foot ring, followed by Paladin and Brownie. Coy pranced at their heels, excited. Paloma had festooned the horses' manes and tails with streamers of bright cloth. The riders were beautifully decked out as well, in big sombreros, short jackets, and beautifully quilled moccasins. "Make the best show you can," Paloma had urged them.

Antonio quickly launched into a fast sea shanty, a jig the

horses knew. Grumble sang the words in English in a fine, round basso:

When I was a little lad and so my mother told me
Way, haul away, we'll haul away, Joe
That if I did not kiss the girls, my lips would grow all moldy
Way, haul away, we'll haul away, Joe.

Hannibal and Sam signaled, and the horses faced each other in the center of the circle, trembling with anticipation. Hannibal lowered his hand in a wide sweep and called, "Dance!"

Antonio strummed and Grumble sang.

King Louis was the king of France before the revolution
But then he got his head cut off, which spoiled his constitution.

On the first line the horses pranced sideways in the same direction in rhythm to the music. On the second they stomped and shook their heads.

Oh, once I had a German girl and she was fat and lazy
Then I got a French gal, she damn near drove me crazy.

At Sam's and Hannibal's hand signals, for the German girl line they pranced the other direction. For the French girl's craziness, they reared and pawed the air.

Now the audience cheered.

Way, haul away, I'll sing to you of Nancy
Way, haul away, she's just my cut and fancy.

To "cut and fancy" they made curvets forward, passed each other, turned, and faced one another from the opposite sides. Sam could almost hear the awe among the Nuevo Mexicans.

Way, haul away, we'll haul away the bowlin'
Way, haul away, we'll haul away, Joe.
Way, haul away, the packet is a rollin'.

Here the mounts reared again, and whinnied—

Way, haul away, we'll haul away together
Way, haul away, we'll haul for better weather.

And finally Paladin and Brownie bowed to one another.
Everyone burst into applause.

As Paladin's head was down, Coy sprinted toward Paladin
and jumped onto her back and stood on his hind legs. Paladin
cantered around the ring, Coy's paws waving at the audience.

The clapping doubled.

Coy barked three times, as though celebrating himself, and
jumped down.

Flat Dog raced into the ring on his own horse for his moment of display. As the pony circled, Flat Dog swung down to
one side, reached under the horse, and shot an arrow into the
sky. When the crowd saw that the arrow displayed the Mexican
flag, they whistled and stomped. Then Flat Dog passed all the
way under the galloping legs and rose back into the saddle.
Sam figured that was the first applause of the Crow's life.

Sam and Hannibal vaulted onto their mounts' backs and
stood up. At first they just waved to the audience. Then, simultaneously, they somersaulted into the air and landed sitting
down. Women in the crowd shrieked. Again and again they did
it—stand, somersault, and land in riding position. When they
did a leaping dismount together, the crowd went wild.

"That was fun," Hannibal said quietly to Sam.

Grumble now stepped forward with a showman's command
of his audience. "And now," he said, "we begin the business of
the day."

Tomás rode one of Paloma's geldings into the ring and did a
figure eight, showing how nicely it reined. On command the
gelding stopped and backed up.

"What are we offered," cried Grumble, "for this fine two-
year-old? I call for five hundred pesos."

"Three hundred fifty," shouted Armijo.

Sam stopped listening and smiled to himself. Paloma's horses
were going to sell for much more than she thought. He and Flat

Dog would do well. And then they got to sell horses from their own herd. Flat Dog said softly, "We're gonna strike it rich today."

"Half rich," Sam agreed.

DINNER WAS A celebration. At Paloma's instruction Juanita cooked the most sumptuous meal she could manage, and the wine flowed freely. Everyone ate heartily and told jokes. Even Tomás, for the first time, seemed to relax and enjoy himself.

After dessert Paloma said, "Thank you all," she said, "today was so very good. Thank you, Mr. Grumble." Here she gave him the amount agreed on—"Plus," she said, "a bonus for cajoling my rich customers into such good prices."

Grumble looked at the coins and said, "Generous. Thank you."

She handed Sam and Flat Dog a stack of coins for their work on the seven saddle mounts she'd sold.

Flat Dog looked at the money and said, "We didn't even get starved or shot at."

"And for putting on such a grand display," she said, "something extra for each of you." Another stack of coins. The friends winked at each other.

"Last," she said, "something for Tomás, and a bit for Juanita, Rosalita, and Lupe for our fine meal, and one coin for Pedro so he can buy himself a treat."

Sam, Hannibal, and Flat Dog also shared a bit of their wealth with everyone. They looked at each other like conspirators. They couldn't get their minds off how much they would buy at the trading posts in town tomorrow.

Then Sumner walked in.

Everyone looked at the expression on his face.

"Don Emilio is awake and talking," he said. "In fact, shouting. He has told the police that the older of the two slave boys bought by me and Sam assaulted him. He demands justice. The police are on their way here now. I rode fast to get here first. They won't have any trouble picking you out, Tomás."

Everyone sat stunned.

Sam thought, *Damn, when we're all a little drunk.*

Grumble cocked his head, waited a moment, and said, "I have an idea."

"What?" said Paloma. This was her home.

"Better you don't know," said Grumble. "Sam, Tomás, let's confer."

Twenty

IN THE CHAPEL Grumble gave Tomás a useful device the boy had never heard or dreamed of. Grumble quickly explained its normal use, which made Tomás look wildly at Sam and grin like a fool. Then Grumble explained how Tomás was to employ it in front of the police, which sobered the young man hugely. For a moment Sam thought Tomás was about to leap into fear and darkness, but then the boy seemed to make up his mind to see the thing through.

Grumble spoke to Sam briefly about the pistol kept in his belt. When Sam understood, he made certain adjustments to it.

"Act it out," said Grumble. "Both of you. An actor sells his reality to the audience."

Sam nodded. Tomás didn't. "It's the only way," Sam said.

Tomás pursed his lips. *"Bueno."*

Then the three of them knelt and prayed, or pretended to.

Sam worried. He eased off on that when he thought how scared Tomás had to be.

They heard Paloma's voice down the hall. "Put your weapons away. Not in my house."

She appeared in the doorway. "The police have come for Tomás."

"Admit them," said Grumble.

That was unnecessary because the officers were already pushing past Paloma.

The candlelight in the chapel was dim, and the officers needed a moment for their eyes to adjust. Sam noticed that their pistols were in their belts.

"Tomás Guerrero," said the tall, fat officer, "you are under arrest for assaulting Señor Emilio Durán."

The three of them rose from their knees.

"The boy has confessed," said Grumble, "and is now ready to yield his fate and his soul to God. He will go with you peaceably."

Sam scowled at Tomás, drew his pistol, and held it against his ribs, assisting the police.

Tomás looked crazily from the policemen to the pistol next to his heart.

"The devil!" he screamed, and swung wildly at Sam's face.

Sam's pistol boomed. The chapel filled with white smoke.

When the smoke cleared and Paloma brought a candle close, everyone saw this tableau: Tomás lay on the stone floor with a shirt bloodied over his heart. Sam stood over him, pistol in hand, with a nasty expression on his face.

Paloma gasped.

"I told you the kid was no good," Sam said in a snarl to Grumble.

Grumble knelt over the prostrate figure and started to pull the shirt away.

At that moment Tomás coughed violently, and blood gouted out of his mouth.

The two officers looked at Grumble. Everyone knew what that meant, a chest wound that made the victim cough up blood.

"Don Emilio is avenged," said Grumble.

"And I paid good money for that little bastard," said Sam.

Grumble felt for a pulse and then spoke to Paloma. "He's gone. We'll get the priest in the morning."

Paloma nodded.

The officers headed back to Santa Fe to give the good news to Don Emilio.

BACK IN THE dining room they had another dessert, more coffee, more wine, and by popular demand a repeat of the performance from Sam and Tomás, the actors, and from Grumble.

First Grumble, the stage director, showed everyone a condom. "They are made from the intestines of lambs," he said.

"Mother Mary," said Paloma, "I heard of them, but . . ."

Then he showed them his vial of chicken blood. He poured some blood into the tip of the condom, knotted it off to the size of a finger joint, and clipped the remainder away.

Immediately, Tomás popped the balloon into his mouth and held it with his back teeth so everyone could see.

"When you clamp down," said Grumble . . .

Tomás did just that. Chicken blood squirted out, making everyone laugh.

"But the wound," said Flat Dog.

"Let me see that," said Paloma.

Tomás did. It was trivial. Still, Paloma clucked and put water on the stove to boil.

"Explain to them," Grumble said to Sam.

"I took the lead ball out of my pistol. All that was left was the powder and cotton patch." He showed them one of the patches normally used for firing a flintlock firearm, a disc the size of the tip of a finger. "When I pulled the trigger, the gun fired. Only the cotton blew out."

Grumble said, "Which hit Tomás hard enough to break the skin, but . . . I've done this before."

"Broke it quite a bit, I'd say," Paloma called from the kitchen.

Now Tomás leapt in eagerly. "I had the other condom in my

hand"—he held his palm out—"and when Sam shot me, I clapped my hand hard against my chest."

They all pondered it.

"Lots of blood," said Tomás.

"The art of illusion," said Grumble.

"And now," said Sam, "what are we going to do with this little criminal?"

"I go with you." Then he repeated, for his first sentence in English, "I go with you."

Sam smiled. But then he thought, *I've already got a kid.*

No one spoke until Hannibal did. "Tomorrow we're going to bury an empty box outside the chapel. Then we're going to buy supplies for rendezvous. And the next day we're going to head for rendezvous. Tomás will be riding with us."

Tomás grinned. *"Bueno,"* he said. *"Bueno.* I am a mountain man."

Twenty-One

"WHAT IS IT?" Hannibal asked Sam.

"Nothing."

Hannibal turned in his saddle and looked back at the casa. "She's standing under the covered entrance, watching us ride away. She's lovely, and the bushes leafing out on each side make her more lovely. The red *ristras* are swaying a little in the breeze."

"I feel like I've spent my whole life riding away."

"Is that it?"

It wasn't just Paloma. They'd said good-bye last night to Grumble and Sumner. The two gamblers intended to get back to California, Grumble said. Sam didn't know when he'd see them again.

He kept his eyes straight ahead. "I've got bigger things to worry about." He swept a hand to indicate all that was in front of him. There was a herd of ninety horses and about three dozen horse colts and fillies. A score of the horses bore packs of trade goods. Two riders led these packhorses on a string, Flat Dog and Gregorio, a hand Paloma had loaned to them. Out in front of the herd was a boy, Tomás. And beside Sam and Hannibal rode Julia, dragging a travois with the thirteen-month-old Esperanza and six-month-old Azul. They were heading down the Santa Fe River to where they would turn north along the Rio Grande, toward Taos.

"Look like enough?"

"Yes, but your mind is back there."

Sam still didn't turn his head. The last thing he wanted was to see Paloma standing in the sun on a fine May morning watching him go.

Sam forced his mind to practical things. "We can't push these horses now—too many haven't foaled yet."

"And when they have, we go easy to let the little ones keep up."

In fact, Paladin herself was one of the mares that hadn't foaled. Sam was riding a stallion he'd trained during the winter, the one that acted like a knothead and needed some kinks worked out.

"What else are you worried about?"

"It might be hard to hire good men in Taos."

All the Nuevo Mexicanos had assured the beaver-hunting Americans that Taos was full of men who had traveled up the Rio Grande and all the way to the Salt Lake to trap beaver, and knew the way well. These men, people assured them, were easy to hire at reasonable wages. Sam's thought was, *They damned well better be.*

"What else?"

"It's a long way to rendezvous with a lot of Indians along the way who'd like to run our horses off."

"And the rivers will be running full this time of year."

They both looked up at the high peaks of the Sangre de Cristo Mountains behind them. Only now was the snow beginning to melt. Soon it would make the rivers flood.

Sam breathed in and out big. "None of this is a big problem."

"We hope."

"Tomás."

They looked at each other.

It was a litany of trouble. Kidnapped, maybe witness to murder. Definitely a witness to rape and suicide. Then attempted murder of his own. Police attempting apprehension. A desperate trick that happened to work. A wound.

"He's got a lot to sort out," said Hannibal.

"Truth is, we don't know what the hell he might do."

"That's right."

Sam looked across at his friend.

"So you worry too."

"Sometimes. But I have a motto I live by."

What's that?"

"Rideo, ergo sum."

Sam shook his head. Whenever Hannibal quoted Latin, it felt like he was a wizard out of a kid's story, with secret knowledge no one else had. "Meaning?"

"I laugh, therefore I am."

Sam laughed. "And if I took up that motto of yours right now, I could stop worrying?"

"Also you could ride back and kiss that beautiful woman good-bye. I saw the way you two parted. Uneasy."

They poked along for a few steps in silence. The last words Paloma Luna had said to Sam were, "Don't come back for a few years. I need the time."

Maybe she was still outside watching. He looked back, but the covered entrance to the house was in shadows. "Rideo whatever," he said to Hannibal.

Sam wheeled the knothead and galloped back to the gate and to the casa. Coy sprinted at his heels.

Still standing on the porch, Paloma smiled and cocked her head at his appearance. "I'm back," he said. He gave her a rip-roaring kiss, and she returned it lustily. She laughed, and he galloped away.

When Sam caught up, Hannibal said, "All right to be going?"

Sam thought and said, "For the first time in two years I'm heading the right direction. Home."

* * *

"IT'S TWO TOWNS," said Sam.

"One Indian, one Mexican," said Hannibal.

The herd was grazing on good grass downstream, not far above the Rio Grande, watched by Flat Dog and Gregorio.

"The pueblo is beautiful." Tomás seemed mesmerized by it.

It was a ramble of multistory buildings, adobe the color of the reddish tan sand and windows and doors painted the light blue of the robes of the Franciscans who had ministered there for two centuries. The Mission San Geronimo stood firmly in the foreground, topped by three crosses. The buildings beyond were a jumble, yet at the same time came together in an attractive way, like boulders rising on a mountain ridge. Ladders jutted out of the kivas, the chambers where the men gathered and the ceremonies began.

"Crosses on a background of kivas," said Hannibal.

"How do they do it?" said Sam. "Take the old religion, scramble it together with Catholicism, and make sense of it?"

"Let's get to it," said Hannibal.

Below the pueblo stretched the Mexican town, a knot where business got done, strings of adobes thrown here and there, and cultivated fields beyond.

In the knot they found the place easily enough, Young and Wolfskill's store. Ewing Young was a Tennessean who had made good money trading between Missouri and Santa Fe and now proposed to make more money by leading parties of trappers throughout the mountains of the Southwest. His store and home were the nerve center of the beaver trade in Taos. Since this country was under the sovereignty of Mexico, however, he had no standing. Governor Armijo took every opportunity to oppose him. So Young had recently gotten Mexican citizenship. Or such was the scuttlebutt Sam and Hannibal had picked up in Santa Fe. Everyone told them that if they wanted experienced guides or trappers, Ewing Young was the man to talk to.

Mr. Young, however, was not in the store. The clerk was a small, sandy-haired teenager. Since he didn't offer his name when Sam and Hannibal introduced themselves and Tomás, Sam asked.

"Kit," the boy said softly.

In answers to questions he was polite but not forthcoming. No, he didn't know when Mr. Young would be back. Yes, he allowed that the town had some men who had trapped the country north on the Rio Grande and west toward the Colorado River, maybe quite a few.

Sam thought the youngster was partly stuck between being a kid and being a man. "Kit," he said, "may I buy you a cup of coffee?" Sam had noticed the potbellied stove and the pot on it.

Kit apologized for his lack of hospitality and poured three cups, no charge. Sam, Hannibal, and Kit sat around the stove like friends. Sam noticed that none was poured for Tomás, who now roamed the room.

"Call me Sam and him Hannibal. Have you done some trapping yourself?"

It turned out that the young man had a good deal of experience trapping. As he spoke, slowly, spending words like hardearned coins, he admitted he'd been over much of the country to the south and west. Mr. Young was a strong leader and determined as a man could be. He'd taken brigades all the way to the Colorado out at the Yuma villages, all up and down the Gila and Salt Rivers, up on the San Juan . . .

Sam revised his estimate of the boy's age from sixteen to eighteen, a small but sturdy eighteen. "You like that life."

The boy nodded. His eyes never sat still on the men he was talking to, but skittered about the store restlessly.

"How about you?" asked Sam. "You've been on the San Juan yourself?"

Kit nodded.

"You know the country—why don't you come with us?"

"My time is promised. I'm going to Chihuahua."

A trading caravan then. Sam supposed it would take slaves. He wondered if Kit cared.

Hannibal was interested. "Is Mr. Young sending a caravan to Chihuahua?"

Kit shook his head no. "Another outfit."

"Will you give us some names then? Men you can recommend?"

"Yes, there's . . ."

Kit pounced and landed right on top of Tomás.

Quick as an eel, Tomás slipped away and shoved his assailant forward.

Kit half banged into a counter, wheeled, ducked under a punch, and tackled Tomás. They crashed to the floor and skidded across it.

Sam and Hannibal got to them at the same time and pulled them apart. Kit was almost more than Sam could handle, though Sam was stronger and half a foot taller.

"Look in his pouch," snarled Kit. "He's a damn thief."

Hannibal held out a demanding hand.

Tomás hesitated, then slipped the pouch off and slammed it into Hannibal's hand.

Hannibal let him go, and Tomás stalked off into a corner.

"He's got a fire steel in there," said Kit.

Hannibal fished inside and held up the steel.

"Come here to rob me, did you, boy?" The voice was a knife blade.

Tomás just glared at Kit.

"Tomás asked me if he could buy a steel," said Sam smoothly. "I've been teaching him to start fires with mine." The second part, at least, was true. "We'll be buying that and some other gear."

Kit looked Sam straight in the face, and the eyes said Sam was fooling with the truth. He set the fire steel next to a pad on the counter.

Kit sat and seemed to calm down. He said, "All right, I'd say Antonio Romero is a good man. He lives over at . . ."

Sam copied down the name and instructions.

"Then there's Esteban . . ."

As Sam wrote, he grinned sideways at Hannibal. He was proud—this was the first practical use for his winter's learning.

In ten minutes they were totaled out and on their way out the door.

Sam turned back. "Kit, I'm sorry for what happened here."

The youngster nodded.

"Why don't you come to rendezvous sometime?"

Kit waited, maybe deciding. "I might do that, Sam."

"What's your last name?"

"Carson."

Before they got to the Romero house, Sam and Hannibal spoke sharply to Tomás about stealing. "Besides," Hannibal said, "didn't you see what that young fellow is like? He'd be a wildcat to fight."

"I said I'm sorry," repeated Tomás.

That night Sam and Hannibal tossed words back and forth about Tomás. He was off kilter. No telling what he might do. They looked at each other helplessly.

THE NEW HANDS were Esteban—a Mexican in his thirties, an old man by mountain man standards—and Plácido, his teenage son. By the time they led the party across from the Rio Grande to the San Juan River and on west, Sam knew the older man was as good a pilot as people in Taos said. He knew the rivers and mountains, knew how to travel in Indian country, and altogether made a good hand. He was worth the fifty dollars he was getting. Plácido? Sam would rather have had another grown man. Both father and son planned to hire on as trappers for the fall season with other outfits when they got to rendezvous.

It was a good time for Sam. He rode behind the herd every day, balancing Esperanza on his lap for as long as she was willing to stay each session. His daughter was learning to talk. She called Julia Mamá. She addressed both Sam and Flat Dog as Papá, which stung.

Good times, though, were to be enjoyed. Spring was gentle and graceful on the land. Since they didn't go over any high passes, the snow was melted into life-giving fluid. Wildflowers sprouted everywhere. The days were warm, the nights crisp. The creeks were running full in a country that otherwise could put a lot of distance between drinks of water. Some days were windy, and they kept an eye out for sandstorms. But they moved along lazily, not rushing the newborn horses. They had no Indian trouble. They thought about the profit they would make at rendezvous. Life had a savory taste.

One evening Sam walked down along the river with Esperanza holding onto his finger. Soon she saw a prairie chicken and ran at it. The damned chicken didn't fly, but just ran around a log and froze. That wouldn't stop Esperanza. Around the log she scampered, knees pumping.

Now the chicken flew—about six feet, back over the log. It went into its disguise as a rock or a clump of dirt. Here came Esperanza back the other way. Sam didn't know whether she wanted to hug it or whack it.

They played this way for half a dozen rounds. Sam had never seen such a crazy prairie chicken, though they were well known to be dumb. Esperanza would have kept on all day, but finally the chicken flew up to the lowest limb of the fir.

Esperanza immediately began to crawl onto the tree. Unfortunately, this was half possible. The trunk was tilted sharply out over the river and barely clung to the bank. Sam grabbed his daughter, sat her down on the log, and took guard position at the base of the fir. She stood up, pointed at the bird, and started talking to it, not words but sounds—squeals, hums, coos, every kind of sound but a word.

Funny that fir—the current had undercut the bank, and some of its roots were exposed. By next spring it would join the river, float downstream, and end up on a sand bar when the flood waters dropped back. He watched the waters froth by. They went on forever. The Crows said only the rocks live forever, but that wasn't true—the waters lived forever, charging down from the mountain peaks, marching out over the plains, joining together with other rivers drumming their way to the sea. There they got picked up, carried back to the peaks, and started the forever circle again.

He watched Esperanza, who was still carrying on a big conversation with the prairie chicken, and the bird was sitting on the limb paying respectful attention. Esperanza would live— this was everyone's plan—in the village where Flat Dog grew up, on the Wind River in winter and in the Big Horn Basin in the summer. Her grandparents, Needle and Gray Hawk, would certainly spoil her rotten. The two pivot points of her life would be the big buffalo hunt in the spring and the huge hunt in the fall, which brought lots of villages together. And the only language she would hear, except sometimes from her two fathers and one mother, would be Crow. She would play entirely with Crow children. She would learn to put up a tipi, dry buffalo meat on a rack, and quill moccasins. She would be raised with the Crow stories, in the Crow religion, and the Crow way of seeing the world.

Sam accepted all this. It was a good road to walk. He hadn't forgotten that he himself carried the sacred pipe and had given a sun dance.

"See," said Hannibal, "she already speaks foreign languages." He was walking toward them, Coy on one side and Plácido on the other.

Now Esperanza, maybe because she had a new audience, started in on her list of words. She had a fair number—"want," "milk," and a baby fistful of other useful words—and she babbled right through them. Then she stood up, stuck her hands out, and said, "Water. *Agua*. Water. *Agua*."

Tickled, Plácido gave her a drink from his canteen.

"Bilingual," Hannibal said, grinning. Sam had learned a lot of out-of-the-way words, hanging around with Hannibal. "She's getting three languages, right in the tipi."

Suddenly Esperanza dropped the canteen to the ground and held her arms up to Hannibal. He picked her up. From her higher stance she pointed at the prairie chicken and launched into a tirade of her sounds that weren't words. She gave that bird a good talking to.

Plácido hooted. Laughing, Hannibal staggered around in a circle, keeping a tight hold on Esperanza.

Sam told Hannibal, "I'm going to take her to rendezvous most years."

"Besides picking up a lot more English, some Spanish, some French, Iroquois, Delaware, she'll be able to talk to all the birds in their own tongues, prairie chicken, raven, hawk, osprey, eagle . . ."

Esperanza reached a climax in her prairie chicken lecture.

Coy yipped, and the bird flew off in search of peace and quiet.

"Down," said Esperanza. Hannibal set her on the ground.

She was good at this word. Every day, riding along with her dad, she got tired of being held and said firmly, "Down." When he dismounted and set her on the ground, she toddled over to the pony drag and crawled onto it. Sam lashed her in. There she could play with her cousin Azul or nap. At the age of six months Azul didn't interest her much yet, but that would come.

Though Julia and Flat Dog had cradleboards, keeping them on the drag was easier.

"Mamá," said Esperanza.

Sam and Hannibal started walking back with her slowly. She didn't want to be carried, but toddled along on her own. Then she forgot her need for mama and stopped to inspect everything interesting along the way.

The next morning, as they were finishing eating, Sam found himself alone by the fire with Tomás. He decided to speak up.

"You know what happened to Maria, none of it . . ."

"You say nothing about my sister."

Sam looked at the kid. Hannibal ambled over with his empty coffee cup.

"Tomás, you have to know your sister didn't deserve . . ."

Tomás stood up and hurled his butcher knife into a nearby aspen. He stalked off. The handle on the knife quivered.

Hannibal walked over to the aspen, studied the knife, and pulled it out. "This far in," he said, holding thumb and forefinger about two inches apart.

Hannibal filled his cup.

Sam looked after Tomás and wondered.

They decided the best way to help Tomás along, whatever his emotional storms were, was to help him learn something. In the evenings either Sam or Esteban rode up whatever creek or river was handy, taking the two teenage boys and setting traps. They showed Tomás and Plácido how to spot beaver signs: the gnawed trees, the slides, the dams. Taught them how to ease into the water well upstream of where they wanted to set the trap. What depth of water to put it in, so the beaver could stand up to smell the bait. How to bait the small stick with medicine out of the stoppered horn. How to set a trap pole stout enough that the big rodent couldn't swim off with it. How to skin the drowned creature.

When they brought beaver back to camp, Julia took over, for she had learned well during her months in the Sierra Nevada. She showed both boys how to scrape the inner side of the hide clean and then stretch it on a willow hoop, so it could be put into a pack and transported on the back of a horse.

The boys got to keep the pelts they brought in, share and share alike. Tomás gradually got outfitted. A pony for five pelts, New Mexico price. A patch knife, a hunting pouch, two horns (small and large) to hold the two kinds of powder, a bar of lead, and a tool to make the lead into balls.

"You catch on quick," Sam told him.

Tomás gave a sly smile. "I am smart," he said.

"Yes," said Sam.

Finally—this was a proud day—he traded Tomás one of the outfit's mountain rifles for two plews.

Being a little older, Plácido already had a rifle and other gear.

The outfit took a nooner every day. The horses did well with a break in the middle of the day, a chance to water and graze. The foals particularly needed time to nurse or do nothing for two or three hours. During times like this Sam taught Tomás to shoot that rifle. How to make a round ball from a bar of lead. How much powder to pour down the barrel, and how to patch that with cloth. How to seat the ball on the patch. How to use the double triggers. Which powder to pour into the pan, and how to make the hammer whack the flint in the pan and create the spark that made the whole thing go *ka-boom!*

The first time Tomás fired the rifle Sam had to giggle at the expression on his face. Between the roar and the cloud of white smoke the boy was bamboozled.

"He's doing all right," Sam told Hannibal that evening.

"Would be good if he made friends with Plácido," Hannibal said. "That kid has a nice calm about him."

"Tomás is only surly about half the time," said Sam.

"He's damn near able to tolerate the man who saved his ass," said Hannibal.

Sam laughed. The truth was, they were both relieved at how the kid no longer seemed about to go twisty at any second.

During the next couple of days Tomás practiced shooting at trees, then at marks on trees. Sam supervised him carefully, instructed him about where to place his left hand on the stock, how to use the sights, how to get steady, and just how to pull the triggers.

Then Sam scraped the bark away from a spot on a cottonwood, and Tomás and Plácido competed shooting at it.

First round: Plácido hit the mark. Tomás missed the tree clean.

Second round: Plácido hit the mark. Tomás missed the tree clean.

Third round: Same result.

Sam could see that Tomás was trembling with rage.

"Enough for today," he said. "Tomás, don't worry about it. That barrel's too heavy for you right now, and you're wobbly. You'll get stronger . . ."

Tomás rammed Plácido in the chest with his head. They went down hard and came up fighting like cats.

"*Pendejo!*" yelled Plácido.

"*Hijo de puta!*" retaliated Tomás.

Sam tackled them both and knocked them to the ground. With a big effort he pushed them apart and got a kick in the *cojones* for his trouble.

"O-o-o-w!" Sam hollered. He kept holding the boys apart and glared at each of them in turn. "Anybody wants to fight, he fights me."

Tomás looked ready to charge. Plácido said, "Looks like maybe this is a good time to fight you, señor."

Sam grinned.

Tomás turned and walked away, mumbling something.

"Don't ask him what he said," Sam instructed Plácido.

SOON THEY WERE herding the horses down El Rio de Nuestra Señora de las Dolores, as Esteban called it.

"River of Our Lady of Sorrows," said Hannibal.

"The name would half keep me away," said Sam.

But it was a lovely stream, a mountain creek, meandering through meadows or bouncing downhill fast. "She comes to the desert," said Esteban. "To the Grand River, above where it flows in and makes the Colorado."

Sam was in no hurry to get back to a desert.

Early one morning just as the sun rose, when the morning smelled truly fresh, Tomás squatted by Sam's blankets. He was coming back from the last watch of the night. "Sam," he said, "your mare, she has her colt."

Sam sat up and saw the dewy-eyed look on the boy's face. "Let's go have a look." Hannibal sat up and went with them.

The colt had Paladin's markings exactly, the dramatic combination of white all over with black around the ears like a hat, black blaze on the chest, and black mane and tail.

"Beauty," said Hannibal.

Paladin was standing, and the foal, a horse colt, was nursing. The mare gave the three human beings a wise, satisfied look.

"Do you think he's Ellie's?"

Tomás knew about the stallion—Hannibal had talked about him a lot when they were putting the horses through their routines for the sale. The boy also knew how much Hannibal missed Ellie.

"The colt is big," said Hannibal. Ellie had been an American horse, not a Spanish pony. "One way you can tell is by counting the vertebrae. Be an extra one. So it's Ellie's."

They watched, wondering, smiling.

Perhaps enchanted, Tomás said, "I want him."

"What?" said Sam.

"I want him for my horse."

"Then you'll have to earn him," said Hannibal.

"Four plews," said Sam. Sam had been thinking of this foal for himself.

Tomás pursed his mouth. "I earn him." Again this was in English. And a little defiant, judged Sam.

*   *   *

ESTEBAN RODE AHEAD with Sam and Hannibal to the Grand River. The sight made Sam suck in his breath hard.

"Damn full," he said. They'd crossed to the north side of the Dolores to get above the confluence.

"Daunting," said Hannibal.

"What you call a beetch," said Esteban in his home-grown English.

It was early June, and the spring runoff was in full swing. The three of them watched the monster slosh against its banks, and out of them, and wondered.

Esteban said, "I know a better place. We must march one day to the north. There two other rivers come in, one on each side. Above that there is a . . . *paso.*"

"Ford," said Hannibal.

Then on north over a divide to the Siskadee, Esteban explained, and up that river to the Uinta Mountains, and into Bear Lake by a route they all knew. A lot of desert ahead. Sam wanted mountains, like the ones in Crow country.

The morning of the crossing dawned fine and clear.

"Going to be hot," said Sam. He rolled out.

He and Hannibal had gotten in the habit of taking the time of predawn light to talk, a good time to be alone.

As soon as Esperanza woke up, she would burst out of the tent and pitter-patter toward Sam's blankets. "Papá," she would call. And Sam would toss her up in the air and catch her.

He was satisfied that the kids would be safe on the crossing. Flat Dog and Julia would carry them in the cradleboards. Sam had ridden Paladin across the ford and back, and the horses could keep their feet the whole way. Still, they'd taken an extra day in camp, to rest the animals and the people.

Everyone knew his job. They made sure of the hitches on the pack animals. Then Sam, Hannibal, Flat Dog, and Esteban moved the loose horses toward the bank. The two boys kept the packhorses well back, and Julia stayed with them. The plan was to take the loose horses across, then the pack animals. Sam was glad to have Paladin between his legs for this job. He trusted her.

He and Hannibal looked across the horses at each other

and nodded. Time. They signaled to Esteban and Flat Dog at the rear.

"Hi-iy-iy!" Sam yelled, and snapped a blanket at the horses. All four men yelled and waved hats and blankets. The herd bolted.

Sam and Hannibal galloped past the leaders and charged into the river. The herd plunged into the water. The river was a melee—horses whinnying, manes and tails flying, water splashing up in barrelfuls—it was crazy. Sam loved it.

Coy ripped along behind, in a rush.

The crossing was over almost before Sam knew it. He was soaked head to toe. *Easy. Hot damn. Let's do it again.*

They got the animals to circle, slowed them down, and took a few minutes to get them settled. The riders grinned at each other. Back across the river. Coy stayed where he was—he didn't like this back and forth stuff.

"Why don't you and Julia go now?" Sam said to Flat Dog. "There's some good shade right over there."

The Crow and his wife got the children in the cradleboards and the cradleboards on their backs. They pussy-footed their mounts down the bank and into the shallow water. "Stay here," said Flat Dog. "We'll be fine."

And they were.

Coy barked across the waters at Sam—what's going on?

The score of packhorses was trickier. A heavily laden animal was more likely to lose its balance in the swift current, and one might bang into another, and several could go down in a tangle.

While Julia sat with the children, the other riders worked the pack animals gently to the bank. Sam and Hannibal put two of the most reliable on lead lines and started them across. Flat Dog and Esteban pushed all the rest from behind. One by one, two by two, the horses stilted into the water. Once there, they looked more comfortable. The two teenage boys, as instructed, rode upstream of the middle of the herd.

Sam turned in his saddle, looking back.

Then he saw it.

A huge fir tree rampaged down the middle of the current,

evergreen leaves dead and brown, roots pointed straight toward men and horses.

"Get out!" Sam yelled, pointing. "Get out!"

Everyone saw the menace. The roots looked like a madwoman's hair violently shaken. The whole tree raised and dived in the waves—it bobbed and sawed back and forth, an immense ramrod gone wild.

There was not one damn thing Sam could do to stop it.

He and Hannibal threw the lead lines away and slapped their packhorses on.

Luckily, some other horses followed. If they had seen the tree, panicked, tried to turn around, milled, done anything but charge straight ahead . . .

Sam turned Paladin and whipped her toward Tomás and Plácido. He shouted, "Go! Go!" Then he remembered. *"Vamonos! Vamonos!"*

Beside him, Hannibal spun Brownie around, but the horse got his feet tangled and fell. Hannibal pitched into the water.

From behind the herd Sam saw Esteban spurring his horse right where Sam was headed.

Tomás whacked his mount with his hat. The pony leapt and cleared the root ball by a whisker.

The roots hit Plácido and his horse dead on.

The horse went down, the boy went up.

Tomás wheeled his mount, but the animal refused to go back.

Tomás dived off the saddle toward the tree.

Plácido landed right where the trunk met the root ball. He grabbed roots with both arms and stuck his legs in among them. He was riding the damn thing!

The root ball clubbed the line of pack animals. Horses screamed. Ropes snapped. Gear ripped in every direction—kegs broke and sprayed their gunpowder, a bundle of wrapped rifles split like twigs, packs of plews got dunked, boxes of beads, bells, awls, and kettles careened into the turbulence. Right below the ford the river narrowed a little, picked up speed, and emptied into a hole.

Tomás grabbed the upstream end of the roots and started heaving himself out of the river.

Sam hollered, "Get out of there! Get out of there!"

He whipped Paladin again with his hat. "Go!" he shouted at her. The tree was no more than twenty feet away and zinging along.

Paladin reared and whinnied. The current hit her or the bottom betrayed her, and she fell on her back.

Sam let go—he dropped The Celt. Paladin ripped her reins away. As he got his footing, a wave knocked him down. He righted himself and launched his body, swimming and wading, toward the fir.

Just before he got to the tree, one edge of the root ball nudged the sand where the river channeled.

The top of the tree swung straight at Sam.

He grabbed branches and pulled himself up. Arms, face, and neck got scratched, but he got on. He looked wildly toward the boys. They were on top, together, and holding on tight. Ride the damn thing—yeehaw!

Then the tree rotated slowly and majestically in the water, and they all rolled to the bottom.

Beneath was madness. Sand and gravel scraped Sam's head and back below. The branches poked and scratched his front. In this universe there was blackness, wetness, insanity, and no air at all. A whole tree, an immense, dead tree beat him down, away from life.

On the surface the tree's tip held, and the fir turned all the way, top downstream and roots upstream.

Hannibal managed, desperately, to get onto the tree. He saw Esteban on it too, nearer the roots. But the human beings were underneath . . .

The tip swung all the way until it hit a gravelly bar and hung up. Now the roots turned inevitably downstream. Serenely, the tree made its complete circle. Then it plunged through the rest of the channel and flumed into the deep hole below.

Hannibal felt it begin another grand spin, once more to . . .

He dived upstream.

From beneath the water, roots, branches, needles, and three people sailed back into the sunlight and air.

Sam's lungs sucked in a world of air.

The tree bobbed gently.

Sam started to claw his way through the branches toward the boys. Were they both alive? He couldn't get down there. Maybe he saw two figures. Oh, hell, Plácido's chest was bloody.

"Jump!" he hollered, and he did.

He came up between two other figures splashing around in the hole—Hannibal and Esteban.

Being in the hole with a dead fir tree about fifty feet long and a dozen kicking horses was like being in a closet with a buffalo herd. Sam got kicked in a dozen places and got clobbered in one calf. Hollering, he swam madly, one-legged, for the near bank. Then he remembered, got to his feet, fell down from the pain, and went back to swimming toward the bank with one leg.

He turned onto his back, craned his head up far enough to see the boys. Tomás and Esteban were pulling Plácido under the arms toward shallow water.

Sam crawled toward the bank, his face sometimes underwater. Coy dashed into the river toward Sam and then leapt back, over and over.

Horses were thrashing and whinnying insanely. Some were probably hurt. Equipment was scattered through the hole like leaves picked up by a dust devil and flung hither and yon.

All Sam wanted was to find out whether Plácido was bad hurt, and hug the hell out of Tomás.

Twenty-Two

FLAT DOG TOOK over. He dragged both boys onto dry land and started rescuing gear from the river, both what floated and what didn't.

Sam crawled to Tomás and embraced him. "You did great."

Tomás was more interested in Plácido's wound. He watched while Hannibal felt it. The gash lay just under the ribs on the left side. "Can't tell anything about it," Hannibal said.

"Bet he got punctured by a limb stub," said Sam. He'd gotten jabbed by a lot of them himself. His arms and face were scratched and gouged, and his shirt was torn.

Plácido was only half-conscious. They didn't know if he had water in his lungs, if he was hurt in the vitals, or if the pain had a grip on him. Hannibal looked into Esteban's eyes. "Nothing to do but wait and see."

Hannibal examined Sam's leg. Sam looked at Hannibal all over while his friend probed the leg. Hannibal was as scratched and bleeding as any of them. Sam didn't want to remember what it had been like, pinned by the tree on the bottom of the river, but didn't think he could ever forget—his dreams would be haunted.

"Not broken," Hannibal said

Sam tried to put weight on it and fell down immediately. "Broke or not, there's no walking on it."

While he was down, Coy licked him in the face.

Paladin stood nearby, and Sam gave her the hand signal to come to him. She did, and he rubbed her muzzle.

Flat Dog came up and handed Sam The Celt.

He had to resist hugging the rifle. "Thank you, thank you," he said. He hadn't thought he'd ever see his father's flinter again.

For once Sam got the privilege of lying on the bank and watching the others work. He looked sideways at Plácido regularly. The boy wiggle-waggled his head from time to time. Sam didn't think his wound was mortal. Maybe he got thunked on the head by a rock when they were on the bottom.

Julia brought the infants up next to Sam. She nursed Azul while Esperanza played. Over and over the girl crawled across Sam's body, back and forth. Once she sat square on his belly, looked at him, and said, "Papá."

Most of the gear came back out of the river. Some of the powder kegs had busted, and the powder was gone. Other kegs were hauled out and the powder spread to dry. Big twists of tobacco and bundles of blankets were laid out in the sun. Some strings of beads were lost, others recovered. Some bundles of butcher knives came out, some kettles, some awls, and so on. Somehow all the barrels of *aguardiente* survived.

"We can't shoot back," said Hannibal, "but we can die happy."

"We won't know what we've lost until we compare what we have to the master list," said Sam.

"You going to do that?" asked Flat Dog.

"Probably not," said Sam.

"It is what it is," said Hannibal.

Two of the packhorses had broken legs. They struggled into shallow water and stood, heads down.

Flat Dog shot them. Coy howled.

Julia left the kids with Sam and set up two racks. Together she and Flat Dog butchered out the horses—women's work, but not in Julia's world—this was a new style, groping toward a new way to live for all of them, white American, Indian, and Mexican. She built a squaw fire, and they laid the strips of meat out to dry in the sun and wind.

Coy licked Sam's face. Evidently, everyone was reasonably glad to see Sam come out of the river. He was more than reasonably glad to be alive.

Tomás wandered by to look at Plácido. "What you did," said Sam, "you were incredible."

The boy beamed.

"I didn't think you liked Plácido."

Tomás shrugged and walked off.

Sam could never quite figure the boy out.

Later that afternoon Sam swung up onto Paladin and found that the pain of weight on the stirrup was bad.

When he limped back to his lazing place, Plácido had started moving around. Tomás was sitting with him, talking. They actually acted like friends. Sam smiled to himself and plopped down.

Esteban sat on his heels next to them. "Tomás," he said, "you saved Plácido's life. I thank you." Now both boys were looking seriously at Esteban. Sam thought maybe Tomás was beginning to understand: When you travel with a man, he sides you and you side him. No matter how hard it gets.

"Tomás," he said, "I want to give you something to show my gratitude. Something big. You think about it and tell me what you want."

Man and boy looked at each other.

Sam was proud of Tomás.

As Esteban started to get up, Tomás said nicely, "I don't have to think. I know."

"Just tell me," said Esteban, and he squatted back down.

"I want Paladin's colt."

When they headed north two days later, Tomás had the colt on a line, teaching him to lead. Esteban had surrendered some dollars of his wages for the colt. Sam also gave Tomás the pony he was riding, as a reward for what he did in the river.

Tomás grinned at him and spoke in English. He chose English whenever he wanted to be sure he was understood, or restate his point, as when he said from time to time, "I'm smart."

Now he said, "I teach him like Paladin, come when I whistle. Later I teach you, come when I whistle."

Twenty-Three

RENDEZVOUS 1828 FELT to Sam like the doldrums.

Part of it was outside things. There was no main supply train that year. Smith, Jackson & Sublette didn't bring one—Bill Sublette had gone to St. Louis with last summer's furs and come straight back with supplies, which arrived in November and got distributed throughout the winter. Normally, when the train arrived, so did enough whiskey for a hundred and more trappers and several hundred Indians. That usually turned rendezvous into a carnival.

Also, Jedediah Smith didn't show up. Nor did any word arrive from him. Diah had left the door open—he might or might not get to rendezvous, since he was heading north out of California—but it worried Sam.

He thought back over his years with Diah and wondered what had happened. Fifteen men under his leadership got killed on the sand bar below the Arikara villages. Another ten lost their lives on the bank of the Colorado. In both cases, Diah escaped by the skinny-skin-skin. Sam had seen both fights, which were more like slaughters. He wondered if Jedediah's luck had finally run out.

Sam felt maybe the doldrums came from inside, though, and he didn't know why.

Everybody was fine, his own leg no longer sore, Plácido's chest healed. Mountain luck, when you thought of what happened to them crossing that river.

Business was good for the Morgan outfit, as the men called it. His tent and another small one run by Joshua Pilcher, the old Missouri Fur Company partisan, were the only ones open for trading. Sam, Hannibal, and Flat Dog sold most of the horses in their herd—the animals had walked for four months to get here—at good prices. The trade goods they'd picked up in Santa Fe sold quickly too, what was left after the river took its bite. What booze they and Pilcher had was quickly gone, and no trapper cared what he paid for it.

The talk of the trade blankets was what the Britishers were doing, or rather how the Hudson's Bay Company was poaching on American territory. The Oregon country, as everybody knew, was a joint occupation with the British—the whole Columbia River area, rich in furs. The Americans wanted to push that way. Those damned Britishers were trapping all the Snake River territory thin, so going west didn't shine for the Americans. Damn Britishers, they claimed everything by prior right, saying they'd been there first. When Americans saw HBC stamped on their property, they took to calling the company Here Before Christ.

When Sam and Hannibal closed the trade blanket for the day and were on their knees putting strings of beads back in their boxes, Hannibal said, "Smith, Jackson & Sublette are going to Flathead country. I want to go with them."

Sam looked up at him quick. Coy lay down and squirmed into the grass, looking from one to the other.

"I want to see Flathead Post, the lake, maybe even work with HBC for a while."

"Here Before Christ. O wise one." Sam said, keeping his voice as light as he could, "You want to see everything."

"That's true," said Hannibal. "One day I'm going to take a trade caravan down the Chihuahua Trail, see the city and the copper mines down below, maybe even Mexico City."

"You go, go, go."

"Vidi, vici, cepi iucunditas."

Sam knew *veni, vidi, vici*—I came, I saw, I conquered—but this was a new one. "What does that mean?"

"I came, I saw, I had fun."

Sam chuckled, but he was pretending.

"So," Hannibal went on, "I'll go to Crow country with you and then on to Flathead country."

Sam nodded.

"Now I better check on Brownie and Paladin."

With that he was off. Coy thumped his tail, looked after Hannibal, started to get up and go, but stayed. His eyes rose to Sam, uncertain.

"You're the only one who has been on all of it with me," Sam said.

When everything was put away in the tent, he just sat and petted Coy. "I am down in spirits," he told the coyote. He mulled. Everything changed all the time. He'd lost Meadowlark and Blue Medicine Horse to death, Third Wing too. Gideon Poorboy had lost his leg below the knee and decided to stay in California. Just this season Sam had started to California with a score of men and left half of them on the riverbank at the Mojave villages. He'd fallen in with Grumble, Sumner, and Abby, but they were off in different directions now. Sam and Hannibal had picked up Flat Dog, Julia, Esperanza, and Azul, but Robber and Galbraith came and then dropped out. Jedediah had taken his entire brigade to kingdom come, or maybe north to the Britishers, whichever he found first.

Sam was glad he had Flat Dog, Julia, Esperanza, and Azul, damned glad, but he was losing people, one after another . . .

He made himself get up and walk around, Coy at his heels.

The good part of rendezvous was seeing old friends, and Sam felt good greeting Tom Fitzpatrick, Jim Beckwourth, Jim Bridger, and a bunch of others. He and Fitz were mates from the first year, when they were in Diah's first brigade. Beckwourth spent a winter in the Crow camp with Sam, the winter he courted Meadowlark, still hard to think about. Bridger, well, Bridger got himself a bad name his first season in the mountains—went off and left Hugh Glass to die, even took his rifle and his possibles. But since that time Jim had proved to be a man who knew what way the stick floated, as they said, and had a reputation as the best storyteller of them all.

Hannibal fell in beside Sam and Coy, Tomás trailing him by a step. "Let's show this boy how much fun rendezvous is tonight," he said to Sam.

"I am not a boy," said Tomás. Since they got to rendezvous, he'd been speaking English all the time. "I am smart."

"Let's find him some company," said Sam.

The Delaware got a lascivious gleam in his eye. "Provide him some beads and vermilion, for the ladies?"

Tomás cackled. He'd heard about Indian women in the willows.

Sam blushed, and knew it. Blushing always made him self-conscious about his white hair. "No, tonight the boys will be telling stories, singing songs."

"Dancing," said Hannibal.

Tomás cackled again.

"Get your mind off that," said Sam. "Or at least Tomás's mind."

They squeezed in around a fire next to Jim Beckwourth. The big mulatto said, "You hear about our scrape with the Blackfeet just coming into camp here?"

"No," said Sam.

"Them Blackfeet," said someone. Everyone was sick and tired of the Blackfeet. Those Indians had been hostile since John Colter fought with them twenty years ago. The American beaver men had made friends with almost all the Indians except the Blackfeet, and were free to trap any country except Blackfoot.

"You want me to tell it?" said Robert Campbell. "I'll tell it straight." Campbell was an Irishman and a brigade leader, capable and serious about his business.

"Straight ain't no way to tell a story," said Beckwourth, and he launched in. "Just a few days ago we was camped maybe eighteen miles above the lake. Cap'n here, he finds the cook facedown and growing Blackfoot arrows out of his back, so he gets us fast up to a place where there's a spring and some rocks we can crouch behind. Me, I don't like hiding in any rocks, I like to go at my enemy out front and hard, but . . . We got to fighting, them shooting at us, us shooting at them. In the long run, though, it was no good, they being five or six hundred—"

"—maybe half that," put in Campbell—

"—and us being maybe thirty. After about half a day I saw someone had to do something."

"*You* did?" said Campbell.

"Cap'n, I'm just giving you a preview of how my grandchildren will receive this story, except maybe the grandchildren that are Blackfoot." He threw a lascivious look around the circle. "I mean to top at least one chief's daughter in every tribe."

Tomás giggled.

"The only thing to do, as I was saying, was ride like the hounds of hell to the main camp here and get help. So, me and Calhoun—"

"—it was Ortega and myself," said Campbell—

"—we took two of the fastest horses and whipped them like banshee devils through the line of Blackfeet. Arrows and lead balls flew thick as hail—the angels themselves must have protected us—and in an hour or so we was here to the lake and roused the men, trapper and Injun alike, and back we rode like a gathering thunderstorm.

"When them Blackfeet saw us, they skedaddled."

"Actually," said Campbell drily, "they'd already left."

"How many men were killed?" said Tomás, his voice throbbing.

Sam couldn't believe the kid had put words out in this crowd, English words.

"One of ours," said Campbell, "and three wounded, and half a dozen horses dead."

"About a score of theirs dead," said Beckwourth with a grin.

"Three or four," said Campbell, "and the same wounded."

"Them Blackfeet," Tomás pressed on, "are they bad Injuns?"

A handful of men said at the same time, "The worst."

"Let me have a small . . . mouth of that," Tomás said to Sam.

"Sip," said Sam. "Or mouthful."

"Thanks."

He handed Tomás the whiskey cup, and the boy drank. "Thanks for the sip," he said.

Tomás was serious about learning English, and he *was* smart.

"Give us a yarn, Gabe." That was what they called Jim Bridger now.

Sam was glad Tomás had a chance to hear one of these stories.

Bridger began in an easy voice, "Me and some un the boys come up Henry's Fork one spring night, time it was nigh getting dark. I knowed the Yellowstone country some, but I got turned around and didn't rightly know where we was. So we stopped along a little crick and made camp in the dark.

"Come mornin', I woke up and saw as fine a place as ever stroked the eye. A big hole, with thick grass reaching off to timbered hills, and the prettiest little stream runnin' through her. Best of all, I seen a bull elk grazin' not a hundred steps off.

" 'Meat,' says I, and rises and throws up Betsy. I shot—and that elk didn't even notice, just kept grazin'. Now Betsy, she shoots center, sure, and I couldn't piece things together in my mind. I crept gentlelike mebbe fifty steps closer, lines up Betsy, and lets fly agin. Same result.

" 'Mebbe that elk is wearing armor,' says I. 'It is sure enough deaf.'

"Riled up, I walks straight over to the elk, raises Betsy like a war club, and swings the barrel right onto the critter's head.

"Old Betsy bounces off harmless.

"Well, I'll be.

"I grabbed the damned elk by the antlers and was about to twist when I realized—these antlers is stone. I kicked the elk and like to broke my toes. Whole damn elk is stone.

"Then I recollects—Black Harris and his story of the putrefied forest. He took a piece of downed tree to Fort Atkinson, and a Dutchman scientist there told him it was putrefied, done turned to stone.

"Now I looks around and sees that our horses are nibblin' at the grass, but their knees are shakin'. I reach down and feels of the grass, and the blades are putrefied. I reach up and feel the leaves of a aspen, and the leaves are putrefied.

"Suddenly, I notice. There ain't no birds making music. I can see birds, but I can't hear 'em.

"I lifts old Betsy again and knocks the nearest jay right off the branch. When I go over and pick up the pieces, I find out even the birds is putrefied. And I can't hear 'em 'cause their songs is putrefied!

" 'Boys!' I holler out. 'Get up! Let's go! This place don't shine!'

"Shortly we is packed up and headed out, afore the horses starve to death and us with 'em.

"But this country, it has ahold of us. We ride north and find the big canyon of the Yellerstone in our way. East, big canyon of the Yellerstone in our path. South, same canyon. West, same thing. We are surrounded by the wide, deep canyon of the Yellowstone River, and no way out.

"Then I gets an idea. Seems good, but I figure I better give 'er a try first, this idea being on the wild side. I backs my horse up a hundred paces, gives her a good kick, and when we get to the canyon edge, I lets out a war cry and reins her up to jump. She does, and pretty as a wildflower in June, we just floats over the whole canyon of that Yellerstone and sets down on the other side soft as cottonwood fluff drifting to the ground.

"Now all the boys get the idea. They back up, stampede the packhorses, and come riding behind 'em hell for leather. At the canyon rim they all sail into the air—horses like wingspread eagles, you shoulda seen it!—and they all light right beside me on the far rim.

"They was all happy to be out'n the trap of that putrefied forest, but they was a mite amazed. 'Gabe,' they says, 'that was right smart, but how did you figure it out?'

"Says I, 'Well, everything in that place was putrefied, animals, grass, leaves, birds, and even the birds' song, so I realized—the law of gravity must be putrefied too!' "

The whole circle broke into appreciative chuckles.

Sam got up and wandered, Coy at his heels. Off somewhere he could hear fiddling, which meant dancing. He had no desire to dance, no desire for a woman, not when he felt Paloma so near behind him and Meadowlark's parents so close in front. But he wanted music, and he had his tin whistle in his hand.

Fiddlin' Red waved Sam over to the log where he was perched. "This old hand," Red announced to the assembly, "last year this time he was starting to shine on that whistle. Give us a tune, Sam, what will it be?"

Sam said, "The Never-Ending Song of Jedediah Smith."

This was the song Robert Evans and Sam and Sumner and all the men of the first California brigade had written together in tribute to their captain. It was a lively affair in 6/8 time, good to dance to, and Sam took it fast.

Lots of men sashayed Indian women around, but no one sang. Sam said, "Don't you remember the words?"

He let Fiddlin' Red take the tune this time, and he sang the words himself.

We set out from Salt Lake, not knowing the track
Whites, Spanyards and Injuns, and even a black
Our captain was Diah, a man of great vision
Our dream Californy, and beaver our mission.

"Now comes the chorus," he cried. "Join in." Coy yipped twice.

Captain Smith was a wayfarin' man
A wanderin' man was he
He led us 'cross the desert sands
And on to the sweet blue sea.

No voice lifted up with Sam's. He plunged onward.

We rode through the deserts, our throats were so dry
If we didn't find water, we surely would die
The captain saw a river, our hearts came down thud
The river was dry, and we got to drink mud.

After this verse, though, he got discouraged. Not a single voice joined in. Didn't they remember the captain, and admire him and the outfit that was the first to go to California? He gave them one more verse with the whistle alone and abandoned music for the night. He felt unaccountably sad, and lonely.

He stopped behind one circle. The boys were playing old sledge, and for a moment Sam thought Tomás was playing. Then he saw that Tomás didn't have a hand and was only watching over one man's shoulder.

A heart was led, and Tomás's player followed with a lower heart.

"Why didn't you trump it?" whispered Tomás.

All four players shushed him.

Sam didn't like this sight. The boy had been fascinated by Grumble's skill with cards.

Tomás said something softly to the player, and the man handed him his whiskey cup. Tomás sipped.

Coy eased up and sat next to Tomás. He gave Sam a begging look.

"Tomás," said Sam, "bedtime."

The boy threw Sam an angry look and then shook his head slowly. "I'm having fun."

Sam walked off and Coy followed. "It's none of my business," he told the coyote.

Coy whimpered.

In the wee hours somewhere Tomás crept into the tent and stretched out on his blankets between Sam and Hannibal. As soon as he lay down, he vomited where he lay.

"God help us," said Sam. He marched the boy to the lake and cleaned him up. Except that Tomás vomited again. They moved knee deep into the lake and Sam held an arm around his waist. Tomás vomited again. And then one more time that seemed to be the last.

Coy stood on the bank, pranced, and squealed.

Sam decided no words were necessary and held the wobbly Tomás on the way back to the tent. Hannibal had moved all three sets of blankets outside—the night was clear.

The boy passed out like a match in a gust of wind.

"Not grown-up yet," said Hannibal.

"Too near and yet too far."

SAM WOKE UP with his mind a muddle. He'd felt out of sorts the entire rendezvous. He could still smell Tomás's throw-up. Everything was askew, and nothing felt right.

He sat up to look around and saw Bell Rock standing a few steps away, gazing at him.

Bell Rock! And behind him four other members of the Kit Foxes.

Sam stood up. Suddenly everything was changed. He must enter a world of Crow customs, Crow manners. This was a time to do things right.

He introduced Hannibal and Tomás briefly and said, "I will take you to Flat Dog's lodge." *Your kinsman, the man you are looking for.*

He could see the questions in their eyes, but it was not his place to speak. In the Crow way Meadowlark was a member of Flat Dog's family, and Bell Rock's. Her husband wasn't her relative, and a relative must bring the news.

They walked to Julia and Flat Dog's tipi, Tomás and Coy trailing. Sam felt an irrational flicker of anger at Tomás.

Flat Dog and Julia were sitting around the outside fire, eating deer meat. The two children played busily. Flat Dog stood up immediately, strip of tenderloin in hand. He looked at his relative and the other Foxes. Sam knew what he was thinking: *This isn't how things are supposed to be done, and now there's no way to do them right.*

Flat Dog motioned for the visitors to sit down, and they did, Tomás next to Sam.

He addressed the five Crow visitors with a thick tongue, "My sister is no longer living."

The Crows were struck silent with the knowledge: *A member of my family is dead—a woman of my village is dead.*

They thought of their responsibilities, how they would inform her parents and all the people of the village, and the grieving that must ensue.

Sam thought, *This is my life. For better and right now damn well for worse.* He reminded himself of correctness.

Azul squalled, and Julia gave him one of her breasts. Esperanza played outside the circle of grown-ups, picking up ants, chewing stems of grass, and letting out the occasional war cry.

At last Flat Dog said to the visitors, "She died giving birth. This is her daughter, Esperanza."

Here was the intolerable contradiction. A life taken, a life given.

Sam knew he must make a gift of horses for the life taken. He wondered how the new life would be received—*My daughter.* Except that Esperanza was not his daughter, not as the Crows saw it—she belonged to Meadowlark's family. Already, in a practical way, she belonged to Flat Dog and Julia. Sam didn't count. His heart twisted like a rag being wrung out.

Flat Dog said, "This is my wife Julia."

Crow eyes took in the woman and the knowledge.

"This is our son Azul."

Eyes smiled at the gift of a new life.

Everyone sat without speaking further. The obligations, mourning and rejoicing—the responsibilities, the grief to come—all was overwhelming.

Sam was swamped with memories. Bell Rock had befriended him, and was his guide to the Crow way of understanding the world. This medicine man introduced him to the sweat lodge, made his pipe, and dedicated it. Most of all, Bell Rock sponsored the sun dance that Sam gave after the death of Blue Medicine Horse. Bell Rock was Sam's spiritual father.

Bell Rock did not have to tell Sam why he and his companions had come to rendezvous. Two years ago Sam had run off with Meadowlark against her parents' will. Red Roan, son of the chief, and her relatives came to Sam and Meadowlark's lodge, where they had spent a few idyllic days absorbed in each other, and took her back by force. After a few days she told Sam that she loved him, but he had to leave the village.

He got out, surrendering Meadowlark in his heart.

At rendezvous a couple of months later, here came Flat Dog escorting Meadowlark. She had run away, and her brother supported her gesture of the heart. Incredible. She and Sam got married in a mountain man ceremony. They were deliriously happy. They went to California so she could see the ocean. And then . . .

An interminable time passed in silence. Finally, Flat Dog asked if the visitors would accept food, and Bell Rock said they would.

When they had eaten, Sam said, "I will go with you to the village, present their granddaughter to Gray Hawk and Needle, and make a gift of horses." In other words, *I will face up to what I have done like a man.*

Bell Rock looked at him for a long moment. Then he said, with sorrow in his voice, "Red Roan has already made a pledge. If you come back to the camp, he will kill you."

Sam tried not to let his surprise show.

"He didn't even know . . ."

Bell Rock held Sam's eyes. "No one will stop him." Meaning, *I cannot help you.*

Everyone stared at these awful facts.

Sam looked at Flat Dog. The Crow raised his eyes. "I am your friend." He took a deep breath and let it go. "I offer to fight Red Roan for you."

They all knew why. The white man would never win that kind of fight.

Sam said only one word. "No."

He reached to one side and rubbed Coy's ears. He stared into space. *The village is against me. Even Flat Dog and Bell Rock cannot defend me. I am finished there.*

SAM AND HANNIBAL prepared for the fight.

They talked first, but that was short.

Hannibal—"Why go there at all?"

Sam—"I have to face up to what I did."

They looked at each other. Going to the village and refusing to fight would never work. Sam would be branded a coward.

Then any man in the village might attack him from behind any tree at any time. An arrow would whiz and . . .

"Tell me about Red Roan."

"Most Crow men are tall and rangy. He's taller and rangier. He's a war leader—*the* war leader in that village—and has lots of coups. He's cocky as hell. Arrogant."

"And what does he think about you?"

"He thinks I'm an ignorant white man who got his cousin killed. And stole his girl."

Hannibal pondered. "What are his advantages?"

"Experience with hand weapons." This would be fought lance, war club, knife, or shield, no firearms, no ability to kill at a remote distance. A face-to-face confrontation, and a true battle of honor. "And he's mostly had the upper hand with me."

"Tell."

Sam was embarrassed to recount the stories. Red Roan courted Meadowlark while Sam skulked in the shadows and watched. Red Roan set up Sam to be humiliated in an arrow-shooting contest with his nephews. And when Sam and Meadowlark ran away for their honeymoon, Red Roan came, snatched Meadowlark away, and marched Sam back to camp as a prisoner.

"He's got mind domination on you," Hannibal said. "He's made you think he's stronger than you."

Sam started to protest, thought, and fell silent. "What do I do about that?"

"Awe him," said Hannibal. "Awe everyone."

So they set out to do what was necessary. First, they traded for a lance, a war club, and a shield made from the thick skin of a buffalo bull's head. Among the Shoshones Sam found a lance and stone war club that felt good. He started carrying them everywhere he went, to get used to the heft and balance. He also practiced all afternoon each day. Throwing a lance at trees didn't seem particularly odd, but bashing them with the war club was very strange. He knew his new skills with his weapon would count for little against the experienced Red Roan.

Second, in the mornings they made some special preparations that might make all the difference. Very special. Before long they were ready, and told Flat Dog so.

Flat Dog had finished the business for the three of them. He sold the last trade goods they wanted to let go of, keeping some back for gifts to Meadowlark's family and for trade to the other Crows. He dealt with Tom Fitzpatrick and got company credit for their share of the beaver they'd traded for. This credit would last Flat Dog, Sam, and Hannibal a good while.

And they got a surprise. Jim Beckwourth asked if he could go along with them. "I like the Crows," he said. Sam remembered that during the winter he spent in Rides Twice's village, the mulatto had had an active social life. They agreed— another hand going to Crow country would be good.

The last evening Sam, Hannibal, and Flat Dog decided to divide up the rest of the horseflesh, twenty animals. When the three got to the herd, Tomás tagging along, Paladin came trotting over to Sam, her colt behind her. Sam spoke one word, and Coy jumped up on Paladin's back and stood up on his hind legs. Tomás burst into laughter—he always loved that trick.

When each man had picked out stallions, mares, colts, and fillies, they started back toward their tents. Sam had picked out four to give to Meadowlark's parents, the obligatory gift. "We're well arranged," Hannibal said.

That did it for Sam. He turned to Tomás. "What are you planning to do, go with Esteban and Plácido?"

The Taoseños had signed on with a group of free trappers intending to trap South Park, the country around Pikes Peak. Then they'd winter in Taos.

The boy shook his head no.

Sam indicated Hannibal. "Go to Flathead country with him?"

Same shake of head.

"Well?"

"I want to be with you."

Sam was flabbergasted. Flat Dog and Hannibal seemed kind of tickled.

Sam waited until they sat at the fire in front of Julia's lodge.

He began with, "In two weeks I may not be alive. Probably won't be."

Tomás looked the other way, but Sam thought his eyes were teary.

"Talk real with me," Sam said. "I probably won't be alive."

Tomás turned to face Sam with a hard expression. "So? I don't have nobody now, I won't have nobody then."

The men looked at each other and at Tomás.

The talk took all evening, with Sam, Tomás, Hannibal, Flat Dog, and Julia. Esperanza toddled around and played in the dirt. Azul crawled around and sometimes ate dirt. The adults talked. Tomás didn't get to say much, and his sullen look didn't help his cause.

In the end it all came down to—well, why not?

"All right, you can hang around. If Red Roan doesn't kill me."

Hannibal said, "If Sam's dead, I'll be glad to have you along."

But Sam had to ask Tomás straight. "Why do you want to be with me?"

"Too soon to separate a colt from its mother," Tomás said with a crinkly smile.

This was a little fraud. Paladin's colt could suckle any of eight or ten mares.

Sam frowned. "Look, I'm a Crow." This was half true. "My daughter is a Crow. I'm a member of the Kit Foxes. I speak the language. I carry the sacred pipe. Don't be fooled by my skin."

"Or your hair?" Tomás asked with a sly smile.

Sam tugged at his white locks. He thought about it. He realized what Tomás's fantasy was. "I think you don't understand. If I survive, I'm not going to be a trapper and roam the country. I'll live in another Crow village. I'll be a warrior like the other young men, and a buffalo hunter."

"¿Verdad?" When Tomás got surprised, he slipped back into Spanish sometimes.

"Yes, true. I want to see my daughter. If I live with another village, I will. Pretty often. Maybe I'll make another family. I like the way the Crows live."

Flat Dog said, "Tomás, I think you like the trapping life. You have no idea if you'll like the Crow life."

Tomás glared at him.

Sam reached out and picked up Esperanza. Coy tapped his tail—maybe he was jealous. "I left Pennsylvania," Sam said, "and found a new home. I made a new family. Now the only family I have is Esperanza." He could hardly believe he was saying this, barely even knew he thought it. "But she's my family, not yours. Why would you want to be around my one little kid?"

Tomás jumped up and ran off. Sam couldn't tell, because he was so quick, whether he was in tears or in a rage.

Nobody spoke for a while. Sam looked at them guiltily.

Flat Dog said, "You have almost no family."

"And she's an infant," Julia said.

"But Tomás," Flat Dog said, "he doesn't have any."

Sam didn't see the boy again until he woke up the next morning. Tomás lay right there, between Hannibal and Sam, looking at Sam.

"I want to go with you," he said. "I bet I can get a Crow girlfriend."

Sam nodded. "Glad to have you."

Tomás grinned.

Coy growled. Sam wondered what the devil that meant.

Twenty-Four

ACROSS THE MOUNTAIN to the Siskadee, over South Pass, down Wind River and through Wind River Canyon. Now they had to do some guesswork. August. Flat Dog, Bell Rock, and the Foxes thought the village would still be up against the mountains. Not until the next moon would they go downriver to join the other villages for the big autumn buffalo hunt.

So the party went up Owl Creek and over the divide to Goose Creek. Sam was saying these names to himself like a litany. Though he barely knew them, really, he had camped on them with Rides Twice's village, he had courted Meadowlark on them, he had given a sun dance on one of them, and for him they were legendary.

He was nervous. At the evening camp on Goose Creek, Flat Dog shot a deer. He was at home now, a man in his own country, and he acted like it. He was expansive and at ease. All the Crows were.

At breakfast, while they roasted fresh deer meat on sticks, Flat Dog said, "What's wrong?"

Sam didn't answer. Julia kept her head down. The two children whined.

"Everybody's on edge," said Beckwourth. "Julia, she meets her new in-laws. She finds out what it's like to live where there ain't no one to empty the chamber pots, not even any chamber pots."

"I gave that up long ago," said Julia. "I wipe dirty baby bottoms all day every day."

"Wouldn't be right if you weren't uneasy." Beckwourth tossed a big grin at Tomás, and handed the boy a strip of tenderloin. Tomás took it and stuffed it into his mouth.

"This boy, he's got a big story, hardly anybody treat him right. What he's gone through . . ."

Sam was about to give Jim a warning look, but the mulatto stopped himself. "Remember, boy, you need someone to side you, I will.

"Now Sam, he's another case. He's just plain afraid. He . . ."

"Jim, that's enough," said Sam.

Beckwourth opened his mouth again.

"I said enough."

Hannibal smiled at Sam.

When they got packed and started for the Gray Bull River, no one's mood was good except Jim's and Hannibal's.

THE VILLAGE WAS right where the Crows expected, where the Gray Bull River came out of the mountain and plunged across the plain toward the Big Horn. They camped on top of the last hill above the camp, and Flat Dog waved his blanket as a signal to the camp. Now people knew the party came bearing news of a death. Sam could think of nothing but the time he and Flat Dog had done this before, reporting the loss of Blue Medicine Horse. It was unbearable.

In due time three Foxes came out. Flat Dog told them the news very factually. Though they were curious about why Meadowlark had gone far west to the big-water-everywhere, they did not ask questions about the death itself. Everyone knew death in childbirth. Soon they and the other Foxes carried the report to the village.

Needle would grieve wildly and cut her hair off, Sam knew, and her mourning would not end until her hair was back to normal length. Gray Hawk might cut a joint off his little finger. But mourning for a passing in the normal course of life—that would not be like mourning for the killing of a young person by an enemy. And the family would carry the grieving, not the entire village.

Sam's task was not to grieve for Meadowlark, not any longer. He and Robert Evans dug themselves graves in the sand of the great desert west of Salt Lake on a blistering afternoon, and he left the blackness of his heart in that hole.

Bell Rock walked back up the hill. With a grave face he said to Sam, "Gray Hawk refuses your gift of horses."

Fine. No surprise. Done.

Sam had one job now—to make himself ready for Red Roan.

THE EVENING FELT never-ending. All through the lingering twilight Red Roan circled the camp, chanting out his plaint like the village crier. "The white-haired man is a coward. The man with white hair is a ghost." This was a great insult. "The white-haired man has brought us only grief. The white man has brought death into our lodge. I challenge him to a fight tomorrow. I challenge him to meet me, the son of the chief of the village of Rides Twice. I challenge the barbarian to come against a war leader of the Absaroka nation and fight until one of us is dead."

He beat out these words over and over, like music to march to. A funeral march.

Hannibal said, "Let's get out of here."

Though Sam couldn't make out the words from here, he knew what was being said. His mind flitted to Gray Hawk and Needle. Like a raven perched high on their lodge poles, he tried to hear what was being said in their lodge, imagine what was going on in their hearts and minds. Nothing good, he knew. Twice now he had brought them death, and they would return to him only death.

A few people in the entire village, perhaps, bore him goodwill. Julia and Flat Dog, Bell Rock and his wife. All other hearts, he knew, were set hard against him.

"Let's get going," Hannibal said again.

Sam got up, The Celt in hand, ready to follow. So did Tomás and Coy.

Hannibal led the way to the river. The three of them sat in the shallows, naked. Coy watched them from the bank and whined. Sam didn't know why Tomás wanted to be with him tonight, but he didn't care.

In the distance Red Roan's caterwauling stopped. Sam smiled at Hannibal. "Flat Dog has done it." Sam asked his friend to go to Red Roan, after his foe had sounded off sufficiently, and tell him that Sam would meet him at dawn.

Sam and Hannibal talked about that easily, comfortably. Then they talked about other things. The two men told stories of their youth, memories of particular pleasure. Hannibal talked about gathering berries with his mother. Sam spoke of wrestling with his younger brother Coy. Hannibal told of his father reading Ovid to him aloud, translating the thoughts into awkward English, and then reading the Latin again, sonorously. Sam recalled his mother's apple pies spiced with cinnamon, left in the warming oven so he could go back for a second piece before bed. On and on they talked, remembering only joys, or transforming sorrows into a kind of joy through the alchemy of understanding.

Sam noticed that Tomás sat fixed on them, completely absorbed, but saying nothing. Sam didn't know why Tomás cared about these stories—he didn't know what stories Tomás himself might have to tell—but tonight he didn't care. He was simply enjoying his own life.

Eventually, they got very tired, arose, wrapped themselves in blankets, and slept on the bank of the Gray Bull River, the water shur-shurring by.

Sam rose with the first hint of light. He and Hannibal made a few preparations. Tomás watched, and Sam could not read the boy's face.

Eventually, the people assembled, a great circle in front of the lodges, every man, woman, and child come to see what might happen.

With his friends Sam walked to the circle with a blanket wrapped over his head, as many of the women came. Hannibal carried his weapons.

Red Roan rode his warhorse into the center of this circle, stripped to a breechcloth, lance in one hand, war club in the other, the shield on the forearm above the club. Again he began to call out the words of challenge.

Sam was ready, and he didn't want to indulge his foe.

He dropped the blanket and reached for the weapons.

"Everything is a roll of the dice," said Hannibal. "Go for it whole hog."

Sam chuckled. He looked into the eyes of his friend. He set the club and shield on the ground and stuck the lance into the earth. Then he turned and stepped into the circle, excited.

Exclamations burst out of the crowd. The white-haired man had come without his mount and without his weapons. People couldn't believe it. An unarmed man on foot stood no chance. Red Roan would ride him down and stomp him under his warhorse's feet.

Sam walked around the circle in the direction the sun went, his eyes on Red Roan. When he started to see impatience on his enemy's face, he whistled.

Paladin galloped into the arena and toward Sam. Hubbub ran through the crowd. The mare was naked of saddle, naked of bridle. Did the white-haired man intend to ride her like this?

As she neared him, Sam whirled one arm from the shoulder and Paladin galloped past him and around the entire arena. Children exclaimed and pointed at the beautiful animal.

This time she stopped beside Sam, and he vaulted onto her back. Paladin went into her show-ring canter, gentle and rhythmic. Sam felt a rush of elation at being on her again. He thought, *By God this is the way to go out!*

Immediately, he was on his feet, riding bareback and standing. He began to sing to Paladin the song that helped them feel the motion together, the lope of horse and—now!—the somersaults of the man. Singing at the top of his voice, Sam leapt into the air, somersaulted, landed with both feet on Paladin's rump, and somersaulted again. Round and round he went, rump to air to rump, bawling out his ecstasy.

The children shouted with glee, and the women covered their gasps with their hands.

Sam could have bounded forever.

Red Roan ended the display with his war cry. Screeching, he spurred his horse directly at Paladin.

Sam dropped into a forked seat and cried to Paladin for speed. Red Roan had speed, but not enough to catch Paladin quickly, or perhaps at all. As Sam rode by his lance, he yanked it out of the ground, turned Paladin hard into the center of the ring, and faced his enemy.

Startled, Red Roan stopped. Sam laughed and hollered in English, "No way can you ever have seen anything like this. What on heaven and earth am I going to do next?"

He charged.

Lance level, eyes on Red Roan's breast, he goaded Paladin forward at full speed.

Red Roan reacted late, but he reacted. He raised his war club and spurred his mount. He would teach the foolish, unshielded white man. He would get even for the white man's stupid antics, for the way he got the people—Crows of Red Roan's own village—to admire him. He would flick the lance aside and smash the white man to a pulp.

At the last moment Sam kneed Paladin, and she swerved in front of the warhorse.

Red Roan found his club on the wrong side! He tried to screw his body around for a swing across his mount, but was too late.

Sam whirled Paladin hard left and rammed her straight into horse and rider.

For a moment Sam's world was topsy-turvy.

Red Roan's horse went down screaming, the warrior under it.

Paladin regained her balance. Sam wheeled her in a desperate turn and bellowed for speed.

Red Roan got to his feet, limping, bewildered.

Sam thundered down on him, lance poised.

At the last instant Red Roan dodged to Sam's left. Sam hurled the lance, but Paladin's neck kept him from changing his aim fully. The lance missed and sank into the earth, its butt quivering.

Sam ran Paladin straight over Red Roan, human and equine limbs flying.

Quickly, Sam brought Paladin full circle and sprinted down on Red Roan again.

Red Roan tried to gain his feet enough for a swing. Sam edged Paladin to the off side, then brought her back and bumped Paladin's shoulder into the warrior hard. He went head over heels, and the war club went flying.

Now Sam circled Paladin wide, watching the stumbling figure. He jumped to his feet on Paladin's back and spoke to her. She sprinted toward Red Roan, who stood gape-mouthed. Just before Paladin ran over him, Red Roan slid sideways.

Sam leapt and kicked Red Roan full in the chest with both feet. Each man landed on his back, but Sam was up like a flash.

Red Roan barely stirred.

Sam pounced on him and sat on his belly.

They looked at each other, wide-eyed.

Red Roan squeezed out a gargly laugh. "You lost your weapon, white man. What are you going to do, scratch my eyes out?"

Sam reached for the belt around his waist, the one that seemed to hold up his breechcloth, and popped the buckle. In front of Red Roan's face he held as sharp and fine a knife as had ever been smithed.

Darkness entered Red Roan's eyes. He gazed at Sam. Finally, he said, "Kill me, white man."

Sam saw moccasins and looked up. Hannibal stood there. So did Gray Hawk. So did Rides Twice, his face grave.

Hannibal nodded yes. So did Gray Hawk.

Red Roan said to his father, "I want to die."

Rides Twice turned away.

Straight and hard Sam drove the blade deep into Red Roan's

throat. Blood bubbled around the handle. Sam drew the blade out, and blood welled.

A long rasp of death eased from Red Roan's mouth.

Sam put the buckle back, looked around, and heard.

Dozens of Crow women were trilling for him.

Scores were silent, glaring.

He walked off. He bent down and petted Coy. He looked into the eyes of Tomás. He felt . . . amazed, incredulous—words couldn't get near it.

Hannibal touched him on the shoulder,

Sam stood back up.

"You were astounding," said Hannibal.

Sam just nodded.

"We'd better get out of here."

"I've got something to do," said Sam.

"I'll get your back," said Hannibal.

Sam walked around the circle of villagers, sunwise. He weaved a little as he went. About a third of the way around he saw Flat Dog and Julia. He padded up to them.

"Thank you, brother," he said to Flat Dog.

"You are welcome, brother."

Sam reached to Julia and took Esperanza. He held her at arm's length and looked at her. The little girl wiggle-waggled her head.

"Hi, Papa," he said in English.

"Hi, Papa," she said, and chuckled.

"Come along too, please," he said to Flat Dog and Julia.

Sam held her close, and the five of them made their way on around the circle. Sam looked at the faces of people he knew. His friend Bell Rock and his wife. Owl Woman, his enemy but a good woman. Her husband Yellow Horn, his enemy and a dangerous man. The boys he competed with once, when they won all his arrows.

At last he came to Gray Hawk and Needle. Gray Hawk stood rigid, his face fixed. Needle held her blanket wrapped over her head against the morning chill.

He looked into their eyes, wanting to be sure he didn't miss anything. Gray Hawk's were dark, impenetrable. Needle's . . . he wasn't sure. Perhaps he saw a hint of warmth there.

He held Esperanza out at arm's length. "I love you," he said. "What I'm about to do, it hurts, but it's for you."

He held her now to Needle. "This is your granddaughter," he said, "Esperanza. I am alone, and a child needs a mother. I give her to her uncle Flat Dog, to her aunt Julia, to you, her grandparents, and to all the people of this village to raise in a good way."

Needle took the child and clutched her close.

Esperanza turned in her arms. "Papa?" she said and reached toward Sam.

He quelled the pain and turned away.

Sam and Hannibal walked the rest of the way around the circle. Sam looked at the faces. When he got back to his blankets and to Tomás, he said, "Now we can go."

Twenty-Five

THEY RODE TOWARD the Yellowstone country. Hannibal had heard about the hot springs and wanted to sit in them. Beckwourth told wild stories about how there were devils just barely under the ground, and they made it tremble, and shot geysers of boiling water into the air. Tomás looked around wild-eyed, uncertain what to believe.

"You'll see the geysers in a few days," Sam told him. "They're crazy, but fun."

They reached the first of the hot springs that very afternoon. "Colter's hell," Beckwourth called it. They sank themselves into the hot water and munched on jerked meat Julia had sent with them. They lounged. They lolled. The water felt very, very good.

"What are you thinking?" Tomás asked Sam. They could see what he meant was, *You won, why aren't you jumping up and down?*

"About Esperanza," Sam told him softly.

Tomás took that in. Then he gave Sam a fine smile. The boy had been beaming all day. "It's all right, Dad," he said. "One day we'll go back and get her."

"Win Blevins has long since won his place among the West's very best."

—Tony Hillerman

❊ ❊ ❊

A Long and Winding Road
Win Blevins

In his decade of roaming the Rocky Mountains, Sam Morgan has made his mark as a trapper, fighter, and survivor. Now he is settled temporarily in Taos, New Mexico, and his lover, the widow Paloma Luna, is dying of cancer. Distraught, Sam sets out to rescue two girls taken captive by Navajo raiders, taking him deep into Indian territory, and to a surprise at the end of the trail.

❊ ❊ ❊

PRAISE FOR WIN BLEVINS

"An entertaining, vivid portrait of frontier America as seen through the eyes of an impressionable youth."

—*Booklist* on *So Wild a Dream*

"The glory years of frontier life, fresh and rich."

—*Kirkus Reviews* on *Beauty for Ashes*

Hardcover
ISBN 13: 978-0-7653-0577-0 • ISBN 10: 0-7653-0577-1
www.tor-forge.com

"As the historian explains why the winning side triumphed, he naturally tends to identify the victor with the most cherished values of the society in which he lives. . . . In American society there are three such values to which historians give adherence: All are convinced that it is a desirable and necessary thing to preserve the American Union; all believe that Negro slavery is an evil; and all profess a faith in democratic government.

"It is not the truth of these beliefs but their juxtaposition which causes the great confusion about the Civil War. Historians, recognizing that Lincoln's government was fighting for the preservation of the Union and for the freedom of the slaves, attribute to it also the third great positive value, the defense of democracy. Such a view is a distortion of the facts . . . the Confederacy, not the Union, represented the democratic forces in American life.

"The democratic tendencies of the Confederacy were all too plainly reflected in its army. Accustomed to regarding themselves as the equals of any men in the world, the Southerners never took kindly to regimented life. Even their appearance showed that they considered themselves individualistic citizens who were temporarily assisting their country. One astonished Englishman . . . gasped: 'Anything less like the received notion, at home, of how a soldier should look . . . never met my eye.' "

—DAVID DONALD

Edited by DAVID DONALD

WHY
THE NORTH WON
THE CIVIL WAR

Essays by
RICHARD N. CURRENT
T. HARRY WILLIAMS
NORMAN A. GRAEBNER
DAVID DONALD
DAVID M. POTTER
With a Foreword by U. S. GRANT III

COLLIER BOOKS, NEW YORK
COLLIER-MACMILLAN LTD., LONDON

Foreword

THIS BOOK makes a very real and important contribution to the appropriate observance of the War's Centennial and to a better understanding of its history. Each article is by a scholar and a specialist in his subject, and deals with an individual disadvantage under which the Confederacy labored and which prevented its ultimate success. Indeed, the title of the publication might better have been *Why the South Lost the Civil War*. But this is a minor distinction like Emerson's difference of the sea seen from the shore and the shore seen from the sea.

Each of the articles here assembled is an authoritative discussion of one of the factors that militated against the Confederacy's final victory. Moreover, these factors, presented from the overall point of view, too generally have been inadequately stressed or even entirely overlooked by many histories of the War. In now bringing these factors to public attention and giving them their proper emphasis lies the importance of this book. Even many "Civil War buffs" may be apprized of facts of which they have heretofore been unaware or to which they have given little thought.

As a footnote to Dr. Williams' excellent article on the military leadership of the North and South, it may be of interest that, on his trip around the world, General Grant said to Mr. John Russell Young: "If the Vicksburg campaign meant anything, in a military point of view, it was that there are no fixed laws of war which are not subject to the conditions of the country, the climate, and the habits of the people. The laws of successful war in one generation would insure defeat in another." And again: "Some of our generals failed because they worked out everything by rule. They knew what Frederick did at one place and Napoleon at another. They were always thinking about what Napoleon would do. Unfortunately for their plans, the rebels would be thinking about something

5

else. I don't underrate the value of military knowledge, but if men make war in slavish observances of rules, they will fail. No rules will apply to conditions of war as different as those which exist in Europe and America. Consequently, while our generals were working out problems of an ideal character, problems that would have looked well on a blackboard, practical facts were neglected. To that extent I consider remembrances of old campaigns a disadvantage. Even Napoleon showed that, for my impression is that his first success came because he made war in his own way."

Inevitably, the articles are special pleas and marshal the evidence in favor of their case. Naturally they do not give much attention to the like disadvantages and difficulties which the North had to overcome, but these are well summarized by the two outstanding English writers on the War, Colonel G. F. R. Henderson in his *Stonewall Jackson and the American Civil War* and Colonel J. F. C. Fuller in his *The Generalship of Ulysses S. Grant*, and which led the latter to write: "The outstanding marvel is that the North ever won."

However, although differences of opinion on military and economic phases and personalities of the War will persist, with the passage of a hundred years such differences of opinion have become academic, and we can well focus our attention on the heroism and self-sacrifice for the cause they thought right shown during those years by Americans on both sides, and take satisfaction in Sir Winston Churchill's summary: "Thus ended the great American Civil War, which must upon the whole be considered the noblest and least avoidable of all the great mass-conflicts of which till then there was record."

As Americans we can all today take pride in the fact that the bitter struggle did end with a reunited country for which the sons of those who fought one another so valiantly have since fought shoulder to shoulder in four foreign wars.

U. S. GRANT III
Major General, U.S.A., Ret'd

Editor's Preface

"THEY NEVER whipped us, Sir, unless they were four to one. If we had had anything like a fair chance, or less disparity of numbers, we should have won our cause and established our independence." This was one Virginian's pithy verdict of the outcome of the Civil War.

The general soul-searching in which many Southerners indulged after Appomattox brought forth other varied explanations of the catastrophe. Some were long-winded and intricate, such as Colonel Robert Tansill's *A Free And Impartial Exposition of the Causes Which Led to the Failure of the Confederate States to Establish Their Independence,* which itemized no fewer than thirteen causes, ranging from excessive "reliance upon foreign recognition and succors" to the election of military officers, "a policy subversive of good order, military discipline and efficiency." Others were more sober and compact, such as "The Causes of the Failure of Southern Independence," by Robert Garlick Hill Kean, former head of the Confederate Bureau of War. Kean listed seven principal reasons for the collapse of the Confederacy, including a bankrupt treasury, want of men, lack of subsistence, incompetency of military men, want of transport, recruiting difficulties, and desertion by slaves.

Later historians continued the argument which contemporaries thus began. Many writers sided with Albert Bushnell Hart, who cogently argued in 1891 that the South was overwhelmed by Northern preponderance in men and resources. Others, like James Ford Rhodes, disagreed, contending that Northern numerical superiority was "none too great" for an offensive war, and found elsewhere the key to Southern defeat.

Relatively few historians have devoted much attention specifically to the sources of Northern strength during the Civil War. Not until the recent publication of Allan Nevins' *The War for the Union: The Improvised War,*

1861–1862 did anyone trouble to list in tabular form the comparative resources of the two sections in 1860. Generations of Lincoln biographers, however, attributed Union victory to the superior political leadership of the North; Rhodes, for example, declared flatly: "The preponderating asset of the North proved to be Lincoln." Such students of military history as J. F. C. Fuller, B. H. Liddel Hart, Kenneth P. Williams, and T. Harry Williams stressed the excellence of Northern military leadership. J. R. Soley contended that the Northern blockade was the chief reason for Southern defeat. E. D. Adams, Frank L. Owsley, and Jay Monaghan maintained that Europe's failure to intervene, whether attributable to superior Union diplomacy or to selfish European economic and political considerations, was of decisive importance in securing Northern victory.

Many more historians have analyzed the weaknesses of the Confederacy. Among those who stressed the economic weaknesses of the South, Charles W. Ramsdell singled out finances as "the greatest single weakness of the Confederacy," Robert C. Black, III, pointed out the failure of the Confederate transportation system, and Frank Vandiver blamed Southern inability to "evolve a command or logistical system adequate to the job at hand." Among the numerous critics of the Confederacy's political leadership, Burton J. Hendrick and Clifford Dowdey are perhaps the most convincing.

Other writers have documented the internal dissensions of the Confederacy. Georgia Lee Tatum stressed the role of desertion and disloyalty in weakening the South, and Frank L. Owsley declared that the tombstone of the Confederacy should bear the inscription: "Died of State Rights." Both Edward Channing and Charles H. Wesley attributed Southern failure to the loss of the will to fight, and Lawrence Henry Gipson maintained that the Southern people, "questioning the justification of secession and still more uncertain as to the end in view," were "distracted unto desperation by internal strife [and were] in need of a great leader." Clement Eaton endorsed a contemporary verdict that the Confederacy lost "because there was no Wisdom in Congress and no Public Virtue among the People." Bell Irvin Wiley felt that the South failed in "flexibility, public information, harmony, morale and leadership."

With so many theories already adduced to explain the collapse of the Confederacy, the authors of the present volume did not set out to invent new explanations for Northern victory. Invited to participate in a conference on this theme at Gettysburg College in November, 1958, each of the five undertook as his assignment the re-examination of one of the familiar interpretations of the outcome of the Civil War. In so doing, they have illustrated the advantages of taking new thought about old subjects. The essays in this book emerged from their contributions to that conference.

Applying contemporary economic theory to an analysis of the economic resources of the two regions, Professor Richard N. Current, of the University of Wisconsin, throws new light on the war-making potential of the North and South. Professor T. Harry Williams, of Louisiana State University, demonstrates that military history has a new significance when interpreted in relation to the main currents of intellectual and social history. Professor Norman A. Graebner, of the University of Illinois, shows how Civil War diplomacy should be reevaluated in terms of the broad European diplomatic tradition. Drawing upon the insights political science offers historians, Professor David M. Potter, of Yale University, suggests the hitherto heretical idea that the North benefited by the presence of two well-organized political parties. My essay indicates that defects in the social and institutional structure of the Confederacy should be considered.

In their reinvestigations of the causes of Southern defeat, the five authors of this book have by no means found themselves in unanimous agreement. Perhaps the basic argument is between Current, who holds that the North's "overwhelming preponderance in most sources of economic power" made Southern defeat "all but inevitable," and the other writers, who believe that, had the Confederacy better managed its resources, Southern independence might have been won. Williams, Graebner, Potter, and I are not, however, agreed as to the source of Confederate weakness. Williams blames Southern generalship, and Graebner tends to agree, stressing that Europe could not intervene "until the South had demonstrated the power to establish and maintain its independence." Potter, on the other hand, accuses Southern political leaders, while I have found the basic fault in too great a respect for democratic liberties in the Confederacy.

The five writers differ also in their allocation of personal responsibility for Northern victory. Williams and I have arrived at adverse verdicts upon Jefferson Davis and his administration, and Potter declares boldly: "If the Union and the Confederacy had exchanged presidents with one another, the Confederacy might have won its independence." But Current concludes: "It is hard to believe, and impossible to prove, that the Southerners did a worse job with economic affairs than Northerners would have done in the same circumstances," and Graebner maintains that neither the deficiencies of the Confederate foreign service nor the skill of Union diplomats, but "the realities of power" determined Europe's decision not to intervene.

All these disagreements, it hardly needs adding, are of an entirely good-natured sort, for none of the five authors is committed to a monolithic scheme of causation and none is blind to the cogent considerations advanced by his colleagues. We hope that these essays, written from five different points of view, will not so much contradict as complement each other. If they do nothing more than demonstrate how complex the problem of historical causation is and how wary writers must be of oversimplification, they will have served their purpose.

All five of us wish to express our gratitude to the officials of Gettysburg College, especially to President Willard S. Paul, Professor Robert Bloom, and Mr. Raymond S. Davis, who did so much to make our conference a successful one. These essays have all been improved by the criticisms of other scholars who participated in the conference: J. Cutler Andrews; Clifford Dowdey; John Hope Franklin; Fletcher M. Green; Warren W. Hassler, Jr.; William B. Hesseltine; David C. Mearns; and Roy F. Nichols. It is unfortunately not possible to convey our deepest appreciation to the original organizer of the Gettysburg College Civil War conferences, for Professor Robert Fortenbaugh died while this book was being prepared for publication.

DAVID DONALD

Princeton University

Contents

God and the Strongest Battalions

Richard N. Current

WHEN WAR BEGAN in 1861, the statistics from the latest federal census decidedly favored the twenty-three states remaining in the Union as against the eleven that had withdrawn from it. In population the North had an advantage of almost five to two, and this advantage appears even greater if the slaves (more than one-third of the Southern people) are counted as somewhat less than the same number of freemen. In wealth and capacity to produce, the North held a still greater edge: in value of real and personal property, more than three to one (even with the inclusion of $2 billion for the slave property of the South); in capital of incorporated banks, more than four to one; in value of products annually manufactured, more than ten to one. The seceded states probably had a much less than proportional share of the national income. Besides, they contained only about a third of the total railroad mileage and practically none of the registered shipping. Though these comparisons are incomplete and inexact, they will serve to illustrate the point that the Union went to war with an overwhelming preponderance in most sources of economic power.

If wars are won by riches, there can be no question why the North eventually prevailed. The only question will be: How did the South manage to stave off defeat so long? Or perhaps the question ought to be: Why did the South even risk a war in which she was all but beaten before the first shot was fired?

Indeed, this last question occurred to at least a few Southerners during the secession winter. For example, the editor of the Lynchburg *Virginian* wrote: "Dependent upon Europe and the North for almost every yard of cloth, and every coat and boot and hat that we wear, for our axes, scythes, tubs, and buckets, in short, for everything except our bread and meat, it must occur to the South that if our relations with the North are ever severed, —and how soon they may be none can know; may God forbid it long!—we should, in all the South, not be able to clothe ourselves; we could not fill our firesides, plough our fields, nor mow our meadows; in fact, we should be reduced to a state more abject than we are willing to look at even prospectively. And yet, all of these things staring us in the face, we shut our eyes and go in blindfold." Of course, the view of the Lynchburg *Virginian* was not the prevailing attitude of Southerners at that time. If it had been, most likely there would have been no war.

Nor was this the opinion of most leading Southerners afterwards, when the war had been lost and they were casting about for reasons why it had been. These men refused to adopt the handy and easy rationalization that the North simply had been too much and too many for the South. These men could not very well accept such an explanation, for it would have convicted them of blindness, stupidity, or even worse in going into a conflict they could not hope to win. In his memoirs General Joseph E. Johnston defended his fellow Southerners against such a possible charge. "That people," he wrote, "was not guilty of the high crime of undertaking a war without the means of waging it successfully."

As Johnston looked back, it seemed to him that the Confederacy had possessed "ample means." Other Southerners agreed with him. General P. G. T. Beauregard, for one, declared that "no people ever warred for independence with more relative advantages than the Confederacy; and if, as a military question, they must have failed, then no country must aim at freedom by means of war." The outcome was not to be explained, Beauregard insisted, by "mere material contrast" between the North and the South. So, too, the Richmond journalist and historian Edward A. Pollard maintained that "something more than numbers makes armies" and that "against the vast superiority of the North in material resources," the South had "a set-off in certain advantages."

Among these presumed advantages of the South, the first was psychological. Her people, fighting as they did for the high ideal of independence, for the protection of their very homes, were moved by a "superiour animation," a more determined spirit than the enemy could attain. The second point in the South's favor was geographic. She possessed rivers, swamps, and mountains that were "equivalent to successive lines of fortification"; she had the "immense advantage of the interior lines"; and, besides all this, she was favored with "one single advantage" which, alone, "should have been decisive of the contest." "That advantage was *space*." Even some economic aspects favored the South: At the beginning of the war it was a "remarkable fact" that "the South was richer than the North in all the *necessaries* of life," producing as she did more corn and livestock per person. The fourth and most important item might be viewed as either economic or diplomatic. This was cotton—a magic word, a magic staple, which theoretically ought to have done wonders for the Confederacy.

If statistics were on the side of the North, history seemed to be on the side of the South. In previous struggles for liberty the Dutch had beaten the Spaniards, the Russians had repelled the French, and the Americans had won out over the British against odds as bad or worse than those the Southerners faced in 1861. "In an intelligent view of the precedents of history," Pollard concluded, "it might safely [have been] predicted that the South . . . would be victor in the contest, however unequally matched in men and the materials of war, *unless the management of her affairs should become insane, or her people lose the virtue of endurance*."

Possibly, then, the Confederacy at last succumbed not because of any economic handicap but because of a loss of virtue, that is, of morale or fighting spirit. This, indeed, is the view of Charles H. Wesley, who discounts the "customary" explanation of the collapse of the Confederacy as due to Northern economic preponderance, and who repudiates the "astonishing conclusion that we must all be amazed that the Confederacy was able to continue the contest for so long a period." According to Wesley, the "psychological factors which entered into the disruption of Southern morale and the inherent political weaknesses of the Confederacy were fundamental" in bringing about the final collapse. But other writers deny that a failure of will was the prime cause of defeat. They point to the fact that Southerners sacrificed far more for the Lost Cause than the Revolutionary patriots had sacrificed for victory over England.

If the defeat was not due to a loss of will to win, then perhaps it was caused by bad management, by human errors, by failures of statesmanship. Certainly the carping Pollard thought so. His book is replete with contemptuous references to the policies of the Jefferson Davis government—with such phrases as "silly prospects," "a new delusion," "silly declamation," "puerile argument," "feeble and mismanaged efforts," "a policy of blunders," "silly devices," and "childish expedients." Pollard, of course, enjoyed the privilege of the second guess. Other similarly privileged critics of the Davis government, while not always agreeing with Pollard in detail, concurred with him in the general proposition that the Confederacy had fallen because of mistakes in the use of its resources and not because of a lack of sufficient resources to begin with.

In economic policy the chief errors commonly attributed to the Confederate government are these: its failure to exploit cotton promptly as a basis for foreign credit; its unwillingness to tax its people and its reliance, instead, on issues of paper money in the form of treasury notes; its impressment, or seizure at arbitrary prices, of the goods of its citizens; and its lack of thoroughness in the promotion of manufacturers and in the control of transportation, especially by railroad. A brief re-examination of these matters may throw light on the question of whether the Confederacy was more handicapped by human or by material shortcomings.

In cotton, the South had a cash crop of great value, and yet, in the midst of war, Southerners reduced their planting, burned some of the bales they had on hand, and discouraged shipments abroad. "Instead of making the best use of this resource," B. J. Hendrick observes, "the Davis government deliberately did all in its power to make it useless." At first glance the policy appears downright insane.

Surely there were alternatives, and in fact the Vice-President of the Confederacy, Alexander H. Stephens, proposed a different course during the war. Take two million bales from the 1860 and another two million from the 1861 crop, Stephens recommended. Pay for these with $100 million in government bonds. Buy fifty ironclad steamers to carry the cotton safely to Europe. Store it there until the price rises to fifty cents a pound, then sell it. Thus, Stephens thought, the Confederacy could net a profit of $800 million! Afterwards General Johnston was positive that this plan, if promptly put into effect, would have won the war. The cotton money, Johnston averred, would have procured arms for half a million men, who could have been ready and in the field by the time the very first battle was fought. The first battle, he implied, might well have been the last. In any event, "the Confederate treasury would have been much richer than that of the United States," and the South would have had the means of eventual success.

That the Confederacy failed to seize this splendid and obvious opportunity during the first year of the war—before the blockade had become too tight—must prove the stupidity if not the insanity of government leaders, of President Davis and his Secretary of the Treasury, Christopher G. Memminger. So it afterward seemed to historian Pollard, who berated Memminger for not having purchased cotton and sent it abroad while he had the chance. Pollard said Memminger had dismissed the Stephens plan as "soup-house legislation," as a scheme of government relief for cotton planters. But historian Pollard forgot a great deal that journalist Pollard had said during the war. Actually, it was Pollard's Richmond *Examiner* which had denounced Stephens for proposing "soup-house legislation." Afterwards, having reversed himself, Pollard put his own words into the mouth of poor Memminger!

The truth is that neither Davis nor Memminger had foisted upon the South the idea of withholding cotton. When the war began, not only these two men but practically all Southern leaders believed that cotton—or rather the lack of it—would win the war for the South. On the Southern staple Great Britain presumably depended for its prosperity, and so did France, and so too did the United States. Without cotton, Great Britain and France would face economic prostration, and to avert this they would have to come to the Confederacy's aid. Without cotton, the United States would suffer the closing of its textile mills and, more important, would have no export crop sufficient for obtaining indispensable foreign exchange. If the notions about "King Cotton" were delusions, they were not the private dreams of Memminger or Davis.

In the light of the times, these ideas were not quite so crazy as they seem in retrospect. True, the cotton shortage failed to accomplish what Southerners had expected it to do. Yet it did create a serious problem for the North, the problem of finding means of payment for necessary imports. Unfortunately for Southern hopes, the North was able to make up for her lack of cotton shipments by means of increased exports of wheat. Unfortunately, also, there were British economic interests that ran counter to the British interest in continued cotton shipments from the South, as Frank L. Owsley had demonstrated.

The Stephens-Johnston-Pollard view regarding cotton exports was at least as visionary as the King Cotton theory itself. There simply was not so much cotton available in 1861 as Stephens estimated: there were not two million bales left over from the 1860 crop, but only a few hundred thousand. Then, too, it is doubtful whether many owners of this cotton would have given it up in return for Confederate bonds. Even if enough money were obtained, the fifty ironclads probably could not have been purchased, and without them the South did not have enough shipping to send the cotton overseas. "Finally," Rembert

W. Patrick concludes, "the idea . . . that with four million bales in storage the price of cotton would have risen to fifty cents a pound, was fanciful."

Granting that Stephens' gigantic cotton-export scheme was not feasible in 1861, there remains the question whether *something* could not have been accomplished by a more prompt and vigorous export policy than was adopted. Whether or not Davis and Memminger should have done more than they did to base financing upon cotton, the fact is that they did more than their critics have credited them with doing. The cotton embargo, it must be remembered, was not the work of the Davis administration or of the Confederate Congress. It was the work of state and local officials and private groups, who had the backing of an almost unanimous public opinion. It did not have the official support of Memminger and Davis, who used their influence to prevent Congress from passing an embargo act, and who encouraged shipments of cotton in so far as vessels were available. Almost from the outset, the Confederate government sought to obtain cotton by purchase or by produce loan, keeping some of it at home as a basis of credit for the purchase of foreign supplies, and sending the rest abroad. The fiasco of the Erlanger loan resulted from an attempt to use cotton for bolstering the foreign credit of the Confederacy. Not until the third year of the war, however, did the government take complete control of cotton exports and push them with determination. If this program had been undertaken earlier, probably Confederate finances could have been made much stronger than they actually became.

Certainly, Confederate financing was much less sound and less successful than Union financing. Of the Confederacy's income, to October 1864, almost 60 per cent was derived from the issue of paper money, about 30 per cent from the sale of bonds, and less than 5 per cent from taxation (the remaining 5 per cent arising from miscellaneous sources). Of the Union's income, by contrast, 13 per cent was raised by paper money, 62 per cent by bonds, and 21 per cent by taxes (and 4 per cent by other means). Thus the Confederacy relied much more upon government notes and much less upon taxation and borrowing than the Union did. Exactly how much paper money was afloat in the wartime South, nobobdy knows for sure. "Even if we knew the successive amounts of Confederate treasury notes in the hands of the public during the war," John C. Schwab remarks, "this would signify little, as they formed but a part of the currency; the State, municipal, bank, corporate, and individual notes formed the other, and . . . no inconsiderable part." The economist Eugene M. Lerner estimates that the stock of money in the South increased approximately eleven fold in the three years from January, 1861, to January, 1864. In any case, the prices of gold and other commodities were multiplied by much more than eleven. The price of gold, in Confederate dollars, rose eventually to sixty-one (in United States greenbacks it never rose even as high as three). The general price level, in Confederate dollars, soared to ninety or a hundred times its original level. The Confederacy suffered the worst inflation that Americans had known since the Revolutionary War.

In its effort to escape the evils of inflation the Confederate government but compounded them. The Funding Act of 1864, designed to force the exchange of treasury notes for bonds by threatening a partial repudiation of the notes, only speeded the loss in value of the currency. The impressment of government supplies, at less than the inflated market price, caused suppliers to withhold their goods and thus lessened the available amount. Unwittingly, the government defeated its own purposes. "The army suffered from want of food," as Schwab has observed, "though in the country at large there was no serious lack of it."

To the later critics of the Davis government it was perfectly obvious that the government should have taxed and taxed and borrowed and borrowed, rather than relying so heavily on the printing of batch after batch of treasury notes. These critics blamed Secretary Memminger, and some historians still blame him (Owsley refers to him as the "measly" Memminger). In truth, however, Memminger was just as well aware of the dangers of inflation as any of his denouncers. They were to have hindsight; he had at least a degree of foresight. But there was little he could do, especially since he lacked the force of personality to carry the Congress with him. As for taxes, he favored them, but at the start of the war he had no going machinery of tax collection to work with, and he was dealing with people who had even more than the typical American's resistance to taxation. Besides, cash was comparatively scarce in the Confederacy. The Secretary and the Congress had little choice but to resort to the 1861 requisition upon the states, which the states raised almost entirely by borrowing instead of taxing. As for issuing bonds to sop up the excess currency, Memminger favored that too, but the plain fact was that the people would not or could not buy the bonds in sufficient quantities. Hence his recommendation of the funding scheme to force the sale of bonds—a scheme that Congress carried even farther than he had intended.

There can be no doubt that the government's fiscal policies failed in their main object, namely, to transfer goods efficiently from private to public hands. There is considerable doubt, however, whether Davis or Memminger or any individual was to blame. There also is doubt whether the paper money issues, alone, accounted for the extent of inflation in the South. Actually, the price rise was uneven, and the prices that rose the most were those of goods in short supply, such as leather, wool, coffee, salt, tea, and drugs. So the actual scarcity of some items, as well as the overabundance of money, seems to have been responsible for soaring prices. Moreover, the flight from the currency, at least during the last couple of years of the war, must have been due in part to a growing popular skepticism as to the chances of the Confederacy's ever winning the war and making good on its promises to pay.

By interfering with the free market, the Davis government unintentionally discouraged production, both agricultural and industrial. At the same time the government

did not interfere enough by means of positive measures to
make the most of manufacturing possibilities. "The failure
of the Confederacy, though predictable from the start,"
Ella Lonn writes, "was immediately attributable to errors
of judgment in not anticipating and justly estimating its
inability to supply certain indispensable necessities." This
is the main conclusion of Miss Lonn in her study of *Salt
as a Factor in the Confederacy*, and it is a conclusion
which may be applied to other items as well as salt. In
controlling manufactures the government never aimed to
do more than provide the army with essential supplies.
Even the efforts in this direction were slow, halting, and
indirect. The chief methods of influencing industrial production were the assignment or withholding of labor
through manipulation of the draft, and the provision or
denial of raw materials through control of the railroads.

Yet the government was "loath to enforce the kind of
transportation policy the war effort demanded." At the
start the railroad system of the South was, of course, defective. There were not enough railroad lines, and few of
these were located where, strategically, they would do the
most good. Besides, there were too many gaps, and there
was too little rolling stock and too few mechanics and
facilities for upkeep or repair. Despite these shortcomings,
the railroads gave as much reality to the concept of "interior lines" as this concept ever attained. At the first
battle of Bull Run the Confederates reinforced an army
by railroad, in the midst of battle, for the first time in
history. In moving General James Longstreet's men from
Virginia to Tennessee before the battle of Chickamauga
the Confederates again made history in the military use
of railroads. Still, in the judgment of R. C. Black, historian of Confederate railroads, "the Confederates by no
means made the best use of what they had." The government delayed too long in taking over and operating all
the lines as a unified system. Confederate transportation
often had to depend on wagons or carts, mule teams, and
dirt roads. Instead of leaving teams and vehicles in the
hands of owners, so as to let the economy go on function-

ing efficiently, the government too often impressed these things for strictly military uses. The resulting transportation difficulties, in the opinion of Charles W. Ramsdell, ranked next to fiscal policies in their "deleterious consequences" for the Confederacy. Without adequate transportation, the geographical advantages of the South were largely lost.

In their handling of finances, manufactures, and transportation, the Confederate leaders made a number of errors that have become clear enough in retrospect. So the question persists: Were the South's economic disasters to be blamed upon human failings rather than material inadequacies? Was Davis inferior to Lincoln, and Memminger to Salmon P. Chase, the Union treasury head, in economic statesmanship? Were Southern civilians inferior to Northern in business ability and capacity for work? It has been said that the Confederate civil leaders in general and Memminger in particular proved themselves incompetent. And yet, if we imagine Chase in Memminger's position, it is hard to believe that he could have made a reputation as a successful financier. Memminger had to deal with problems in comparison with which those of the Union treasury were almost child's play. As for the Southern people as a whole, they unquestionably lagged behind Northerners in business experience and in education and literacy, if not also in physical health. Yet it is hard to agree with the emphasis of Pollard when he concludes: "He who seeks to solve the problem of the downfall of the Southern Confederacy must take largely into consideration the absence of any intelligent and steady system in the conduct of public affairs; the little circles that bounded the Richmond administration; the deplorable want of the commercial or business facility in the Southern mind."

It is hard to believe, and impossible to prove, that the Southerners did a worse job with economic affairs than Northerners would have done in the same circumstances. It is unimportant and unnecessary to try to prove this. The point is that the North had an economic strength several times greater to start with. In order to overcome this handicap and attain even so much as equality in economic power, the civilians of the South would have had to be *several times* as able, man for man, as those of the North. And this, obviously, is too much to have expected of any people, however willing and determined they might have been.

If the South could not meet the North on anything like an equal economic footing, she would have to compensate in some other respect. She would have to be blessed with better luck or higher achievement in matters political, diplomatic, military, or psychological. A mere glance at these other considerations reveals at once that they cannot be appraised apart from one another, or the economic apart from any of them. These categories, after all, are purely arbitrary: we distinguish among them only for our own convenience.

In waging war, the Confederacy faced problems of politics and government that vastly complicated its problems of economic mobilization. Always the Southerners had to struggle with the incubus of John C. Calhoun, with the idea of state rights, with that fatal principle upon which their new government had been based. A Confederacy formed by particularist politicians could hardly be expected to adopt promptly those centralist policies—for marshaling resources and transportation—which victory demanded. Even apart from this ideological handicap, the Confederacy faced insuperable difficulties in attempting to set up, from scratch, a going administration in the midst of war. Professor Ramsdell has put the matter admirably: ". . . the southern people and their governments failed, with a few exceptions, to conserve, develop, and efficiently administer their resources; but it must be said that these were gigantic tasks, intricate, complex, and baffling. That they did not succeed better is not surprising when we remember the simplicity of southern economic and political organization before secession. There was not time, while a powerful and determined enemy was crashing at the gate, to reorganize their whole system and, without previous experience, create a complex administration, and train administrators. Problems had to be met as they arose. . . . All in all, it is not surprising that they could not be solved, or that, in the end, the collapse was complete."

By successful diplomacy, by winning the support of Great Britain or France, the South most likely could have canceled out all the economic advantages of the North. The Confederate financial policies, by the way, were not always easy to distinguish from the Confederate foreign policies. Thus, for example, the Erlanger loan, at least from the point of view of Judah P. Benjamin, was more a diplomatic than an economic measure, intended to elicit the support of France rather than, primarily, to raise funds. To explain why Southern hopes for foreign aid finally were dashed, it is necessary to look into a tangle of international economic relationships. It is necessary also to look into the world politics of the time, especially the divergent interests of Great Britain, France, and Russia. It is necessary even to look into the internal politics of England.

Certainly the economic history of the Confederacy cannot be told without including also the military and naval history (nor, for that matter, the military and naval without the economic). Bad as Southern transportation was at the start of the war, it soon was made worse by the advance of Union forces on land and sea. River and coastal waterways were occupied or blockaded and thus rendered useless to the Confederacy. Rail centers, like Chattanooga and Atlanta, were taken and new gaps thereby made in the already defective railroad system. The capture of New Orleans, only a year after the fighting had begun, meant the loss of the Confederacy's financial heart. As the Union armies took over more and more Southern territory, there was a continual shrinking of the area within which Confederate notes passed as money. And as this area contracted, the quantity of paper money in it increased even more rapidly than the treasury put forth new issues, for Southerners living in the occupied territory got rid of their Confederate money by sending it to places

where it still had at least a little value—to places where
the Stars and Bars still waved. The more ground the Confederacy lost in battle, the worse the problem of inflation
became. Meanwhile, in filling her armies, the South had
to draw off from the economy a much higher proportion
of her manpower than the North did of hers. The South's
capacity to produce, already so small by comparison, was
made even smaller by a disproportionate reduction of her
labor supply. While Union military power was weakening
the Southern economy, Union naval power had the same
effect in perhaps even greater degree. The blockade, by
bringing about serious shortages in strategic items, not
only added to the inflationary trends but also frustrated
efforts to maintain the transportation network and to increase industrial output. And, toward the end of the war,
the Southern loss of faith in victory, as has been seen,
contributed to the currency depreciation and to the economic disorganization that ensued.

Thus psychological influences, resulting from military
events, fatally affected economic conditions. The reverse is
equally true. Economic conditions gave rise to psychological influences that seriously affected military events.

Strategy itself at times conformed to economic facts.
When the South resorted to the draft, in April, 1862, the
congressional critics of Davis blamed him for having made
such an extreme measure necessary. They charged that he
had adopted a strategy of the "dispersed defensive" and
that this, in turn, had chilled the enthusiasm of Southern
men, who would have volunteered in ample numbers for
an aggressive, concentrated campaign against the North.
In reply to his critics Davis explained that the Confederacy lacked the means for such a campaign. "Without military stores," he said, "without the workshops to create
them, without the power to import them, necessity not
choice has compelled us to occupy strong positions and
everywhere to confront the enemy without reserves."

Soldier morale, presumably hurt by the dispersed defensive, was further damaged by economic developments
behind the lines. As General Johnston remarks, "after the

Confederate currency had become almost worthless" the married soldiers from the farms "had to choose between their military service and the strongest obligations they knew—their duties to wives and children." The dilemma of these soldiers was made especially poignant by the actions of Confederate impressment officials. Those officials, as Johnston says, frequently preyed upon the most defenseless of the citizens, especially upon farm women whose husbands were away in the army. Hard beset by inflation and impressment, wives summoned their soldier-husbands home, and, faced with a torturing choice of loyalties, the soldiers often placed family above country. In other ways, too, the fiscal policies of the Confederacy no doubt impaired the morale of both soldiers and civilians. Amid the wild inflation some people grew rich overnight, at least on paper, and others lost their fortunes just as suddenly. A gambling spirit infected the land, and almost everybody became a speculator of some kind. Those gamblers who lost—and practically all of them lost in the end—naturally were prone to feelings of bitterness and envy. And they directed these feelings against one another as well as against the Yankee foe.

Since so much of the Southern despair was induced by objective conditions and events, on the battlefield and on the home front, it is difficult to accept the Wesley thesis that the Confederacy collapsed because of a failure of the spirit. In most respects the loss of morale seems to have been a secondary rather than a primary cause of defeat.

The prime cause must have been economic. Given the vast superiority of the North in men and materials, in instruments of production, in communication facilities, in business organization and skill—and assuming for the sake of the argument no more than rough equality in state-craft and generalship—the final outcome seems all but inevitable. At least, it seems to have become inevitable once two dangers for the Union had been passed. One of these was the threat of interference from abroad. The other was the possibility of military disaster resulting from the enemy's superior skill or luck on the battlefield, from his ability to make decisive use of his power-in-being before the stronger potential of the Union could be fully developed and brought into play. Both dangers appear to have been over by midsummer, 1863, if not already by autumn, 1862. Thereafter, month by month, the resources of the North began increasingly to tell, in what became more and more a war of attrition.

True, the victory is not always to the rich. The record of mankind offers many an example of a wealthy and fat and decadent people overcome by an enemy who was poor and lean and vigorous. Indeed, these historical examples heartened those Southerners who, at the outset, assumed that all Yankees had been corrupted by commerce and industry, that the "mudsills" of the factory and the money-grubbers of the counting-house would lack the fortitude that victory required. On the other hand, many in the North looked upon Southerners as a people debased, debauched, and incapacitated by contact with the institution of slavery. Today, at this distance in time, we can see that the two sides must have been about even in virtue and vice, devotion and disloyalty, human strength and weakness.

For the North to win, she had only to draw upon her resources as fully and as efficiently as the South drew upon hers; or, rather, the North had to make good use of only a fraction of her economic potential. Her material strength was so much greater that she could, as it were, almost lick the South with one hand tied behind her back. In fact, the North during the war years did devote a large part of her energies and resources to nonmilitary enterprise. Once the financial crisis of late 1861 was past, the Union entered upon an economic boom. She actually grew in material strength, while the South wasted away. From 1861 to 1865 nearly 5,000,000 acres of the public domain in the West were transferred to settlers and corporations. Railroad mileage lengthened from about 31,000 to more than 35,000 miles—an increase of approximately one-eighth. The value of imports for the North alone in 1864 was almost as great as it had been for the entire country, the South included, in 1860.

With justifiable pride President Abraham Lincoln boasted of the wartime progress and prosperity in his annual message to Congress of December, 1864. "It is of noteworthy interest," Lincoln declared, "that the steady expansion of population, improvement, and governmental institutions over the new and unoccupied portion of our country have scarcely been checked, much less impeded or destroyed, by our great civil war, which at first glance would seem to have absorbed almost the entire energies of the nation." He noted the sales of public land, the work on the Pacific railroad, the discovery and exploitation of gold and silver and mercury in the West. "The important fact remains demonstrated," he concluded, "that we have *more* men *now* than we had when the war *began*; that we are not exhausted, nor in process of exhaustion; that we are *gaining* strength, and may, if need be, maintain the contest indefinitely. This as to men. Material resources are now more complete and abundant than ever. The national resources . . . are unexhausted, and, as we believe, inexhaustible."

Jefferson Davis could not truthfully have said the same of the South in 1864. At that time the Confederacy was not yet beaten on the field of battle, but already economic exhaustion was setting in behind the lines. As Ramsdell has remarked, ". . . the Confederacy had begun to crumble, or to break down *within*, long before the military situation appeared to be desperate."

From Ramsdell's observation it is but a step to the conclusion that economic rather than strictly military superiority was the basic reason for the ultimate victory of the North. At the start the North had possessed no significant advantage in a narrowly military sense—certainly no advantage comparable to that of her economic power and potential. This vast productive ability made the Union armies the best fed, the best clothed, the best cared for that the world ever had seen. This economic might made it possible for the North to field the stronger forces and, when the final test came, to place at every crucial point, as A. B. Hart has said, "more officers, more men, more camp followers, and more army mules."

Some Northerners used to cherish a simple—and, it would seem, an irrefutable—explanation of the Northern victory. God had willed that the Union be preserved. Surely, in view of the disparity of resources, it would have taken a miracle, a direct intervention of the Lord on the other side, to enable the South to win. As usual, God was on the side of the heaviest battalions.

The Military Leadership of North and South

T. Harry Williams

GENERALS AND THEIR ART and their accomplishments have not been universally admired throughout the course of history. Indeed, there have been some who have sneered at even the successful captains of their time. Four centuries before Christ, Sophocles, as aware of the tragedy of war as he was of the tragedy of life, observed: "It is the merit of a general to impart good news, and to conceal the bad." And the Duke of Wellington, who knew from experience whereof he spoke, depreciated victory with the bitter opinion: "Nothing except a battle lost can be half so melancholy as a battle won."

Civil War generals were, of course, not considered sacrosanct—were, in fact, regarded as legitimate targets of criticism for anyone who had a gibe to fling. Senator Louis T. Wigfall was exercising his not inconsiderable talent for savage humor, usually reserved for the Davis administration, on the military when he said of John B. Hood: "That young man had a fine career before him until Davis undertook to make of him what the good Lord had not done— to make a great general of him." One can understand Assistant Secretary of War P. H. Watson's irritation when the War Department could not locate so important an officer as Joe Hooker on the eve of Second Manassas, while also noting Watson's patronizing attitude toward all generals in a letter to transportation director Herman Haupt stating that an intensive search for Hooker was being conducted in Willard's bar. "Be patient as possible with the Generals," Watson added. "Some of them will trouble you more than they will the enemy."

And yet in the final analysis, as those who have fought or studied war know, it is the general who is the decisive factor in battle. (At least, this has been true up to our own time, when war has become so big and dispersed that it may be said it is managed rather than commanded.) Napoleon put it well when he said, perhaps with some exaggeration: "The personality of the general is indispensable, he is the head, he is the all of an army. The Gauls were not conquered by the Roman legions, but by Caesar. It was not before the Carthaginian soldiers that Rome was made to tremble, but before Hannibal. It was not the Macedonian phalanx which penetrated to India, but Alexander. It was not the French Army which reached the Weser and the Inn, it was Turenne. Prussia was not defended for seven years against the three most formidable European Powers by the Prussian soldiers, but by Frederick the Great." This quotation may serve to remind us of another truth about war and generals that is often forgotten: That is that tactics is often a more decisive factor than strategy. The commander who has suffered a strategic reverse, Cyril Falls emphasizes, may remedy everything by a tactical success, whereas for a tactical reverse there may be no remedy whatever. Falls adds: "It is remarkable how many people exert themselves and go through contortions to prove that battles and wars are won by any means except that by which they are most commonly won, which is by fighting."

If, then, the general is so important in war, we are justified in asking, what are the qualities that make a general great or even just good? We may with reason look for clues to the answer in the writings of some of the great captains. But first of all, it may be helpful to list some qualities that, although they may be highly meritorious and desirable, are not sufficient in themselves to produce greatness. Experience alone is not enough. "A mule," said Frederick the Great, "may have made twenty campaigns under Prince Eugene and not be a better tactician for all that." Nor are education and intelligence the touchstones to measure a great general. Marshal Saxe went so far as to say: "Unless a man is born with a talent for war, he will never be other than a mediocre general." And Auguste Marmont, while noting that all the great soldiers had possessed "the highest faculties of mind," emphasized that they also had had something that was more important, namely, character.

What these last two commentators were trying to say was that a commander has to have in his make-up a mental strength and a moral power that enables him to dominate whatever event or crisis may emerge on the field of battle. Napoleon stated the case explicitly: "The first quality of a General-in-Chief is to have a cool head which receives exact impressions of things, which never gets heated, which never allows itself to be dazzled, or intoxicated, by good or bad news." Anyone who knows the Civil War can easily tick off a number of generals who fit exactly the pattern described next by Napoleon: "There are certain men who, on account of their moral and physical constitution, paint mental pictures out of everything: however exalted be their reason, their will, their courage, and whatever good qualities they may possess, nature has not fitted them to command armies, nor to direct great operations of war." Karl von Clausewitz said the same thing in a slightly different context. There are decisive moments in war, the German pointed out, when things no longer move of themselves, when "the machine itself"— the general's own army—begins to offer resistance. To overcome this resistance the commander must have "a great force of will." The whole inertia of the war comes to rest on his will, and only the spark of his own purpose and spirit can throw it off. This natural quality of toughness of fiber is especially important in measuring Civil War generalship because the rival generals were products of the same educational system and the same military background. As far as technique was concerned, they started equal, and differed only in matters of mind and character. It has been well said: "To achieve a Cannae a Hannibal is needed on the one side and a Terentius Varro on the other." And one may add, to achieve a Second Manassas a Robert E. Lee is needed on the one side and a John Pope on the other.

When Marshal Saxe enumerated the attributes of a

general, he named the usual qualities of intelligence and courage, and then added another not always considered in military evaluations—health. It is a factor that deserves more attention than it has received. Clifford Dowdey has recently reminded us of the effects of physical and mental illness on the actions of the Confederate command at Gettysburg. A comparison of the age levels of leading Southern and Northern officers in 1861 is instructive. Although there are no significant differences in the ages of the men who rose to division and corps generals, we note that, of the officers who came to command armies for the South, Albert Sidney Johnston was fifty-eight, Joseph E. Johnston and Lee were fifty-four, John C. Pemberton was forty-seven, Braxton Bragg was forty-four, and P. G. T. Beauregard was forty-three. Of the Union army commanders, Hooker was forty-seven, Henry W. Halleck and George G. Meade were forty-six, George H. Thomas was forty-five, D. C. Buell was forty-three, William S. Rosecrans was forty-two, William T. Sherman was forty-one, U. S. Grant was thirty-nine, Ambrose Burnside was thirty-seven, and George B. McClellan was thirty-four. Hood and Philip H. Sheridan at thirty represent the lowest age brackets. Youth was clearly on the side of the Union, but obviously it cannot be said, with any accuracy or finality, that the generals in one particular age group did any better than those in another. Nevertheless, when Grant thought about the war in the years after, he inclined to place a high premium on the qualities of youth, health, and energy, and doubted that a general over fifty should be given field command. He recalled that during the war he had had "the power to endure" anything. In this connection, it may be worthy of mention that during the Virginia campaign of 1864 Lee was sick eleven of forty-four days, while Grant was not indisposed for one.

The Civil War was pre-eminently a West Pointers' fight. Of the sixty biggest battles, West Point graduates commanded both armies in fifty-five, and in the remaining five a West Pointer commanded one of the opposing armies.

What were the men who would direct the blue and gray armies like in 1861? How well trained were they for war? What intellectual influences had formed their concepts of war and battle? A glance at the Point curriculum reveals that it was heavy on the side of engineering, tactics, and administration. The products of the academy came out with a good grounding in what may be termed the routine of military science. They knew how to train and administer a force of troops; or, to put it more accurately and to apply it specifically to the Civil War, they had the technical knowledge that enabled them to take over the administration of a large force without imposing too much strain on them or their men. It should be emphasized, however, that none of the West Pointers had had before 1861 any actual experience in directing troops in numbers. Not a one had controlled as large a unit as a brigade, and only a few had handled a regiment. Except for a handful of officers who had visited Europe, the men who would lead the Civil War hosts had never seen an army larger than the fourteen thousand men of Winfield Scott or Zachary Taylor in the Mexican War.

One subject which was taught but not emphasized at West Point was strategy, or the study of the higher art of war. The comparative subordination of strategy may be explained by the youth of the cadets and the feeling of the school's directors that it was more important to impart a basic knowledge of tactics and techniques to the boys. Nevertheless, many of the graduates enlarged their knowledge of the topic by reading books on military history while stationed at army posts. The strategy that was presented at the Point and studied by interested graduates came from a common source and had a common pattern. It was the product of the brilliant Swiss officer who had served with Napoleon, Antoine Henri Jomini, universally regarded as the foremost writer on the theory of war in the first half of the nineteenth century. Every West Point general in the war had been exposed to Jomini's ideas, either directly, by reading Jomini's writings or abridgments or expositions of them; or indirectly, by hearing them in the classroom or perusing the works of Jomini's American disciples. The influence of Jomini on the Civil War was profound, and this influence must be taken into account in any evaluation of Civil War generalship. There is little exaggeration in General J. D. Hittle's statement that "many a Civil War general went into battle with a sword in one hand and Jomini's *Summary of the Art of War* in the other."

Here it is impossible to attempt more than a summary of Jomini's ideas and writings. Essentially his purpose was to introduce rationality and system into the study of war. He believed that in war rules prevailed as much as in other areas of human activity and that generals should follow these rules. He sought to formulate a set of basic principles of strategy for commanders, using as his principal examples the campaigns and techniques of Napoleon. The most convenient approach to Jomini is through the four strategic principles that he emphasized, the famous principles that many Civil War generals could recite from memory:

(1) The commander should endeavor by strategic measures to bring the major part of his forces successively to bear on the decisive areas of the theater of war, while menacing the enemy's communications without endangering his own.

(2) He should maneuver in such a way as to engage the masses of his forces against fractions of the enemy.

(3) He should endeavor by tactical measures to bring his masses to bear on the decisive area of the battlefield or on the part of the enemy's line it was important to overwhelm.

(4) He should not only bring his masses to bear on the decisive point of the field but should put them in battle speedily and together in a simultaneous effort.

It is, perhaps, unnecessary to remark that much of this was not new. Xenophon had said about the same thing to the Greeks, and the definition of strategy as the art of bringing most of the strength of an army to bear on the decisive point has been fairly constant in the history of war. But it should be noted that Jomini envisioned the decisive point as the point where the enemy was weakest. This is often true but not always. There are occasions in war when the decisive point may be the strongest one, as Epaminondas demonstrated at Leuctra and the American strategists in the cross-Channel attack of World War II.

To explain how his principles should be applied in war, Jomini worked out an elaborate doctrine based on geometrical formations. He loved diagrams, and devised twelve model plans of battle; some Civil War generals actually tried to reproduce on the field some of these neat paper exercises. In all Jomini's plans there was a theater of operations, a base of operations, a zone of operations, and so forth. The smart commander chose a line of operations that would enable him to dominate three sides of the rectangular zone; this accomplished, the enemy would have to retire or face certain defeat. Jomini talked much of concentric and eccentric maneuver and interior and exterior lines, being the first theorist to emphasize the advantage of the former over the latter.

At times, especially when he discussed the advantage of the offensive—and he always stressed the offensive— Jomini seemed to come close to Clausewitz's strategy of annihilation. But a closer perusal of his writings reveals that he and the German were far apart. Although Jomini spoke admiringly of the hard blow followed by the energetic pursuit, his line of operation strategy allowed the enemy the option of retiring. In reality Jomini thought that the primary objectives in war were places rather than armies: the occupation of territory or the seizure of such "decisive strategic points" as capitals. He affected to be the advocate of the new Napoleonic ways of war, but actually he looked back instead of forward. It has been rightly said of him (in R. A. Preston, S. F. Wise, and H. O. Werner, *Men in Arms*): "By his emphasis on lines of operation Jomini, in effect, returned to the eighteenth-century method of approaching the study of war as a geometric exercise. . . . In emphasizing the continuance of traditional features he missed the things that were new.

There can be no doubt that this interpreter of Napoleonic warfare actually set military thought back into the eighteenth century, an approach which the professional soldiers of the early nineteenth century found comfortable and safe."

Jomini confessed that he disliked the destructiveness of the warfare of his time. "I acknowledge," he wrote, "that my prejudices are in favor of the good old times when the French and English guards courteously invited each other to fire first as at Fontenoy. . . ." He said that he preferred "chivalric war" to "organized assassination," and he deplored as particularly cruel and terrible what he called wars of "opinion," or as we would say today, of "ideas." War was, as it should be, most proper and polite when it was directed by professional soldiers and fought by professional armies for limited objectives. All this is, of course, readily recognizable as good eighteenth-century doctrine. This could be Marshal Saxe saying: "I do not favor pitched battles . . . and I am convinced that a skillful general could make war all his life without being forced into one." Eighteenth-century warfare was leisurely and its ends were limited. It stressed maneuver rather than battle, as was natural in an age when professional armies were so expensive to raise and maintain that they could not be risked unless victory was reasonably certain. It was conducted with a measure of humanity that caused Chesterfield to say: "War is pusillanimously carried on in this degenerate age; quarter is given; towns are taken and people spared; even in a storm, a woman can hardly hope for the benefit of a rape." Most important of all, war was regarded as a kind of exercise or game to be conducted by soldiers. For the kings war might have a dynastic objective, but in the thinking of many military men it had little if any relationship to society or politics or statecraft.

Many West Pointers—McClellan, Lee, Sherman, and Beauregard, among others—expressed their admiration of Jomini and usually in extravagant terms. Halleck devoted years to translating Jomini's works, and his own book on the elements of war was only a rehash of Jomini, in parts, in fact, a direct steal. William Hardee's manual on tactics reflected Jominian ideas. But the American who did more than any other to popularize Jomini was Dennis Hart Mahan, who began teaching at West Point in 1824 and who influenced a whole generation of soldiers. He interpreted Jomini both in the classroom and in his writings. At one time Jomini's own works had been used at the academy but had been dropped in favor of abridgments by other writers. In 1848 Mahan's book on war, usually known by the short title of *Outpost*, became an official text. Most of the Civil War generals had been Mahan's pupils, and those older ones who had not, like Lee, were exposed to his ideas through personal relationships or through his book. Probably no one man had a more direct and formative impact on the thinking of the war's commanders.

Mahan, of course, did little more than to reproduce Jomini's ideas. He talked much of the principle of mass, of defeating the enemy's fractions in succession, and of interior lines. But it should be emphasized that his big point, the one he dwelt on most, was the offensive executed by celerity of movement. Mahan never tired of stressing the advantage of rapidity in war—or of excoriating "the slow and over-prudent general" who was afraid to grasp victory. "By rapidity of movement we can . . . make war feed war," he wrote. "We disembarrass ourselves of those immense trains." There was one operation that could change the face of a war, he said. When one's territory was invaded, the commander should invade the territory of the enemy; this was the mark of "true genius." (This passage makes us think immediately of Lee and Stonewall Jackson.) Jominian strategy as interpreted by Mahan then was the mass offensive waged on the battlefield, perhaps with utmost violence, but only on the battlefield. It cannot be sufficiently emphasized that Mahan, like his master, made no connection between war and technology and national life and political objectives. War was still an exercise carried on by professionals. War and statecraft were still separate things.

The Jominian influence on Civil War military leadership was obviously profound and pervasive. But before considering its manifestations, it may be helpful to dispose of a number of generals who do not meet the criteria of greatness or even of acceptable competence. This perhaps too brutal disposal will be performed by means of some undoubtedly too sweeping generalizations. These generals fell short of the mark partly because, as will be developed later, they were too thorough Jominians, and partly because they lacked the qualities of mind and character found in the great captains of war. Of the generals who commanded armies we can say that the following had such grave shortcomings that either they were not qualified to command or that they can be classified as no better than average soldiers: on the Union side—McClellan, Burnside, Hooker, Meade, Buell, Halleck, and Rosecrans; on the Confederate side—Albert Sidney Johnston, Beauregard, Bragg, Joe Johnston, and Edmund Kirby Smith.

McClellan will be discussed later, but here we may anticipate by saying that he did not have the temperament required for command. Burnside did not have the mentality. Hooker was a fair strategist, but he lacked iron and also the imagination to control troops not within his physical vision. Meade was a good routine soldier but no more, and was afflicted with a defensive psychosis. Buell was a duplicate of McClellan without any color. Halleck was an unoriginal scholar and an excellent staff officer who should never have taken the field. Rosecrans had strategic ability but no poise or balance; his crack-up at Chickamauga is a perfect example of Napoleon's general who paints the wrong kind of mental picture. A. S. Johnston died before he could prove himself, but nothing that he did before his death makes us think that he was anything but a gallant troop leader. Beauregard probably was developing into a competent commander by the time of Shiloh, but his failure to win that battle plus his personality faults caused him to be exiled to comparatively minor posts for the rest of the war. Bragg, the general of the lost opportunity, was a good deal like Hooker. He created favorable situations but lacked the determination to carry through his purpose; he did not have the will to overcome the inertia of war. Kirby Smith made a promising start but seemed to shrink under the responsibility of command and finally disappeared into the backwash of the Trans-Mississippi theater. The stature of Joe Johnston probably will be argued as long as there are Civil War fans to talk. But surely we can take his measure by his decision in the Georgia campaign to withdraw from a position near Cassville that he termed the "best that I saw occupied during the war" merely because his corps generals advised retiring. A great general, we feel, would have delivered the attack that Johnston originally planned to make. Johnston undoubtedly had real ability, but he never did much with it. It is reasonable to expect that a general who has sustained opportunities will sometime, once, achieve something decisive. Certainly Johnston had the opportunities, but there is no decisive success on his record.

Of the lesser generals, it is fair to say that James Longstreet and Stonewall Jackson were outstanding corps leaders, probably the best in the war, but that neither gave much evidence of being able to go higher. Longstreet failed in independent command. Jackson performed brilliantly as commander of a small army but probably lacked the administrative ability to handle a large one. In addition, he was never fairly tested against first-rate opposition. Thomas and W. S. Hancock stand out among Union corps generals. Thomas also commanded an army, but his skills were of a particular order and could be exercised only in a particular situation. He excelled in the counterattack delivered from strength. J. E. B. Stuart, Sheridan, N. B. Forrest, and J. H. Wilson were fine cavalry leaders, but we cannot say with surety that they could have been anything else. On the one occasion when Sheridan directed an army he displayed unusual ability to handle combined arms (infantry, cavalry, artillery), but he enjoyed such a preponderant advantage in numbers over his opponent as to be almost decisive. He was never really subjected to the inertia of war. In the last analysis, the only Civil

War generals who deserve to be ranked as great are Lee for the South and Grant and Sherman for the North.

We can now turn to an examination of the influence of Jominian eighteenth-century military thought on Civil War generalship, first directing our attention to the first Northern generals with whom Abraham Lincoln had to deal. It is immediately and painfully evident that in the first of the world's modern wars these men were ruled by traditional concepts of warfare. The Civil War was a war of ideas and, inasmuch as neither side could compromise its political purposes, it was a war of unlimited objectives. Such a war was bound to be a rough, no-holds-barred affair, a bloody and brutal struggle. Yet Lincoln's generals proposed to conduct it in accordance with the standards and the strategy of an earlier and easier military age. They saw cities and territory as their objectives rather than the armies of the enemy. They hoped to accomplish their objectives by maneuvering rather than by fighting. McClellan boasted that the "brightest chaplets" in his history were Manassas and Yorktown, both occupied after the Confederates had departed, because he had seized them by "pure military skill" and without the loss of life. When he had to lose lives, McClellan was almost undone. The "sickening sight" of the battlefield, he told his wife after Fair Oaks, took all the charms from victory. McClellan's mooning around the field anguishing over the dead may seem strange to the modern mind, but Jomini would have understood his reactions. Buell argued, in the spirit of Marshal Saxe, that campaigns could be carried out and won without engaging in a single big battle. Only when success was reasonably certain should a general risk battle, Buell said, adding: "War has a higher object than that of mere bloodshed." After the Confederates retired from Corinth, Halleck instructed his subordinates: "There is no object in bringing on a battle if this object can be obtained without one. I think by showing a bold front for a day or two the enemy will continue his retreat, which is all I desire." Meade, who confessed shame for his cause when he was ordered to seize the property of a Confederate sympathizer, thought that the North should prosecute the war "like the afflicted parent who is compelled to chastise his erring child, and who performs the duty with a sad heart."

With an almost arrogant assurance, Lincoln's first generals believed that war was a business to be carried on by professionals without interference from civilians and without political objectives. It is no exaggeration to say that some of the officers saw the war as a kind of game played by experts off in some private sphere that had no connection with the government or society. Rosecrans gave a typical expression of this viewpoint when he resisted pressure from Washington to advance before the battle of Stone's River: "I will not move until I am ready! . . . War is a business to be conducted systematically. I believe I understand my business. . . . I will not budge until I am ready." But, as might be expected, the classic example is McClellan. He refused to retain General Charles Hamilton in his army when Lincoln requested him to, even after, or more accurately, especially after the President emphasized that there were weighty political reasons for assigning Hamilton a minor position. When McClellan conceived his Urbanna plan, he did not tell Lincoln about it for months. He did not seem to know that it was his job to counsel his political superior on his plans; in fact, he did not seem to know that there was any relationship between war and politics. In the winter of 1861–1862 Lincoln implored McClellan to make a move, even a small or diversionary one, to inspire public opinion with the belief that more decisive action was contemplated later. McClellan refused on the grounds that he was not yet completely prepared. That the public might become so discouraged that it would abandon the war impressed McClellan not at all. With him the only question was when the professionals would be ready to start the game.

Lincoln's early generals also accepted blindly the Jominian doctrine of concentration. As they interpreted it, it meant one big effort at a time in one theater. McClellan's

proposal to mass 273,000 troops in the eastern department in 1861, a physical and military impossibility at that
time, was a typical piece of Jominian thinking. Of course,
each commander was convinced that the one big push
should be made by him, and each one demanded that
other departments be stripped of troops to strengthen
his own army. It would be possible to argue that the apparent caution of every Union general in the first years
of the war, and the consequent inaction of Union armies,
was the result of each commander's conviction that he
did not possess enough strength to undertake the movements recommended by Jomini. But this feeling of the
generals brought them into conflict with their commander
in chief, who was no Jominian in his strategic notions,
and their differences with Lincoln will be discussed later.

When we examine the psychology of the Northern generals, the thought immediately occurs that the Southern
generals were not like this, and inevitably we ask, why
not? Had the Southerners freed themselves from Jomini's
dogma? Were they developing new ways of war? The
answer to both questions is no. The Confederates were,
if possible, more Jominian than the Federals. They simply
gave a different emphasis to the traditional pattern of
strategic thought. Whereas the Federals borrowed from
Jomini the idea of places as objectives, the Confederates
took from him the principle of the offensive. Moreover,
the Southern generals were fortunate in being able to make
enemy armies the object of their offensives because Confederate policy did not look to the acquisition of enemy
territory. The influence of Mahan, with his doctrine of
celerity and the headlong attack, is also apparent in Confederate strategy, especially as it was employed by Lee.
In addition, the poverty of Southern resources had the
effect of forcing Southern generals to think in aggressive
terms. They could not afford to wait for a big build-up
in men and equipment, but had to act when they could
with what they had. Paradoxically, the Industrial Revolution, which would have so much to do with bringing
about the advent of total war with all its destructiveness,

had the immediate consequence of making the Northern generals less inclined to deal out destruction. They could secure material so easily that they refused to move until they had received more than they needed—after which they were often so heavily laden they could not move.

Far from departing from Jomini, the Confederates were the most brilliant practitioners of his doctrine. If we look for successful applications of the principles that Jomini emphasized—the objective, the offensive, mass, economy of force, interior lines, and unity of command—we find them most frequently in the Confederate campaigns and most particularly in the Virginia theater. Lee, the Confederacy's best general, was also its greatest Jominian. Probably it is because Lee embodied so precisely the spirit of traditional warfare that he has been ranked so high by students of war. Military historians are likely to be as conservative as generals. The English writers, who have done so much to form our image of the war, have been especially lavish in their praise. It may be suspected that their attitude stems largely from a feeling that Lee was a gentleman, English style, although for a long while the British, when they faced a possible combination of superior continental powers, studied Lee's strategy because of its application of the principle of interior lines. Cyril Falls said that Lee was a master combination of "strategist, tactical genius, leader of the highest inspiration, and technician in the arts of hastily fortifying defensive positions superbly chosen." Falls added: "He must stand as the supreme figure of this survey of a hundred years of war." Colonel A. H. Burne was more restrained, but spoke admiringly of Lee's audacity, his use of the offensive, and his skill at concentration. The opinions of G. F. R. Henderson and G. J. Wolseley are so well known as not to require quotation.

Let us concede that many of the tributes to Lee are deserved. He was not all that his admirers have said of him, but he was a large part of it. But let us also note that even his most fervent admirers, when they come to evaluate him as a strategist, have to admit that his abilities were

never demonstrated on a larger scale than a theater. Cyril
Falls, after his extravagant eulogy of Lee, falls on his face
in attempting to attribute to his subject gifts for "large-
scale strategy": the only example he can find is Lee's rede-
ployment of forces between the Shenandoah Valley and
Richmond during the Peninsula campaign! Lee was pre-
eminently a field or a theater strategist, and a great one,
but it remains unproven that he was anything more or
wanted to be anything more. "In spite of all his ability, his
heroism and the heroic efforts of his army," writes General J. F. C. Fuller, "because he would think and work
in a corner, taking no notice of the whole, taking no interest in forming policy or in the economic side of the war,
he was ultimately cornered and his cause lost." For his
preoccupation with the war in Virginia, Lee is not to be
criticized. He was a product of his culture, and that culture, permeated in its every part by the spirit of localism,
dictated that his outlook on war should be local. Nevertheless, it must be recognized that his restricted view
constituted a tragic command limitation in a modern war.
The same limitation applied to Southern generalship as
a whole. The Confederates, brilliant and bold in executing
Jominian strategy on the battlefield, never succeeded in
lifting their gifts above the theater level.

In many respects Lee was not a modern-minded general.
He probably did not understand the real function of a staff
and certainly failed to put together an adequate staff for
his army. Although he had an excellent eye for terrain,
his use of maps was almost primitive. He does not seem
to have appreciated the impact of railroads on warfare or
to have realized that railroads made Jomini's principle of
interior lines largely obsolete. His mastery of logistics did
not extend beyond departmental limits. In February, 1865,
he said that he could not believe Sherman would be able
to move into North Carolina. The evidence of Sherman's
great march was before him, and yet he was not quite
sure it had really happened.

The most striking lack of modernity in Lee was his
failure to grasp the vital relationship between war and

statecraft. Here the great Virginian was truly a Jominian. Almost as much as McClellan, he thought of war as a professional exercise. One of his officers said admiringly that Lee was too thorough a soldier to attempt to advise the government on such matters as the defense of Richmond. When late in the war a cabinet member asked Lee for his opinion on the advisability of moving the capital farther south, the general replied: "That is a political question . . . and you politicians must determine it. I shall endeavor to take care of the army, and you must make the laws and control the Government." And yet what could be a more strategic question than the safety of the capital? Lee attained a position in the Confederacy held by no other man, either in civil or military life. There was little exaggeration in the statement General William Mahone made to him: "You are the State." But Lee could not accept the role that his eminence demanded. He could never have said as Pitt did: "I know that I can save the country and that no one else can." It has been suggested that Lee did not try to impose his will on the government because of his humility of character, and this may well be true. But it would also seem to be true that he did not know that a commander had any political responsibility.

Lincoln's first generals did not understand that war and statecraft were parts of the same piece. But none of the Confederate generals, first or last, ever grasped this fact about modern war. The most distinguishing feature of Southern generalship is that it did not grow. Lee and the other Confederate commanders were pretty much the same men in 1865 that they had been in 1861. They were good, within certain limits, at the beginning, and they were good at the end but still within the original limits. They never freed themselves from the influence of traditional doctrine. The probable explanation, David Donald has suggested, is that the Confederates won their first battles with Jominian strategy and saw no reason to change and that the Southern mind, civil and military, was unreceptive to new ideas. The North, on the other hand, finally brought forward generals who were able to grow and who could employ new ways of war. Even so doctrinaire a Jominian as Halleck reached the point where he could approve techniques of total war that would have horrified the master. But the most outstanding examples of growth and originality among the Northern generals are Grant and Sherman.

The qualities of Grant's generalship deserve more analysis than those of Lee, partly because they have not been sufficiently emphasized but largely because Grant was a more modern soldier than his rival. First, we note that Grant had that quality of character or will exhibited by all the great captains. (Lee had it, too.) Perhaps the first military writer to emphasize this trait in Grant was C. F. Atkinson in 1908. Grant's distinguishing feature as a general, said Atkinson, was his character, which was controlled by a tremendous will; with Grant action was translated from thought to deed by all the force of a tremendous personality. This moral strength of Grant's may be news to some present-day historians, but it was overpoweringly apparent to all who were thrown into close association with him. Charles Francis Adams, Jr., like all his family not disposed to easy praise, said that Grant was really an extraordinary person, although he did not look it. In a crisis, Adams added, all would instinctively lean on Grant. Lincoln saw this quality in Grant clearly: "The great thing about Grant, I take it, is his perfect coolness and persistency of purpose. I judge he is not easily excited, —which is a great element in an officer." But the best tribute to Grant's character was paid by the general who knew him best. In a typical explosive comment to J. H. Wilson, Sherman said: "Wilson, I am a damn sight smarter than Grant. I know a great deal more about war, military history, strategy, and administration, and about everything else than he does. But I tell you where he beats me, and where he beats the world. He don't care a damn for what the enemy does out of his sight, but it scares me like hell." On the eve of the great campaigns of 1864 Sherman wrote to Grant that he considered Grant's strongest feature was his ability to go into battle without hesitation, doubts, or reserve. Characteristically Sherman added "It was this that made me act with confidence."

In this same letter Sherman confessed to a reservation that he had had about Grant: "My only points of doubt were as to your knowledge of grand strategy, and of books of science and history; but I confess your common sense seems to have supplied all this." Common sense Grant had, and it enabled him to deal with such un-Jominian phenomena as army correspondents and political generals. Unlike Sherman, Grant accepted the reporters—but he rendered them harmless. "General Grant informs us correspondents that he will willingly facilitate us in obtaining all proper information," Junius Browne wrote S. H. Gay, then added significantly that Grant was "not very communicative." Unlike McClellan, who would not accept General Hamilton for political considerations urged by Lincoln, Grant took John A. McClernand at the President's request. He could not imagine why Lincoln wanted a command for McClernand but assumed that there must be some reason important to his civil superior. He put up with McClernand until he found a way to strike him down to which Lincoln could not object. In this whole affair Grant showed that he realized the vital relation between politics and modern war.

It was Grant's common sense that enabled him to rise above the dogmas of traditional warfare. On one occasion a young officer, thinking to flatter Grant, asked his opinion of Jomini. Grant replied that he had never read the master. He then expressed his own theory of strategy: "The art of war is simple enough. Find out where your enemy is. Get at him as soon as you can. Strike at him as hard as you can and as often as you can, and keep moving on." After the war Grant discussed more fully his opinion of the value of doctrine. He conceded that military knowledge was highly desirable in a commander. But he added: "If men make war in slavish observance of rules, they will fail. No rules will apply to conditions of war as different as those which exist in Europe and America. . . . War is progressive, because all the instruments and elements of war are progressive." He then referred to the movement that had been his most striking departure from the rules, the Vicksburg campaign. To take Vicksburg by rules would have required a withdrawal to Memphis, the opening of a new line of operations, in fact, a whole new strategic design. But Grant believed that the discouraged condition of Northern opinion would not permit such a conformity to Jominian practice: "In a popular war we had to consider political exigencies." It was this ability of Grant's to grasp the political nature of modern war that marks him as the first of the great modern generals.

The question of where to rank Sherman among Civil War generals has always troubled military writers. He is obviously not a Jominian, and just as obviously he is not a great battle captain like Grant or Lee. Colonel Burne points out that never once did Sherman command in a battle where he engaged his whole force and that he never won a resounding victory. Conceding that in the Georgia campaign Sherman displayed imagination, resource, versatility, broadness of conception, and genuine powers of leadership—all fundamental traits of a great commander —Burne still contends that Sherman exhibited two serious failings: that of pursuing a geographical rather than a military objective and that of avoiding risk. B. H. Liddell Hart, on the other hand, depicts Sherman as the greatest general of the war because more than any other commander he came to see that the object of strategy is to minimize fighting. Part of this evaluation can be written off as an attempt by Liddell Hart to glorify through Sherman the British strategy of the "indirect approach." And yet he is right in saying that Sherman had the most complete grasp of the truth that the resisting power of a modern democracy depends heavily on the popular will and that this will depends in turn on a secure economic and social basis. Sherman, a typical Jominian at the beginning of the war, became its greatest exponent of economic and psychological warfare. Nobody realized more clearly than

Sherman the significance of the techniques he introduced. Describing to Grant what he meant to do on his destructive march, he said, "This may not be war, but rather statesmanship." At the same time we must recognize that Sherman's strategy by itself would not have brought the Confederacy down. That end called for a Grant who at the decisive moment would attack the enemy's armed forces. As Burne puts it: "Sherman might help to prepare the ground, but it was Grant who struck the blow." The North was fortunate in finding two generals who between them executed Clausewitz's three objectives of war: to conquer and destroy the enemy's armed forces, to get possession of the material elements of aggression and other sources of existence of the enemy, and to gain public opinion by winning victories that depress the enemy's morale.

It remains to touch on the military leadership of the North and the South at the highest levels where strategy was determined—at the rival Presidents and the command systems they headed. In supreme leadership the Union was clearly superior. Lincoln was an abler and a stronger man than Davis. The Northern President illustrated perfectly the truth of Clausewitz's dictum that "a remarkable, superior mind and strength of character" are the primary qualifications of a director of war. The North developed at an early date an over-all plan of strategy, and it finally devised a unified command system for the entire military machine. The South was unable to accomplish either one of these objectives. But its failure should not be set down as the result of a shortage of brains among its leaders. Here again we need to remind ourselves that ways of making war are always the product of cultures. For the nationalistic North it was comparatively easy to achieve a broad view of war. Conversely, it was natural for the localistic South to adopt a narrow view and to fight a conservative war. Confederate strategy was almost wholly defensive, and was designed to guard the whole circumference of the country. In military jargon, it was a cordon defense. Probably the South's best chance to win its independence by a military decision was to attempt on a grand strategic scale the movement its generals were so good at on specific battlefields—the concentrated mass offensive. But the restrictions of Southern culture prevented any national application of the one Jominian principle that might have brought success.

Just as a cordon defense was the worst strategy for the South, a cordon offense was the best strategy for the North. This was the strategy that Lincoln had pressed upon his generals almost from the beginning of the war —to make enemy armies their objective and to move all Federal forces against the enemy line simultaneously. An offensive along the entire circumference of the Confederacy would prevent the enemy from moving troops from one threatened point to another and would inevitably achieve a break-through. It was an eminently sensible strategy for the side with the greater numbers and the superior lines of transportation and for a war fought over such a vast theater. When Lincoln proposed his plan to general after general, it met with polite scorn. It violated the Jominian principle of concentration in one theater for one big effort. It was the product of a mind that did not know the rules of war.

Not until he found Grant did Lincoln find a general who was original enough to employ his strategy. Grant's master design for 1864 called for an advance of Federal armies all along the line. It was the operation that broke the back of the Confederacy. When Grant explained his plan to the President, he remarked that even the smaller Federal forces not fighting would help the fighting by advancing and engaging the attention of the enemy. We have dealt much with maxims here, and we may fittingly conclude with one. Lincoln grasped Grant's point immediately and uttered a maxim of his own. At least for the Civil War it had more validity than anything written by Baron Jomini. "Those not skinning can hold a leg," said the commander in chief.

Northern Diplomacy and European Neutrality

Norman A. Graebner

MAJOR ROBERT ANDERSON'S surrender of Fort Sumter in April, 1861, placed an unprecedented burden on American diplomacy. Not since the American Revolution had the foreign relations of the United States been reduced to a defense of the Republic's very existence. Diplomacy, to be sure, was only one element in the vast arsenal of resources upon which Northern leadership could draw to frustrate the South's determination to sever the Union, but from the outset of the struggle it assumed a primary importance. Even limited European power, thrown effectively into the scale against the North, could have rendered the Southern cause successful. The nation's future, therefore, rested on the efficiency of its diplomatic as much as its military corps.

Europe's involvement in the American Civil War comprised a persistent danger to the Union, for the Southern independence movement threatened all the fundamental power relationships between the Old World and the New. Despite its tradition of isolationism toward Europe, the American Republic had become by 1861 a significant force in world politics. Cassius Clay, President Lincoln's choice for the court at St. Petersburg, wrote in April, 1862, that it was "useless to deceive ourselves with the idea that we can isolate ourselves from European interventions. We became in spite of ourselves—the Monroe Doctrine—Washington's farewell—and all that—a part of the 'balance of power.'" To European leaders the United States was a nation of consequence in world affairs, but the relationship of American strength and American traditions to the precise interests of Europe varied from country to country.

London promised to become the focal point of all wartime diplomatic maneuvering, for Britain was the dominant power of Europe and her control of Canada and the sea lanes of the north Atlantic created extensive commitments in the New World. France was equally concerned over events in America but lacked the power to escape the British lead. Keeping such interested and calculating nations neutral became the chief task of Northern diplomacy.

Fortunately for the North, Anglo-American relations had never been more cordial than they were in 1861. But this was no guarantee of British neutrality. Britain's powerful conservative classes, always cynical toward the democratic experiment of the United States, recognized the fundamental meaning of the American Civil War. Democratic institutions were on trial. The United States as a nation had passed beyond the normal control of Old World power, but if the American people were determined to destroy their national greatness and demonstrate the failure of their institutions, the least that reactionary Europe could do was to encourage them in their effort so that the work of destruction might succeed. British aristocrats had long regarded the American democratic example as a threat to their estate. For them the breakup of the American Union would impede the expansion of democracy everywhere. In July, 1861, *Blackwood's Magazine* declared: "It is precisely because we do *not* share the admiration of America for her own institutions and political tendencies that we do not now see in the impending change an event altogether to be deplored."

British conservatives resented American power and truculence as much as American institutions. What disturbed them especially was the growth of the United States into a formidable maritime rival. Edouard de Stoeckl, the Russian Minister in Washington, lamented in January, 1860, that in the approaching dissolution of the Union Great Britain would experience one of those "strokes of fortune" which occur but rarely in history. England, he predicted, would benefit more than any other nation from the disintegration of American power. "The Cabinet of London," he warned his government, "is watching attentively the internal dissensions of the Union and awaits the result with an impatience which it has difficulty in disguising." From St. Petersburg Cassius Clay warned Lincoln, "I saw at a glance where the feeling of England was. They hoped for our ruin! They are jealous of our power. They care neither for the South nor the North. They hate both."

Western Europe, moreover, had long been indignant at the American effort to keep the Western Hemisphere off limits for further European encroachment. For the ambitious Louis Napoleon of France, especially, events in America were encouraging, for they seemed to be rendering the Monroe Doctrine inoperative. No American fleet would block the contemplated movement of French troops to Vera Cruz or demolish his dreams of establishing a vassal empire in Mexico. A strong and friendly Confederate States of America would create a buffer between what remained of the United States and his new Mexican possessions. Secession appeared so consequential to Europe because it again exposed the western world to European partition. It was no wonder that Stoeckl advised his government in April, 1861, that "England will take advantage of the first opportunity to recognize the seceded States and that France will follow her."

In Washington, Henri Mercier, the French Minister, favored immediate action. He advised his government that in recognizing the Confederacy it would give the American conflict the character of a war and thereby extend to French seamen the benefit of neutral rights. The United States could not complain, he added, because it had recognized the revolutionary governments of Spanish America. Certainly this nation could not be offended merely because other nations accepted its democratic principles of self-determination. Yet Mercier was a realist. He admonished the French Minister in Paris to formulate his American policy only in agreement with the other powers of Europe.

Russia alone of the European states made the preservation of the Union a matter of conscious policy. For Stoeckl the destruction of the Union threatened the equilibrium of world politics. The United States, ran his argument, had become Europe's best guarantee against British aggression and arrogance. Traditional Russian-American friendship had been based on a mutual rivalry toward Great Britain. It had been the case of the enemies of a rival becoming friends. George Mifflin Dallas, when United States Minister at the Czar's court during the Van Buren administration, had recorded this significant phrase of Nicholas I, "Not only are our interests alike, our enemies are the same."

After the outbreak of the Civil War the *Journal of St. Petersburg,* official organ of the Czarist government, declared: "Russia entertains for the United States of America a lively sympathy founded on sentiments of mutual friendship and on common interests. She considers their prosperity necessary to the general equilibrium." Nothing, the Imperial Cabinet agreed, should be permitted to weaken this powerful counterpoise to England. Prince Gortchakov, the Russian Foreign Minister, instructed Stoeckl in July, 1861, to assure the American nation that it could assume "the most cordial sympathy on the part of our August Master, during the serious crisis which it is passing through at present." This *entente cordiale* between the world's greatest despotism and its leading democracy was *Realpolitik* at its diplomatic best, for despite the incompatibility of political principles, it served the best interests of both nations.

William H. Seward, Lincoln's Secretary of State, assumed the essential task of preventing the introduction of European power into the American Civil War. His diplomacy had but one objective—the preservation of the Union. Seward's devotion to this cause was so intense that in April, 1861, he recommended to Lincoln a foreign war, perhaps against Spain and France, to rally the seceded states around the American flag and thus reforge the Union. Lincoln tactfully ignored the proposal, but the Washington diplomatic corps was amazed. Lord Lyons, the British Minister, warned the Foreign Office in London that Seward would be "a dangerous foreign minister."

Thereafter the British government regarded the American Secretary with suspicion. Charles Francis Adams, the American Minister in London, reported that Seward was viewed there as "an ogre fully resolved to eat all Englishmen raw." Lord John Russell, the British Foreign Secretary, addressed Lyons in February, 1861: "The success or failure of Mr. Seward's plans to prevent the disruption of the North American Union is a matter of deep interest to Her Majesty's Government." From the opening guns of the war Seward's leadership was a matter of grave concern to the chancelleries of Europe.

To forestall European interference in American affairs after the fall of Sumter, Seward denied officially the existence of any war between North and South. "There is here, as there always has been," he informed the British and French governments, "one political power, namely, the United States of America, competent to make war and peace, and conduct commerce and alliances with all foreign nations." What existed, he explained, was an armed sedition seeking to overthrow the government. Its suppression did not constitute a war or in any manner modify the character, rights, and responsibilities of either the United States or foreign nations in their diplomatic relationships. Seward admitted that international law permitted the recognition of established *de facto* governments; he merely denied that one existed in the South.

What endangered Seward's rigid position toward Europe was the rapid expansion of the conflict between North and South onto the Atlantic. It was fundamental in Lincoln's strategy to weaken and destroy the Southern economy by cutting off Southern shipments of cotton to Europe through a blockade of the Southern ports. Shortly after the crisis of Fort Sumter the Confederate government issued a proclamation calling for privateers, and Lincoln announced his blockade. Seward warned Lyons that the North would tolerate no further European commerce with the South, but he denied that a formal blockade destroyed his own claims that war did not exist. Yet the United States could hardly proclaim a blockade without declaring itself a belligerent and claiming rights over foreign vessels admitted only in time of war. Lyons was disturbed, for the blockade imposed on Europe the choice of recognizing the Confederacy or submitting to the interruption of its commerce with the South.

Britain, fearful of being trapped in a maritime war, took immediate steps to protect her commerce. On May 13, 1861, without awaiting the arrival of Minister Adams, Queen Victoria issued a declaration of neutrality which called upon British subjects to avoid hostilities between the North and South. Soon France, Spain, the Netherlands, and Brazil followed the British lead. This recognition of Southern belligerency granted to Southern ships the privileges in neutral ports accorded the ships of the Federal government.

Washington was shocked at this British action, for it not only suggested collusion between Britain and France but also presaged the diplomatic recognition of the South. Charles Sumner, the Massachusetts Senator, termed the Queen's proclamation "the most hateful act of English history since the time of Charles 2nd." Seward's reaction was even more violent. "They have misunderstood things fearfully, in Europe," he wrote home in May. "Great Britain is in great danger of sympathizing so much with the South for the sake of peace and cotton as to drive us to make war against her, as the ally of the traitors. . . . It will be dreadful but the end will be sure and swift." Through Adams in London, Seward warned the British government, "If any European power provokes war, we shall not shrink from it."

Similarly Seward advised Mercier that French recognition of the Confederacy would result in war with the United States. This nation might be defeated, he admitted bluntly, but France would know that she had been in a war. To William L. Dayton, the American Minister in Paris, Seward wrote: "Foreign intervention would oblige us to treat those who should yield it as allies of the insurrectionary party and to carry on the war against them as enemies. . . . The President and the people of the

United States deem the Union, which would then be at stake, worth all the cost and all the sacrifices of a contest with the world at arms, if such a contest should prove inevitable."

European interference meant war, but Seward offered the Old World powers the carrot as well as the stick. He reminded both Britain and France of their long tradition of friendship with the United States and assured them that this nation had cherished that peace. The American Republic, he instructed Adams, was "anxious to avoid all causes of misunderstanding with Great Britain; to draw closer, instead of breaking, the existing bonds of amity and friendship. There is nothing good or great," he added appealingly, "which both nations may not expect to attain or effect if they may remain friends. It would be a hazardous day for both branches of the British race when they should determine to test how much harm each could do the other." The Secretary extended similar assurances to the French: "We have no hostile or interested designs against any other state or nation whatever, and, on the contrary, we seek peace, harmony, and commerce with them all." Seward repeated ceaselessly his contention that the United States was one, and that the nations of Europe should not view themselves as neutrals between two imaginary belligerents in America, but as friends of the United States.

Seward's warnings were not without effect. When Lord Russell learned of the arrival in London of William L. Yancey, the Confederate Commissioner seeking recognition for his government, he wrote to Lyons in Washington: "If it can possibly be helped, Mr. Seward must not be allowed to get us into a quarrel. I shall see the southerners when they come, but unofficially and keep them at a proper distance." But even the unofficial reception of Yancey was too much for Seward. His next letter to Adams was so menacing that Lincoln revised certain passages and removed others. Nor would the President permit Adams to read the dispatch to Russell. Even in revised form the dispatch was little less than an ultimatum.

It suggested that Adams break off his relations with the British government if Russell persisted in seeing the Confederate Commissioner. Not content with this warning, Seward invited William Russell, the noted Washington correspondent of the London *Times,* to his home and read to him deliberately the long dispatch with its insinuations that Britain would destroy the American Republic if she could. Russell, he hoped, would not keep his impressions to himself.

Adams regarded the Secretary's warning as little less than a declaration of war. "I scarcely know how to understand Mr. Seward," he admitted. "The rest of the Government may be demented for all I know, but he surely is calm and wise." Adams informed Lord Russell in London that further relations between the British government and the "pseudo-commissioners" of the Confederate States, whether unofficial or not, would be regarded as a manifestation of hostility by the United States. Lord Russell did not receive the Southern Commissioner again. In May the British Minister announced a hands-off policy: ". . . we have not been involved in any way in that contest . . . and for God's sake, let us if possible, keep out of it."

Through Dayton, Seward informed the French Minister that the United States would regard any further communications of his government with the Southern Commissioners as "exceptional and injurious" to American dignity and honor. Even an unofficial reception of the emissaries of disunion, he complained, would give them encouragement to prosecute their effort to destroy the American Republic. Perhaps a warning would be sufficient to relieve the United States of further action, for Seward declared that this nation could not tolerate, whatever the consequences of its resistance, the recognition of the Confederacy by the French government.

Mercier and Lyons in Washington, still determined to commit their nations to a settlement of the American conflict, suggested mediation, with their governments serving as umpires between North and South. Lord Russell judiciously declined and Seward caused the diplomatic corps abruptly to drop what remained of the scheme. In a statement to the governor of Maryland he made it clear that the Federal government would accept no foreign arbitrament in settling its differences with the Confederacy. The American Constitution, he reminded the Europeans, provided all the required means for surmounting internal disorders. Arbitration would endanger the nation's integrity by substituting non-Constitutional devices for the normal functioning of the American system.

United States relations with Britain were unnecessarily disturbed in December, 1861, when Captain Charles Wilkes of the Federal warship *San Jacinto* stopped the British mail steamer *Trent* off the coast of Cuba and removed two Confederate leaders, James M. Mason and John Slidell. These men, among the South's ablest, had been dispatched to London and Paris respectively to replace the earlier commissioners. To the zealous Wilkes their capture was an unprecedented coup, but unfortunately he had broken the cherished maritime principle for which this nation supposedly had fought the British in the War of 1812. In London Henry Adams, son of the American Minister, saw the issue clearly, writing to his brother: "Good God, what's got into you all? What do you mean by deserting now the great principles of our fathers, by returning to the vomit of that dog Great Britain? What do you mean by asserting now principles against which every Adams yet has protested and resisted?"

Seward was embarrassed. He faced the necessity of satisfying the British who were wronged and at the same time of protecting American prestige abroad. "If I decide this case in favor of my own government," he admitted, "I must disavow its most cherished principles, and . . . forever abandon its essential policy. The country cannot afford the sacrifice. If I maintain those principles, and adhere to that policy, I must surrender the case itself." Seward soon decided on the latter course and conceded to the British with remarkable grace, for nowhere did the *Trent* case challenge his Union policies. "In coming to my conclusion," he wrote to Adams, "I have not forgotten that if the safety of this Union required the detention of the captured persons it would be the right and duty of this government to detain them. But the effective check and waning proportions of the existing insurrection, as well as the comparative unimportance of the captured persons themselves, when dispassionately weighed happily forbid me from resorting to that defense." Federal officials released the two Confederates promptly and sent them on their way. Lord Russell was relieved. He wrote, "I do not believe that Seward has any animosity to this country. It is all buncom."

What gave the South the presumption of success in its effort to secure European recognition was the alleged economic power of cotton. Southern writers in 1861 assumed that Britain would break the Northern blockade to guarantee the flow of cotton into England. "Cotton," declared the Charleston *Mercury,* "would bring England to her knees." *De Bow's Review* in June predicted that a blockade of the Southern ports would be "swept away by the English fleets of observation hovering on the Southern coasts, to protect English commerce, and especially the free flow of cotton to English and French factories." If cotton were king, the South had only to place an embargo on that commodity to force Britain to destroy the blockade. "Foreign nations will not recognize the independence of the Confederate States," admitted one Southern governor realistically, "until commerce with the Confederate States will become not only desirable, but necessary to their own prosperity." The Confederate Congress refused to establish an embargo, but Committees of Public Safety in the Southern seaport towns effectively halted the export of cotton to Europe.

By the spring of 1862 King Cotton had compelled neither Britain nor France to recognize Southern independence or break the blockade. Confederate efforts to force action in the British government by depriving Lancashire of raw cotton actually had the opposite effect. As one British leader observed, "I wonder the South do not see that our recognition *because* they keep cotton from us would be ignominious beyond measure, & that no English Parlt could do so base a thing." But the British resolve not to break the blockade resulted from a far more fundamental motive than a willingness to dispense with cotton, for the blockade defied America's own precedents and doctrines of neutral maritime rights. In undermining the principle of the Declaration of Paris that blockades to be binding must be effective, the United States was releasing England in a future conflict from this burdensome feature of the past. American action weakened the stand of the smaller maritime powers in their perennial effort to force Great Britain to recognize neutral rights in time of war.

Historians have agreed that cotton failed as a diplomatic weapon because Britain enjoyed too much lucrative trade with the North, requiring especially huge quantities of Northern grain, and because the textile workers most affected by the cotton famine remained staunch friends of the Union. Professor Ephraim D. Adams has accounted for the allegiance of English workingmen to Lincoln's wartime leadership by citing the general threat to democratic progress imposed by Southern secession. Either the North would triumph or democracy everywhere would be in jeopardy. The eventual Northern success vindicated the democratic system so completely, says Adams, that it led directly to the British Reform Bill of 1867.

Lincoln's Emancipation Proclamation, although designed, at least partially, to influence European attitudes toward the Union cause, had little effect on European sentiment and none on European action. British conservatives thought it foolhardy and anticipated a servile insurrection. Even William E. Gladstone was unmoved by Lincoln's action, reiterating his conviction that "negro emancipation cannot be effected, in any sense favourable either to black or to white by the bloody hand of war, especially of Civil War." British liberals, abolitionists, and workingmen lauded the Proclamation, but these groups had always favored the Union because it represented the cause of democracy. None of these groups, moreover, wielded influence over British policy. Northern diplomatic success found its fundamental explanation less in specific interests and doubts than in a great diplomatic tradition.

Europe's diplomatic tradition cautioned against any recognition of the Confederacy until the South had demonstrated the power required to establish and maintain its independence. Without the assurance of ultimate Southern success, European involvement would assume the risk of either an eventual ignominious retreat from a declared diplomatic objective or an unlimited military commitment to guarantee the achievement of Southern independence. Confronted with Europe's traditional realism, the Southern diplomatic cause in London and Paris could be no more successful than the Southern military cause in Virginia and Pennsylvania. Diplomacy reflects the status of power, and Southern power never appeared greater than during the summer and autumn months of 1862.

News of General George B. McClellan's retirement from before Richmond in the early summer of 1862 merely confirmed a general European conviction that the American Union was doomed. To European military experts, diplomats, and statesmen, Northern power seemed incapable of overcoming the defensive nature of the Southern military commitment. The North, Europe understood, enjoyed an immense industrial superiority, but the advantages of strategy, terrain, and leadership appeared to lie with the South. Confederate armies had no obligation to conquer the North, but only to beat off the Union forces. This they appeared capable of doing. In June, 1862, the London *Times* broached the issue of European intervention, convinced that Southern independence was inevitable. "It is plain," said the *Times,* that the time is approaching when Europe will have to think seriously of its relations to the two belligerents in the American war. . . . That North and South must now choose between separation and ruin, material and political, is the opinion of nearly every one who, looking impartially and from a distance on the conflict, sees what is hidden from the frenzied eyes of the

Northern politicians." Recognition of a successful cause could be both legitimate and effective.

For many British editors and politicians, McClellan's retreat from the peninsula during the summer of 1862 was like redemption. So dominant was the pro-Southern trend in British opinion that Henry Adams wrote from London, "There is no doubt that the idea here is as strong as ever that we must ultimately fail, and unless a very few weeks show some great military result we shall have our hands full in this quarter." Only a decisive Northern victory, he observed, could prevent European intervention. Public hostility, Charles Francis Adams wrote on July 18 to his son in America, was "rising every hour and running harder against us than at any time since the Trent affair." There was nothing to do but retreat. "I shut myself up," he lamented, "went to no parties and avoided contact with everyone except friends." Reports in the British press of the capture of McClellan's entire army, Adams believed, had been fabricated "to carry the House of Commons off their feet" as it commenced its crucial debate on William Shaw Lindsay's resolution calling for a more vigorous pro-Confederate British policy.

In defense of his resolution, Lindsay pointed to the inevitability of final separation between North and South. He declared that the Southern cause was just and that the North would now accept mediation. Lancashire was in distress. Lindsay quoted from a letter written by a mill hand, "We think it high time to give the Southern States the recognition they so richly deserve." Friends of the North were assured that the British Ministry would not be influenced by the parliamentary debate and therefore chose the strategy of permitting the pro-Confederates to wear themselves out against a stone wall of silence. After two days of verbal effort Lindsay asked for a postponement of his motion to "wait for king cotton to turn the screws still further." Somehow the debate created a strong impression in England that public opinion favored intervention.

That critical summer found the European diplomats confused and divided. Napoleon pondered the Southern victories, convinced that the moment for intervention had arrived. He informed the British Ministry that France would recognize Southern independence if the London government would follow. Edouard Antoine Thouvenel, the French Minister in Paris, did not share the Emperor's enthusiasm for intervention. He doubted that the French public had any interest in such involvement or that the Confederacy would win. He warned that French intervention, unless supported by both Britain and Russia, would result in an overcommitment of French power. Russia, he surmised, would reject every proposal for joint action. He was correct. Prince Gortchakov made it clear that his government would regard the dissolution of the Union as a catastrophe. In an interview with Bayard Taylor of the American Embassy in October, 1862, he said: "You know that the government of the United States has few friends among the Powers. England rejoices over what is happening to you; she longs and prays for your overthrow. France is less actively hostile; her interests would be less affected by the result; but she is not unwilling to see it. She is not your friend. . . . Russia, alone, has stood by you from the first, and will continue to stand by you. We are very, *very* anxious that some means should be adopted—that *any* course should be pursued—which will prevent the division which now seems inevitable."

In Washington Mercier, still counseling mediation, stood alone. Lyons had no interest in confronting Seward with that issue again. To Stoeckl he observed, "We ought not to venture on mediation unless we are ready to go to war." Lyons did not share the European hostility toward the American Union. During his visit to England in the summer of 1862 he wrote to the British chargé d'affaires in Washington, with reference to McClellan's defeat, "I'm afraid no one but me is sorry for it." He believed that the debate on British policy in Parliament was ill-timed. "I do not think we know here sufficiently the extent of the disaster [to McClellan] to be able to come to any conclusion as to what the European Powers should do," ran his warning. Stoeckl concluded that the ravages of war would prompt the North eventually to beg for mediation, but not yet. He doubted, moreover, that British or French recognition of the South would achieve anything. "It will not end the war and what is more," he predicted, "it will not procure cotton for them, and the distress of the manufacturing districts will not be lessened. It can be accomplished only by forcing open the Southern ports, thus leading to a clear rupture with the North."

In London Mason, misled by the public evidence of British interventionism and unmindful of the disturbing doubts in the Foreign Office, moved to drive home his apparent advantage. He dispatched a brief note to Lord Russell requesting an interview. This Russell refused, assuring Mason that no advantage would result from it. In a second dispatch the Confederate Commissioner phrased his position in great detail, but again Russell replied that the moment for recognition had not arrived. For Mason the official British position had suddenly become clear. The Ministry would not alter its policies until the South revealed its ability to gain and maintain its independence, and reports from America indicated that the South was faltering at New Orleans, Memphis, and Shiloh. From Vienna John Lothrop Motley observed with accuracy that diplomacy would continue to reflect the course of war in America.

In Paris Slidell met with equal opposition. Thouvenel convinced him that it would be unwise even to ask for recognition. France, he said, was involved in Italy, but Slidell understood clearly the cause for French hesitancy. To the Confederate government he wrote on August 24: "You will find by my official correspondence that we are still hard and fast aground here. Nothing will float us off but a strong and continued current of important successes in the field." England, he warned, would avoid intervention until the North and South had become entirely exhausted. "Nothing," he lamented, "can exceed the selfishness of English statesmen except their wretched hypocrisy. They are continually casting about their disinterested magnanimity and objection of all other considerations than those dictated by a high-toned morality, while their entire policy is marked by egotism and duplicity."

Despite the lack of conviction in Europe's judgment of Confederate prospects, Southern victories were prompting the British Ministry to consider intervention. Russell admitted that nothing less than further Confederate successes would force mediation on the North. "I think," he wrote to the Embassy in Washington, "we must allow the President to spend his second batch of 600,000 men before we can hope that he and his democracy will listen to reason." Russell was convinced privately that October, 1862, would be the anticipated time for action. Stonewall Jackson's victories in Virginia prompted him to inform Lord Palmerston, the Prime Minister, that "it really looks as if he might end the war." Palmerston agreed, writing on September 14: "The Federals . . . got a very complete smashing . . . even Washington or Baltimore may fall into the hands of the Confederates. If this should happen, would it not be time for us to consider whether in such a state of things England and France might not address the contending parties and recommend an arrangement upon the basis of separation." The British Cabinet awaited word from France.

Before Napoleon could commit France to intervention, the British government passed the moment of decision. The wise and respected British politican, Earl Granville, warned Russell that involvement would mean war. "I doubt," he cautioned, "if the war continues long after our recognition of the South, whether it will be possible for us to avoid drifting into it." If Granville's words lacked conviction, Northern arms did not. Before the end of September news reached London of McClellan's success at Antietam and Lee's retreat down the Shenandoah Valley. Russell, who had been the ministry's most vigorous spokesman for involvement, now admitted, "This American question must be well sifted." Palmerston's support of Russell's position had been conditioned on the Southern invasion of Maryland. Now on October 2 in a letter to Russell he also acknowledged the wisdom of Granville's argument. Since mediation would favor the Southern position, its acceptance in the North hinged on Southern triumphs. Ten days earlier the necessary conditions seemed impending; now Palmerston counseled delay. He had no interest in exposing Canada and British commerce to a war against the United States. Nor would he venture into a quarrel without the support of France and Russia. "The whole matter is full of difficulty," he concluded, "and can only be cleared up by some more decided events between the contending armies."

William E. Gladstone, Britain's liberal cabinet leader, continued to urge British involvement in the American conflict as a moral obligation. At Newcastle on October 7 he declared: "Jefferson Davis and the other leaders have made an army, they are making, it appears, a navy, and they have made what is more than either, they have made a nation." Gladstone denied that British mediation would be met by insult or war, for, he predicted in a memorandum to the Prime Minister, "America would feel the influence and weight of a general opinion on the part of civilized Europe that this horrible war ought to cease." Whatever the immediate Northern reaction, the British proposal would produce a powerful effect on opinion and alter affairs in America in favor of peace. But perhaps Gladstone was motivated by more than a moral revulsion to war. He had recently toured the North of England and was fearful that the unemployment in the cotton districts would produce a violent upheaval. By serving the cause of peace the great liberal might also serve the cause of the British cotton textile industry.

Palmerston, under pressure from the Cabinet, sought the advice of the Earl of Derby, leader of the opposition. Derby vigorously opposed both mediation and recognition. He reiterated the fundamental conviction of European conservatives that either action would merely irritate the North without advancing the cause of the South or procuring a single bale of cotton. Mediation, he added, would gain its apparent objective only if England were prepared to sweep away the blockade and invite a declaration of war from the Lincoln administration. Intervention was hopeless because there was no way in which England could influence events in America short of military involvement. Palmerston's decision reflected this fundamental reality. Britain, he informed Lord Russell, "could take no step nor make any communication of a distinct proposition with any advantage." The North, he pointed out, demanded no less than restoration of the Union and the South no less than independence. To offer mediation would merely pledge each party in the conflict more firmly to its uncompromising objective. Russell added his conviction that no British action would be effective unless it were supported by Russia, Prussia, Austria, and France. For nations of such diverse interests agreement on interventionist policy was impossible.

During the crucial months of October and November, 1862, Napoleon never disguised his sympathy for the Confederate cause. But sentiment and policy are not synonymous, and the French Emperor balked at involvement in the American conflict. He complained to Slidell of troubles in Italy and Greece and acknowledged his fear that if he acted alone England would desert him and would attempt to embroil him in a war with the United States. Slidell assured him that recognition would not be regarded by the North as a *casus belli* and that with his powerful navy he could defend French interests on the seas without difficulty. To Slidell joint mediation was worthless, for he had no faith in England or Russia. Napoleon answered with a proposal acceptable to the Southern Commissioner. France and Britain might seek a six-month armistice in the American Civil War in the interest of humanity. Napoleon's final program for joint action was dispatched to both London and St. Petersburg.

In London the tripartite proposal threw the Cabinet into confusion. Palmerston was displeased, for he no longer had any interest in European intervention. Lord Russell favored action provided European leaders could discover terms upon which the warring sections in America would agree. In lieu of this elusive formula he favored a Cabinet discussion of the French dispatch. At the Cabinet meetings of November 11 and 12 Russell conceded the issue to Palmerston. Reported Gladstone to his wife: "The United States affair has ended and not well. Lord Russell rather turned tail. He gave way without resolutely fighting out his battle." In its reply to the French government, the British Ministry declared that mediation in any form was useless since Lincoln would not accept it.

At issue in the final Cabinet decision was the attitude of Russia. As early as November 8, St. Petersburg had informed the Foreign Office that the Russian government has rejected Napoleon's proposal. Prince Gortchakov advised the French that it was "essential to avoid the appearance of any pressure of a nature to offend American public opinion, and to excite susceptibilities very easily roused at the bare idea of intervention." Russell yielded on this key question to Palmerston when he wrote, "We ought not to move at present without Russia." Russia's inflexibility created the basis for a harmonious decision within the British Cabinet, and even Gladstone could write, "As to the state of matters generally in the Cabinet, I have never seen it smoother."

Throughout the months of decision in Europe, Seward exerted relentless pressure on the British and French governments. When Mercier transmitted a French offer of mediation to him in July, 1862, the Secretary warned that "the Emperor can commit no graver error than to mix himself in our affairs. At the rumor alone of intervention all the factions will reunite themselves against you and even in the border states you will meet resistance unanimous and desperate." It was not in the French interest, he continued, to compromise the kindly feeling which the United States held for France. Mercier thereupon advised caution in Paris, adding that intervention could easily result in war. When Mercier apprised Seward of Europe's reaction to McClellan's withdrawal from Richmond, the Secretary again stormed back: "I have noticed it but as for us it would be a great misfortune if the powers should wish to intervene in our affairs. There is no possible compromise ... and at any price, we will not admit the division of the Union." Seward acknowledged the kindly sentiments of Europe but replied that the best testimony of those sentiments would be Old World abstention from American affairs. When Mercier suggested that restoration of the Union was impossible, Seward told him: "Do not believe for a moment that either the Federal Congress, myself or any person connected with this government will in any case entertain any proposition or suggestion of arrangement or accommodation or adjustment from within or without upon the basis of a surrender of the Federal Union."

Above all Seward sought to disabuse European leaders of their conviction that a Northern victory was impossible. Nothing had occurred, he once wrote to Dayton in Paris, to shake the confidence of the Federal government in the ultimate success of its purpose. To those Europeans who insisted that the United States was too large for one nation, Seward retorted that it was too small for two. When Europe gave evidence of interventionist tendencies in August, 1862, Seward wrote to Adams: "The nation has a right and it is its duty, to live. Those who favor and give aid to the insurrection, upon whatever pretext, assail the nation in an hour of danger, and therefore they cannot be held or regarded as its friends. In taking this ground, the United States claim only what they concede to all other nations. No state can be really independent in any other position."

In denying Europe the right to intervene, Seward insisted that he was defending the principle of civil government itself, for at stake was nothing less than the existence of the United States. "Any other principle than this," he said, "would be to resolve government everywhere into a thing of accident and caprice, and ultimately all human society into a state of perpetual war." American policy was dictated by the law of self-preservation, and no nation, he added, "animated by loyal sentiments and inspired by a generous ambition can ever suffer itself to debate with parties within or without a policy of self-preservation."

Seward, therefore, instructed Adams not to debate, hear, or receive any communication from the British government which sought to advise the United States in its relations with the Confederacy. This nation was fighting for empire, he admitted in October, 1862, but it was an empire lawfully acquired and lawfully held. "Studying to confine this unhappy struggle within our own borders," he wrote to Dayton, "we have not only invoked no foreign aid or sympathy, but we have warned foreign nations frankly and have besought them not to interfere. We have practised justice towards them in every way, and conciliation to an unusual degree. But we are none the less determined for all that to be sovereign and to be free."

Seward's reaction to the British Cabinet debate of November revealed both confidence and dismay. It was not pleasant for a loyal American, he admitted to Adams, to observe an English cabinet discuss the future of the American Republic. But the United States, he added, enjoyed the right and possessed the power to determine its own destiny; never before was it better prepared to meet danger from abroad. The wheel of political fortune continued to turn. England had once desired American friendship; she would do so again. "Neither politicians nor statesmen control events," the Secretary concluded. "They can moderate them and accommodate their ambitions to them, but they can do no more."

After November, 1862, all wartime diplomacy receded into insignificance. Whatever Southern hopes of European intervention still remained were shattered by the Confederate disasters at Gettysburg and Vicksburg in July, 1863. In September Mason informed Russell by note that his mission had been terminated. The British Secretary replied coldly: "I have on other occasions explained to you the reasons which have inclined her Majesty's Government to decline the overtures you allude to. . . . These reasons are still in force, and it is not necessary to repeat them." Europe's final refusal to involve itself in the American struggle was nothing less than a total vindication of Seward's diplomacy. Whatever the North's diplomatic advantages, he had understood them and exploited them with astonishing effectiveness. He made it clear that any European nation which committed itself to the destruction of the American Union would pay dearly if it sought to fulfill that commitment.

In one sense there was nothing unique in the diplomatic issues raised by the American Civil War. Many nations in the past had undergone internal revolution in which elements seeking power had sought either to overthrow the established government or to establish the independence of some portion of its territory. Such uprisings had succeeded and failed, but when major power was involved they had demonstrated invariably that other nations, whatever their moral and material interests, really could not intervene diplomatically without running the risk of military involvement.

Unfortunately Union diplomacy after 1861 placed this nation in the unprecedented and embarrassing position of appearing to defy its own democratic principle of self-determination. Americans in the past, Europe recalled, had not only made declarations in favor of the Greek and Hungarian revolutions and applauded such revolutionary leaders as Louis Kossuth, but they had furnished them money for the declared purpose of assuring new disorders. Now Americans were compelled to recognize what they had often denied Europe—that governments cannot exist without authority and that, to maintain their authority, they must resort to force. Cassius Clay, to explain American purpose, once declared that the United States was fighting for nationality and liberty. To this the London *Times* replied sarcastically that it was difficult to understand how "a people fighting . . . to force their fellow citizens to remain in a confederacy which they repudiated, can be called the champions of liberty and nationalism." The Confederates were fighting for their independence, observed the *Times,* adding, "But with the Northerners all is different. They are not content with their own. They are fighting to coerce others."

Europe might have recalled that idealism had never established the official diplomatic tradition of the United States toward revolution and oppression. Whatever the concern of individual Americans toward events abroad, the nation's dictum since Washington's presidency had been one of abstention. John Quincy Adams had given it classical form in his Marcellus letters of 1794: "It is our duty to remain, the peaceful and silent, though sorrowful spectators of the European scene." Again in July, 1821, Adams declared that "America is the well-wisher to the freedom and independence of all. She is the vindicator only of her own." All national leaders prior to the Civil War, when holding positions of responsibility, agreed that any foreign intervention in behalf of liberal causes might well commit the United States beyond its national interest. President James Monroe recognized this when he refused to render aid to the revolting states of Latin America. They would receive recognition, he informed them, when they had demonstrated sufficient strength to establish their own independence. Palmerston was merely reflecting this diplomatic tradition when he admitted in October, 1862, that Britain "must continue merely to be lookers-on till the war shall have taken a more decided turn."

Tangible British and French interests were involved in the Southern struggle for independence, and to that extent neither nation could ignore events across the Atlantic. But until the South could demonstrate, as did the Latin American republics, that it could overcome the power and purpose of the North, European recognition would have defied one of the most significant and thoroughly established traditions of modern diplomacy. Except for one fleeting period in 1862, neither Britain nor France revealed any serious intention of breaking from their own past and assuming commitments which would endanger their territorial and commercial interests in the New World. Had Europe given expression to its moral sentiment by supporting the cause of the seemingly oppressed, it would merely have magnified the horror and confusion. Of this Seward left no doubt. He warned Europe in May, 1862, that its involvement in the affairs of the United States would not serve the interests of humanity. "If Europe will still sympathize with the revolution," he wrote, "it must now look forward to the end; an end in which the war ceases with anarchy substituted for the social system that existed when the war began. What will then have become of the interests which carried Europe to the side which was at once the wrong side and the losing one? Only a perfect withdrawal of all favor from the insurrection can now save those interests in any degree. The insurrectionary states, left hopeless of foreign intervention, will be content to stop in their career of self-destruction, and to avail themselves of the moderating power of the Federal government. If the nations of Europe shall refuse to see this, and the war must therefore go on to the conclusion I have indicated, the responsibility for that conclusion will not rest with the government of the United States."

Seward here touched the central issue of Europe's relationship to the conflict in America. If after the summer of 1862 it was still within the power of the Old World to bring injury to the North, it was beyond its power to bring salvation to the South. There were no inexpensive means available to Europe to achieve the liberation of the South against the North's determination to hold it. Those Europeans who sought to cast from the South the yoke of alien rule might have been moved by the moral sentiment of Gladstone, but they had no influence on Palmerston. And since the realities of power are always the determining factors in international affairs, a Gladstone in office, whatever his sentimentalism and faith in moral pressure, could have influenced the internal affairs of the United States, wrapped in civil war, with no more success than the masters of *Realpolitik* who rejected such purpose as a matter of principle.

Died of Democracy

David Donald

HISTORIANS HAVE EXPLAINED Confederate defeat in a variety of ways, but even as they blame the South's weaker economic resources, declining morale, defective strategy, and feeble political leadership, they have a faintly apologetic air. They know that, had the Confederacy gained its independence, they would be writing, with equal cogency, to explain the Southern victory. The historian, in other words, is a camp follower of the successful army.

As the historian explains why the winning side triumphed, he naturally tends to identify the victor with the most cherished values of the society in which he lives. He may describe the defeated cause as courteous, chivalrous, and romantic (maternal virtues which we admire but do not respect), but he attributes to the victor the masculine traits of strength, power, aggressiveness, and tough-mindedness (paternal assets which we may not like but necessarily respect). In American society there are three such values to which historians give adherence: All are convinced that it is a desirable and necessary thing to preserve the American Union; all believe that Negro slavery is an evil; and all profess a faith in democratic government.

It is not the truth of these beliefs but their juxtaposition which causes the great confusion about the Civil War. Historians, recognizing that Lincoln's government was fighting for the preservation of the Union and for the freedom of the slaves, attribute to it also the third great positive value, the defense of democracy. Such a view is a distortion of the facts. If we could free ourselves of the notion that democracy (a "good" thing) must inevitably have been connected with the winning (hence "good") Lincoln government, we would discover abundant evidence that

79

the Confederacy, not the Union, represented the democratic forces in American life.[1]

The democratic tendencies of the Confederacy were all too plainly reflected in its army. Accustomed to regarding themselves as the equals of any men in the world, the Southerners never took kindly to regimented life. Even their appearance showed that they considered themselves individualistic citizens who were temporarily assisting their country. One astonished Englishman, after seeing his first Confederate soldiers, gasped: "Anything less like the received notion, at home, of how a soldier should look . . . never met my eye."

Like all American soldiers in all wars, the Confederate disliked military discipline. Mississippi volunteers shirked assignments which they found tedious, declaring "they did not enlist to do guard duty but to fight the Yankies." At the outbreak of the war, when wealthier soldiers received onerous orders, some coolly instructed their Negro servants to carry them out, meanwhile uncomplainingly taking "upon themselves the duty of sitting on the fence and superintending the work." Others hired substitutes to perform their chores. "The two or three men of the overseer class who were to be found in nearly every company," George Cary Eggleston recalled, "turned some nimble quarters by standing other men's turns of guard-duty at twenty-five cents an hour."

The Southern soldier reserved his democratic right to interpret his orders broadly. The British observer, Colonel J. A. L. Fremantle, at first thought Confederate sentries "quite as strict as, and ten times more polite than, regular soldiers" because they efficiently challenged him when he entered James Longstreet's camp. But when he complimented the Confederate commander, Longstreet "replied,

---

[1] I am using "democracy" in this essay precisely as Alexis de Tocqueville used it in *Democracy in America;* it includes not merely such political manifestations as the extension of the suffrage, but all antiauthoritarian, individualistic, "levelling" tendencies in nineteenth-century American society.

laughing, that a sentry, after refusing you leave to enter a camp, might very likely, if properly asked, show you another way in, by which you might avoid meeting a sentry at all."

Southern soldiers simply disobeyed orders which they deemed unreasonable. Unconvinced that it was necessary to carry heavy packs, they carelessly tossed irreplaceable equipment aside on long, hot marches. Even the idea of marching at a regular rate in tidy lines offended their sense of individuality. "Our great embarrassment," Robert E. Lee reported to Jefferson Davis, "is the reduction of our ranks by straggling, which it seems impossible to prevent. . . . Our ranks are very much diminished—I fear from a third to one-half of our original numbers."

The Southern soldiers who volunteered at the outbreak of the war considered it their right to determine for themselves the length of their service. After a victorious battle in the early days of the war "many would coolly walk off home, under the impression that they had performed their share." When Jefferson Davis attempted to construct a more stable army through conscription, he probably lost more than he gained. "This Conscript Act will do away with all the patriotism we have," an indignant South Carolinian wrote in April, 1862, "A more oppressive law was never enacted in the most uncivilized country or by the worst of despots." Other Southern soldiers expressed their resentment by deserting in droves.

Unwilling to have their liberties curtailed by the Confederate government, Southern soldiers were also heartily opposed to undemocratic exercise of authority by their officers. They obeyed orders on the battlefield, but they saw no reason why officers should give themselves special airs in camp. Privates both resented and envied the privileges which officers enjoyed. The common soldier had "the hardships to undergo," a hungry Alabaman complained, while the officers had "bacon to eat, sugar to put in their coffee and all luxuries of this kind." An Englishman reported that he had never heard such handsome cursing as when Confederate privates, off duty and "squatted cross-legged on beds," spent their evenings damning their superiors' "eyes and limbs."

Often the Confederate soldiers were in a position to put their officers in their places. Sometimes they petitioned for the resignation of unpopular commanders; occasionally they rode an especially objectionable officer on a rail until he promised better behavior. Chiefly, however, the Confederate privates relied for redress upon their sovereign democratic right to elect their own officers. The elective system, a carry-over from the old peacetime militia, seemed perfectly reasonable to these democratic individualists. The theory behind it, as Eggleston remarked, was "that the officers were the creatures of the men, chosen by election to represent their constituency in the performance of certain duties, and that only during good behavior."

Though professional military men unanimously disapproved of the election of officers, politicians, sensitive to the democratic aspirations of the Southern fighting man, fought to continue the system. Southern soldiers "are not automatons," a Confederate congressman insisted, "dancing to the turning of some official organ grinder. The best *mind* and the best *blood* in the country are in the army, and much of both are found in the ranks. They have not lost the identity of the citizen in the soldier." Even Jefferson Davis agreed: "The citizens of the several States volunteered to defend their homes and inherited rights . . . the troops were drawn from the pursuits of civil life. Who so capable to judge of fitness to command a company, a battalion or a regiment as the men composing it?"

The result of the elective system was further to demoralize Confederate discipline. The men spent much of their time in quasi-political campaigning. "Authorize a squad of six men to elect a Lance Corporal," one observer commented, "and five of the number will at once become candidates." Secretary of War James A. Seddon pointed out that the elective system inevitably produced "an undue regard to popularity, especially among the non-commissioned officers, and a spirit of electioneering subversive of subordination and discipline." An Alabama congressman agreed: "I have seen a company rendered inefficient for months because of the opportunity of exercising the elective franchise in the choice of a lieutenant."

Of course the Confederacy was not alone in having these problems of discipline. Billy Yank was in most ways astonishingly like Johnny Reb, and both Civil War armies were, by modern standards, shockingly disorganized and maladministered. Yet in the Northern armies the respect for soldiers' individual rights never quite led to chaos. For one thing, the Lincoln government moved much more speedily to end the system of electing officers. What is more important, the Union administration had at its disposal two sizable reserves of manpower, neither of which had much experience in democracy nor much tendency toward individualism. The Federal armies recruited heavily from European immigrants. By 1864 one out of every four or five Union soldiers was of European birth, many of them newly arrived immigrants. Relatively uncontaminated by American notions of democracy or individualism, they were prepared to serve in a regular and subordinate fashion in the Union armies.

At the same time Federal enrolling officers were recruiting Negroes. By 1865 the Union army included 178,895 colored soldiers—roughly five times the number of men in Lee's army when he surrendered at Appomattox. These "Negroes make good soldiers," a lieutenant in one of the colored regiments wrote home to his wife. "They are docile and quick to learn . . . and they have a decided advantage over our white soldiers in the fact that they are taught *obedience* to every command, especially when that command comes from a white man. The trouble with *our* [white] volunteers, is, that they have always been accustomed to do as they pleased and to have their own way about everything and it is very hard work to come under the yoke of army discipline. With the Negro it is right the reverse."

Foreign observers almost invariably commented that the Union army was a far less colorful and interesting aggregation than that of the Confederacy. So it was, but it was also a far better organized and disciplined fighting force. The Southern soldier was a democratic, liberty-loving individualist; his Union counterpart became a cog in a vast machine.

The Confederacy's tolerance of democracy was not confined to military affairs. In civil rights, too, the South had an astonishingly libertarian record. Though engaged in deadly war, Davis' government preserved the traditional civil rights of freedom of speech, freedom of the press, and freedom from arbitrary arrest, even when the government itself was debilitated by these rights.

Let no one romantically conclude that the Southern government permitted criticism and dissent because all its people were loyally united behind the lost cause. Quite the contrary. Both Davis and his government were subjected to tirades of abuse. Davis, said T. R. R. Cobb of Georgia, was "the embodiment and concentration of cowardly littleness [which] he garnishes over with pharasaical hypocrisy. How can God smile upon us while we have such a man [to] lead us." The editor of the influential Richmond *Examiner,* E. A. Pollard, described Davis as "a literary dyspeptic who had more ink than blood in his veins, an intriguer, busy with private enmities." Robert Toombs, the Confederacy's first Secretary of State, declared: "Davis's incapacity is lamentable. . . ." The Vice-President of the Confederacy, Alexander H. Stephens, announced that Davis was simultaneously "weak and vascillating [*sic*], timid, petulant, peevish, obstinate, but not firm." "How God has afflicted us with a ruler!" exclaimed Linton Stephens, the Vice-President's brother, a leader in the Georgia House of Representatives. "He is a *little, conceited, hypocritical, snivelling, canting, malicious, ambitious, dogged,* knave and fool."

Not one of these, nor any of the other critics, of the Confederate President had his liberty of utterance impaired. Davis was well aware of the enmity of his critics and thought that most Southern newspapers were partisan and venal; Lee scathingly remarked that, from the tone of the press, the Confederacy had "put all our worst generals to commanding our armies, and all our best generals to editing newspapers"—but neither man did anything to curb the Southerners' limitless democratic right of free expression. "When Davis's advisers were to urge that anti-Administration papers be restrained, he would not hear of it," Hudson Strode points out. "As a democrat, he believed in maintaining complete freedom of the press." It is true that in January, 1862, the Confederate Congress did pass a law forbidding the publication of unauthorized news of troop movements, but even this slight regulation was bitterly protested and flagrantly ignored. No Southern newspaper was ever suppressed by the Confederate government for its opinions, however critical or demoralizing. The ardent wish of Secretary of War George W. Randolph was realized: that "this revolution may be . . . closed without suppression of one single newspaper in the Confederate States."

More significant militarily was the Confederacy's insistence upon maintaining the cherished legal rights of freedom from arbitrary arrest and upon preserving due process of law. This sentiment was so strong that, though the Confederacy was invaded and Richmond was actually endangered, President Davis did not dare institute martial law until he had received the permission of his Congress. While General George B. McClellan was about to assault the Confederate capital in 1862, the Southern Congress debated the question and concluded that their President was "subject to the Constitution and to the laws enacted by Congress in pursuance of the Constitution. He can exert no power inconsistent with law, and, therefore, he cannot declare martial law." Grudgingly Congress permitted Davis to suspend the privilege of the writ of habeas corpus for three brief periods—once when McClellan was within sight of Richmond, again during the Fredericksburg-Chancellorsville threat, and once more when Grant was pushing through the Wilderness. Even then he was allowed to suspend the writ only in limited areas, not throughout the Confederacy. When he came to Congress for a renewal of his authority during the grim winter of 1864–1865, he was refused, lest too much power in the hands of a dictatorial president curb the democratic rights of the people.

The result, of course, was that disloyal elements throughout the South had almost unrestricted freedom. If a member of the Peace and Constitution Society, the Order of Heroes, or any of the other disloyal bands that centered in the hill country of the South was arrested, he was tried by civil process before a jury of his peers—many of whom probably belonged to the same disloyal organization as himself. The influential Confederate bored with army service could often secure from a judge of his own persuasion a writ of habeas corpus, which released him from military duty. The planter who hoarded grain, the merchant who traded with the enemy, the blockade-runner who brought in laces and perfumes rather than desperately needed medicines—all were equally secure. And when Davis reluctantly considered cracking down on these disloyal elements, a newspaper controlled by his own Vice-President came out with a black-bordered edition, as if in mourning, and exclaimed: "Georgians, behold your chains!—Freemen of a once proud and happy country, contemplate the last act which rivets your bonds and binds you hand and foot, at the mercy of an unlimited military authority."

Again, one does not suggest that the North was free from these troubles of disloyalty and sedition, nor should he imply that the Lincoln government handled them with the same grim efficiency which was shown during the later Woodrow Wilson and Franklin D. Roosevelt administrations. Yet, in comparison with the Confederacy, the Union government did curtail civil liberties. As soon as the fighting started, President Lincoln, without delaying to consult Congress, suspended the privilege of the writ of habeas corpus, at first for a small area in the East, later for the entire nation. At a subsequent date he reported his *fait accompli* to Congress: "These measures, whether strictly legal or not, were ventured upon, under what appeared to be a popular demand, and a popular necessity; trusting then, as now that Congress would readily ratify them." Congress had little choice but to ratify, and the disloyal citizen no alternative but to acquiesce. At least 15,000 civilians were imprisoned in the North for alleged disloyalty or sedition. They were arrested upon a presidential warrant and were kept incarcerated without due process of law. It did the disaffected citizen no good to go to court for a writ of habeas corpus to end his arbitrary arrest. On orders from President Lincoln himself, the military guard imprisoning him refused to recognize a judicial writ even when it came from Chief Justice Roger B. Taney.

Freedom of the press was also seriously abridged in the North. To be sure, Northern editors abused President Lincoln as "a slang-whanging stump speaker," a "half-witted usurper," a "mole-eyed" monster with "soul . . . of leather," "the present turtle at the head of the government," of "the head ghoul at Washington"—but they did so at the acknowledged risk of having their papers suppressed and going to prison. Over three hundred Northern newspapers were suppressed, for varying periods, because they opposed the administration's policies or favored stopping the war.

But in painting this picture one must be careful not to exaggerate. If, as J. G. Randall noted, "Legally the Civil War stands out as an eccentric period, a time when constitutional and legal restraints did not fully operate and when the 'rule of law' at least partially broke down," one must also add that "civil liberties were not annihilated" and "the traditional attachment of the American people to the 'rule of law' as a principle had its steadying effect." Lincoln was no dictator. He disliked the arbitrary procedures which he felt compelled to employ, and he carefully used them for no selfish or self-promoting purpose. Furthermore, few Nothern citizens were affected by these curbs on civil rights. Enthusiastic in their support of the Union cause, most neither knew nor cared that freedom of the press was abridged or that arbitrary arrests were numerous. Yet the test of civil liberties is not the freedom of the majority but that of the dissenter. In the Confederacy the dissenter retained his democratic rights down to Appomattox.

Political democracy, too, was unimpaired in the Confederacy. Jefferson Davis took care to abridge no Southerner's political rights. Elected provisional president through no solicitation of his own, re-elected as the first— and only—regular President of the Confederacy, Davis did not believe that he should interfere in politics, either to solicit votes for his friends or to win support for his measures. Davis' political record as president is almost exclusively negative. He endorsed no congressional candidates, and he discouraged the formation of political parties in the South. When North Carolina held a critical gubernatorial election in 1864 to choose between Zebulon Vance, pledged to sustain the war effort, and William W. Holden, dedicated to withdrawing the state from the Confederacy and making an independent peace, Davis expressed no public preference between the candidates. Nor did he make any attempt to secure the defeat of Governor Joseph E. Brown, of Georgia, though Brown, with the backing of Vice-President Stephens, did all he could to hamstring the Richmond government, announced that the people must check Davis' "fearful strides towards a centralized government with unlimited powers," and urged a convention of the "sovereign, equal, and independent states" to make peace with the Union. Davis did not try to replace his arch-rival, Stephens. In the South, the soldiers knew it was wartime, but not the politicians.

The record of the Lincoln government is in marked contrast. Lincoln regularly used patronage to build up a political machine, dedicated to supporting his policies. At first he tried not to intervene in the elections themselves, but his hands-off policy, comparable to that pursued by Davis, resulted in a disastrous defeat for the Republican party in the congressional elections of 1862. The key states of New York, Pennsylvania, Ohio, Indiana, and Illinois were lost to the Democrats. The newly-elected Democratic legislators in those states began condemning the Lincoln administration for catering to the Negro and for ruthlessly kidnapping white citizens, who were "cast into dungeons . . . to remain, sicken and die." They announced: "War alone is no remedy for the evil of disunion."

Rapidly Lincoln moved to reverse his policy by strengthening the hands of his friends. When Republican Governor O. P. Morton of Indiana was faced in 1863 with a hostile Democratic majority in the state legislature, which threatened to curb his appointing powers and his control of the state militia, the Republicans, by prearrangement, walked out of the chamber, leaving the legislature without a quorum and unable to transact any business. The Democrats then adjourned the session, believing that Morton, in order to carry on the government, must call them promptly back. Instead, the Indiana governor made a flying trip to Washington, saw Lincoln and Secretary of War E. M. Stanton, and returned to Indianapolis bearing $250,000 extracted from war department funds, on which he ran the state government until the next election, blithely ignoring constitutional regulations and majority rule.

Having learned a lesson from 1862, Lincoln was prepared to take a more active, preventive role in the presidential election two years later. When he saw that the Northwestern states were going to show a closely balanced vote, he wrote in September, 1864, to General W. T. Sherman, whose army was in a tight spot before Atlanta: "Any thing you can safely do to let [your] soldiers, or any part of them, go home to vote at the State election, will be greatly in point." Although Lincoln added that "this is, in no sense, an order," he was clearly giving a directive, and it was one which Sherman promptly obeyed. The Republicans carried the Northwest by narrow majorities. In Pennsylvania, too, the Democrats were threatening, and it was found possible to furlough several thousands from Grant's army before Richmond. Not all the soldiers were Republicans, to be sure—but Democratic soldiers found it strangely difficult to secure furloughs.

In 1864 a number of Northern states permitted their

soldiers to vote in the field. Republican canvassers were afforded every facility for getting to the front, but Democratic politicians were often harassed by long delays in Washington. Lincoln himself took a great interest in the soldier vote. When Secretary of War Stanton gruffly refused, on grounds of military security, to disclose the location of New York regiments to the official canvassers from the Empire State, they complained to the President, who at once interceded in their behalf. When they commented on the alacrity with which the President had overruled his Secretary, E. B. Washbourne, an old friend from Lincoln's Illinois period, explained the facts of life: "Why that would beat Mr. Lincoln. You don't know him. While he is a great statesman, he is also the keenest of politicians alive. If it could be done in no other way, the president would take a carpet bag and go round and collect those votes himself."

The collapse of the Confederacy, then, came not from deficient economic resources, insufficient manpower, defective strategy, or weak political leadership. All of these were handicaps; but none was fatal. The real weakness of the Confederacy was that the Southern people insisted upon retaining their democratic liberties in wartime. If they were fighting for freedom, they asked, why should they start abridging it? As soldiers, as critics of their government, and as voters they stuck to their democratic, individualistic rights. In the administration of the Southern army, in the management of Southern civilian affairs, and in the conduct of Southern political life, there is, then, extensive evidence that we should write on the tombstone of the Confederacy: "Died of Democracy."

Jefferson Davis and the Political Factors in Confederate Defeat

David M. Potter

THE QUESTION "Why did the North win the Civil War?" is only half of a question by itself, for the other half is "Why did the South lose the Civil War?" Was one side more crucial than the other? Did the North win because the South was a natural loser, or did the South lose because the North was a natural winner? Is one side of a watch crystal concave because the other is convex, or is one convex because the other is concave? Shall we explain the results in terms of what the North did to the South, as Kenneth P. Williams tended to do in *Lincoln Finds a General*, or in terms of what the South failed to do to the North, as Douglas S. Freeman tended to do in his studies of *R. E. Lee* and *Lee's Lieutenants*?

The answer to these questions is easier in theory than it is in application. In principle it is clear that the outcome of a contest between two parties results not from the qualities of either taken alone, but from the differentials between them. Yet to measure these differentials, one must give a kind of bifocal attention to both parties at the same time. This is an ambidextrous feat which historians of the Confederacy and historians of the Union have alike found hard to attain. Consequently, most of the answers come to us in terms of the strength of the Union or the weakness of the Confederacy, rather than of the relative qualities of the two.

Where differentials are examined, they can be measured more precisely in economic terms than in any other, and historians have long been impressed by the great economic superiority of the North. Here there are innumerable measurements—of manpower, of wealth, of railroad mileage, of industrial capacity—all of which point up the overwhelming advantage on the side of the Union. These comparisons have led many writers to conclude that the South was fighting against the census returns and that Northern victory was inevitable from the beginning.

One-sided as these statistical comparisons are, even they fail to reveal in full the economic handicaps of the South. No statistics can measure, for instance, how much the Confederacy suffered from the fact that it had the kind of economy that is prostrated by war, in contrast to the Union which had the kind of economy that flourishes under wartime conditions. War invigorated the Northern economy by stimulating a leading form of Northern economic activity, namely industrial production. Thus the conflict brought prosperity to the civilian population, and civilian morale remained good largely because civilians had nothing to be demoralized about. But in the Confederacy, war paralyzed the chief form of economic activity, which was the cultivation of cotton. As the flow of income from cotton dried up, the economy languished, the economic welfare of civilians suffered, and their morale deteriorated. In the end, the economic morale of the people collapsed before their military morale was exhausted.

In terms of economic logic, it can perhaps be demonstrated that the Confederacy, hopelessly overmatched by almost every measure of strength, was doomed to defeat. But history not only shows that in war the lighter antagonist sometimes defeats the heavier, it also shows that what seems logically certain often fails to happen. Thus, if we survey the course of the Civil War, do we not find that, in actuality, the Confederacy developed very formidable striking power—power impressive enough to make Lincoln doubt, even as late as 1864, that the Union would be saved? Do we not find the effective power of the opposing forces balanced so evenly that sometimes great results seemed to swing on the hinge of relatively trivial events? If a Confederate soldier had not shot Stonewall Jackson in the dusk at Chancellorsville, if Gouverneur Warren had not had a quick eye for Little Round Top, if a duplicate copy of Lee's plan of campaign in September, 1862, had not been used by someone on D. H. Hill's staff to wrap three cigars, might not a delicate balance have swung the other way in spite of all the statistics?

In weighing the question whether inescapable forces doomed the South in advance, it is well also to remember that the question is not what the South might have done during the last twenty-one months of the forty-eight-month war. For in fact, the result had been registered after Gettysburg and perhaps even after Sharpsburg, and all the South could hope for then was that the Northern people might fail to notice that they had won—as indeed the Northern Democrats did fail to notice in the election campaign of 1864. But for fourteen months before Lee came to high command, and for perhaps thirteen months after he did so, the result often appeared to be in real doubt, and it seems legitimate to question whether more effective political policies by the Confederates might at that time have made a crucial difference.

If the balance was, in fact, a delicate one, the analysis of forces must go far beyond the *à priori* arguments of economic determinism. While no one will deny that economic factors gave to the North an immense advantage, the precise question is whether other countervailing factors could possibly have offset it. For instance, could superior military and political skill on the Confederate side have done so? Reducing this question still further: Was there a differential in military performance in favor of the South which tended to offset, in part, the economic differential in favor of the North? The preponderance of historical opinion has agreed that the answer to this question is yes. For four long years, Lee's army did stave off defeat. But was the differential in political performance also in favor of the South? If it was, then one can say that Southern military and political prowess were hopelessly overmatched by the Union's sheer economic weight. But unless the effectiveness of the Confederate government equalled or surpassed that of the Union government, we cannot rest the evaluation of Confederate policy, as some historians have done, with the affirmation that Confederate leaders should not be blamed for their mistakes since the problems that they faced were insuperable. Instead, we shall have to say that economic and political factors, in conjunction, produced the final result, despite military factors which had a contrary tendency. Can we not go a step farther and ask whether the difference between Union and Confederate political performance was not as great as or greater than the economic disparities—whether in fact, the discrepancy in ability between Abraham Lincoln and Jefferson Davis was not as real and as significant as the inequality in mileage between Union and Confederate railroad systems?

The danger of a question like this is that it tends to displace one explanation with another, and to minimize the truly immense handicaps of the Confederacy. No just appraisal would ever underestimate the dead weight of those handicaps, but on the other hand, an appreciation of the magnitude of the South's problems should not stand in the way of a recognition that Confederate policy sometimes aggravated these problems instead of diminishing them, and that mistakes of policy as well as the handicaps of given conditions weakened the Southern cause.

In a number of the situations in which the Confederacy failed, it is fairly evident both that the problems were essentially insurmountable and also that government policy made them even worse than they would otherwise have been. In the matter of raising public revenue and controlling inflation, for instance, it was inevitable that a new government with no gold reserves and no revenue laws would face financial crisis, and also that the scarcity of goods in a blockaded, nonindustrial country would cause an inflationary rise in prices. But while no government could have wholly averted these evils, almost any government could have done more than the Confederacy did. Hesitating to resort to taxation, it called on the states for funds, and they met the requisitions largely by borrowing. In the end, only about one per cent of Confederate revenue was raised by taxation, which is a smaller proportion than any modern government in wartime has raised in this way. In spite of this abuse, the Confederate dollar held up almost as well as the Union greenback during the first two years of the war, which suggests that a sounder financial policy might have sustained it somewhat longer.

A similar combination of unavoidable difficulties on the one hand, and mistaken choices between policy alternatives on the other appears in the treatment of what had traditionally been the South's major economic asset—namely the cotton crop. In 1861, this asset was worth $225 million in gold, or nearly ten times as much as the actual gold supply in the Confederacy. Every one of the 4,500,000 bales, if exported and held in a European warehouse, would have helped to pay for vital Confederate purchases overseas. The loss of a considerable part of this value was inevitable, because shipping could not have been procured to export the whole crop before the Union blockade became operative. It was fantastic to suppose, for instance, as did Alexander H. Stephens, that fifty iron-bottomed boats could have been bought and used for the export of 4,000,000 bales. But while lack of shipping forced the Confederate leaders to keep a part of the cotton at home, they willingly embraced a fallacious belief—the King Cotton delusion—which caused them voluntarily to keep all of it at home. This belief that, by withholding their cotton, they would force Britain and France to intervene in the war, failed to face up to the question whether there were commodities which the Confederacy would need even more urgently than Britain and France would need cotton fibres.

There were realistic men in the Confederacy who perceived the fallacy in the cotton policy. As early as April, 1861, Secretary of the Treasury C. G. Memminger resolutely opposed the cotton embargo and expressed his disapproval "of any obstruction to commerce in our ports." During 1862, the Commissary Department faced the reality that supplies were vital and must be procured even if it meant trading cotton to the enemy—a far more serious matter than selling it abroad. According to R. G. H. Kean, in November, Commissary General Lucius B. Northrop reported that "he could not supply the Army unless allowed to purchase bacon from the enemy at Memphis with cotton," and the Quartermaster General wanted to procure blankets in the same way. The Secretary of War, George W. Randolph, had already become convinced of the necessity of a cotton trade limited to the bureau in question. By April, 1863, Secretary of State Judah P. Benjamin broke sharply away from the King Cotton doctrine, asserted that it was a matter of primary importance to bring in army supplies at Confederate ports, and proposed a definite export of cotton "to be received by the merchant vessels of France at certain designated points." Before the end of the war, even General Lee strongly recommended to President Davis that the trade which was already bringing New York bacon to his army should be widely extended to secure other supplies.

These men perceived the point of a problem posed by Kean: "The question is simply whether they [the North or the British and French] suffer more for the . . . cotton . . . or we for the indispensable articles of salt, meat, clothing, medicines." But Kean also reported, "The President resisted it [the proposal for trade] in toto." In March, 1863, he noted in his diary that "the President has yielded at last on the subject of getting meat from the enemy for cotton"—this in connection with Generaly Kirby Smith's trade at the mouth of the Río Grande. But Kean added, "Too late to do much good." Nearly a year later, he was still criticizing Davis for placing upon the cotton trade, restrictions which made it almost impossible to conduct. As he reported, regulations for the trade were drawn very carefully in the War Office, and sent to the President, but "they came back so modified as to destroy the trade by their stringency."

In the end, cotton responded to the laws of necessity, and a vast amount was traded through the lines. In fact, this trade became an important factor in sustaining the armies in the West, and Memphis took its place as "a greater outfitting point for Confederate armies than Nassau." Private families—even patriotic ones—found that by smuggling out a single bale they might escape starvation, while quartermasters and commissaries and state officials learned that this was sometimes the only way to keep Southern armies in the field. Therefore, it cannot be said that Jefferson Davis succeeded in imposing a policy based upon the King Cotton doctrine. All that he did succeed in doing was to reduce the cotton situation to chaos. In this chaos, the Confederate government lacked control of the cotton in the South and lacked a constructive overall policy for utilizing such cotton as it did control. Consequently, private owners smuggled large amounts of cotton through the lines, thus breaking the partial embargo, demoralizing the citizens who were too patriotic to smuggle, and creating competition against their own government in bidding for the goods which cotton would buy. At the same time, the government itself survived by accepting, more or less unwittingly, the fruits of a trade conducted mostly on an unsanctioned basis by desperate or imaginative minor officials. But while permitting enough trade to break its own embargo, the government never faced the question how best to reap the potential advantage of the cotton supply as a whole. At the end of the war, 2,500,000 bales had been destroyed to prevent them from falling into the hands of the enemy; less than 1,000,000 probably had been exported through the blockade; and an incalculable amount had been smuggled through the lines, more for the gain of private parties than for the good of the cause. Such was the ultimate destiny of what everyone recognized as the greatest economic asset of the Confederacy.

The same pattern of initial handicaps compounded by mistaken policy appears in the procurement of supplies and foodstuffs for the Confederate Army. The initial handicap lay in the fact that there were many commodities, especially those produced abroad, which were inevitably scarce, or even unobtainable. The mistaken policy lay in the fact that even the goods which might have been produced in sufficient quantity became scarce because of restrictive economic measures. In this connection, it is important to recognize that, as the war developed, Southern farmers turned from the production of cotton to the production of grain, and there was no overall deficiency of food. But in procuring food for the army the Confederacy found it-self in the dilemma that if it purchased supplies on the open market at an uncontrolled price, inflation would mushroom, while on the other hand, if it requisitioned supplies at an arbitrary price, productive output would be discouraged and the loyalty of the producers would be impaired. Caught between these alternatives, the government chose to give priority to avoiding inflation. Accordingly it set up a system of impressment, which partook of legalized confiscation, since it permitted military officers to seize draft animals or foodstuffs at a fixed price which was sometimes less than half of the market value. The net result of this was to encourage corrupt practices, to place civilian morale under an almost intolerable strain, and to discourage production without noticeably slowing the pace of inflation. As men either hoarded their crops, or stopped planting altogether, severe shortages developed. By March, 1863, these shortages were so acute that Kean wrote: "The Army will be starved and famine will ensue in the cities unless the Secretary changes his policy and buys in the market for the best price. The government will have to outbid the traders; else *neither* will get anything of the present scanty stock and no future stock will be produced."

The failures of the impressment system have received full recognition at the hands of historians, but another error in economic mobilization, which has largely escaped notice, was the failure of the Confederacy to assert control over the use of a labor force which constituted more than one-third of its manpower—namely that part which consisted of Negro slaves. Where manpower was white, the government did not hesitate very many months before adopting conscription laws which made the allocation of the labor of such men subject to public control. These laws drew most men of military age into the army, but they left others, whose occupations were deemed to be essential, in a civilian status. But where manpower was Negro, conscription did not bring it under similar control. Because of the *idée fixe* that slaves were property and not persons, the allocation of nearly 40 per cent of the Confederacy's total manpower was left to the whim and discretion of individual slaveholders. This produced great inequalities of sacrifice, for manpower meant earning power on the farms. Conscription had taken the manpower, and thus the earning power of the nonslaveholding families, who suffered great privations during the war. It left most of the manpower and thus the earning power of the slaveholding families, whose privations were usually much less severe.

It is an ironical comment on the blind refusal of the South to regard slaves as men that when resentment flared up against this system, it took the form of protest not against the failure to conscript slaves—whether for military or nonmilitary service—but against the exemption from military service of one white man as overseer for every twenty slaves whose labor had to be supervised. The disgruntled men who said bitterly that this was "a rich man's war and a poor man's fight," resented deeply the fact that a limited number of white men were allowed to remain in noncombatant employment as overseers, yet they apparently did not resent at all the fact that the labor of several million black workers continued to be used for the benefit of their owners, while the labor of white workers was subject to the demands of the Confederacy. The failure to include Negroes in any overall system of public allocation of labor was both a fundamental source of inequality of sacrifice on the part of the people and a basic flaw in the plan of economic mobilization. It is in some ways surprising that Jefferson Davis seems to have grasped this point, for in a message to Congress in November, 1864, he observed that slaves were sometimes treated as property, subject to impressment for short terms, but that "the slave . . . bears another relation to the state— that of a person. . . . In this [war] aspect, the relation of person predominates so far as to render it doubtful whether the private right of property can consistently and beneficially be continued and it would seem proper to acquire for the public service the entire property in the labor of the slave, and to pay therefor due compensation."

These failures, if failures they be—the failure to tax, the failure even to attempt an effective use of the cotton supply, the failure to achieve effective use of resources and manpower—all stemmed from attitudes which prevailed widely in the Confederacy. Insofar as they were errors, they were the errors of the South in general and not of the Confederate President nor any other one man in particular. In fact, the general level of political leadership in the Confederacy left much to be desired—as witness the parochialism of men like Governor Joseph E. Brown, who never really perceived that the defense of Georgia lay beyond the territorial boundaries of the state, or the negativism of men like Senator Henry S. Foote, whose futile ranting presented a painful anticlimax to the great tradition of Southern political excellence in the Federal Congress in the decades before the war.

But in appraising the part which political factors played in the failure of the Confederacy, it is necessary to look beyond the questions of formation of policy to the more human question of the quality of leadership. At this level, as distinguished from the policy level, there is a great deal of evidence to justify placing a considerable share of the responsibility for the Confederacy's misfortunes directly at the door of Jefferson Davis.

This is not at all the same thing as to say that the strictures of his critics were valid. In fact, the narrowness, pettiness, and lack of realism of men like Alexander Stephens, Brown, and Foote make the narrowness of Davis seem broad-gauge by comparison. Moreover, when these critics assailed him, they usually did so for the wrong reasons. Men who least understood what the South needed were the most vocal in attacking him, while the men who, like Lee and Benjamin, most clearly perceived his real shortcomings were the least vocal because they were also the ones who understood that whatever was to be accomplished must be accomplished through him. With his most acute critics always silent and his most obtuse ones never so, he enjoyed a brand of criticism which, however galling it may have been at the time, has helped his historical reputation, since history must vindicate him if he is measured by some of the accusations brought against him by his critics—accusations of despotism and too much centralization. But if he is measured, instead, by the tests which history itself would apply to the appraisal of leadership, what do we find? We find, it may be argued, a record of personal failure significant enough to have had a bearing on the course of the war.

Davis failed in three important ways—in his relations with other Confederate leaders and with the people, in his fundamental concept of his job as president, and in his specific handling of his politico-military role as commander in chief. In every one of these respects, Lincoln offered a striking contrast and presented superlative qualities of leadership.

Concerning Davis' relations with the Confederate leaders, Clifford Dowdey has remarked that he had only two first-rate minds among his advisers—Robert E. Lee and Judah P. Benjamin. Both men had to employ a disproportionate amount of their time and energy in exercising the supreme tact which was necessary in working with Davis. Benjamin was never permitted to bring his originality and resourcefulness into play, and he was forced to forfeit his influence with the public by silently accepting blame for measures which Davis chose not to explain to the people. As for Lee, he was held in peripheral commands or at a desk in Richmond until fourteen of the twenty-seven months during which the South still retained some striking power had passed. Davis never allowed him a post of overall command such as Winfield Scott, George B. McClellan, Henry W. Halleck, and U. S. Grant all enjoyed under Lincoln. When Congress adopted a bill establishing the office of general in chief, intended for Lee, Davis vetoed it.

Compare this record with that of Lincoln, who took both William H. Seward and Salmon Chase into his cabinet, who kept Charles Sumner on his side while at the same time holding border state moderates like Edward Bates, who formed a cabinet with four former Democrats and three former Whigs and blandly remarked that he could balance the elements since he was an old Whig himself. Compare, too, Lincoln's forebearance when Seward was trying to run the administration, Chase was conducting a presidential campaign against Lincoln from his post in the Treasury, and the Blair family was waging its bitter family feuds from the postmaster-general's office.

Again, it is revealing to compare Davis' attitude toward P. G. T. Beauregard when he felt that the Creole general was blaming him for the failure to reap the fruits of First Manassas, and Lincoln's attitude toward Joseph Hooker when he believed that Hooker was saying there ought to be a dictator at Washington. Davis wrote to Beauregard that he was "surprised" at that general's report of the battle "because if we did differ as to the measure and purposes of contemplated campaigns, such fact could have no appropriate place in the report of the battle; further, because it seemed to be an attempt to exalt yourself at my expense."[1]

The accusation was very likely valid, but Lincoln would not have made it. When he wrote to Hooker, it was to say: "I have heard, in such a way as to believe it, of your recently saying that both the army and the government needed a dictator. Of course it was not for this, but in spite of it, that I have given you the command. Only those generals who gain successes can set up dictators.

[1] It must be conceded that both Joseph E. Johnston and Beauregard gave Davis great provocation, and that he was sometimes astonishingly patient in replying to them, but he was also capable of being very starchy in his rebukes. When Brigadier General Whiting protested the policy of giving each brigade a commander from its own state, and declined the command of such a brigade himself, and when Johnston forwarded Whiting's letter to Richmond, Secretary Benjamin replied: "The President has read with grave displeasure the very insubordinate letter of General Whiting, in which he indulges in presumptuous censure of the orders of his commander-in-chief and tenders unasked advice to his superiors in command. . . . The President requests me to say that he trusts you will hereafter decline to forward to him communications of your subordinates having so obvious a tendency to excite a mutinous and disorganizing spirit in the army."

What I now ask of you is military success, and I will risk the dictatorship. The government will support you to the utmost of its ability, which is neither more nor less than it has done and will do for all commanders."

Just as Davis could not really work with other Confederate leaders, so also he could scarcely even communicate with the people of the Confederacy. He seemed to think in abstractions and to speak in platitudes. It is suggestive, I think, to recall his appeal to the men who had fought, suffered, lost their faith, and gone through hell under the command of Braxton Bragg and who wanted no more of their commanding general. Davis' way of dealing with these hard-bitten and badly demoralized soldiers was to praise in flowery language their virtues as fighting men and then, as a climax, to urge them: "Crown these [virtues] with harmony, due subordination, and cheerful support of lawful authority."

One reason for Davis' failure to communicate was that he could seldom admit he was wrong. He used an excessive share of his energy in contentious and even litigious argument to prove he was right. He seemed to feel that if he were right that was enough; that it was more important to vindicate his own rectitude than to get results. When a matter could not be explained without admitting a mistake, as for instance in the case of the loss of Roanoke Island, it simply did not get explained at all, and the people were alienated by the feeling that the administration dared not trust them with the truth. As a critic of Davis, Edward Pollard of the Richmond *Examiner* often displayed rank prejudice, but he came close to the truth when he said that Davis "has not told the people what he needed. As a faithful sentinel, he has not told them what of the night."

The contrast presented by Lincoln shows up clearly in a letter of Lincoln to Grant at the end of the Vicksburg campaign. "When you first reached the vicinity of Vicksburg," said Lincoln, "I never had any faith, except a general hope that you knew better than I, that the Yazoo Pass expedition, and the like, could succeed. When you got below, and took Port Gibson, Grand Gulf, and vicinity, I thought you should go down the river and join General [N. P.] Banks; and when you turned northward east of the Big Black, I feared it was a mistake. I now wish to make the personal acknowledgement that you were right and I was wrong."

This letter has no counterpart in the correspondence of Jefferson Davis.

If Davis failed in his relations with people, he failed also in his concept of his task as President. In April, 1861, history cast him in the role of a revolutionary leader. What such a role requires of a man is that he shall concentrate intensively upon the essentials, with a bold indifference to all that is irrelevant to the cause; that he shall hold to the level of overall leadership, leaving matters of detail to his subordinates; and that he shall have a driving instinct for success and a readiness to adopt the innovations which will bring success. Although Davis possessed talent and intelligence, it would have been hard to find a man more lacking in these qualifications than he.

Davis was a conservative leader, not a revolutionary leader; a man with a strong sense of protocol and convention, but with a weak sense of innovation; a man who was much happier with details than he was with overviews; a man who loved order and logical organization better than he loved results which are achieved by unorthodox methods; above all, a man who thought in terms of principles rather than of possibilities and who cared more about proving he was right than about gaining success.

All these qualities showed up in his handling of his duties as commander in chief. In that role, his other weaknesses were accentuated by his firm conviction that he possessed real military talent and that he should give his attention primarily to the close guidance of the operations of all the Confederate armies. Because of this conviction, he ran the war office himself and all six of his war secretaries were either nonentities or transients—even Benjamin seemingly exercised little initiative while in this post. For the same reason the giant, Lee, was never permitted to hold a general command such as even Halleck held under

Lincoln. The same irresistible temptation to run military operations himself also led Davis to descend to points of detail where he lost sight of the larger issues with which he should have concerned himself. Consequently, two of the severest criticisms of Davis have come from men who were in the War Department in Richmond. After serving Davis as secretary of war, George W. Randolph said that, despite all his attention to this area of activities, the President had "no practical knowledge of the workings of our military system in the field." Even more contemptuously, Robert G. H. Kean, an official of the department, said that Davis wasted time on "trash that ought to be dispatched by clerks."[2]

This attention to military detail resulted in something far more serious than the waste of presidential time. It meant that Davis made decisions in Richmond which should have been made in the field and that he hampered his field commanders by limiting their functions too narrowly and by interfering with their command. Not only did he sometimes visit battlefields and change the disposition of regiments while combat raged, but he sometimes sent orders to subordinate generals without consulting, and even without informing, their field commanders.[3]

A striking contrast to Davis' constant intervention appears in the policy of Lincoln, who was always concerned with military policy and often admonished his generals,

[2] On February 1, 1862, J. E. Johnston wrote to Benjamin: "I have been greatly surprised today to receive an order from the War Office detailing a private for a working party here. I hazard nothing in saying that in time of war, a Secretary of War never before made such a detail."

[3] On February 14, 1862, replying to a protest by J. E. Johnston, Davis said: "While I admit the propriety in all cases of transmitting orders through you to those under your command, it is not surprising that the Secretary of War should, in a case requiring prompt action, have departed from this usual method in view of the fact that he had failed more than once in having his instructions carried out when forwarded to you in the proper manner." This comes close to suggesting that, when a field commander is slow to obey orders, the proper remedy is to bypass him without informing him that he has been bypassed.

but who avoided details and refrained from giving orders. Lincoln's whole philosophy was expressed in a letter to Grant in 1864 in which he said, "The particulars of your plans, I neither know nor seek to know." By this statement Lincoln in no sense abdicated his authority as commander in chief. Rather, he clearly defined the true division of function between commander in chief and field commander. His role was to consider overall questions of military policy. The operational particulars were the business of the generals in the field. Lincoln knew this without learning it by experience. Davis never learned it despite his experience at West Point, in the Mexican War, and as secretary of war under Pierce.

If Davis had developed a military policy which would produce victory, his compulsion to run everything himself might not have mattered. But his decision to be his own secretary of war and his own general in chief meant that he was the author of Confederate military policy, and that he incorporated into this policy two fatal principles. One was the principle of departmentalization; the other, allied with it, was the principle of dispersion of force for the defense of territory, rather than concentration of force for the defeat of the enemy.

The principle of departmentalization appealed naturally to a man who thought in formal and static terms rather than in functional and dynamic ones. Like the dedicated bureaucrat that he was, Davis loved a symmetrical table of organization. Consequently, he did not hesitate to carry on the peacetime practice of assigning the units of the army to completely separate geographical departments, each one reporting solely to the war office and each operating independently of all the others. Sometimes this led to strange results. For instance, Lee, commanding in a department north of the James, and Beauregard, commanding in a department south of the James, converged in 1864 to defend Petersburg, but they continued to communicate with one another through the War Department in Richmond. But in fact, Lee and Beauregard did cooperate, despite the mechanical awkwardness of their situation. What was more serious was that, in general, the departmental commanders sought reinforcements for their own departments and looked to the defense of them without much regard for the needs of their fellows in other departments. One reason for the loss of Vicksburg was the fact that help had not come from the Trans-Mississippi Department, and Davis had rebuked Secretary Randolph for trying to bring help from that quarter. In June, 1863, Kean wrote: "The fatal notion of making each military department a separate nation for military purposes without subordination, co-operation, or concert—the same on which in point [of fact] the President and General Randolph split—has lost us Mississippi."[4] Dowdey, who also regards this departmentalization as one of the decisive factors in Confederate failure, remarks: "When Lee took over the War office, on hilly North Street, across from Capital Square [in 1862] Davis had a dispersal of forces in Virginia which, counting subdivisions of armies, had eight separate forces arranged in separate parts of the state. . . . The Confederate forces in Virginia were ready for anything except to fight a battle."

When accused of practicing dispersal, Davis denied that this was his policy, and he might have claimed, in extenuation, that the state governors exerted great pressure upon

[4] On July 12, Kean wrote further: "The radical vice of Mr. Davis's whole military system is the separate departmental organization, each reporting only to him. It makes each department depend only on its *own* strength and deprives them of the mutual support and combination which might else be obtained. It appears from a recent report of Richard Taylor that Vicksburg *might* have been relieved from that side; that the whole situation was treated with a levity incomprehensible when the vast stake is considered! Mr. Seddon remarked yesterday that he thought there was more blame on the command on the west than on the east side of the [Mississippi] river for its loss. It was a difference on this very principle of co-operation across the Mississippi, at this very point, Vicksburg, in connection with which General Randolph's resignation was brought about. His instruction to Holmes, who then had the command Smith now has, to cross over when necessary to produce the best results, and by virtue of his rank to take command of the combined force, was the thing of which the President so pointedly disapproved, and *countermanded*."

him to assign troops for local defense throughout many parts of the South. But he was committed to defensive action by temperament, if not by conviction. He never initiated the daring concentrations which Lee was willing to risk. He always thought in terms of repelling the invader rather than of smashing the enemy, and he was slow to recognize the fearful cost of defending fixed positions, as at Vicksburg. He never showed the compelling urgency of a man who knows that time is on the side of the enemy and that victory must be gained before the enemy's potential strength can be brought into play.

Once again the contrast with Lincoln is illuminating—and damaging to Davis. To my mind, it has been conclusively demonstrated that Lincoln had a sounder concept of the overall military objectives of the Union than any of his generals. He was impatient with the endless maneuvering and seeking of positional objectives which so completely dominated the thought of many of the generals, and he seldom lost sight of the ultimate goal of defeating the enemy's forces. T. Harry Williams quotes his message to Hooker: "I think Lee's Army, and not *Richmond,* is your true objective point. . . . Fight him when opportunity offers. If he stays where he is, fret him and fret him." Many months later, Lincoln wrote again, this time to General Halleck: "To avoid misunderstanding, let me say that to attempt to fight the enemy slowly back into his intrenchments at Richmond, and then to capture him, is an idea that I have been trying to repudiate for quite a year. . . . I have constantly desired the Army of the Potomac to make Lee's army and not Richmond, its objective point. If our army cannot fall upon the enemy and hurt him where he is, it is plain to me it can gain nothing by attempting to follow him over a succession of entrenched lines into a fortified city."

Many passages might be quoted to underscore the extent of the difference between Lincoln and Davis. But it would be hard to find any quotation which focuses the contrast quite as clearly as Lincoln's statement of what he liked about Ulysses S. Grant. I do not mean his curt:

"I can't spare this man; he fights," though that is apposite enough. What I am referring to is his observation: "General Grant is a copious worker and fighter but a very meager writer or telegrapher." If Davis was anything, he was a copious writer and telegrapher—so much so that Pollard said he had ink instead of blood in his veins—and what is more to the point, he seemed to cultivate this quality in his commanders. But he was a meager worker and fighter in terms of bringing about results, or even of clearly perceiving the results that needed to be brought about.

Fundamentally, Davis always thought in terms of what was right, rather than in terms of how to win. There is no real evidence in all the literature that Davis ever at any one time gave extended consideration to the basic question of what the South would have to do in order to win the war. He said almost nothing on this subject in his messages to Congress, which abounded in passages designed to prove the iniquity of the North and the rectitude of the South. By contrast, Lincoln wanted victory and wanted it so badly that in order to get it he was willing to co-operate with men who had shown they hated him. As he said, "I need success more than I need sympathy and I have not seen so much greater evidence of getting success from my sympathizers than from those who are denounced as the contrary." Lincoln thought of the war as something to be fought, but Davis thought of it as something to be conducted. There was no instinct for the jugular in Davis. That is why one seldom finds him pressing his generals to engage the enemy and never finds him striving for the concentration which might make possible a knockout blow.

In the light of Jefferson Davis' conspicuous lack of an instinct for victory, his lack of a drive and thrust for action and results, his failure to define his own office in terms of what needed to be accomplished, it hardly seems unrealistic to suppose that if the Union and the Confederacy had exchanged presidents with one another, the Confederacy might have won its independence. In this sense, is it not justifiable to doubt that the overwhelming statistical advantages of the North predestined the Confederacy to defeat? Historians have never developed a really satisfactory way of dealing with the relationship between the vast, impersonal, long-range social and economic forces of history and the immediate, close-range, somewhat accidental factors of personality; but here is certainly a case where the factors of personality played an important part in guiding the impact of the impersonal social and economic forces.

A political scientist might well object that it is superficial to emphasize these factors of personality without considering the question of what there was in the political system of the South that prevented the development of any viable alternative to the leadership of Davis. As we all know, any government may occasionally have the bad luck of putting an unsuitable man in a position of leadership. England, in 1939, had her Neville Chamberlain. No system can wholly prevent this from happening. But an effective political system, and especially an effective democratic system, is supposed to contain a mechanism which makes it possible to substitute new leadership when the existing leadership fails. England may have entered the Second World War with Chamberlain at the helm, but she ended with Winston Churchill dominating the scene. Granted there was no mute, inglorious Churchill waiting in the wings of the Confederacy, still there is abundant evidence that before the end of 1862 widespread and deep-seated dissatisfaction with Jefferson Davis was rife in the Confederacy. A great many people—perhaps the majority of informed men—knew that the choice of president had been a mistake. Yet there was no constructive opposition. The petulant, short-sighted, narrow-gauge, negativistic, vindictive quality of the criticisms of Davis made him seem, with all his shortcomings, a better man than most of those who assailed him. The Congress was little better than a bear garden, where Senator Benjamin Hill hit Senator William L. Yancey in the face with an inkwell, where a subordinate clerk of the House shot and killed the chief clerk on the capitol grounds, where a "lady" horsewhipped Senator George G. Vest, and where Senator Foote fought promiscuously with anyone who would fight him. Why did no legislative leader emerge to claim a legislative receivership for the bankrupt office of the executive?

This is a major question which suggests several lines of thought. For one thing, it tempts one to wonder to what extent the long years of defending slavery and building protective legalistic safeguards for the South as a minority section within the Union may have impaired the capacity for affirmative and imaginative action on the part of Southern leaders generally. How much had the vaunted statesmanship of the South suffered in this process? There is another suggestion which comes to mind. This is the possibility that the Confederacy may have suffered real and direct damage from the fact that its political organization lacked a two-party system. In the crisis of war, Southerners professed to regard it as a source of strength that they were not divided by party dissensions, but functionally a two-party system has important values. Where parties do not exist, criticism of the administration is likely to remain purely an individual matter; therefore the tone of the criticism is likely to be negative, carping, and petty, as it certainly was in the Confederacy. But where there are parties, the opposition group is strongly impelled to formulate real alternative policies and to press for the adoption of these policies on a constructive basis. In 1863 in the South, new Congressional elections were held, and, though history has neglected these elections most scandalously, we do know that they constituted a sharp rebuke to the administration and its followers.

Alternative leadership at that point, or even earlier, might have found a very substantial backing and might have been able to dominate policy. But the absence of a two-party system meant the absence of any available alternative leadership, and the protest votes which were cast in the election became mere expressions of futile and frustrated dissatisfaction rather than implements of a decision to adopt new and different policies for the Confederacy. Thus, the political leadership could not be altered, and Jefferson Davis continued to the end in his distinctive role—not a role which destiny fatalistically forced upon him, but one for which his qualities and temperament peculiarly fitted him and which he fulfilled in a very functional sense—the role of the leader of a Lost Cause.

For Further Reading

Studies devoted primarily to explaining the reasons for Northern victory in the Civil War are not numerous. Among the most interesting are Robert Tansill, *A Free and Impartial Exposition of the Causes Which Led to the Failure of the Confederate States to Establish Their Independence* (Washington, 1865, a rare pamphlet in the Clarendon MSS, Bodleian Library, Oxford University); Albert Bushnell Hart, "Why the South was Defeated in the Civil War," *New England Magazine,* V (new series, 1891); Duncan Ross, "Why the Confederacy Failed," *Century Magazine,* LIII (1896); Lawrence Henry Gipson, "The Collapse of the Confederacy," *Mississippi Valley Historical Review,* IV (1918); Charles H. Wesley, *The Collapse of the Confederacy* (Washington, 1937); Charles W. Ramsdell, *Behind the Lines in the Southern Confederacy* (Baton Rouge, 1944); and Bell Irvin Wiley, *The Road to Appomattox* (Memphis, 1956).

Of course, every general history of the Civil War period contains, either explicitly or implicitly, some judgments on the reasons for Southern defeat. Some basic interpretations are: John W. Burgess, *The Civil War and the Constitution, 1859–1865* (New York, 1901); James Ford Rhodes, *Lectures on the American Civil War* (New York, 1913) and *History of the Civil War, 1861–1865* (New York, 1917); Edward Channing, *The War for Southern Independence (A History of the United States,* Vol. 4 [New York, 1925]); A. C. Cole, *The Irrepressible Conflict, 1850–1865* (New York, 1934); Carl Russell Fish, *The American Civil War: An Interpretation* (London, New York, 1937); George Fort Milton, *Conflict: The American Civil War* (New York, 1941); J. G. Randall, *The Civil War and Reconstruction* (Boston, 1953); Allan Nevins, *The Statesmanship of the Civil War* (New York, 1953) and *The War for the Union: The Improvised War, 1861–1862* (New York, 1959); and Bruce Catton, *This Hallowed Ground* (New York, 1956).

The best general histories of the Confederacy are Ellis Merton Coulter, *The Confederate States of America, 1861–1865* (Baton Rouge, 1950); Clement Eaton, *A History of the Southern Confederacy* (New York, 1954); and Clifford Dowdey, *The Land They Fought For: The South as the Confederacy, 1832–1865* (New York, 1955).

The many economic difficulties which confronted the Confederacy are well analyzed in John Christopher Schwab, *The Confederate States of America, 1861–1865: A Financial and Industrial History* (New York, 1901); Robert C. Black, III, *The Railroads of the Confederacy* (Chapel Hill, 1952); Richard C. Todd, *Confederate Finance* (Athens, Ga., 1954); and Ella Lonn, *Salt as a Factor in the Confederacy* (New York, 1933). Important articles are Eugene Lerner, "The Monetary and Fiscal Programs of the Confederate Government, 1861–1865," *Journal of Political Economy,* LXII (1954), and "Money, Prices, and Wages in the Confederacy, 1861–1865," *ibid.,* LXIII (1955).

Jefferson Davis has been a source of much controversy among historians. His own *Rise and Fall of the Confederate Government* (2 vols., New York, 1881) is revealing, not merely for what it includes, but for what it neglects. Dunbar Rowland compiled his correspondence and public papers in *Jefferson Davis, Constitutionalist* (10 vols., Jackson, Miss., 1923). Edward A. Pollard, his bitter critic, wrote a harshly adverse *Life of Jefferson Davis, with a Secret History of the Southern Confederacy* (Philadelphia, Chicago, St. Louis, Atlanta, 1869); and his wife, Varina Howell Davis, presented what is perhaps the most convincing favorable portrayal yet to appear in her *Jefferson Davis, Ex-President of the Confederate States of America, a Memoir by his Wife* (2 vols., New York, 1890). Twentieth-century biographers have been rather favorable and not very searching in their appraisals. The most recent and most laudatory of these is Hudson Strode, *Jefferson Davis* (2 vols. to the year 1864; New York, 1955, 1959). The reader is likely to find more actual insight into Davis' policies as war president in Burton J. Hendrick, *Statesmen of the Lost Cause: Jefferson Davis and His Cabinet* (Boston, 1939); and Rembert W. Patrick, *Jefferson Davis and His Cabinet* (Baton Rouge, 1944). James Z. Rabun, "Alexander H. Stephens and Jefferson Davis," *American Historical Review,* LVIII (1953), is an important study of Davis' principal critic. Two diaries kept by minor officials in the Confederate War Department afford remarkable insights into the operations of the Davis administration: John Beauchamp Jones, *A Rebel War Clerk's Diary* (2 vols., Philadelphia, 1866); and Edward Younger (ed.), *Inside the Confederate Government: The Diary of Robert Garlick Hill Kean* (New York, 1957).

A full political history of the Confederacy has yet to be written. Albert Burton Moore, *Conscription and Conflict in the Confederacy* (New York, 1924), gives a good general account of local opposition to Davis' policies. For the Vance-Holden contest, see Richard E. Yates, *The Confederacy and Zeb Vance* (Tuscaloosa, 1958). On affairs in Georgia, Louise Biles Hill, *Governor Joseph E. Brown and the Confederacy* (Chapel Hill, 1939) and T. Conn Bryan, *Confederate Georgia* (Athens, Ga., 1953) are excellent. Also outstanding are Charles Edward Cauthen, *South Carolina Goes to War, 1861–1865* (Chapel Hill, 1950); John K. Bettersworth, *Confederate Mississippi* (Baton Rouge, 1943); and Jefferson Davis Bragg, *Louisiana in the Confederacy* (Baton Rouge, 1941). William M. Robinson, Jr., *Justice in Grey* (Cambridge, 1941) is an exhaustive treatment of Confederate judicial and constitutional problems.

The social and economic problems confronting the Union government have not been thoroughly explored by recent scholars. The best general discussion is still Emerson D. Fite, *Social and Industrial Conditions in the North during the Civil War* (New York, 1910). Wesley C. Mitchell, *A History of the Greenbacks* (Chicago, 1903) remains the standard work. See also Milton Friedman, "Price, Income and Monetary Changes in Three Wartime Periods," *American Economic Review,* LXII (1952); and Marshall A. Robinson, "Federal Debt Management: Civil

War, World War I and World War II," *ibid.,* XLV
(1955).

The literature on Lincoln is vast. The best guides to it
are Jay Monaghan (ed.), *Lincoln Bibliography, 1839–
1939* (2 vols., Springfield, 1945); Paul McClelland Angle,
A Shelf of Lincoln Books (New Brunswick, N.J., 1946);
and Ralph Newman, "Basic Lincolniana," *Civil War History,* III (1957). The definitive compilation of Lincoln's
writings is Roy P. Basler (ed.), *The Collected Works of
Abraham Lincoln* (9 vols., New Brunswick, N.J., 1953–
55). The best one-volume biography is Benjamin P.
Thomas, *Abraham Lincoln* (New York, 1952); and the
most satisfactory full-length study is J. G. Randall and
Richard N. Current, *Lincoln the President* (4 vols., New
York, 1945–55). Recent writers have stressed Lincoln's
political sagacity: Harry J. Carman and Reinhard H.
Luthin, *Lincoln and the Patronage* (New York, 1943);
David Donald, *Lincoln Reconsidered* (New York, 1956);
Burton J. Hendrick, *Lincoln's War Cabinet* (Boston,
1946); William B. Hesseltine, *Lincoln and the War Governors* (New York, 1948); Richard Hofstadter, "Abraham Lincoln and the Self-Made Myth," in his *The American Political Tradition* (New York, 1948); T. Harry Williams, "Abraham Lincoln: Principle and Pragmatism in
Politics," *Mississippi Valley Historical Review,* XL
(1953); and William Frank Zornow, *Lincoln and the
Party Divided* (Norman, Okla., 1954).

New studies of most of the Northern states during the
Civil War period are badly needed. Of the existing books
Frederick Merk, *Economic History of Wisconsin during
the Civil War Decade* (Madison, 1916) and Arthur C.
Cole, *The Era of the Civil War, 1848–1870 (The Centennial History of Illinois,* Vol. 3 [Springfield, 1919]) are the
most useful. Kenneth M. Stampp, *Indiana Politics during
the Civil War* (Indianapolis, 1949) is an incisive and
provocative work.

On civil rights in the North, the standard work is J. G.
Randall, *Constitutional Problems under Lincoln* (Urbana,
Ill., 1951). See Robert S. Harper, *Lincoln and the Press*

(New York, 1951) for editorial attacks on Lincoln, and J. G. Randall, "The Unpopular Mr. Lincoln," *Lincoln the Liberal Statesman* (New York, 1947) for other contemporary criticisms.

The literature on Civil War military history is massive, but little of it gives attention to the cultural and intellectual forces that shaped the generalship of the war. David Donald's "Refighting the Civil War," *Lincoln Reconsidered,* is an attempt to explore the influences of Jomini upon Confederate and Union strategy. A perceptive essay on Jomini appears in Edward M. Earle (ed.), *Makers of Modern Strategy* (Princeton, 1944), Chapter 4, "Jomini," by Crane Brinton, Gordon A. Craig, and Felix Gilbert. Jomini and his background are also treated in R. S. Preston, S. F. Wise, and H. O. Werner, *Men in Arms* (New York, 1956). The best source for Jomini's thought is his own writings: J. D. Hittle (ed.), *Jomini and His Summary of the Art of War* (Harrisburg, 1947). For a convenient introduction to other writers on the art of war see Thomas R. Phillips (ed.), *Roots of Strategy* (London, 1943). Valuable secondary treatments are Cyril Falls, *A Hundred Years of War* (London, 1953); and F. E. Adcock, *The Greek and Macedonian Art of War* (Berkeley, Calif., 1957), especially Chapter 6, "Generalship in Battle."

Civil War high command and strategy are treated in E. W. Sheppard, "Policy and Command in the American Civil War," *The Army Quarterly,* XXXVI (1939); Sir Frederick Maurice, *Statesmen and Soldiers of the Civil War* (Boston, 1926); and T. Harry Williams, *Lincoln and His Generals* (New York, 1952). Frank E. Vandiver dissects the Confederate military hierarchy in *Rebel Brass: The Confederate Command System* (Baton Rouge, 1956). Particularly good for its discussion of the three greatest military figures of the war is A. H. Burne, *Lee, Grant, and Sherman* (New York, 1939). The best analysis of Grant's generalship, which sometimes turns into a too ardent defense, is J. F. C. Fuller, *The Generalship of Ulysses S. Grant* (London, 1929), and *Grant and Lee* (London,

1933). Also good on Grant are C. F. Atkinson, *Grant's Campaigns of 1864 and 1865* (London, 1908); A. L. Conger, *The Rise of U. S. Grant* (New York, 1931); and Kenneth P. Williams, *Lincoln Finds a General* (5 vols., New York, 1949–59). In *Sherman* (New York, 1929), B. H. Liddell Hart explores Sherman's development from a Jominian to a prophet of total war, in the process finding support for his own strategic doctrine. Douglas S. Freeman details Lee's military career in *Robert E. Lee: A Biography* (4 vols., New York, 1934–35) and evaluates his subject's generalship in Chapter 11, Volume IV, "The Sword of Robert E. Lee."

On the common soldier in the Civil War the outstanding works are Bell Irvin Wiley, *The Life of Johnny Reb* (Indianapolis, New York, 1943), and *The Life of Billy Yank* (Indianapolis, 1951), both distinguished for thorough research and careful analysis. David Donald discusses democratic tendencies in the Southern army in "The Confederate as a Fighting Man," *Journal of Southern History,* XXV (1959). On the Federal army the standard work is Fred A. Shannon, *The Organization and Administration of the Union Army, 1861–1865* (2 vols., Cleveland, 1928). Jack Franklin Leach, *Conscription in the United States: Historical Background* (Rutland, Vt., 1952) is valuable. Dudley Taylor Cornish, *The Sable Arm* (New York, 1956), is the best study of Negro troops in the Union Army. Ella Lonn has fully discussed the role of Europeans in the Civil War in *Foreigners in the Confederacy* (Chapel Hill, 1940) and *Foreigners in the Union Army and Navy* (Baton Rouge, 1951).

There are two standard works on Europe's relationship to the American Civil War. E. D. Adams, *Great Britain and the American Civil War* (2 vols., London, 1925) is a detailed and scholarly study of the British position, whereas F. L. Owsley has analyzed the Southern effort to secure recognition in his *King Cotton Diplomacy* (Chicago, 1931). Concerned with European opinion toward the American struggle are D. Jordan and E. J. Pratt, *Europe and the American Civil War* (Boston, 1931); L. M. Case (ed.), *French Opinion on the United States and Mexico, 1860–1867* (New York, 1936); and W. R. West, *Contemporary French Opinion on the American Civil War* (Baltimore, 1924). Enlightening articles on various segments of British attitudes are W. D. Jones, "The British Conservatives and the American Civil War," *American Historical Review,* LVIII (1953); J. H. Park, "The English Workingmen and the American Civil War," *Political Science Quarterly,* XXXIX (1924); and M. P. Claussen, "Peace Factors in Anglo-American Relations, 1861–1863," *Mississippi Valley Historical Review, XXVI* (1940).

Much has been written on the maritime issues raised by the Civil War. On the *Trent* affair are C. F. Adams, Jr., "The Trent Affair," *Massachusetts Historical Society Proceedings,* XLV (1911); Thomas Harris, *The Trent Affair* (Indianapolis, 1896); V. H. Cohen, "Charles Sumner and the *Trent* Affair," *Journal of Southern History,* XXII (1956); and W. W. Jeffries, "The Civil War Career of Charles Wilkes," *Journal of Southern History,* XI (1945). On questions of neutral rights and freedom of the seas, see F. L. Owsley, "America and the Freedom of the Seas, 1861–1865," in Avery Craven (ed.), *Essays in Honor of William E. Dodd* (Chicago, 1935); J. P. Baxter, "The British Government and Neutral Rights, 1861–1865," *American Historical Review,* XXXIV (1928) and "Some British Opinions as to Neutral Rights, 1861–1865," *American Journal of International Law,* XXIII (1929); and D. H. Maynard's two articles, "Union Efforts to Prevent the Escape of the *Alabama,*" *Mississippi Valley Historical Review,* XLI (1954) and "Plotting the Escape of the *Alabama,*" *Journal of Southern History,* XX (1954).

Perhaps the best analysis of Seward's leadership can be found in Samuel F. Bemis (ed.), *The American Secretaries of State and Their Diplomacy* (New York, 1925), VII. Another useful survey is Frederic Bancroft, *The Life of William H. Seward* (New York, 1900), II. For Lincoln's role see Jay Monaghan, *Diplomat in Carpet Slippers* (Indianapolis, 1945). On Adams in London, see W. C. Ford (ed.), *A Cycle of Adams Letters, 1861–1865* (2 vols., Boston, 1920) and the fascinating journal of one member of the legation, S. A. Wallace and F. E. Gillespie (eds.), *The Journal of Benjamin Moran, 1857–1865* (2 vols., Chicago, 1949). On another American diplomat of the period see Margaret Clapp, *Forgotten First Citizen: John Bigelow* (Boston, 1947). For a good evaluation of two British diplomats see Lord Newton, *Lord Lyons* (2 vols., London, 1913) and Spencer Walpole, *Life of Lord John Russell* (2 vols., London, 1891). On Slidell's fruitless mission to Paris, see L. M. Sears, "A Confederate Diplomat at the Court of Napoleon III," *American Historical Review*, XXVI (1931). W. H. Russell, *My Diary North and South* (2 vols., London, 1863) is an interesting analysis of wartime diplomacy from the viewpoint of a leading British correspondent.

Index

Index

Adams, Charles Francis, 59, 60, 74–75; distrusts Seward's belligerency, 61–3; on anti-Union sentiment among British, 67

Adams, Charles Francis, Jr., 50

Adams, E. D., 65

Adams, Henry, 63, 67

Adams, J. Q., 77

Atkinson, C. F., 50

Banks, N. P., 104

Beauregard, P. G. T., 36, 106; on failure of the South 16; admires Jomini, 40; appraised as general, 42; quarrels with Davis, 102

Benjamin, J. P., and Erlanger loan, 27; plans control of cotton trade, 96; relations with Davis, 100–101, 104

Black, R. C., III, 24

Blackwood's Magazine, 56

Blockade, as factor in defeat of Confederacy, 27, 28, 59–60

Bragg, Braxton, 36, 42, 43, 103

Brown, J. E., 88, 100

Browne, Junius, 51

Buell, Don Carlos, 36, 42, 44

Burne, A. H., 47, 52

Burnside, Ambrose, 36, 42

Calhoun, John C., 26

Charleston *Mercury*, 64

Chase, Salmon P., 25, 101, 102

Chesterfield, Lord, 40

Civil rights, in Confederacy and Union, 84–88

Clausewitz, Karl von, 35, 39

Clay, Cassius M., on European interest in American affairs, 55–6; on English distrust of United States, 56–7; on Union war objectives, 76

Cobb, T. R. R., 84

Confederacy, economic resources of, 15; advantages of,

in war for independence, 16–18; fails to exploit cotton resources, 18–21, 95–8; financial policy of, 10, 21–3; fails to regulate production, 23–4; fails to regulate transportation, 24–5; generalship in, 33–54; pursues King Cotton diplomacy, 64–5; seeks European recognition, 68–9, 72, 75; democratic tendencies in armies of, 80–4; civil rights in, 84–7; fails to handle financial problems, 94–5; mismanages impressment policy, 97–8; fails to conscript Negroes, 98–9; political leadership in, 100–12

Cotton, not exploited by the Confederacy, 18–21, 95–7

Davis, Jefferson, condemned by Pollard, 18; cotton policy of, 19–20; as financier, 22–3; as strategist, 28–9; 53–4; defends election of officers, 82; refuses to curb critics, 84–6; and martial law, 85; refuses to intervene in politics, 88; mismanages cotton trade 96–7; on need to impress Negroes, 99–100; fails in relations with Confederate leaders, 101–3; fails to communicate with Southern people, 103–4; fails in conception of presidency, 104–5; fails in duties as commander in chief, 104–10

Dayton, William L., 60, 74, 75

De Bow's Review, 64

Democracy, as factor in Confederate defeat, 79–90

Derby, Earl of, 71–2

Diplomacy, as factor in Confederate defeat, 27, 55–78

123